Magic is believing in yourself, if you can do that, you can make anything happen. "

Johann Wolfgang von Goethe
Playwright, Poet, Novelist and Dramatist, 1749-1832

SOME EXCERPTS FROM 5 STAR REVIEWS
ON AMAZON KINDLE

Love, romance, family, adventure, fantasy and science rule in this fascinating story of a man who strives to reconcile his reality and his knowledge. …Stan Law will take you to places you never imagined and help you to explore enchanting thoughts and possibilities. I highly recommend it!

Amy Taylor (Amazon.com, USA)

The book is so well written that reading it over again and again is an absolute treasure. "Alexander" is both whimsical and brilliant and is the perfect successor to "Alec."

Kevin Linter (Amazon.com, USA)

This is not light reading, but for readers who like something to get their teeth into or perhaps enjoy new perspectives, …this is the book for you. It enters the realms of the paranormal, laying the path to Book III of this Trilogy, "Sacha."

Joan A. Adamak VINE VOICE (USA)

Alexander is yet another brilliantly thought provoking book that unravels in such a mind bending way. …Superior writing that I highly recommend!

Mary Leckie (Amazon.com, USA)

… The author has keen abilities to observe all the external (marriage, parenting, career) and inward (conscious, subconscious and super conscious) mile markers of development of a man, and to illustrate both inward and outer barriers, including physical manifestations of inward struggle, as with Alex's paralysis.

To have all of this woven into the fabric of a story that is compelling at the surface plot level as an educated man constructs a life a meaning while experimenting with compelling mystical experiences, along with very witty and fun passages (such as sparring wryly with Freud!) is a soul treat, indeed.

Alex Prosper (Amazon.com, USA)

The novel blends classic science fiction elements with fantasy, drama, romance, action and adventure. The writing is both emotionally charged and deeply adventurous in tone; creating a fast-paced story that feels fresh and new.
…it left me wanting to dive headfirst into the last book in the Alexander Trilogy.

L. Clifford (TOP 1000 REVIEWER, USA)

…I'm a huge fan of Stan I.S. Law's books… I simply cannot say enough good things about this book or this author. He has captured perfectly the essence of a teenage boy on his journey of self-discovery. Get this book, you will be glad that you did! I highly recommend.

M. Brown (TOP 500 REVIEWER, USA

By the same author

ALEC (Alexander Trilogy, Book I)
ALEXANDER (Alexander Trilogy, Book II)
SACHA—The Way Back (Alexander Trilogy, Book III)
YESHUA—Personal Memoir of the Missing Years of Jesus
PETER AND PAUL (An intuitive sequel to Yeshûa)
ONE JUST MAN (Winston Trilogy Book I)
ELOHIM—Masters and Minions (Winston Trilogy Book II)
WINSTON'S KINGDOM (Winston Trilogy Book III)
THE AVATAR SYNDROME (Prequel to Headless World)
HEADLESS WORLD—The Vatican Incident
(Sequel to *The Avatar Syndrome*)
MARVIN CLARK–In Search of Freedom
THE GATE—Things My Mother Told Me
NOW—Being and Becoming
GIFT OF GAMMAN
THE PRINCESS
ENIGMA of the Second Coming
WALL—Love, Sex, and Immortality (Aquarius Trilogy Book I)
PLUTO EFFECT [Aquarius Trilogy Book II]
OLYMPUS—Of Gods and Men [Aquarius Trilogy Book III]

Short stories

THE JEWEL & OTHER STORIES
CATS AND DOGS
Sci-Fi Series 1
Sci-Fi Series 2

Non-fiction Books by Stanislaw Kapuscinski

VISUALIZATION—Creating Your Own Universe
KEY TO IMMORTALITY
[Commentary on the Gospel of Thomas]
BEYOND RELIGION: Volumes I, II and III
[Collections of essays on perception of Reality]
DICTIONARY OF BIBLICAL SYMBOLISM
DELUSIONS—Pragmatic Realism

Poetry in Polish
[with illustrations by Bozena Happach]
KILKA SŁÓW I TROCHĘ GLINY
WIĘCEJ SŁÓW I WIĘCEJ GLINY

INHOUSEPRESS, MONTREAL, CANADA
http://inhousepress.ca

ALEXANDER
Alexander Trilogy Book Two

Sequel to
ALEC
Prequel to
SACHA—THE WAY BACK

A novel by

Stan I.S. Law

INHOUSEPRESS, MONTREAL, CANADA

Published by
INHOUSEPRESS
http://inhousepress.ca

This book is a work of fiction.
Names, characters, titles, places and incidents are
either the products of the author's imagination
or used fictitiously.

ISBN 978-1-987864-05-2

Paperback Edition 2015
INHOUSEPRESS

CONTENTS

Prologue

The Beginning

Remembering

Time

The Return

The Epilogue

Prologue

Dr. Alexander Baldwin is a young, brilliant physicist, determined to unlock the secrets of the Universe. Yet, his scientific training is at odds with the memories of his youthful exploits that repeatedly drew him into the realm of irrepressible, often unbridled, imagination. He is only vaguely aware of having become a radically different person from the one of his youth.

Awkward, unseen elements from his past seem to pop up, as though to justify the present; elements that Alec has not experienced in his present life; elements so strong as to be pushing him with inexorable force. There are forces at play that he'd forgotten existed—forces akin to sorcery and Black Magic.

As the memories of his adolescent jaunts demand recognition, his mind and his emotions refuse to travel the same paths. His inner and outer selves are on a collision course. Ultimately, cajoling his wife and his son into his enigmatic reality, they all come very close to unlocking the secrets of the true nature of being.

***

The Beginning

I knew a man… such an one caught up to the third heaven.

2 Corinthians 12:2-4.

1
Peek-a-boo

The noise was overwhelming. The lightning struck repeatedly with blinding determination, frothing the water; steam rising in near vertical cones, joining with angry, convoluting clouds.

"Bastards," he thought. "I deserve better than that."

He did. He also dared to be original. Really original. Way past what the stereotype professors upholding the scientific *status quo* were capable of. No matter.

"I'll show them!" he murmured through his teeth.

In the next instant, his anger left him. The sky resumed its serene countenance, the lustrous water stretched out to the northern slopes of the distant Adirondacks. Moments later, he couldn't see that far. The western sun produced a shimmering sheen on the lake, barely disturbed by the dying breeze. The horizon closed in, the sky touching the water with blissful amity.

Had anyone told him that he had anything whatever to do with what happened moments ago, he would have denied it. After all, he was a hardnosed scientist, not some practitioner of hysterical mumbo-jumbo. What if he hadn't been awarded *summa cum laude*? He was a Master of Science. A Magister. And down south, in the US of A, at Caltech, they recognized his intent. His potential. More so that the local upstarts.

"I really wish you wouldn't do that!" Suzy's tone of voice was much sterner than her face.

She was certainly disoriented but, all in all, she was beginning to get used to it. It wasn't the first time that Alec had shifted from place to place in, what appeared to be, less than a second. One instant he was in one place, the next in another. It didn't make any sense.

"I'm sorry, you know..." he started.

"Yes, I know. But it's still getting on my nerves. It's disconcerting."

"I'm..." he began, reaching out for her waist in an attempt to embrace her, "...sorry."

This time she sighed.

"At least I wish you wouldn't do that when I am around. And especially when other people are coming. Surely you can do that for me?"

Yet, there was a poorly veiled threat in her plea. Not a threat of hell and damnation, but a festering omen of her unpredictable temper that she still managed to hold in relatively strong reins. Evidently even his Suzy had her limits. He regarded her azure eyes momentarily turning to tempered steel, only to relax in a smile that seldom left her face—the face he loved since he was a boy; ah, yes, a boy flexing his muscles to impress her. But it was her hair what really beguiled him. Long, flowing, tresses, now catching the rays of the evening sun which laced her golden filaments with streaks of red.

Alec smiled. For a briefest of moment their eyes studiously avoided each other. He knew that look in her eyes.

The 'other people' were Suzy and Alec's parents. The occasion was his Master's degree in physics, which he had just won at McGill University. His parents had decided to have a sort of Coming of Age party, before he'd leave to write his doctorate at Caltech. Alec wasn't all that keen on both sets of parents paying court to their easy-going existence. His mom, Alicia, would repeatedly drop her usual hints such as: 'isn't it time you two lovebirds tied the knot?'

Dad, looking tired lately, a slight stoop down to Alec's height hiding his conspiratorial smile, would whisper suggestions that it was high time Alec made an honest woman out of Suzy. 'Not for me, you understand, son, but you know how mother is.' Dad would follow this remark with a knowing wink.

As far as Alec knew, having lived together, on and off, for some five years, they were as honest with each other as anyone could be. But he would never say that to his dad.

Suzy's parents seemed more understanding, or perhaps just more tolerant. Officially, or theoretically, he and Suzy had moved in together for practical, namely financial, reasons, just after Suzy started teaching French at the CEGEP. But neither of them ever thought that practicality had anything whatever to do with it. It just felt like the right thing to do. At any rate, Suzy's mother seemed more preoccupied with her make-up than with her daughter's marital status. Only Mr. Norman, Mr. John Norman, with whom Alec still found it impossible to get on first name terms, was as discrete as any father could be. Alec strongly suspected that, although Mr. Norman was well aware of their living arrangements, to him, the doting father, Suzanna remained the eternal, and eternally innocent, Vestal Virgin.

In a peculiar, indefinable way, Alec thought that the old man was right. There was a strange innocence in Suzy that, in spite of her occasional bouts of temper, made her almost child-like. This innocence combined with her complete, unabashed, and almost overwhelming femininity, made her totally irresistible.

At least to him.

"I really don't find your peek-a-boo tricks amusing," she threw over her shoulder on her way to the kitchen. She still had to finish two large plates of *canapés*.

"Next you'll be accusing me of sorcery, or black magic," he mumbled, finding the idea as amusing as it was ridiculous. Luckily, by then Suzy was out of hearing. He once saw her reading up on Black magic, making it quite clear that she equated Black with Evil.

Nevertheless, her parting shot brought Alec back to his purported, if disconcerting, habit of shifting from one chair to another, or from one end of the room to the other side. He'd tried to explain to her, more than once, that, in spite of the many assurances of various talented Sci-Fi writers, there was no such thing as instantaneous traversing of space, any more that it was possible to travel through time. At least not backwards. We all travel through time forward. When we stop, it's because we have just dropped dead. As for the first two cases, it is not just that science has not as yet found a way of doing so, but it never would. Time travel would create a paradox, which would forever remain irreconcilable. The concept of time travel made for good fantasy stories, but that's all they were. Stories. And traversing from one side of the room to the other in-no-time-at-all would be equivalent to travel in time. Backwards. In this material universe of ours this could never happen, he'd repeated many times.

Except for his childhood experiences…

Alex shrugged. He wished his lingering memories would leave him alone.

Getting back to the real world, it was the same paradox as with the velocity of light. One couldn't reach it for the simple reason that it would take infinite force to move mass at such velocity. And any object possessed of any mass would become infinite if it reached the magic C. The velocity of light. Albeit the stretching into infinity occurs only at right angles to the direction of travel—but infinite is infinite—in whatever direction. Nevertheless, Alec did, on occasion, appear to deny the laws of physics. At least in Suzy's judgment. But Black magic? *Bah and Humbug* as his father would say. His dad was a great admirer of Ebenezer Scrooge—both, before and after Ebenezer's metamorphosis.

But Suzy had her own ideas.

"You scientists are playing around with dangerous things. I've warned you before. Stop before you do yourself harm," she'd insisted, on a number of occasions.

Suzy finished the appetizers and busied herself arranging flowers in the living room vase. She still contended that his peek-a-boos had something to do with the brand new 10TeV accelerator the experimental physicists were using in an attempt to find the Higgs particle. Alec had been invited on a tour of the monster only last month, to witness a series of experiments. The 10TeV accelerator yielded 10 trillion electron volts; hopefully enough to smash atoms into smallest particles known to man: the Higgs particles. A very excited Alec Baldwin Jr. had been the only undergraduate student invited.

"Darling, I told you..."

His voice trailed off into silence. He could hardly tell her that he had absolutely no idea what it was that she was seeing. He was not in the least bit aware of ever having 'space-shifted' in any way whatever.

"They will be here soon. Do I look all right?"

She hit him with an almost overwhelming wave of femininity. Her polka-dot dress, taken directly from a late 60s Hollywood musical, gave her a look of carefree girlishness. Her eyes grew larger, disarmingly innocent; her lips parted in a supplicatory smile, her head turned coquettishly over one shoulder. He said nothing but again tried to take her in his arms.

"Darling, not now. You'll ruin my make up!"

She wiggled out, though not too fast, from his embrace. She must be nervous about tonight, Alec thought. She seldom if ever wore any make up. She didn't need to.

Anyway, time travel was limited by similar constraints as space and light. As time is a factor of space, the two are inexplicably interwoven into spacetime. The only way to experience anything in another timeframe would necessitate a step outside space, outside time, and thus outside the material or physical universe. And that, according to all laws of physics, was impossible also.

"Oh yes? And what about the Black Holes?" Suzy had once asked. She seemed to capitalize the last two words.

She was right of course. No one knew what happens inside those singularities. No one knew everything. Not yet. That was precisely why Alec loved physics so much. The more you learned, the greater unknowns bubbled to the surface. It was as if the universe and its laws were playing their own game of peek-a-boo. Sometimes he thought he grasped some new concept, gained a fresh understanding, construed a new insight—the next instant, it would be gone. And, as with the Cheshire cat, only the grin lingered behind, suspended in the rarified space of theoretical physics—a vague aroma of things to come.

"That's the fun with infinity," he murmured under his breath. "It's infinite!"

Suzy agreed with his arguments, she just didn't believe them. She trusted the evidence of her own eyes. She knew that occasionally Alec moved outside the limits imposed by time or space, or any laws of physics, for that matter. On one occasion, he'd even changed his shirt on the way across the room. *In no time at all.* One moment he was standing by the window, pulling on the blinds, and the next instant he was by the door wearing a dark blue shirt. The white shirt he'd been wearing at the window had vanished into thin air. She saw it happen. No matter what he said later. Her mind was not constricted by his vast knowledge of physics. Sometimes he envied her. She could be so sure...

And when Suzy was sure, Alec knew better than to argue with her.

If Suzy's observations were right, then his shifts in location could not be due to his incredibly fast movement from one armchair to another. No. So-called, telepathy was involved—if such were possible. The only theory that fitted the facts was that he was rebuilding, or reconstituting, his physical body from the available energy extant in the environment to which he was returning. From where? The posting address was of no consequence. Matter and energy were indestructible but interchangeable. If he was not present in one place, he had to be in another. But how? Should he be able to move backwards even one second in spacetime, the same principle would apply. Only then it would be more than easy to reconstitute his physical body in the exact location it was a second ago. In fact, in any duration of less than a few millennia, the same would apply. More or less. There could be tides or currents in the fabric of spacetime, of course; energy fields, gravitation, perhaps still unknown forces that, on occasion, could upset the laws of physical universe. The exceptions only served to prove the rule. But all this was theory. A figment of his overactive imagination. To date, it was not a part of physics. He should know. He was about to write his thesis.

Once or twice he attempted to explain the theory of his speculations to Suzy. He couldn't tell her everything, because, well, on the face of it, it didn't make sense! It was not a matter of mathematical logic, more like a... well, like an act of faith. Once you assumed that he'd done it, that Suzy's peek-a-boo observations were not figments of her imagination, it seemed perfectly logical, but you needed that assumption based on faith...

On the other hand, perhaps it had me she, and not him, who resorted to some kind of shady magical practices. She was certainly beautiful enough to be a witch and get away with it.

Alec recalled when, as a boy, he just couldn't accept that an object heavier than air could fly, like a 747, for instance. Or how could a boat or a ship made of steel or ferrocement float? But he'd seen planes fly, heavy ships float. He accepted these facts with his intellect but not with his emotions. At some level of his young perceptions, he still couldn't accept it. Emotionally, it just didn't make sense. Gradually his feelings caught up with his mind. But until that time, the principle of the vacuum created by the airfoil, and displacement governing the possibility of floatation, remained just acts of faith. Like his imagination. When he closed his eyes, he could fly. But only with his eyes closed.

Suzy knew Alec was struggling in a reality other people recognized as 'normal', but she didn't like it. And when Suzy didn't like something, Alec often found it safer to let it go. Lately he did—and he paid for it.

And then the doorbell chimed.

"Darling..." His mother's opening salvo reverberated in the hall. "You look absolutely gorgeous. But then you always do, darling. You always do."

When she's right, she's right, Alec nodded from afar. She always did. Look gorgeous, that is.

Alicia didn't look bad either. If it hadn't been for the slightly excessive makeup, particularly the rouge underlining her cheekbones, she could have been Suzy's elder sister. Not much older, either. Her figure was fantastic, the curve of her neck, patrician. It had been three months since Alec had last seen his mother. He wasn't sure he would see much of her today. Suzy was bound to lead her to the cocktail cabinet where dear mom would be happiest. Not that she 'drank'. She'd been known not to touch a drop of the hard-stuff for weeks at a time, just to be able to let herself go when an occasion presented itself.

"Alexander, darling!" his mother said, offering her cheek to be kissed. "Alec, doesn't he look just wonderful?"

She'd taken to calling Alec—Alexander, when her son first left home. She felt it was more appropriate, more mature. Continuing to call her own husband Alec did not seem contradictory to her. After all, everyone knew how masculine Alec Baldwin Sr. was. "Not that there is anything..." She once tried to explain but lost her thought.

Alec Sr. dutifully agreed. Dad usually did. It was the best policy. And dad was very good at carrying out policies. He'd just retired as the Chief Engineer in charge of administration of Air Atlantic, the only real competitor of Air Canada. This involved both formulating and carrying out countless policies, as well as constant negotiations with VIPs. He still claimed it had been more exiting than living with a slide-ruler in his pants. His younger assistants had been brought up on computers. They probably had no idea what a slide-ruler was.

Alec held dad in vaguely grudging respect. His father had never struck him as an epitome of mental dexterity. He was good at his job, or had been while still working, and he made his mother happy. Slightly taller than Alec, about six-foot-two, he still presented a striking figure of robust masculinity: broad in the shoulders, still able to suck in his protesting waist, and still drawing glances from women half his age. He could hold his own in any crowd, hold up his end of any conversation, even if he lacked the deeper knowledge to venture his own opinion. People found him congenial, pleasant, a good man to have around.

Only he did look a little tired, lately.

And, to repeat, dad made Alec's mother happy. He was the rock she could lean on in moments of stress, when the currents of life seemed to drift away from her striving grasp. As was happening now. Nevertheless, while Alicia thought that her son should get married, settle down, his father reminded her gently that had he done so himself, then he and Alicia would never have met, let alone gotten married.

"He is twenty-four, dear. At this age I was in England, trying to make up my mind what to do with my life."

For a moment Alec Sr.'s eyes drifted, lingering on some old memories.

"Yes but... " Her voice was almost plaintive.

"...but Alec, ah... Alexander, on the other hand, just graduated; he's won a scholarship to Caltech. He is acclaimed the best scholar graduating this year at McGill, and he seems perfectly happy to stick with Suzy, without venturing into the playing-field, which nowadays seems replete with more 'gentlemen's' diseases than was the case when I was his age."

Alicia seemed to feel better under the onslaught of her husband's quiet logic.

"Do let me offer you a drink, Mother," Suzy pulled Alicia firmly towards the cocktail cabinet. "Alec, you will give me a hand?"

More often than not, Suzy addressed both women as 'mother', both men as 'dad'. Somehow, she'd managed to avoid confusion.

Suzy suspected that Alicia was waiting for the opportunity to break her self-imposed fast. As for assistance, she was addressing Alec Sr. They had been on first name terms almost since they all met, that day, in Sloop Bay off Valcour Island, on Lake Champlain. Some ten years ago.

Alexander couldn't help but smile at the ease with which Suzy killed two birds with one stone. She made both his parents happy with a single request. Being left momentarily alone, his thoughts drifted back to the matter that was beginning to prey on his mind.

Frankly, he couldn't blame Suzy.

Living with a man who did things which, according to the sane majority, could not be done, could not be easy. At least Alec no longer drifted into his imaginary travels, a habit he had when they first met.

Yet, of late, she often seemed to feel lonely.

There was nobody with whom she could share her knowledge of Alec's youthful exploits. Now, even in hindsight, they seemed impossible, at the very least improbable. One had to know his past to be able to understand the internal battle he was waging within himself. Battle between the world of the mind and the spirit. Or was it logic versus imagination?

"Why must these two be always at adds?" she often mused, her perennial smile losing some of its luster.

There was no one she could lean on, confide in. No one, that is, if you exclude the bifocalled staff member, a Ph.D. she'd presumed, at the friendly local psychiatric ward. She'd tried. They'd listened politely, asked her if she had any other symptoms that disturbed her, and what medication she was taking for her delusions. It had been obvious that no one had believed her. Alec was her problem and her problem alone. It wasn't easy.

Unfortunately, Alec was very new to this shifting game. He was only just beginning to sort out what was happening. He hardly believed some of his conclusions himself. It was like flying and floating. He did it, but couldn't quite believe it. Not in his heart. Or so it seemed. After years of nuclear physics, later particle physics in which atoms appeared like giants compared to the subatomic quarks and mesons and a host of other nuclear debris...

And yet, weren't atoms virtually empty space? And if so, wasn't all this taking place in his mind? In Suzy's mind?

For the two of them, the story did not start when he began studying physics. It started a good few years earlier when he'd met his Princess. Princess Sandra.

It now seemed so very, very long ago. He missed having Sandra to ask questions. There was a time, when he thought of Sandra as his own soul. As his own inner being, incontrovertibly united with his own psyche. Not many people had a chance to meet their own inner selves. Not in 'real' life. The last thing he remembered was her admonition to 'just live'.

But that was then. There was no room in his present life for souls or inner beings. Now, he was a scientist. A man guided by this mind, and mind alone. And in the realm of scientific logic there is no room for sudden, inexplicable space shifting, in gross denial of laws of nature.

Alec had opened the door before Mr. Norman pressed the bell. Suzy's parents arrived punctually. Actually, his own mom and dad had arrived a little early. Mother probably wanted to give the apartment the once-over, before being forced to share her first impressions with anyone. It was, after all, her first visit to their new place.

John Norman embraced Alec as though he were his own
son. There seemed to be a genuine friendship between the
older man and Alec. Mr. Norman was a good twenty years
older than Alec's father. More like a granddad, really. A
granddad Alec had never had. Suzy was the youngest of the
Normans and had come fairly late in Mr. Norman's life. Her
nearest brother was sixteen years her senior.

"God, I missed you, son. It's really good to see you." He
finally let Alec go.

"Good of you to say so, Sir." Alec took Suzy's father's
coat.

"John," John Norman corrected.

"Ah, yes, sorry Sir, I mean...."

Mrs. Norman was only a little more reserved in her
attitude towards Alec. She still thought Alec was too young;
"She needs a strong hand, you know," she'd told Alec on a
number of occasions. "She's our youngest, you know," she
assured him repeatedly. "One tends to spoil the youngest..."

"How is my little girl?" she asked Alec, after bending his
head down to her ample bosom in a motherly embrace.
"Remember what I told you about spoiling her?" She looked
up at him sternly when he came up for air. She was a good
eight inches shorter than Alec.

"Yes, Mrs. Norman. But I really don't think Suzy is
spoiled at all. She's as mature and responsible as any woman
her age!" Alec tried to cheer up his prospective mother-in-
law, quite unaware of his qualifying statement.

"And just how many women Susan's age have you met,
young man? Well? Well?" she prompted. And as Alec stood
flustered, Joan Norman burst into laughter.

"Gotcha!" she blurted and pushed past Alec into the
living room.

Before joining his wife, John Norman took a step back
and pressed the door chimes. He had liked the sound they
made when Suzy showed him the apartment last week, on
condition that he wouldn't tell anyone.

"Do I hear wedding bells?" Alicia asked raising her glass.

This time Suzy was the only one who'd noticed. All six of them were sitting along the full length of the balcony, admiring the distant hills, now shrouded in haze, only just visible across the water. And then it happened. Alec was at the very end of the balcony, sipping his Scotch and water, and then...

Well, it was strange to say the least.

He was telling his dad about the benefits of USLA when, in the middle of his sentence he'd changed positions: from one end of the balcony to the other. Normally such an inexplicable shift might have been ignored, but the balcony was less than five feet wide. He would have had to climb over Mr. & Mrs. Norman's stretched out legs to get to the other side—the other end of the balcony. One instant he was talking to his dad, and the next he was smiling at Susan's mother.

At first, seemingly, no one had noticed anything. The human mind tends to dismiss things that do not make sense. And Alec might have gotten away with it, had it not been for the plate of *canapés*. It left Suzy's hands and descended by the shortest route towards his feet. He caught it just in time.

"Perhaps you will offer one to your mother?" Suzy asked sweetly. Her eyes, however, told quite a different story. As she brushed by him on her way into the living room, she whispered, "You promised you wouldn't. Not with people around?"

Alec had never promised anything of the sort. Nor could he. Quite the contrary. He assured her, again and again, that he had absolutely no control over whatever it was that she'd noticed. Or thought she had. He'd spent countless hours trying to translate her observations into some semblance of logic, all to no avail. What Suzy described made no sense.

For a moment he played with the idea of asking the others if they'd noticed something, anything peculiar taking place, but that would really make Suzy mad. And it was unwise to make Suzy mad. For whatever reason, and in front of others, family or not, it was equivalent to suicide. His—not hers. Well, practically...

Or maybe it was all Suzy. Maybe she was suffering from some sort of mental aberration that prompted her to see things that didn't happen. Neither of the parents had said anything. But he didn't dare suggest it to her. Anyway, what purpose would it serve?

"Won't you have one, Mrs. Norman?" he proffered the tray.

"Can't I have two?"

"Of course, Mrs. Norman."

"Three...?" This time she looked closer at Alec's eyes. "What is it, son?" There was astute concern in her eyes.

"It's nothing," he lied. "Really, Mrs. Norman."

"Son!" his father called. "Why did you take away our *canapés*?"

Could it be that his father only now noticed his absence from his side? Perhaps Suzy was right. My God, whatever is going on? "Sandra..." he whispered. And then the moment was gone. Suzy came back with another tray while everybody was still busy doing justice to the bottle of Black Label Alec had gotten on his way back from the States. As a libertarian at heart, he considered buying off-duty liquor his patriotic duty. At the present rate, the Scotch would die a sudden death before Suzy had had a chance to serve dinner. Returning to the balcony, she looked perfectly calm and in high spirits. Alec smiled his thanks.

As it often happens at such gatherings, at any one time the three men would chat at one end of the balcony, the three women amused each other at the other. The three women in Alec's life. Susan, with her long, blond hair, was much closer in appearance to Alicia than to her own mother. What was more, she was relatively tall, as was his mother: slim, almost statuesque, while Mrs. Norman tended towards the short and cuddly variety. Not fat, but well, perhaps just very well endowed with generous pulchritude. Suzy probably inherited the same features but they were distributed on a frame about six inches taller, which, frankly, made an enormous difference. A goddess, versus a mother goddess. His own mother also gravitated, or rose is a better word, to the first variety. Of course, Mrs. Norman had given birth to four children—Suzy had three much older brothers she hardly ever saw—while he was an only child. This could, at least in part, account for the difference in the two mothers' proportions.

Strangely, the two mothers were about the same age, but Joan Norman had married a much older man. He'd been established by the time they'd met, while Alicia and dad had climbed the ladder together. Now his dad was also retired, but this was partly due to an inheritance he'd received from the Old Country. Apparently being an only child ran in his family, as he was the sole heir to the estate of his grandfather, who'd spent a good part of his life in India, amassing his fortune. Not a great fortune, but enough to allow dad and mom to do the travelling they'd always been drawn to. And, of course, the new boat was much bigger. From a twenty-seven-foot O'Day, dad has upgraded to a thirty-seven-footer, by the same builder. Central cockpit, a 'real bedroom' astern, and room enough to swing a cat. Two cats if need be. Not as agile (the boat, not the cats), nor as maneuverable, but what comfort! "If I'm in a hurry, I'll take a jet," dad liked to assure anyone who questioned his choice of locomotion. But he wasn't quite fair. With a good breeze the new 37 would leave the old 27-footer well behind, and Alec Sr. liked that a lot.

Yet, the yacht was practically dad's only folly, if such it was. In all other respects, it was almost a shame that Alec Sr. exhibited virtually no interest in money. It was necessary, it was utilitarian, it was practical. Often it was a nuisance, particularly at income tax time. Like father—like son. Alec Baldwin Jr. loved mathematics, but hated accounting.

Soon after finishing an enormous pile of steamed shrimps served with individual bawls of garlic butter and French fries— which they ate sailor-wise: with their fingers—both parental couples left. It was a long-standing custom that no dessert would be served. A small cognac with coffee, a single Belgian dark chocolate, and they were gone. Alec and Suzy cleared the dishes together and returned to the balcony. It was that time of the year when the evenings were still warm, but cool enough to cuddle up in each others arms for extra comfort. They had a hemispherical chair, resembling a satellite-dish, which only just fitted on the narrow terrace but was eminently suitable for such occasions.

"Tell me about her?" Suzy whispered, her head resting on Alec's shoulder.

"Her?"

"Her."

Alec knew she was talking about Sandra. There was no other 'her' in his life. He'd already told Suzy a little about Sandra, now and then, more as a memory of his youthful exploits than as a vibrant part of his life. Frankly, he was ready to leave that part of his life behind. As far as he was concerned, Sandra was an imaginary figment of his youth.

She no longer belonged to the scientific coordinates of his mind.

What could he tell her that she didn't already know? Some things could not be shared. Not for unwillingness, but well, some feelings cannot be translated into words. He recalled a saying he'd once heard: the intellect calculates, the soul feels. Perhaps poets can do justice to the feelings, but Alec was a hard-nosed physicist. Or… tried to be? He may have inherited a lighter, more artistic side from his mother, but not enough to be able to speak, with facility, of the unspeakable.

"All too often, Sandra seemed well beyond words..." Alec began. He never felt comfortable talking about her. Not even with Suzy.

Suzy cuddled even closer. His eyes drifted across the expanse of the lake, and then beyond.

"My contact with Sandra, if I can be call it that, began when I was no more than fourteen. At the time, I had developed a habit of escaping into a wild, imaginary world; a world that I seem to have populated with great achievements, conquests on unprecedented scale, with heroism and daring, mostly, if not exclusively, designed to escape a reality which, at the time, I did not find particularly exciting."

He smiled a little sadly.

"Since those days, my schooldays, I'd learned that such an imaginary world is a form of escapism not altogether unknown to child psychologists. Adults tend to compensate for their limitations, real or perceived, by realities supplied by the prodigious imagination of celebrated authors of books of fiction, by prolific screenwriters, poets and musicians. They sate their need for adventure by identifying with the bushwhacking heroes of yesteryear, by the exorbitant worlds of science fiction, by losing themselves in romance novels populated by the bold and the beautiful. At the bottom end of this escape funnel, the frustrated housewives turned countless innocuous starlets, propped up by aging ex-stars of afternoon soaps, into multi-millionaires.

"And you found a different way to compensate for your perceived inadequacies?" She smiled up at him. In her heart Alec had no inadequacies. Well… almost, she smiled at her own thoughts.

He ignored her interruption, but drew her even closer, planting a gentle kiss on her upturned lips.

Frankly, she was right. Any other boy with Alec's talents and achievements would find no reason to escape reality. He might well have wallowed in his scholastic achievements, sport championships, and even a happy, close-knit family life. But Alec had not been an ordinary boy. Not by a long shot. In fact, even in his early teens he would find the word "ordinary" as distasteful as would any promising artist or musician. From as early as six or seven years of age, Alec had exhibited extraordinary characteristics, a heritage that even now he found challenging to live up to.

"The real story began when I met Sandra..."

"When you *imagined* you met Sandra?" she corrected.

"No, Su! When I *met* Sandra. She was as real to me then, as you are now."

Then she felt his muscles relaxing again.

"I first saw her reflection in a mirror, then in a dark pane of my bedroom window. My life was never the same since. It seems that my overactive imagination took me on ever wider escapades, all seemingly propagated by my rapport with my... with my imaginary, if you insist, Princess Sandra, who seemed to appear and disappear at will, exposing me to ever wider views of the universe." By now his voice sounded as dreamy as the stars swirling his eyes. "Together we traversed time and space as easily as closing my eyes and letting imagination take me, take us, to the very end of the rainbow."

Suzy's lips tightened, just a fraction. She felt a pang of inexplicable jealousy. She scolded herself, *I mustn't be jealous of figments of his imagination.*

"And what a pot of gold had invariably awaited me there!" Alec affirmed, now lost in the world of yesteryear.

He didn't tell her that this strange period in his life, lasting no more than a few months, coincided with his incipient maturity, perhaps stimulated by the hormones that demanded some strange metamorphosis in his body. In his inner worlds, as he called them, he and Sandra had crossed galaxies, traversed eons of time, cringed frozen, terrified, while suspended over the green slime of the primordial earth, only to return with more questions than he had before. Only in those days, Sandra was there to answer many of his questions.

Now, Sandra was gone.

Alec could recall virtually all the details of his experiences under Sandra's tutelage. What he experienced became indelibly etched on his young mind.

"You must understand, Su, that the inner-world I had seemingly created for myself was as real as anything I had ever experienced with my five physical senses. In fact, those very same senses seemed infinitely more acute, sharpened to diamond hardness, honed to perfection in the worlds where no mundane distractions diluted their effectiveness."

He took a deep breath. There seemed an eerie silence around them, as though nature herself was listening to the secrets of the inner worlds.

"Yet, as far as Sandra was concerned, there is one other trait that set her apart from all the other characters I had played, or played with, or indeed had created in my imagination. For surely, in spite of the palpable reality of my inner worlds, it must have been just imagination." He smiled sadly. "What else? You do not scale Mt. Everest and conquer the North Pole in the same day, indeed, within the same hour or two…"

His voice grew quiet, hardly above a whisper.

"What really set her apart from all the other imaginary characters was, or had been, that she alone had not succumbed to my will. She had not appeared at my bidding, had not acted in a manner that in any way implied that I was, or had been, the creator of her presence. If anything, I'd felt subjected to her will, her desires, her bidding…"

He couldn't tell her, not his dear, dear Suzy, that he recalled making himself available to Sandra's every whim. Or so it had seemed at the time. And what was equally as strange was that this indelible impression that Sandra left on his awareness has been etched on his mind after only a few months. She'd come, she'd conquered, and she was gone. All in his dreams. Or daydreams. No matter. She was more real to him, even now, than any other experience that ever touched his awareness.

"And when I finally began to understand the possible reasons for her presence, she bid me her final farewell."

His mind retreated into a realm he'd once called his own. What an incredible farewell it had been. He was no longer talking to Suzy. He was reliving the experience he would carry for the rest of his life.

"We both hovered among an infinity of stars. Suspended, weightless... The black velvet of outer space, as wide and as deep as my inner senses would reveal to me, surrounded us on all sides. Then, as though it were the most natural thing in the world, she merged into me, imbued me with the presence of her utterly overpowering intensity; melted into my beingness. It was as though her own individuality was no more, as though her very sense of being became my own. But she did not die: quite the contrary. From that day, from that strangest of all my experiences, I became one with her, joined into a single amalgam, into a precious alloy that could never be set apart."

The rest he couldn't share, not even with Suzy. He closed his eyes...

Even as he became aware of Sandra losing her individuality within his, from that day on he remained convinced that, should he die, he in turn would lose his individuality within her. Like an evolving vortex—a partnership of being and becoming. Like two peas in a single pod. For of one thing Alec was as sure as of day being followed by night: Sandra was immortal. She also seemed to be all-knowing, omnipresent, or at least present wheresoever Alec found himself in any of the inner or outer worlds. Somehow, at some level of perception, she was with him, an inseparable part of his own being.

"Alec? Alec, come back..." Suzy was shaking his arm. "Alec!"

His eyes opened slowly. He smiled at his love.

"Don't worry, darling. All this happened more than ten years ago, when I was just stepping on the road toward manhood."

In a way, one could say that Sandra, a girl, a woman, an incredibly beautiful Princess, made him a man. In another way, she was none of these, yet, she was all of them at the same time.

As fate would have it, at about that same time, Alec had also met Suzy.

Both blondes, both beautiful, but that is where the likeness ended. Even as Sandra conquered and ruled his inner worlds, Suzy was the supreme queen of his passion. Suzy was as physically enchanting as Sandra was adept at sating his more esoteric needs.

Ten years...

Although Alec had not given up his imaginary travels for some years, Sandra had never again appeared in them. And yet, in a strange way, he'd always held a deep conviction that she was here, and there, and wherever he went, with him. Perhaps she really was one with him. Though in what way, by what blending of atoms or subatomic particles, he couldn't explain.

"So you see, Pet, she is not a woman of whom you can be jealous."

"Who, me?" She managed to convey innocence mixed with absolute denial. "Jealous?" She was almost convincing.

Alec held Suzy closer to his chest. "There is a school of thought that within every man there is an anima, even as an animus is in every woman. They are one, only my anima became personalized in my imagination...."

Suzy looked up at him. This time there was no doubt in her eyes. No doubt at all.

"I suppose," he added ponderously, "you might think of her as the feminine part of my own self. As part of me. Whatever part Sandra plays in my life, it is as much at your disposal as any other aspect of my being. Do you believe me?"

She nodded. Alec breathed a sight of relief, although his conclusion was not quite accurate. He rationalized his feeling this way, but, if it hadn't been for the fact that he was a physicist, that he was totally committed to scientific research, he would simply have said that it was Suzy who ruled his heart.

There was one other thing he couldn't tell her. For some inexplicable reason he felt that Sandra, the Sandra within him, was a source of quite incredible power. A power that was neutral, amoral, and, in equally as strange way, at his disposal. Only he had no idea how to use it, let alone how to control it. Yet, it seemed, it was a power that demanded recognition.

Yes, he nodded to himself. Suzy ruled his heart, but Sandra, Princess Sandra, ruled his soul.

A week later Alec left for Caltech.

He was hoping to leave youthful fancies behind.

**

2
Alexander Baldwin Ph.D.

From the synchrocyclotron at Columbia University to the monster atom-smasher at Waxahachie in Texas, was a long journey. During the intervening years, the Tevatron at the Fermi National Accelerator Laboratory, which measured some four miles around, dominated the field of nuclear physics. Finally the Superconducting Super Collider, the SSC, at Waxahachie, was built to measure more than fifty miles in diameter. "Don't mess with Texas" is the saying down South. Texas likes to be big. The biggest—if at all possible. Well, Alec had no intention of messing with Texas or with the SSC. An opportunity to peek at the installation was all he could hope for.

And as he discovered later, there was a great deal to peek in on.

Already, after only a few years in the field, Alec found that there were many approaches in the advancement of research. Some, perhaps one could put Texans in this category, appeared to measure success in size. Others counted the number of years; still others stressed the degree of intensity. In physical terms, the SSC was the biggest but measured in years, in experience, it was a mere baby. No one knew for certain what doors it might open, what secrets of science it might unveil. After all, in terms of duration 'modern' physics may be said to have begun around 430 B.C., when Democritus of Abdera declared that '*Nothing exists except atoms and empty space: everything else is opinion.*'

Perhaps. Opinions vary.

Alec thought that if we chose to measure the generations of knowledge by intensity, then we would have to pay homage to a group of people who formed part of the Manhattan Project. While their objective could be described as ignominious—the building of the atom bomb—it brought together the *créme de la créme* of scientific minds of the time. Robert Oppenheimer, Niels Bohr, Enrico Fermi, after whom the Fermilab was later named, John von Neuman, Hans Bethe, Richard Feynman, Eugene Winger.... Some called this group the greatest gathering of intellects since ancient Greece.

Other scientists assigned value to larger chunks of history.

There were those who called the XVII century the age of genius. Johannes Kepler, Galileo Galilei, Rene Descartes, William Harvey, Christiaan Huygens, Baron von Leibniz, Robert Boyle, Sir Isaac Newton, Sir Francis Bacon, John Locke... the list seemed endless, a roster seldom if ever surpassed in any century of intellectual endeavour. Alec smiled at the thought of where he might have been today if it weren't for those men. We all stand on the shoulders of giants, he thought. Without them we are nothing.

Alec always relied on intensity. He found that time is flexible, while intensity is like a pebble thrown into a pond. It creates concentric waves, ever increasing, ever bearing fruit in the field of human progress. The consequences of greatness leave their indelible mark on humanity as a whole.

Yes—intensity was always affecting time, while time might leave no mark on humanity at all. Like the stagnation of the Dark Ages.

But science was only one factor that stirred Alec's hunger.

Though he would never admit it to his colleagues, the experiences of his early teens were also firmly anchored in his subconscious. While he fully accepted the limitations imposed by the material world, he refused to prejudge the physical reality as the only reality. Somewhere, there was a bridge waiting to be discovered, perhaps crossed. It was a bridge only for the daring, for the stout of heart. But, he felt certain in his own heart that, when discovered, it would be a real, solid, scientific bridge. A bridge that would justify his choice of profession, and would somehow, someway, integrate it with the demands of his psyche.

He didn't expect it to be easy.

For the next few months, Alec tried to lose himself in his work. Researching a thesis was not something that could be carried out on a part time basis. It demanded full effort, total concentration and commitment. His great advantage over the other researchers was his relative maturity. Perhaps due to being a single child, Alec had been forced to spend a lot of his early years in the company of adults. This alone advanced his mental development well ahead of his biological years. As for the usual hormonal interferences—and powerful interferences they had been—he discharged them, so to speak, during the three intervening years between his sexual awakening and moving in with Suzy. At McGill he found *les* girls as exiting as would any virile young man. His reasonably athletic physique was generally regarded as attractive. His academic standing belied his somewhat scatterbrained appearance with the signature mop of disorderly hair hanging over his rugged features. He'd tasted the forbidden fruit and found it interesting, stimulating, but not overwhelming. For a while he experimented with the different aspects of the feminine mystique, until he discovered, to his utter amazement, that not one of his passing romances came even close to the enchantment that Suzy radiated. It was a moment of such powerful epiphany that he called her that same day and asked her to marry him.

She refused. He remembered that day, as that same evening, and extending well into the night, an electrical storm raged over Montreal with unprecedented fury. Next morning, the meteorologists were at a loss to explain the heavy storm, that didn't deposit a single drop of precipitation.

She'd said that she would never marry a man she couldn't trust. He recalled the conversation. He recalled most things that concerned Suzy. Even when he was with other girls.

"You mean you don't trust me? Why on earth not?" He wasn't really hurt; rather surprised.

"I didn't say that."

He couldn't decide whether she was coy or serious. His mathematical mind worked more in black and white than in shades of gray. Suzy's mind was multi-hued.

"Yes, you did. You said..."

"I said I could never marry a man I didn't trust."

"Well?"

"Well...? How am I supposed to know if I can trust you or not?"

"But... but... don't you trust me?"

"I don't know. Should I?"

The funny thing was that he'd never really thought about it. To be quite honest, his relationship with Suzy matured from a youthful infatuation to an almost sisterly relationship, to mad sailing cruises in beguiling moonlight, to.... He really didn't know where he stood exactly. Suzy was as much a part of his life as eating and drinking. Perhaps, even more so. She was like a fresh breath of spring he inhaled in moments of euphoria.

Did any of this advance him towards marriage?

"I would never break a promise to you."

"I suppose you wouldn't. But you also wouldn't break a promise given to anyone else. Would you?"

"Of course not."

"Then we cannot take this as the sole postulate for marriage."

"I never said it was sole..."

"Alexander." She only used his full name when she was about to say or ask something very important. "Why do you want to marry me?"

"Because I love you, of course."

"There is no 'of course' about it. Many people get married for many more obscure reasons. They are bored, lonely, insecure, afraid, to face the world alone. Are you any of these?"

"I... I don't think so. Why are you asking me all this? Don't you want to get married?"

"Frankly... not today."

"Tomorrow?"

"Alexander!"

"Oh, all right. I'll do it your way. Tell me what it is and I'll do it."

"Let me think about it and I'll let you know. Give me a couple of weeks."

Alec spent the next fortnight sitting on pins and needles. It was utterly absurd. Normally he would go to see her; they would dine together, go for a walk, with luck he might get lucky, as they say. He did fairly often. Suzy was no pushover, but she wasn't a prude. In fact she was disarmingly honest. There was no 'not tonight, I've got a headache' nonsense about her. If she wanted him she said so. If for whatever reason the atmosphere wasn't quite right, she was also open about it. Perhaps that is why whenever they did make love, it was always special. Something to be remembered—almost cherished. Suzy was a very special lady.

Finally, after exactly two weeks the telephone rang.

"Let's move in together," she said. No 'hello', no 'how are you?'. Just that. A proposal—rather a proposition. He wasn't sure which.

That was almost three years ago. He'd just turned twenty-one. It was a good time to try something new. They moved in together the next day without actually getting rid of their old places. For some unknown reason, at least unknown to Alec, she wanted it that way. It had to be a different place.

A new beginning. Their new place was small, worse than they've been used to, but they were together. It lasted three weeks. It was not quite the same as seeing each other on special occasions. No matter how often.

They'd joined forces some six more times, not counting occasional weekends. Once they'd lasted almost four months. It had been then that she'd said that she was considering giving up her own apartment. Alec took her to dinner and got rather tipsy. Somehow he'd considered it a major victory. For all his previous philandering, Alec had never discovered that women mature much faster than men. A year later she'd told him that finally he'd started acting like a man. That he'd matured. That he was still young wine, but the vintage showed promise.

"And before?"

"Before, my boy, you were a boy."

And that was that.

The first thing Alec had to do was to get his subject approved. He'd selected the California Institute of Technology, in Pasadena, because this illustrious university boasted, in his opinion, the top physicist in the world, Dr. Desmond McBride, whose acumen did not stop him from acting, on occasion, like a sour Scotsman—Scot, as he preferred to be called. Dr. McBride never tired of reminding people that it was self-evident that he was a man, whereas the word Scot denoted his affiliation to a Gaelic tribe of Northern Ireland, which migrated to Scotland in the fifth century. Regardless of his heritage, Dr. McBride, McDes as he was called behind his back, dared to talk and write things in scientific papers on subjects that others feared. He did not regard the present advancement of knowledge to be the alpha and omega of human endeavour. Quite the contrary. To many of his equally illustrious colleagues and to anyone who would listen, he also never tired of saying that physics had barely scratched the surface of knowledge.

"Nuts! My boy," he assured Alec, wrapping one of his arms over Alec's shoulder, which was about a foot higher than his own. "Nuts to them and to all theirr cohorrts. They wouldn't rrecognize a quarrk if it were squirrted into theirr nostrrils."

Professor McBride liked Alec the moment he laid eyes on him. The feeling was mutual. It could have been that they shared an affinity for disheveled mops over their equally high foreheads. It could have also been the seemingly scatterbrained look they shared, no matter how misleading. Alec knew that with the Professor, with McDes, he could dare to go where no man had gone before. Only in the opposite direction to Captain James Kirk. The good Captain had gone outwards. Alec was directing his spaceship inwards. As far in as he could possibly go. He completely ignored the fact that some of the post-docs working at Caltech referred to the Professor not as McDes, but McDeath. The Professor didn't mince words when he saw mediocrity. He called a spade a spade. And, even in the field of physics, there were many spades around that should have been shoveled away.

Alec wasn't deterred.

When Alec finally summoned enough courage to ask the Professor to supervise his thesis, the man smiled and replied, "I thought you'd neverr ask!" There was a surreptitious sense of humour fomenting under that grey mop of hair that seemed to make the impossible more acceptable. And, when Professor McBride talked, all things sounded possible. At least to Alec's ears.

"You'rre a young'un, me lad. You can go wherre an ol' coot can harrdly venturre any morre." There was a hint of sadness in the Professor's tone.

Dr. McBride still tended to roll his r's in the Scottish fashion, though Alec suspected this was just to add flavour to his other eccentricities. As for his allusion to quarks, that was a little more involved.

A quark is a subatomic particle. Its size is less than 10^{21} centimeters. That's one divided by one with twenty-one zeros. Quarks and leptons are as small as a point drawn by an *imaginary* pencil. Nothing you can imagine is as small as a quark. Collectively quarks and leptons are called fermions. Although none of them can be seen or smelled or tasted, the scientists assign them three colours that have nothing to do with colour. They might as well have a smell or a taste. Colour was introduced by Murray Gell-Mann to explain certain experimental results, and to predict others. Speaking of others, other scientists also allotted quarks delightful names such as 'charm' and 'strange' and 'up' and 'down'. Leptons have more prosaic names such as muons and neutrinos (tau), and the ever-popular electrons.

And so on, and so forth...

The reason these things are mentioned here at all is that since Democritus said, as is erroneously suggested, that the atom is the smallest indivisible particle, if we add up the eighteen quarks, six leptons, twelve gauge boson force carriers, then add to this list all the antiparticles, then you can see that there is a lot of room to explore in the invisible world of quantum mechanics. As for Democritus he never claimed that the 'atom' was the smallest particle. All he said was that a-tom is the smallest particle. In Greek 'a-tom' *means* the smallest, *indivisible* particle. Whatever it might be. Like possibly a quark or a lepton, only smaller...

Only they, those smaller 'wee ones', as Dr. McBride once referred to them, might, just might, consist of strings, and superstrings... which had only two dimensions, as long as you didn't try to measure them...

And this is the world that fascinated Alexander. The world within; within all matter. A world as invisible as any reality of his private inner travels, his inner visions, actions, aspirations. As invisible as Sandra, only much, much less real.

The other reason Alec had hoped to get into Caltech to do his thesis was that the Institute was the 'home' of Richard Feynman. It wasn't that the late physicist had come as close to fathoming Quantum Theory as anyone ever had; nor that Dr. Feynman was the Nobel Prize winner in physics. It was Richard Feynman 'The Man' that fascinated Alec. This Nobel Laureate once suggested that all physicists put a sign in their offices to remind them how little they know, or rather how much they don't know. He also warned his students to 'Learn from science that you must doubt the experts...'

But above all, Richard Feynman seemed to humanize physics. He once warned his listeners not to take his lecture too seriously. He said: '...*if you will simply admit that maybe she (nature) does behave like this, you will find her a delightful, entrancing thing. ...Nobody knows how it can be like that.*'

This is very much the awe Alec held in his heart for physics, but also for the whole universe. When Alec was alone, and no one could hear his most secret thoughts, he dreamed of following in Dr. Feynman's footsteps.

He never thought, nor would he ever dare to even suspect, that one day he would go much, much further.

Not all great minds have been enamoured with Quantum Theory. Albert Einstein, for instance, was a classicist. He believed in cause and effect. God doesn't play dice with the universe, he'd said. Others might well think that God can do anything She bloody-well wants. With the universe or with anything else. Nevertheless, Einstein expected predictable results. In Quantum Theory only probabilities are predictable. Einstein didn't like that.

To vent his spleen, or perhaps just his humour, as far back as 1936 Albert invited his pals, Boris Podolsky and Nathan Rosen to put together, what else but... the Einstein-Podolsky-Rosen Paradox. The original intent of the 'EPR Paradox' was to show that at least one of the implications of Quantum Theory was to Einstein and his buddies quite unacceptable. The three classicists wouldn't accept that measuring a photon in one place could have an instantaneous physical consequence on another photon somewhere else.

Sometime after Dr. McBride accepted Alec's subject for his thesis, Alec tried hard to explain to Suzy the substance of the EPR Paradox. It wasn't easy. Frankly, it took him almost four years at McGill to understand the implications of his involvement.

"What bothered Einstein was," Alec began, "that if one were to treat photons as real objects, rather than waves, awkward implications would creep into the field of physics."

He recalled Suzy's eyes shimmering as photons bounced off her irises.

"You know, of course, that the purpose of Polaroid sunglasses is to allow some photons to go through and some to be stopped. Right?"

"Yes, Professor," she smiled like a dutiful student. Alec ignored that.

"So right here, we regard photons as individual particles. Problems start when we realize that we have no way of knowing which photons will go through and which won't."

"Is that bad?" she asked innocently.

"Not as such," he tried not to lose his train of thought. To explain even the simple connotations of Quantum Theory was not as easy as one might think. "We can predict that half of the photons will go through, but we can never be sure what an individual photon will do."

"Fancy that..." Suzy then noticed the concentration on Alec's face and shut up.

"Now we get to the interesting part. Imagine that we entangle a pair of photons polarized at right angles to each other. Until you measure them, you have no idea what their polarizations are. They could be horizontal or vertical or at any other angle. All you know is that they are at ninety degrees to each other. Are you with me so far?"

"I think so. The photons are at ninety degrees to each other, but you don't know in what relations they are to you, so to speak." Her brow became knit in two delicate furrows.

"Good enough. Now the real fun starts. You now—this is all theoretical you understand—fire these photons off towards polarizing filters set up in opposite directions. OK?"

She nodded.

"Now if one photon passes through a horizontally polarized filter, it simply means that it was, originally, horizontally polarized. Right?" Another nod. "But, since the photons were polarized at 90 degrees to each other, this means that the other photon must have been polarized vertically. The second photon, therefore, would pass through any vertical filter, but not through a horizontal one."

"Makes sense to me. But where's the paradox?"

"Wait for it." Alec smiled. "The problem is that until the first photon hits the filter, we have no way of knowing whether it has been polarized vertically or horizontally. You might even say, the photon didn't know either, until it actually passed the filter."

"So?"

"So how did the second photon travelling in the opposite direction know what filter to pass through? How did it know whether it was polarized horizontally or vertically before the first photon passed the filter?"

"It didn't, I suppose," Suzy admitted.

"And yet, at the precise instant of the first photon arriving at its filter, its counterpart instantly became its opposite. Remember, the second photon could not have known what the first photon would do until it actually did it."

Suzy's face remained blank. She blinked repeatedly.

"I think I understand the physics of this, but aren't you anthropomorphizing the photons?" she said at last. "You make it sound as if they are making a choice?

"Don't you see, darling? There had to be some communication between the two photons? And what's more, the communication must have been instantaneous."

"Peek-a-boo?"

"What?"

"Never mind."

There ensued a prolonged silence. They sat facing each other, Alec's mind whirling within the mysteries of Quantum Mechanics, Suzy growing in admiration for her man. Yes, she confirmed to herself. Definitely my man.

"And your thesis...?" she asked at last.

"I don't know, really." He shook his head. "I mentioned the EPR to Professor McBride and all he said was 'About time'. As if he was just waiting for someone to get his or her teeth into the paradox. I suppose I just volunteered."

"But you do want to tackle it, don't you?"

His eyes finally settled on her lovely face.

"Yes, darling. For some unknown reason I want to get my teeth into it more than anything else in the world." And he kissed her with passion he had lately reserved only for subatomic particles.

"And peek-a-boo to you too," she whispered, when she finally came up for air.

Some 11,500 strenuous hours later, many of them passed as sleepless nights, after some 20 trips to Montreal and 10 visits from Suzy to Caltech, Alec became known as Dr. Alexander Baldwin, the youngest Ph.D. in Caltech's history. But he took residence in Montreal. During the same period of time he hadn't thought about Sandra even once.

Not even once.

Also, during this period, there had been not a single report of unexplained inclement weather. Alec was happy.

***

3
The Top of the World

After two and a half months of togetherness, Alec's first job came out of the blue. A telephone call from Professor McBride came as a surprise. He'd missed the old man. On a number of occasions Alec had been at the end of his tether, literally ready to give up, and ol' McDes had taken him by the elbow, lead him to his private office and practically forced a hefty drop of malt Scotch down Alec's throat.

"What's the matterr, Alec m'lad. Got stuck in the heatherr?"

The professor operated metaphors quite strange to Alec's ears.

"Heather, Sir?"

"Got blown off the heath?"

Alec had no idea what the professor meant. Of one thing Alec was very sure. Whatever it was, the ol' man meant well. And eccentric or not, the man was still brilliant.

"You'rre lucky, young man. Rreally lucky!"

The professor smacked his thin lips. The Scotch, as always, was first class. Sometimes Alec thought that the professor was just waiting for one of his charges to get depressed so as to have an excuse to partake in another drop of the hard stuff.

"I feel more depressed than lucky, Sir."

"Aye... I rememberr it well... " Dr. McBride was obviously wandering off on a tangent. "I was most deprressed the day beforre they nominated me forr the Nobel Prrize. Aye, that was most deprressing."

"Excuse me, Sir, but I fail to see how a nomination for Nobel Prize could depress anyone?"

"You can't, can you? Well, they also nominated that old fusspot from Irreland who couldn't tell the differrence between a lepton and a leprrechaun. A boson and a bozo. A Quarrk and a quack. A meson and..."

"I get the message, Sir. You were not delighted at having to share the Nobel Prize with someone you didn't particularly admire."

"Admire? Admirrre??? Arre you trrying to insult me young man?"

"No, Sir. I am sorry, Sir. Nothing was further from my mind?" Alec rose to his feet. The old man seemed ready to hit him over the head with the bottle of Scotch.

And then McDes smiled.

"I got you going, therre. Just ferr a minute I think I got you going rratherr nicely, eh son? Get yourr glass closerr to me, son. You want me to spill?"

The refilled glasses were followed by a prolonged, high-pitched laughter over the rim of the professor's glass. Alec just wagged his head. He felt like an ass, and he had no tail.

"You see, lad. The imporrtant thing, the exciting thing, is the trrip. Once you get therre, therre's nothing morre. Nothing until you get the next bee under y'rr bonnet. And then it starrts all overr again."

This scene had taken place no more than six months ago. Now Professor McBride's voice seemed to be coming from very far away.

"I'll be here for another couple of days. Why don't you drop in and join me?"

"Where, Sir?"

"You can pick up a helicopter. It will drop you right at the hotel." The Professor's Scottish elongated r's were conspicuously missing.

"Dr. McBride? Do you mind telling me where are you calling from?"

"Didn't I tell you? From the top of the world."

"What?"

"From Machu Picchu, lad. From the top of the empire. Bless my heart it's beautiful here. You won't believe it till you get here. I got your room all booked for tomorrow night."

"But, Sir..."

"Oh, and by the way," the Professor went on as if nothing was out of the ordinary, "I thought you might care to give them a lecture in Lima. They've got their pants all twisted over your conclusions on the EPR thing. The money isn't that good, but it'll be good experience for you. I'll see you!"

The EPR thing was, of course, the substance of Alec's, Dr. Alexander Baldwin's, doctoral thesis. Thanks to Dr. McBride it had been published on three continents in quite a few languages. The Professor was not just brilliant; he was a really good friend.

"Anyway, therre'll be enough left overr ferr a drrop of the harrd stuff, he, he..."

And the phone went dead. The resurrected rolling r's and all.

For a while Alec sat staring at the silent receiver he still held in his hand. He was on the verge of doubting if the call had really just happened. Perhaps he was reverting to his youthful daydreams, only the subject matter had changed. Then he shook his head.

"Eccentric? Mad as a hatter!" And then Alec laughed long and hard. "God I love that man," he said out loud. "I just love that man!" And he called the airline to book himself a flight.

For a moment he thought he would ask Suzy to come with him but, since his doctorate, he hasn't managed, as yet, to bring in his share of the loot. Suzy was keeping up her end, while he was lagging behind. He hoped the fee for the lecture would cover his ticket and the hotel. He didn't dare spend any more of Suzy's money.

On her return from the CEGEP, Suzy, bless her heart, was overjoyed at the news from the professor. Rather than being jealous, she wished Alec Godspeed, every success, and happy hunting.

"But just one look at a *señorita* and you're dead meat. You know that, don't you, sweetheart?"

"Not if she was standing naked at the top of the highest mountain," he swore.

"Then how would you know that she was naked?"

Suzy drove him to Dorval Airport that evening. He was booked on the 7 o'clock flight to Miami, changed there to AeroPeru and continued on to Lima. From there, he hoped to get a helicopter connection to Machu Picchu. If worse came to worst, he'd catch a local flight to Cuzco, and pick up a rotor from there.

The tickets set him back more than he could afford.

"Don't worry, darling. The beginning is always a bit difficult. And anyway, what would you do with all that money." Suzy smiled, seeing his frazzled expression.

"What money?"

"The money we wouldn't have spent on the tickets?"

He thanked his lucky stars for having met her, knowing her, for being with her. He would have stayed in Montreal, by her side, if she'd said a single word. But he was grateful to her for not having asked. He had no way of advising Dr. McBride that he wouldn't be coming.

"Will you marry me?" he asked for the thousandth time.

"I just might. Your name sounds much better with a Pheee'd after it. Ask me again after you get back."

"You can count on it."

To everyone's amazement, the airplane took off on time. Alec leaned back and tried to spot Suzy's car speeding home. Obviously, he couldn't. But his thoughts followed her all the way. Would anything change when they got married? He doubted it. A piece of paper didn't seem that important. Many people appear to rely on just such a document to get their share during divorce proceedings; but hardly to stay happy. Still, he liked the sound of Mrs. Alexander Baldwin. Except Suzy would probably keep her father's name. Mrs. Susan Norman. He hoped she wouldn't stick to the Ms. honorific. Perhaps she would hyphenate her name with his. Oh, well. Beggars can't be choosers. He sighed deeply just as an airhostess bent over him to avoid another person in the aisle.

"Are you all right, Sir?" she asked, a look of concern on her motherly face.

"I am now!" he quipped.

It was good to be alive.

He landed in Miami in early evening. Luckily, the connecting time was just three hours away. Soon he was settled in the AeroPeru, a Scotch on the rocks in his hand, an extra pillow under his head. After a light, and almost tasty, meal, he tried to get some sleep.

He dozed off almost at once.

He saw himself standing on a very high stage, towering over a great hall filled with students, all dressed in Incan national costumes, the colourful topacus. He was delivering a lecture on the EPR paradox. Now and again, he flew down and shot through a polarizing screen, emerging unscathed on the other side. He then reversed polarity and rose instantly to his elevated desk.

"And that's all there is to it," he assured his young audience. "You just reverse polarity and you get back to wherever you were."

There followed a tremendous applause that woke him up. It turned out that the engines were working overtime into the prevailing wind. For the last ten years or so, there'd been talk of the earth twisting a few degrees on her axis and severely upsetting the usual wind patterns. Something to do with the transfer of weight after a lot of ice had melted at both polar caps.

He fell asleep again. This time it was the captain's voice that woke him up.

"Ladies and gentlemen. We are now making our approach to the Aeropuerto Internacional Jorge Chávez. Please raise your tables and seats to an upright position and attach your seatbelts..."

Then he repeated all that in Spanish. It was a smooth landing.

Leaving the Lima airfield was another story. The customs officials had to deal with their returning citizens, who seemed determined to bring with them half of the United States annual export to South America, most, if not all of it, in carry-on baggage. The exit from the plane was blocked solid for half an hour. This was followed by a good 90 minutes at the customs. The funny thing was that Alec had only one small piece of hand luggage, yet he had to follow the mountains of overloaded natives piled before him. So much for AeroPeru organization.

The next problem was to get a connecting flight to Cuzco, or directly to Machu Picchu. Alec's Spanish was fair, but by no means perfect. After about a ten-minute haggle over the cost of a taxi, he was sped to the small helicopter airport on the outskirts of the city. Surely, he thought, the very idea of a helicopter is to get you into the centre of town; not dump you at the outskirts?

No matter.

He survived the trip, though barely. It was a hair-raising ride in which the dilapidated taxi crossed at least 40 red lights at an average speed of a 100 kilometers an hour. He was playing with the idea of letting him drive all the way to Cuzco, but decided to stay alive instead. If the breaks had failed, he would have made it to Cuzco by shear momentum.

The large ex-US army Sikorsky took less than two hours to get him and the other tourists to Cuzco. The whole idea was to take a helicopter directly to Machu Picchu. The pilot decided otherwise. Anyway, at Helicuzco, an appendage to the Alejandro Velasco Astete International Airport, there weren't that many choices. Alec learned later that helicopters didn't fly all the way to Machu Picchu. Some years ago the authorities had decided that the vibrations created by the rotors, or perhaps the noise as such, had a detrimental effect on the ruins. Just as well, thought Alec. By the time they'd reached Cuzco, the noise of the rotors was making him deaf.

"You must taka smallerr birrd," the pilot told him. "Anyway, too mucho winda. Anda rrain. Anda foga." The pilot sounded as if he'd learned his English in Italy. He also sounded a little like Professor McDes after he'd had one too many.

Rather than taking a smaller 'birda', Alec decided to take the train, which would take him to Aguas Calientes. From there, a short bus ride would deposit him in his waiting Professor's arms. He'd been to Europe, twice, but had never visited South America, and he wanted to see as much as he could.

Alec wasn't sorry about the delay. He looked around.

What a completely different atmosphere, he mused. Not just the culture but also the feel of the place was steeped in a different history. At the time of Columbus, Cuzco was the vibrant, powerful capital of the Inca Empire. At 3326 meters above sea level, one soon learned to breathe deeper than one would normally. It was the highest Alec had ever been. The city now sports about 300,000 people; most of them bent on trying to squeeze, quite aggressively, the very last dollar from throngs of tourists. The resulting hustle was in stark contrast to the serenity descending from the pale blue, almost cloudless sky.

He walked to the *estacion* San Pedro in good time to get his lungs filled with acrid smoke, even before mounting the train. Watching his shoulder-bag and pockets, he got his ticket and climbed into the compartment. This was already 'out of season', the 'dry season', so he was lucky to get into the 'autovagon', which, he'd been assured, was less smelly than a regular coach.

It wasn't true.

When two hours later the train came alive, Alec felt a strange thrill. He was on the Machu Picchu train. The most frequently used train in Peru. The autovagon would take three hours to get to Aguas Calientes. Some trip. Slowly, very slowly it began zigzagging up a gentle serpentine climb. There was not enough room for the train to climb in one continuous sweep or curve. The prehistoric locomotive advanced some distance pushing, stopped and pulled in the opposite direction, and then climbed the next ramp. This exercise was repeated four times until the train cleared a cloud suspended halfway up the mountain. Cuzco was built by the Incas at almost eleven thousand feet above sea level, and the train was moving upwards from there—a strenuous climb, indeed.

For three hours Alec gazed on high mountainous valleys. They reminded him of the Alps, only here there were hardly any people. Just nature on all her volcanic, rapacious glory: a most enchanting journey. The train descended with audibly less effort, relatively gently, towards *estacion* Puentas Ruinas, some four thousand feet lower than the highest point they'd climbed. On his left, Alec saw the deep gorge carved out by the Urubamba River. On his right, the mountains soared as high as Mount Veronica, its white peek touching 5750 meters, almost a kilometer higher than Mt. Blanc, which dominated the Alps. Alec sighed a silent thank you for not being able to fly directly to Machu Picchu. This mountain pass was out of this world. It had that inaccessible feel about it, reserved for places where mere mortals were not allowed to tread with impunity.

Approaching Aguas Calientes the train passed a station, strangely enough, bearing the name Machu Picchu. Just a clever trick the Peruvians employed to mislead the unsuspecting tourists. The station is miles away from the ruins, but a useful place to disembark if you were looking for a cheap place to spend the night.

At long last, the autovagon stopped at its destination. Alec got out and gratefully stretched his legs. He took a stroll to clear his poisoned bronchial tubes. Peruvian trains have very low chimneys, which enable them to fit under and through tight tunnels carved through solid rock. Unfortunately, this also allows the smoke from the ancient coal engines to drift directly into the coach windows. Periodically, bouncing off a soaring tor the wind changes. The windows get opened, but a single gust from around the corner fills the compartment with the acrid fumes again. A while later you again open the windows to clear the smoke, only to be hit with more smoke, smack the face, a minute later. It keeps you busy.

You are free suffocate inside or outside, at no extra charge.

A half-hour later Alec was on a bus, once again zigzagging upwards, some 700 meters, towards the ruins. He wondered how and where he would find the professor. He breathed easier once he'd learned that there was but one hotel right at the foot of the tourist shrine. His eyes were still burning from the smoke. So far he'd refused to close them for want of taking in all the exotic views. Now, for just a few minutes, he did lower his eyelids. The next moment the bus stopped. Unwittingly, he must have dozed off.

Alec walked straight up to the reception desk. Dr. McBride had left him a note to go up to his room and take a nap. He found that the Professor had taken a suite with two interconnected rooms. It suited him fine. Apart from being tired and hungry, most of all Alec needed at least a short nap. The snooze on the bus just hadn't been enough. He dropped his bag and fell back on the bed. He had no idea what happened next.

"The dinnerr is serrved, Doctorr Baldwin," Alec heard from afar, his eyes still firmly closed. Then a gaunt grip shook him by the shoulder. "By my calculation, you've had a

good two-hourr nap. That should be quite enough ferr a
strrapping lad such as you, my boy."

The professor's smiling face was looking down at Alec
who, for a brief moment, was convinced that he'd fallen
asleep in the professor's office. He jumped up before
remembering his whereabouts.

"My, you have such rred eyes grrandma. Like the devil
himself. It's a good thing that mop y'rre wearring is hiding
y'rr horrns, eh, lad?" Dr. McBride seemed to be enjoying
himself. "You didn't take my advice and fly to Aguas
Calientes, I see."

Alec stifled a yawn. He's been on the go since seven
o'clock last night. With a three-hour stop over in Miami, two
at customs in Lima, another two at the heliport, and probably
two more on the way to the train. The rest of the time he was
flying or being tossed about in a bus or train. He had a right
to be tired. It was fun but it was tiring.

"I know the trrain ride is fun, but it plays havoc with y'rr
vision. Still. At y'rr age, come morrning you'll be as good as
new." McDes smiled as though remembering the good old
days. "Up you come, now, we've got to eat. A good steak and
maybe a wee drrop of that rred stuff they elaborrate in
Arrgentina."

Alec went to the bathroom they shared, stripped, washed
first with hot then rinsed with cold water. The thin layer of
soot from the train swirled away. He felt much better. After
all, he was just 25, and at that age, a two-hour nap is usually
enough to conquer the Matterhorn.

They dined in the main ballroom—or at least it looked
like one. As the professor commanded all of his attention
Alec didn't have time to examine it for any architectural
merit. Dr. McBride allowed him a single Scotch and two bites
into the steak before getting down to business.

"So, you know why I called you here," he affirmed, as
though thinking aloud. "It is vital that you talk your head off
before the heat dies down." He swallowed a small bite of
steak and washed it down with the 'rred stuff from

Arrgentina,' a full-bodied Cabernet Sauvignon, before going on. Alec noticed, again, that the rolling r's were gone.

"You see, when you break into a new field, the establishment is apt to turn against you. And your thesis is going to upset many people. Many important, established people."

He let that sink in. They resumed eating, and continued in silence until the steaks were gone. Only then the professor sat back and smiled.

"So how do you like the rred stuff?" He was now alternating between being himself and being ah... himself. Take y'rr choice, Alec thought.

"You really think I broke new ground, Sir?"

"Des. I was Sir when I knew twice as much about everything as you did. Now there is a field where you know more. Desmond if you like, but I prefer Des."

"Yes, Sir."

The old man gave Alec a dirty look.

"Yes, Des. I am honoured. I really mean that."

"Blah, blah, blah. I bet you called me McDeath behind my back many a time. Eh?"

"Maybe once..."

They both laughed. The wine was warming their bones, which in the mountains, at night, needed warming. Then Dr. McBride's face got serious again.

"I accepted your thesis not just because it was solid, but because you dared to do it. It is about time someone crossed the bridge."

Alec thought he knew what the Professor was talking about. When Alec took on the subject of the Paradox, his unspoken, perhaps even fully unrealized, dream was to propose a different attitude towards time. He knew that even the experiences of his youth could not be accepted by any scientific concepts known to man. Either man was wrong, or his experiences were due to unremitting schizophrenia. He refused to accept the second, thus, as Sherlock Holmes would say, he had no choice. He put his thoughts into words.

"If you eliminate all other possibilities, then the remaining one must be true."

"It's not the way I would put it, but I agree. The problem is that before you get an army of post-docs digesting and experimenting with your theories, you've got to get a bit famous. Lima is a good place to start. I have a friend there who did his post-doc with me. After Lima I've got you scheduled for Rio, Buenos Aires, and Bogota. Then, by the time I approach Harvard, you'll have a string of lectures behind you. Semi-public lectures, but you've got to start somewhere. The darn problem is that you're so darn young, damn it!"

Alec was flabbergasted. He swallowed hard, and leaned back in his chair.

"But... b-but..."

"No buts. I had my secretary scan the Internet to see if you were doing anything yourself and she found nothing. We can't have that. You've got to strike that iron while it's hot." The professor swallowed the rest of his wine.

"Frankly, Sir, I mean Des, I got scared. Just plain scared. To tell you the truth, I never thought I would really get my Ph.D. for the stuff I wrote."

"You silly boy. You silly, silly boy. You were brilliant!"

Alec slept very, very well that night. Night air at the top of the world is as good as it gets.

The next morning they took breakfast at seven. It was better to visit the ruins before eleven, at which time the hordes arrived. True, there were still some heavy patches of fog, but it was better than crowds of tourists. Today was a holiday; tomorrow Alec would be on an airplane. The Professor would attend his lecture in Lima, fly with him to Rio, as he had his own business to attend to there, and then Alec would be on his own for Buenos Aires and Bogota. Over breakfast the old man also handed him a credit card with a limit of $10,000 US.

"Use it, don't abuse it," he warned. "I got you on my post-doc program. Didn't I tell you that? Must have slipped my mind. Your salary is $80,000 US. It, of course, entails a teaching position, and I expect you to put in some ninety-hour weeks. Expenses extra, well, some of them. At least to start with. Do you find that acceptable?" There was a twinkle in his eye that would light up a sunny room.

"I don't know what to say, Sir, Desmond, Des..."

"Any one of them will do, but as I said, I prefer Des."

"Thanks."

"Don't mention it. Shall we go?"

"Just one thing, Des."

"Yes?"

"How does one give a lecture?"

"Didn't you ever listen when I gave one?"

"Yes, of course, but..."

"You must go easy on the buts. Be yourself. If you managed to fool me then you will fool most other people. Don't you think?"

"I suppose so..." And Alec realized that the old man got him again. "Fool you, Sir...?"

"Let's go."

And they went.

Machu Picchu was awaiting them in all its morning glory.

* * *

4

The Information Theory

Frankly, the morning glory turned out to be a thick
drizzle. They donned plastic ponchos offered by the
hotel free of charge. Judging by the prices Alec saw on
the menu last night, this was just about the only thing that the
hotel offered for free.

Just as well. Machu Picchu is nestled in a thick, dense
rain forest. Thick! And very wet. And incredibly green. It
rained almost daily for ten months out of the year. You might
argue that mist, as dense as the jungle itself, added to the
mystery. Well, it did. Only the closer stones and rocks were
visible. The rest was forbidden to the eyes. No sunrise over
the ruins; no distant views shrouded in enigmatic yesteryear.
Just rain. And fog. And wet, slippery stone paving.

"Neverr mind," the professor seemed to have read
Alecs's thoughts. He also appeared to be enjoying some
private joke. "Come on lad, at this rrate we'll neverr get
therre." And the 'old man' doubled his pace. There was an
awful lot of spring in his step.

Alec wanted to ask 'Where's there?' but bit his tongue.

About fifteen minutes later, still climbing, they met some
youths coming down from the Inca Trail. The four lads, and
two girls, all looked half-frozen and very miserable. The
apparent leader asked Alec for directions! Alec replied in his
best Spanish. They didn't seem to understand a word. No
matter. Alec didn't really understand the question.

"Strraight down, bearring to the rright. You'rre almost
therre," Dr. McBride threw over his shoulder.

"Thanks!" they replied in unison.

Slowly, very slowly the mists rose—or perhaps fell.
They seemed to dissolve, be absorbed by the stones
themselves. Larger shapes emerged, loomed out of the

vapours, as though emerging from the hoary past. Before the first busload of 'organized' tourists arrived, Alec was given unforgettable glimpses of the mysterious city. Empty—but for the ghosts of the past. It was as riveting as he'd always suspected. Above them, all around, still shrouded in gradually dissipating mists, towering, near-vertical walls of pointed crags jutted over snow-white clouds, like gods standing guard over their own.

They walked in silence.

Here and there the professor sat on a flat rock, his eyes as misty as the surrounding jungle. There was more, much more to the old man than met the eye. Alec again felt a strange affinity with the professor. During the last eighteen months they'd hardly spoken, yet now there was nearness, a rapport between them that was hard to explain. Karma? Reincarnation? Could their lives have crossed in the past? Perhaps right here, right at this Sacred Plaza, where they now sat and rested. Alec looked down at the house of the High Priest. A place where there was no past and no future. There was only an intangible now.

And then Alec's mind wandered into a realm he hadn't visited for a long time. To a place that was not at all like Machu Picchu. Not physically, yet in almost every other way—it was. It was a place where dreams were made. Generated, enhanced, elevated to a realm where everything was possible. A realm where you didn't measure plans by your presumed ability to realize them, but by the scope of imagination itself. A place where all that you could dream of could become reality. It was up to you or, in his case, up to Sandra, the Princess of his youth. Had the Incas been like that? Had gods raised the veils of mystery from their eyes and given them the power to realize their dreams? To the full?

And then the clouds parted and a single ray of sun blinded Alec's eyes. He shook cobwebs out of his head. Just two words lingered on in his mind. Home Planet. These two words had meant a great deal to him once. It also was a place of dreams, of imagination. Was it real? Ever?

A place where all things were possible. Like here. At least, for as long as you suspended your disbelief. Even for a short while. Here—time stood still...

Time, time itself, at Machu Picchu, was by far the greatest enigma. Perhaps Alec's work would one day help to solve some of its mystery.

By noon, in a state half way between shock and euphoria, the two physicists were riding back to the heliport at Aguas Calientes. The bus was fighting a losing battle with a deeply sun-tanned ten-year-old, who greeted them at every corner with a resonant gooood-byyyye...

The boy ran straight down, while the bus descended in a continuous zigzag. Finally, the lad boarded the bus for a few *soles'* reward.

"I bet he's a futurre champion. Prrobably overr long distance, but could be a thrree-thousand-meterr steeplechaserr," the Professor commented expertly. He gave the boy five times the expected amount. Dr. McBride enjoyed shocking people. Particularly youngsters. And the look in the boy's eyes was his generosity's ample reward.

They only just made it to the heliport on time. The rotors were already spinning, the noise deafening. As they climbed aboard, the helicopter rose straight up, then leaned to one side to show them, deep down, the thin, wiggly line of the Urubamba, snaking its way through the canyon.

All too soon they were at the Alejandro Velasco Astete International Airport. They had to rush again. Here, all arrivals and departures had to take place in the morning. In the afternoon, the climatic conditions made landing and takeoff too difficult. The two physicists made it by the skin of their teeth.

They were ushered into an airplane virtually without any formalities. Perhaps they already knew the professor? The seats on board weren't numbered and there was plenty of room. The professor got some papers out to look over, while Alec, with sleepy eyes, tried to organize his thoughts.

What would he remember about Machu Picchu? A lot less than he would like. The whirlwind the Professor had injected into his life was more than he could take in his stride. His brain was working overtime. Last night's dreams had repeatedly placed him in absurd situations, all concerned with his forthcoming lectures. Once he'd woken up during the night finding it hard to breathe. He'd dreamt he was delivering a lecture from the inside of his listeners. He reverberated inside their heads, pulsated in their veins, controlled their micro-voltaic synapses. Only around two in the morning had he escaped into a deep, dreamless slumber. He'd woken up stiff but strangely elated.

On waking, he remembered that he hadn't given the professor any money, nor had he spent any of his own.

"Des, how much do I owe you?"

"In round figures about three dollars. It may not sound like much but a Peruvian can get a good pizza for such money and have enough left over to feed the rest of his family for a week."

"The hotel, Des. The dinner. I owe you…?"

"It has been taken care of. Don't forget to mention Machu Picchu in your lecture. That's the only way we can write it off."

The usual twinkle was dancing in the Professor's eyes from early morning, but the rolled r's were missing. He seemed more exited about Alec's forthcoming lecture than Alec was himself. If only that were possible.

The flight was uneventful. A taxi deposited them at the Sheraton, in the centre of old Lima. There was no time for sightseeing. Alec had with him all the papers for the lecture he was hoping to give one day, but now that the moment was at hand, he was counting on the Professor to polish them up. They spent the afternoon in the Professor's room, bent over closely typed sheets, selecting the material suitable for Alec's maiden discourse. It was not a question of what to talk about. Alec had enough material for about three weeks of a continuous yammer. The problem was to maintain a scientific approach, while making it acceptable to the general public. A feat a lot more difficult than it seemed.

Finally they decided to keep the lecture short and rely on questions from the audience to make up the missing parts. If they didn't ask, that meant they weren't interested. If necessary, Alec could always fall back on the many different slants that the original arguments of Einstein, Podolsky and Rosen had generated over the years.

By seven o'clock, they both felt tired. Alec proposed a walk in the Old City to clear his head. Dr. McBride declined. He still had some of his own work to do—a fact he failed to mention, as he had given Alec's problems priority. He felt responsible for Alec's success. He also cared for him—a lot.

Alec intended of going for a stroll in the park adjoining the hotel, just to get away from his papers. Once outside, he changed his mind and walked instead to the *Parque Universitario*. He wanted to picture, smell, to 'case the joint', where tomorrow his fate might well be sealed. Perhaps not sealed, but either launched or relegated to an 'also-ran'.

"Which is exactly where I am right now," he mused, smiling at his somber thoughts. Then, as he walked on, he briefly examined his present life. "On the other hand, it's not such a bad place to be..." he muttered under his breath.

On the other hand...

Later, in his own room, Alec dialed his home number. Suzy was not in. He left a message:

"I love you. Have great news. Love you. See you in about a week. Love you." And he put down the receiver.

The lecture was scheduled to take place at noon, to enable the general public to attend during their siesta. The actual dissertation would take less than an hour; the questions would take as long as they took. Since Alec already knew the way to the *Sala de Conferencias*, they both walked. It was only some months later that Alec learned that Dr. McBride had been a regular visiting lecturer in the very same hall some years ago. When Alec finally learned about it, it went a long way to explain the reception that Dr. Desmond McBride received when he stepped on the stage to introduce Dr. Alexander Baldwin. The applause was thunderous. No wonder. At least four of the past and present Professors of physics at the University of Lima came from his personal roster. Dr. McBride was as famous here as Alec was unknown. Nevertheless, when finally Alexander Baldwin did face the audience, the polite, if not over-enthusiastic, applause was long enough to help him calm his nerves. A little.

And then there was absolute silence.

"Distinguished..."

There followed a litany of titles, given him by the Professor, which belonged to distinguished people who, Alec was certain, were in attendance only because Dr. McBride was present. Finally Alec concluded the list with:

"...Señores, Señoras," here he looked up, then left and right, and added: "Señoritas", which generated one or two giggles. "The Incas in Machu Picchu, as well as in a number of other famous places, managed to erect stones with a greater precision than our present-day architects and masons. They had knowledge that continues to baffle our best archeological minds. The information is lost. I think that's a pity. A great pity.

And yet, we are said to have entered the so-called 'Information Age'.

Perhaps this is why I've decided to concern myself with the nature of information. Not specific bits, or quanta, but with its basic structure. I am not talking about computers, which provide mechanical storage of data, but with the essence of information itself.

I wish to stress this point.

I am not concerned with the nature of atoms or subatomic particles but with information that the atoms and the subatomic particles carry. This has to do both with the continuity of information, with its primary characteristics, and with its basic structure. Historically, we tend to associate information with our mind, brain at best. I propose that information, in its purest form, lies at the crossroads between the Quantum and the Continuous universes and their structures. All matter can be reproduced, but only if the information is available.

Last year, I was privileged to have the opportunity of visiting a very unique laboratory in Waxahachie, Texas, in, ah... the United States of America. (A slight giggle from the back row). As you know, everything that comes from Texas must be big. This holds true, of course to the supercollider, affectionately known as the SSC or the Superconducting Super Collider. The SSC is designed to operate at about 40 TeV, which, for our friends who have forsaken their siestas to hear this, T stands for tera or trillion, and eV, for electron volts. The reason this is of some considerable consequence is that as the energy goes up, the size of the particle goes down. Ultimately, the infinitely large would interact with the infinitely small. Something doesn't work with this equation.

A sort of poetic justice, or karmic balance."

Alec glanced at Dr. McBride. The Professor was leaning back, a blissful smile on his perfectly relaxed face. Or—he could have been sleeping.

"The SSC at Waxahachie can generate enough energy to recreate conditions extant in the first millionth of a second after the Big Bang. What has not been taken into consideration is that, as in the EPR apparent paradox, the subatomic particles carry information. Whatever information was disseminated at the time of the big bang must be, by inverse logic, available today. The problem to resolve is how to recover it.

And this takes us to the heart of the matter."

Alec went on for another half-hour or so. The auditorium was filled with such an incredible silence that, on a later occasion, he swore he could hear his own heart beat. Finally his lecture was over. He arranged his papers, squared them, and looked over his audience. No one stirred. The silence continued.

"Are there any questions?" he asked, his voice somewhat shaky from the long-sustained tension.

More silence.

Then a hand went up. A young lady rose, blushing.

"I am Carla Rodrigues, physics, second year. Are you suggesting, Doctor Baldwin, that we can expect time travel to be possible in the near future?"

There was a stir in the audience.

"No, Miss Rodrigues. What I am saying is that information does not appear to be bound by the considerations of space or time."

"So information can travel through time?"

"It does already."

"How do you mean, Doctor Baldwin?"

"You might have heard Doctor Baltimore refer to viruses as little more than information."

Dr. Baltimore was not only the past president of Caltech, he was a Nobel Laureate who was endowed with an enormous knack for explaining the complex in terms that ordinary mortals could understand. Alec, who made a point of attending lectures on many subjects outside his own discipline, admired him greatly.

"He argues that viruses pass on information through time with the greatest of ease. Don't you agree?" Alec was playing with the student.

"That is not quite what you have in mind, is it, Doctor?" Miss Rodrigues persisted.

"Quite true. I would prefer to say that information is here and there, so to speak, already..."

This time there was a considerable stir. A wave of heads were looking at the girl, then again at Alec. A number of hands went up and then were withdrawn, as though the questions weren't quite right.

"Sir, Sir..." a young man at the back of the hall was waving his arms. Alec didn't recall ever being called 'Sir'. Certainly not in public. He actually blushed.

"Yes, the young man with the waving arms," he tried to cover his embarrassment.

"But if you can send info through time, then you can recreate the object specified at different...." The young man lost his line of thought.

"I think we are jumping ahead of ourselves here. There is a difference between photons responding to information over distance in zero time, and making a lamp out of them. But your question is valid. If there is matter and energy available, then, given information, we can expect to be able to..."

"To do anything!" the young man blurted. Then he sunk into his chair as low as he could.

"I think we must distinguish..."

Just for an instant there Alec felt a pang of anger. He wasn't even sure why. Could it be at himself for some failure to develop his own theory still further? He shrugged and followed his mentor.

Dr. McBride got up and slowly made his way to the podium. Alec was grateful. He forgot that some four years ago he was as enthusiastic as the young man who had just disappeared from his view. This was beginning to sound like a Sci-Fi convention. As the professor mounted the stage, silence returned to the hall.

"I am sure we are all grateful to Dr. Baldwin for sharing with us his unique view of the Information Theory. I am equally as sure that you'll allow him to have lunch as neither he nor I have had anything to eat since seven this morning."

After a momentary silence, the auditorium resounded with long, spontaneous applause. Alec had stirred the imagination not only of youngsters, but also of people who had heretofore been stuck in a rut. He showed them that there is yet a further horizon for which they can aim.

And there was.

They ate in the academic dining room. Alec was seated between Dr. Juan Wiseman, the Dean of the Department of Physics, and Dr. McBride. They didn't talk much about physics. They enjoyed the food and the wine. Alec listened as his seniors exchange ideas on every subject under the sun, and some a lot further away. The so-called establishment couldn't have been as stagnant as Professor McBride had suggested. And then Alec recalled that Dr. Wiseman was one of Desmond's earliest successes. Only in those days he was known as John Wiseman.

At three they walked back to their hotel. Rather than going to their respective rooms, Desmond took his young colleague directly to the lobby bar.

"Two large Glenfidish, one lump, no soda," he ordered. As the man delivered the two crystal glasses, the professor raised his to his lips. Before taking a sip, he mumbled over the rim: "Now that wasn't too bad, was it lad. Cheerrs to you. Cheerrs and congrratulations." And he emptied his glass in a single gulp.

Alec, still drowsy from emotions generated by the intensity of recent events did exactly the same. Then he leaned back. The Scotch was what the doctor ordered. After a little while, his heart resumed the normal, steady rhythm.

"Aye, Desmond my dearr frriend. Perrhaps it wasn't as bad as all that," he said, waving to the waiter for another round. This time just singles.

"Arre you taking the Mickey out of me, laddie?"

"I wouldn't darre, Sirrr."

"Aye, I guess you wouldn't at that."

When the drinks came, Alec raised his glass to the professor.

"Thank you, Sir. You are a true friend, Des. A true friend, indeed." And he emptied the glass again. The professor smiled and took a tiny sip. He was old enough to know when to stop.

"Better go easy on that, lad. You've three more lectures to go."

And suddenly Alec felt very tired. Until this moment he seemed to have been coasting, at times galloping, on emotions alone. Now, the flights, the crazy taxi ride, the helicopter followed by the train with its acrid smoke, the emotional visit to Machu Picchu, and finally the large auditorium of people hanging on his every word, all this and more, was suddenly too much. And on the top of all that, his unexpected appointment as the post-doc research scientist to the top brain in the business of theoretical physics was more than his young emotions could take.

"I guess you're right, Professor. If you don't mind I'll turn in."

He excused himself and almost staggered back to his room. He intended to call Suzy and tell her all about it. All about everything. But when he got to his room, he walked to his bed, sat on it, and leaned back just for a moment. Just for a few seconds....

He woke up at three a.m. Although the hotel was in the very center of town, he was surrounded by absolute silence. And then his mind saw distant peeks shrouded in circular clouds, like puffs of smoke from some gigantic cigars. And he knew that he was, once again, on the Home Planet.

Only he was quite alone. He missed Sandra. He suddenly released that he'd ignored her, ignored the memory of her, for some time. Even here, on the Home Planet, he seemed to remain a hard-nosed scientist. Yet, this was his reality. Here, or anywhere, he was the creator. And today he was just too tired. Or maybe too many of his dreams had been already realized? Back there, on the dear old planet Earth. He closed his eyes and slept on until a none-too-gentle knock on the door brought him back to earth.

"The bathroom is free, lad."

And that's exactly how Alec felt. He finally felt rested and free. But mostly just wonderfully free. He remembered a phrase he'd heard somewhere: Just live. He repeated the two words as though they formed some secret mantra.

"Just live!" he repeated. And then he called almost as an afterthought: "Coming, Des. Give me five minutes."

"Thought you'd neverr come. I knocked on y'rr doorr a dozen times," the Professor said digging into *dos huevos rancheros*. How did you sleep anyway, lad?"

"Like a log would be quite an inadequate metaphor. More like a ton of bricks fell on me."

"Aye," Desmond looked at him over the cup of black coffee. "But you do look a lot better, m'lad. A lot betterr."

Alec did feel a lot better, except for one thing. Over the last few days, he'd noticed an increasing stiffness of his joints. Not enough to really slow him down, but enough to be aware of them virtually all the time. A sort of dull, nagging pain. At first he thought it was due to his extensive travelling in relatively cramped positions. But now he was beginning to wonder. I'll have to see a doctor when I get home, he thought. Right now, he was too busy to give his bones any more thought.

"Like a new born baby," Alec agreed.

"Ah, 'tis good to be young..." Doctor's wise eyes drifted to some distant place Alec had never visited. And then he just said: "aaah..." And that was that. The next moment he was giving Alec instructions about their impending departure for Rio.

Whatever the Professor's age and memories, Dr. McBride lived in the present.

To the fullest.

***

5
Family Reunion

Finally, **after three days** in Rio de Janeiro, two in Buenos Aires, and two in Bogota, Alec collapsed on his own bed, in his own apartment. His back hurt as though he'd been playing tennis for hours on end. His shoulders and elbows were competing with his legs and hips for degrees of stiffness. By the time he got back to Montreal, the dull pain was beginning to affect his ability to concentrate. He was sure a short rest would be as good as a cure.

His anger was rising.

Four lectures do not a reputation make, but it was a start. According to Des, a good start. Alec thought otherwise. The upstarts dared to question his assumptions. Just who were they, the has-beens, the never-having-made-it critics?

Next month he was booked at Harvard and the week after that he'd been invited to the Mecca of the daring, the think-tank Desmond called the Santa Fe Institute.

"If you can make it there, you'll make it anywhere," the Professors assured him, which was enough to scare the living daylights out of Alec and his budding career.

"Shouldn't we wait then?" he asked wearily.

"What, and get some upstart ham to steal your idea?"

What idea, Alec mused, but tried hard not to show his frustration. Most of them didn't even begin to understand it. Still, the professor must have been very serious because the rolled 'rs' were missing.

Alec couldn't really object to becoming Desmond McBride's personal project. In truth he needed the advice and the expertise. Specifically, he was told, in no uncertain terms, to stay away from any mention of psychophysics, telepathic projections, or quantum-psychotics.

"Apart from it sounding silly, it isn't what you're doing, in spite of the ravings of the popular press." And the Professor threw before Alec a headline from the local rag:

CANADIAN SCIENTIST
TRAVELS THROUGH TIME
A new Theory of Information

The mention of "Theory of Information" was miniscule, almost illegible. The Sci-Fi angle sold the newspapers—it did nothing to help Alec. It could well have hindered his progress.

He clenched, then grinded his teeth. He did his best to calm the storm was brewing inside him. Thankfully, Desmond had just given him two weeks off to collect his thoughts, and to spend some time with Suzy. God knows, he needed that. He flew to Canada by the first available seat.

And what a reunion it was!

Alec's airplane was scheduled to arrive so late that he chose not to tell Suzy about his arrival in case she'd offer to pick him up at Dorval. It was a good half-hour drive to and from the airport, plus the usual waiting after an international flight—at three in the morning no fun at all. He took a cab, crept into the apartment and then, into the bed. He was sure he hadn't wakened Suzy until... until she threw one arm over his chest and whispered in a drowsy, amorous voice.

"You must hurry, darling, my husband might be home any minute."

He liked the 'husband' bit, but... He bit his lips.

The next minute Suzy relaxed them with a prolonged, hungry kiss.

"Gotcha!" she said. He could see her grin in the moonlight.

For the next three days Alec had to continue reassuring her that he was actually never fooled. It wouldn't do to admit that for a split second his heart did stop beating. Perhaps a little longer. After all, how could she have known that it was

him? Anyway, he'd missed her 'something awful'. He missed
her touch, her look, her humour—even when he was on the
receiving end of it. But most of all he missed that way she
looked at him when he described the events of the past ten
days. The way her eyes searched his face, he felt as though he
was the most important person in the whole world. In the
universe. It wasn't something he'd earned, or deserved. It was
a free gift that she bestowed on him. It was just one of the
multitude of reasons why he loved her.

And then, after three full days of dodging corny remarks,
he asked her point blank.

"Just how did you know that it was me, climbing into
your bed?"

"Oh, that? Dr. McBride called me. Apparently you were
in such a state when he left you in Rio that he wanted to make
sure you'd given him the right telephone number."

"So you knew all along..."

"The Prof sounds like a really nice man. But he does
speak with a funny accent."

"Only when he wants to," Alec murmured, his mind
trying to connive a way to get even with her. And then he
gave up. After all, he could have asked her the same question
three days ago, couldn't he?

"Dare say you're right. He's probably the nicest man I've
ever met. In the scientific community, anyway," he agreed.

"Second nicest," and suddenly she was in his arms, all
demure. "Have I told you lately that I love you?"

"Not during the last ten minutes. Anyway, I expect no
less what... with eighty K flowing into our bank account?"

"Eighty thousand dollars US," she corrected.

"Whatever," he said. He had more important things to do
than to argue, when she was in his arms. Much more
important.

As for Suzy, her routine was a lot less exciting. She
taught, she went to see her parents, once dropped in on his.
His father was ill—something to do with lungs. They, the

physicians, weren't sure but apparently emphysema had set in. There was a time when dad had smoked quite a lot. He quit more than twelve years ago, but living downtown in Montreal didn't help either—a city proliferated with open fireplaces and barbecues.

She asked Alec if she could invite them all to a family reunion; she's asked him not to solicit his permission, but rather to find out if he felt up to it, so soon after his trip. She thought they had so much to celebrate. Although they shared about a dozen friends, as is so often with avid sailors, none of them lived within an easy travelling distance. They had many acquaintances, but she wanted to share their good news just with the family. Alec, of course, agreed. It would have been the wrong time to tell her about his lingering aches and pains. At times, he felt as though something was eating him on the inside. Anyway, he expected them, the pains, to go away, any time now.

They set a date for next Saturday. Suzy had Friday off, and together they would take time to do the shopping and prepare a sumptuous meal. Alec also made sure that there was a Magnum of Champagne. Well, of *brut* bubbly, anyway. Made in Spain.

"Let's do this properly," she agreed. "Do you realize that we never celebrated your Ph.D.? We're way behind in drinking to your health."

"A punishable offence," he agreed once again.

And then, quite out of the blue, she asked him, "Have you been peek-a-booing lately?"

In the tumult of the last week he'd completely forgotten about his reputed little peccadilloes. Also, he still had some reservations if his purported space-shifting was not part of Suzy's overactive imagination.

"Why, no... I suppose not. No one has said anything. Why, have I?"

She looked at him carefully. "I am not sure."

"Then, why do you ask?"

This time the pause was longer. She sat down on the settee and pulled him down next to her. After a while she seemed to have made up her mind.

"I've been thinking."

This was enough to make Alec nervous. Usually, virtually always, Suzy was as direct as anyone he'd ever met. This sudden hesitation was not like her.

"Promise you won't be angry?" she prodded.

"Why on earth should I be angry? I don't hold monopoly on thinking..." he tried to be flippant, but luckily Suzy ignored that.

"It has to do with Sandra."

"What?" He half rose to his feet.

"Relax, darling. It's nothing sinister. And it's not jealously. I've had lots of time to think while you were gallivanting all over romantic South America. Some thoughts came to me, and I would like to share them with you. OK?"

"Of course, go right ahead."

But he was still nervous. Admittedly he'd spent altogether too much time recently thinking about Sandra. He hadn't meant to, but, well, there was Machu Picchu, the recurring memory of the Home Planet... One way or another, it all had to do with Sandra. But his thinking had to do with getting rid of Sandra from his memories, with freeing himself from childish distractions.

"You realize that all I know—I know from you. My understanding could be going off on a tangent. But I've been watching you. Most of the time you are relaxed, almost boisterous, and then your eyes seem to drift away as if your thoughts, your very soul were elsewhere. Are you aware of that?"

He didn't answer other than clearing his throat. Her observations may have had something to do with his attempts to cover his overall physical stiffness.

"Well, from what you told me, way back, there are a number of characteristics that Sandra exhibited on different occasions. Briefly, she said that she was always with you, yet you did not always see or detect her presence. Then, she seems to have an incredibly wide knowledge not only about your own activities, but also about just about anything you cared to mention. She was, I hesitate to say, omniscient?"

She looked at Alec seeking confirmation. He nodded slowly. His memories of Sandra flooded his mind in successive waves. Even as Suzy talked, his imaginary Princess was taking shape as though the years since he was fourteen melted into oblivion. It was hard to believe that his time with Sandra, real or imaginary, had taken place more than ten years ago. And that it had lasted for less than a year. How come it had left such an indelible mark on his memory? He tried to push the memories back where they belonged. Way back.

"Then, we have her ability to travel through time, or, what is more fascinating, she seemed well-aware of your travels even when you thought you were on your own."

As Suzy persisted with the subject, Alec withdrew his resistance and allowed memories of Sandra to fill his awareness. Almost immediately he felt better. Even the stiffness in his joints seemed to recede, if only slightly. All within seconds. Apparently hysteria is not limited to women, he thought.

"She did say she was always with me," he interrupted for the first time.

"Exactly. Invisible, often not manifesting her presence in any way, virtually omnipresent, omniscient... does this remind you of anything?"

Alec remained silent. Sandra had been very, very real. On the Home Planet, as real and as solid as he was. He said as much.

"And yet..." Suzy looked down at her hands playing with his own. "And yet, she was equally as invisible as the air, when she chose to be."

"That's true."

This time Suzy's eyes seemed to drift away and rest on something far away. "And yet, from the moment you and she became one, from the moment you merged, she lost her will."

He, himself, was beginning to shine, as though all the galaxies within him emitted their own heretofore-constrained radiance. For an ephemeral instance he saw himself, as though, from outside. He saw a brightness of a thousand stars, ney... a billion points of light dancing a dance of celestial harmony.

"What do you mean by that?" He was startled. He was also fighting back memories with all his might. It was a losing battle. He wanted to shout at Suzy to stop. Yet his throat was dry.

In the essence of this brightness that burned his eyes he saw Sandra.... made up exclusively of light. Purest of all light. In the next instance he merged with this radiant phantom. They fused into a single entity. An entity of light.

"Up to the time of, let us call it, merging, she was the one who'd chosen whether you'd see her or not. She was the master, mistress—might be a better word—of her 'life' so to speak. And now? Can she still do all she wants? Or is she limited by... well, by your limitations."

"I love you, my Prince," he detected the very last emotive thought as if coming from the outside of his own being. And as he consolidated his oneness with the glorious body of light he whispered with the same ardour: "I love you for ever more, my Princess. You are my life."
In the next segment of eternity they become one.

'One doesn't limit a Princess,' was his first conscious thought. It felt as though a great load was lifted from him only to return with an even greater weight. Or was it commitment? A greater duty? Responsibility?

"Why are you saying all that...?" he said in a halftone, his mind slowly returning to the present.

"Because I think Sandra is asking for a fair shake."

What a strange way of putting it, he thought. Why does it sound so right?

Then he shrugged. I'm a scientist, he told himself. But at some level of perception, he was beginning to feel himself slipping into a groove. Brilliant ideas of his immediate past remained just there—in the past. He felt himself being drawn into the entrenched mentality of The Establishment. Scientifically, I'm an old man, he mused. I've done it all. There is nothing new for me to do. Even my bones tell me that. And it's all Sandra's fault. I'm sure of it!

Was Sandra asking to play a greater part in his life? Was she demanding that he fulfill his allegiance, his sworn promise of eternal love? How does one love a part of oneself? Isn't that a form of exalted egocentricity? A form of Narcissism gone wild?

Even worse if Sandra was in fact a figment of a boyish imagination...

And then a strange thought shot through his mind—the next instant it was gone. The thought didn't make sense. It was neither deductive nor inductive; it was as fleeting as a wisp of smoke on a windy day...

What if I am a figment of her imagination?

Am I a butterfly dreaming I'm a man, or am I a man dreaming I'm a butterfly, was his last thought before finally falling asleep.

The next moment he felt wide-awake. He was paralyzed from the neck down. He couldn't move. What's happening to me? He saw himself lying in a double coffin next to his father. Am I dead? Is this what being dead feels like?

And then something kind, very kind and loving seemed to caress his tired nerves. He felt the comfort a baby feels in his mother's womb. It was dark and cozy and warm. And restful. And very, very safe.

I must still be asleep, he thought. Please God. Let me be asleep.

When Alec awoke, breakfast was ready. It was nice to be spoiled. It didn't happen that often, if ever. As Suzy was working, he prepared her breakfast more often than she did his. He smiled at the thought. He wondered if Suzy, now that he'd become the official breadwinner, would continue to work.

"Sue," he asked, over the second cup of coffee. "Do you think you'd find time to take a trip or two with me? I mean on my lecture tours. We could afford it, you know?"

"And what would happen to my poor Anglophones starving for the word of Molière?"

"Dare I say no one is indispensable?" he prodded.

"It's nice to think one is, at least sometimes." Her tone was almost hurt.

"You are to me, Sue. I miss you when I'm away..."

He watched her from the corner of his eye. Would she see through his charade and laugh?

"You are striking just the right chords, my lord. But I can see through your game. You want to make me into a kept woman so that I'll have to marry you."

"The thought never crossed my mind!" he protested.

Only later, well after breakfast, did Alec realize that the stiffness in his joints had receded into some murky past. The dull pain felt like a distant memory. He also had a strange feeling that he'd been forgiven. Only he had no idea for what...

Mom and mom, dad and dad, all four, gave a good impersonation of a coop of agitated peacocks for whom, or for which, the walls of the apartment were too constricting. John Norman walked in holding cuttings from at least two dozens articles mentioning Alec's name. He appeared to have bought out the Peruvian, Brazilian, Argentinean and Colombian presses in addition to anything he could get a hold of from Canada and the US. Judging by his tone and demeanor, he considered himself solely responsible for Alec's meteoric rise to fame.

"I knew it," he rambled, "I always knew it!" he proclaimed, his voice filled with pride and authority.

He wielded the evidence before everyone's eyes, translating, rather badly, the Spanish and Portuguese words immediately preceding, and those following, Alec's name. The subject itself seemed of lesser importance. The value lay in the number of times Alec's name and title appeared in every article. The old man was as proud as Punch. His own dad brought double the number of computer printouts, and proffered them as indisputable evidence that he'd sired, all by himself, an irrefutable genius. The two moms danced around Alec as if he was a Hollywood celebrity, only much more important. They both laid claim to having foretold his magnificent future, present at present, yet undeniably even brighter future.

There may have been just a grain of truth, in this spontaneous adulation. Taking time off from his work, sequestered in Suzy's arms, Alec had no idea what effect his lectures had had on the world outside his apartment.

His dad was the first to propose a toast.

"I am sure I speak for all of us..." he began, knowing full well that John would much rather speak for himself, as would probably the two ladies. He spoke of Alec's youth, the cups he'd won at tennis, the medals bestowed on Alec's chest for swimming, the top marks he boasted at school.

"May he live long and prosper!" Dad said, even as a frog seemed caught in his throat. There was no time for him to delve into his son's academic achievements, because John Norman rose, raised his own flute and said in his deep, sonorous voice, "Ladies and Gentlemen, I give you Dr. Alexander Baldwin, Ph.D."

"Dr. Alexander Baldwin," echoed Alicia and Joan. Their eyes were shining, their cheeks flushed, their faces filled with wonder.

And they all raised their glasses.

During all this canonization Suzy sat quietly, gazing at her man. Alec had changed little from the time when she'd first met him on Lake Champlain. The mop of hair was just as disheveled. The rest of him seemed to have enlarged in proportion to his age, too. About a foot and a half taller and broader, somehow more muscular, looking more like a professional football player than a scientist of fledgling reputation. No one would ever suspect that he was completely dedicated to scientific research. No one except herself, who knew him better than his own mother—by now, much better. There had been times when she'd mothered him herself, when she'd given him gentle nudges in the right direction. And now she knew that it was all worth it. Alec no longer needed her motherly concern. He was a man through and through, independent, with considerable self-assurance, confident of his ground. I wonder, she mused, I wonder when he'll ask me next. I wonder....

"Speech, speech..." they echoed each other.

Alec had no choice. Obediently he rose to his feet.

"Dear mothers, dads... I love you all. In many ways, whatever I've managed, so far, is as much your achievement as mine. But...." he looked down at Suzy who succeeded in finding something terribly interesting on her plate, "but of one thing I am more certain than of anything else in my life. If you're raising your glasses to me, then you must raise them to Suzy. She was my inspiration, my friend, my haven when I felt lost. She pulled on the tiller when I was loosing wind in my sails. I give you my toast. Suzy!"

And over 'bravo!' and 'Suzy!' they all rose again and emptied their flutes.

Suzy blushed and then laughed, and laughed, and then cried. And then both ladies cried and the men found a great need to blow their noses.

"This damn bug is getting to me," said John.

"Same here," Alec's dad seconded. "The damn bugs..." And they both blew a frightful cacophony.

Suddenly Alec Baldwin Sr. leaned over his plate. His glass toppled as he tried to prop himself on one elbow. In a single leap Alec was at his side.

"This way dad, come and lie down," he commanded.

"I'm all right, I tell you." But his voice was raspy and he didn't resist Alec's arm.

Too many emotions? Was dad just too happy?

As he rested on three pillows, colour slowly returned to his face. The voices in the living room were muted until he told them to speak louder because he couldn't hear them. The boisterous atmosphere returned, but not fully.

"He's all right," said Alicia. "He'll be alright. Just let him rest. He got overly excited with Alec and all the good news." Regardless of her words there was such concern in her voice that Suzy embraced her and gently stroked her hair.

"Of course he is, Alicia. Of course he is."

But he wasn't. He died later that day.

Sandra... Sandra, Alec whispered. Suddenly he felt terribly alone. And then thoughts flooded his unresisting brain with succeeding waves. What is death? Is it the end or the beginning? Or is it just part of a continuous cycle, neither terminating nor initiating life? Surely, we cannot define death until we discover the nature of life. Alec had never had to face the death of someone close to him.

Is life no more than a biological function endowed with the ability to self-reproduce? Or is life more than a means of maintaining and propagating the genes we carry in our bodies? Are we more than mobile robots constructed as complementary units designed to assure the immortality of this basic gene... robots endowed with the facility to move, from place to place, in search of basic materials to assure the gene's survival?

Sandra... What is life?

In Bally, at the foot of the Himalayan Mountains, they maintain that both life and death are an illusion. A strange religion, Alec thought, but is this not what he'd once attempted to escape, the illusion of life? Have his own inner travels been more than an illusion? The Ballynese might espouse a strange religion, yet all religions, even as secular systems, failed to sate man's hunger for knowledge. Is this what life really is? A search for knowledge? Is this what I am doing by turning to physics? Will my Theory of Information finally lead man to a greater, fuller, more satisfying life?

Or just to yet another illusion...

The doctor Suzy called arrived, obviously, too late. He certified the death and left with the standard words of sympathy. What more could he have done? "Arise Lazarus," he could have said. "Arise and walk, in the name..." But he had no power. He was a physician not a healer. He transcribed chemical compounds to those we call still alive. He was helpless in death. Death is death. It seemed so final.

What is death? What is death, Sandra?

Bless Suzy. She called the doctor. She called the funeral parlour. She saw to it that everything was done. The body of Alec Baldwin Sr. was lifted and placed on a collapsible trolley by four black-clad gentlemen; black, except for a fringe of white shirt underscoring a black tie. They moved quickly, quietly, on rubber soles, with the efficiency and economy of motion required of those who deal with matters we pretend do not really exist. She led her own parents to the door, assuring them that everything would be all right. After the body was taken out she sat with Alicia, then made the bed up for her to stay overnight, longer if she wished. She gave

Alec a large Scotch and sat next to him, saying nothing, just being there to lean on.

Was father really gone, or was it just that his body was missing? Why did I dream I was lying next to him in a double coffin? Am I also that close to death?

Alec looked at the chair from which his father had risen not three hours ago to propose the toast to his life. Life! What a sardonic twist. A dying man toasting life.

"May he live long and prosper!" The echo still rung in Alec's ears.

"Thanks, dad, thanks…" He hadn't even had the time to say it.

Time is such an enigmatic concept. It seems to arrange some events in a sequence, yet leaves others out. Is that by accident or on purpose?

Alec had to face the concept of death in his studies. Not death in an emotional context, but as a factor contributing to the event horizon, such as defines a Black Hole. In purely scientific sense, we hover on the thin line between living and dying all the time. For some reason, most people call this 'life'. As consciousness is withdrawn from our body, the body stops recreating itself. It glides along for a short while, like a cart pushed along a smooth ground. Soon the body stops dividing and regenerating its cells. Cells break down into molecules, then into atoms and sub-atomic particles. Ultimately those same atoms will combine into new molecules, new cells, form other bodies. At some level we already are immortal.

So what is missing?

Apparently consciousness. No wonder the great biologist, Dr. David Baltimore, found it the most fascinating question of all. He seemed to suggest that science was on the verge of getting its teeth into the question of what constitutes consciousness.

To most people, man is the embodiment of an enigmatic soul; a word few people manage to endow with any meaning. To Alec, to Dr. Alexander Baldwin, a man is a universe of trillions upon trillions of bits of information, encapsulated in atoms and subatomic particles and their relationship to each other, held together by forces vaguely known to physics. This is consciousness. This is life.

So what happens to our consciousness when it withdraws itself from the swirling universe of atoms?

Alec had never had to face this problem so close to his heart. Was dad's consciousness immortal even as atoms appeared to be? Does consciousness, on vacating the body, retain its characteristics? Does it retain any form of individuality? What happens to it? What happens to the information stored in a photon and how does it transfer its knowledge, the knowledge of its polarization, to another photon elsewhere? We all emit photons, all the time. We radiate energy. We absorb it, we reflect it, and we radiate it... at some level of our awareness.

"What is my father's consciousness doing right now?"

Alec smiled. Nothing physical ever disappears in the universe—although the black holes raise an interesting question, he had to admit, an enigmatic smile reflecting his musing. Would this be true also of non-physical manifestations such as emotions, thoughts or ideas? Do they linger in the virtual universe ever ready to be reentered, 'reused' for the purpose of gathering new information—even as atoms are? And again he asked himself the same question: Is this what life is—a process of gathering information? And if so, what for? For fun or out of necessity? Is it a condition, *sine qua non*, for survival? But if neither matter nor emotions nor ideas ever dies, then who or what sustains them? And if all of them, all the bits of information, are immortal then they have no beginning. They just are.

Is my dad immortal, in some form or another?

"I am," he muttered under his breath.

"Darling, it's time you got some sleep. It's late."

"It seems, that we are stuck in the eternal process of becoming," he said aloud.

"Shhhh, your mother is already asleep. I gave her a couple of pills..."

Alec's eyes had that far away look that Suzy had noticed on so many occasions. He was perfectly entitled to have that look today, she thought. Poor darling.

"You know, Sue, I'm in danger of loving you forever...."

"Yes, dear. Me too. Now go to sleep."

And she led him by the hand to the bedroom. She left him there to check on Alicia. When she returned, Alec was lying prone on the side of the bed, fully clothed, fast asleep.

She didn't wake him. For a while she stood, looking down at her husband to be. For some reason, she felt that Alec's life was predicated on the assumption that he is special and that therefore the events of his life have meaning and value. Without that assumption their relationship would be little more than a ramble. Like most lives.

***

6
Stormy Night

Alec had a surprisingly good night. The stiffness of
the joints he'd felt for more than a week hardly
bothered him. 'Must be doing something right,' he
told himself.

Somehow he wasn't as distressed about his father's death
as he always imagined he would be. Living on his own, away
from his parents since he was seventeen, may have had
something to do with it. He'd lost the immediacy of their
previous relationship. He still loved his dad just as much, but
his father was no longer part of his everyday life. It helped.

He was much more concerned about his mother. Perhaps
he needn't have been. It was his mother who had originally
taught him to live in the present. To enjoy whatever life
offered at any particular time. He was hardly surprised when
Alicia, just three days after the funeral, decided to go to
Europe. She still had some family there and thought that it
would be a good time to visit them.

"No one needs me here, Ali. I might as well stretch my
wings," she said.

There was a peculiar, almost uncanny peace about her. A
serenity that comes with the acceptance of what must be. Not
under duress, but with an open mind.

"He'd had problems for the last two years, you know",
she added. "He always presented a brave face to the world,
but he never really liked it here. To the very end he missed
the Old Country. He was a Brit through and through."

Alec thought he'd known his father. He remembered
dad's British idiosyncrasies, little sayings, witticisms, habits,
but he had never paid much attention to them. He thought
they were just that: idiosyncrasies—quaint, nothing to be
taken too seriously.

"He resented that he couldn't quite cut it back home." Alicia looked far into the distance. "In a way, I killed him. I convinced him to come to Canada. At least I should have pushed him to continue working after the inheritance came. He needed his work. He found pride in doing something useful."

"You mustn't talk like that, mother. Dad was a grown man..."

"Why can't I? He doesn't mind any more. And frankly, I still think we had a good life together. He fought his demons, and most of the time he was on the winning side. We all have them, you know, Ali. We all reach out for the unknown, often for the forbidden."

The mention of demons struck an eerie chord in Alec's heart. He sensed anger, a tumultuous gathering of clouds, a roar of distant thunder, then... as quickly as they came, the darkness that was drawing him in with inexorable force, was replaced by calm. As if those momentary visions belonged to someone else, with Alec being no more than a spectator.

"Demons, M-mother?"

Alicia looked at her son with guilt in her eyes.

"We were both trying hard to protect you from them..." she said softly. "Dad was the kindest of man, but, at times, he had to struggle." And then, as though shrugging cobwebs of her past, she whispered. "There is good and evil in this world, Ali. In equal measure." Then she looked at Alec with her usual, carefree smile. "He's all right now. He's resting."

During all the years he'd lived at home Alec had never heard his mother talk like this. He wondered if he'd ever truly known either of his parents. Does one ever really know anyone? Alicia always presented her light, almost whimsical side to the world. To everyone she encountered she gave the impression of a flighty, light-hearted woman. In many ways she was. Might be. Yet at some deeper level...

At some deeper level we're all deeper, Alec thought, even my dear mother. He was growing aware of having demons to subdue in his own personality, but dad?

To spend more time with Alec, and generally to help, if need be to look after Alicia, Suzy had taken two weeks off work. They didn't like her doing so, but when she'd offered to resign, the administrators found a substitute teacher with no trouble at all. Some days later, after driving Alicia to the airport, Alec called Dr. McBride, and having assured himself that he was not in immediate demand, he rented a boat just south of the border, on Lake Champlain. He felt a little more relaxed, the physical and mental exhaustion he'd experienced recently was still tugging at the corners of his mind. At least that's what he thought it was. Exhaustion. He also wanted to get away. To break the pace. Just for three days. He thought it would be nice to visit the old bays, old anchorages. Old memories.

Suzy was delighted.

"Darling, what a wonderful idea. I'll meet you all over again!" She had a marvelous ability to smile with her mouth, her eyes, even with the tone of her voice.

They used to sail a lot more in the past. Her father still kept a boat near Kingston, on mighty Lake Ontario, but her memories were really of Spoon Bay, where she and Alec first met. He was a scrawny lad, with a big mop of hair. Long or short, it seemed to stand on end at the slightest provocation. A gust of wind, an open window, or even just his fingers running through it. A mop became Alec's logo, an ever-present feature. Even now. Only now it was much farther away from his feet.

They drove down to the lake the next day. It was the very end of summer. In a week, two on the outside, the boats would be hauled out onto the hard, to spend the winter away from the crushing ice. But there was still a little time.

The weather was glorious.

Just a suggestion of autumn colours, here and there, to force you to enjoy the last days of summer. Every single ray of sunshine was precious. Actually, autumn had officially started last week. They were four days into the golden season.

This time of the year the wind tended to be stronger, gusts more unpredictable, the sail more challenging. But they both thought of themselves as old salts, as weathered sailors.

Suzy made sure that they carried enough food and ice, not to mention Scotch and wine, to last them a week. Well, almost. But they wouldn't have to economize on anything. The boat had a good icebox, no refrigeration, but with just three days this was of no consequence. Particularly this late in the season. The sloop was similar to the O'Day his dad had bought over ten years ago, only three feet longer. The OAL was thirty feet, a good size for the lake. They transferred their provisions on board at once, filled the icebox with ice, and cast off within an hour of arriving at the marina.

The gentle purr of the diesel was soon silenced as Suzy hoisted the main, while Alec unfurled the Genoa. The wind was kindly at ten knots from north by northwest, an ideal tack to take them south, to their beloved Valcour Island. Some say that the South Pacific hosts the most romantic islands in the world. Not in their opinion. Not by a long shot.

By three in the afternoon Alec dropped anchor in Smuggler Harbor, a tiny bay where one left one's bow facing the lake and tied the stern to a convenient tree. Actually someone had embedded iron rings to tie their warps to, but a tree was far more romantic. Sort of 'wilder'. They both shed a dry tear for not anchoring in Spoon Bay, the place of their original meeting, but with wind predominantly from the north it would hardly give them enough protection. Anyway, there was not a single yacht in the tiny Harbor. The cove was as idyllic as any they could wish for.

Alec was the first (and, as it happened, the last) to dive overboard.

He almost screamed on contact with the water. He was about a month too late to enjoy the warm waters they'd been used to. But, when you're in your mid-twenties, a Scotch awaiting you on board not to mention a beautiful woman, the water was just right. In spite of his assurance regarding its quality, Suzy did not join him. Instead, she prepared some tidbits to go with the drinks, and then encouraged him to stop showing off and join her in the cockpit.

He didn't need much coaxing. He pulled himself up the metal rungs just in time to enjoy his Scotch in the last rays of sunshine. The little Harbor faces east, and the trees of the Island cast an early shadow over the bay. No matter. After a single drink they took the dinghy to the shore and spent the next two hours walking the winding footpaths. They had the island to themselves. In mid-week, and at the tail end of summer, most people had given up sailing for the year. Perhaps a short cruise on the weekend, but no one would want to spend a night on board, away from their marina. But, Suzy and Alec had each other, and this magic combination kept them as warm as they chose to make it.

The next morning they weighed anchor at nine and took a leisurely cruise around the island peeking into every cove and bay on the way. They beat north to the Sloop Cove, then jibed over the Tiger Point to enjoy the aft wind on the way south, rounded the point to say hi to the Garden Island, and beat again to the bay south off Bluff Point where they stopped for lunch. An hour later, Alec weighed anchor again but because the westerly wind was picking up in force, they decided to ignore the beauty of the cove north of Bluff Point. By two in the afternoon, the radio announced a gale warning. Alec laughed it off and continued past the northern point of Valcour Island. Of course, he had little choice. There was no protection on the west side of the island from a westerly gale. He could have sought protection in the Snug Harbor at Olde Valcour, but this would be equivalent to giving up. Beating north became harder, but finally, on reefed sails they reached their 'private' Spoon Bay.

"With the wind veering from north to west by northwest the western shore of the bay should offer us sufficient protection," Alec said. It had to.

After all, this is where their memories began to intertwine.

Alec was at least half-right. Had he known, he would have continued to Smuggler Harbor. By five o'clock the wind was howling at a good thirty knots. It whined and whistled through the shrouds at the top of their mast. But way down, the water remained calm. And for as long as the prevailing direction of the wind remained westerly, they would be snug and cuddly.

And then the sky grew dark.

He had his pick of good spots. Once again, they were the only boat in the bay. With a draft of less then four feet, he could get within thirty feet of the protective shoreline. Just two hundred yards east, the water was already angry. Further out still, the white crests spoke of a dark and stormy night.

The rain that came lasted a thunderous, intensive hour. The heavens opened and emptied itself right over their heads. From the moment they heard the first distant thunder, to the almost continuous blinding flashes accompanied by a cacophony of hallow explosions, they hardly had time to make sure all was fast on deck. The rainstorm itself may have lasted less than an hour, but the wind remained. It sang in the trees, it whistled erratic, wistful airs, it made them feel that they were miles away from anywhere, on a distant desert island, where no man's foot had as yet dared to tread. It wasn't what they'd planned, but a sailor's life is an unpredictable one. Also, for some reason, Alec was watching and listening to nature's tantrums with a sense of strange familiarity.

After making sure that everything was properly tied down on deck they both retreated to the cabin to wait out the storm. Alec was disappointed until a strange thought crossed him mind. *Is nature getting even with me?* The next moment he chuckled at his own thought.

"I'm becoming presumptuous, in my old age," he murmured.

"You're what, darling?"

"I'm becoming pissed off with this…"

"Don't be silly, it's beautiful!" Suzy insisted, feeling like an intrepid sailor of the seven seas. "Beautiful," she repeated, her eyes flashing in accord with the lightning.

After such a wonderful first night Alec wasn't looking forward to spending the evening cooped up inside the small cabin. He had little choice but to resign himself to an evening of reading. And... if it hadn't been for Suzy, that's exactly what he would have done.

Luckily, she knew exactly what to do. By the time Alec had finished inspecting the ship and changed into dry clothes, she'd lit a couple of candles, put in a compact disk full of their favourite tangos, and dressed herself in luscious expectation awaiting what might develop.

Soon enough, developments took their predictable course. Alec took one look at her, and muttered, "Why did I bother to get dressed again...?"

The yacht was too small to allow dancing, down below. You might have just tried it if you absolutely had to. But once you lowered the table in the main cabin—and the table was needed for the wine, the cheese and the candles—the only way you could enjoy the tango was in a horizontal position, on port or starboard berth, on either side of the table. And, predictably, in a relatively short time, though not *for* a short time, Alec gave new meaning to the old expression that a tango is a vertical expression of a horizontal desire. Only in their case, the desire and the expression followed the same orientation. This matter is of some considerable importance because it had a direct bearing on the rest of their lives.

It was a dark and stormy night.

A night never to be forgotten.

Memories were made on nights such as these. Why?

Because nine months later, to the day, Alexander Baldwin III was born.

On their return to Montreal, a message was waiting from Dr. McBride. Alec should report back to Caltech within the next few days. Next week he was to give a lecture at MIT, as scheduled, but also at UCLA where he would share the podium with a Russian physicist who was also dabbling in the consequences of, or generated by, the EPR paradox. Dr. McBride had no idea if their fields were compatible or in competition, and in fact if they would support or contradict each other. Although it would have been much easier to fly directly to MIT, it was vital that Alec got back to work and find out.

Alec didn't mind. By now he considered himself to be an experienced globetrotter.

The recorded message finished in Des's usual style: "And that's all therre's to it, lad. And don't forrget to give best regarrds to yourr charrming lassie frrom me."

And that was that.

"I told you he was nice," Suzy smiled.

"And a slave driver to boot," Alec added with a grin.

At Dorval airport she leaned against him as if to whisper something into his ear. He lowered his head, expecting some sweet-little-nothing as a parting gift, or perhaps a goodbye kiss. He put his arms around her.

"You know, darling, I've been watching you all the time," she half-whispered with a tone of satisfaction. "You haven't peek-a-boo'ed even once!"

Alec was taken aback. "I've been too busy," was all he could come up with. *Or I was not getting on Sandra's toes?* He kept the latter thought to himself.

But then he got his kiss anyway.

The EPR paradox was a motivation for Alec's research, not his soul nor his guiding light. Since the beginning, Alec had thought of using it as one uses a baton to conduct an orchestra. It wasn't the music, but it helped to create it.

Upon arriving at Caltech, he was shown to his own office. His name was engraved on a brass plate and appended to the metal door at about the level of his throat. Evidently, the majority of the staff was well below his six-foot-two stature. Six foot-ten, if you counted the hair.

He found three piles of paper neatly stacked on 'his' desk. Documents to sign, papers to read, newspaper cut-outs, university programs, and all sorts of other printed matter that seemed destined for the proverbial file 13. Shuffling through this last stack, Alec found references to Dr. Alexis Goudoff with whom he was to share the podium at UCLA.

Soon he discovered that the good Doctor was more concerned with the popular vote than with scientific research. At least not with science as Alec knew it. Dr. Goudoff seemed to hover on a thin line between Bell's Inequality Principle and Cosmic Consciousness, with some rather esoteric connotations. Bell's Inequality Principle was interesting enough, until it ventured into the experimental confirmation that reality doesn't have locality with CFD. CFD stands for Counterfactual Definiteness. Frankly Alec found this, as well as the Quantum Nonlocality and the Possibility of Superluminal Effects, rather confusing. He was not interested in faster than light effects, but with instantaneous effects. There is a vast difference. He thought that one distorted the laws of the universe, the other reached outside them. Both mathematically and under laboratory conditions.

The visiting physicist wrote about Cosmic Consciousness as though it was some sort of Quantum Myth. Alec suspected that the Doctor wouldn't have been invited to speak if it hadn't been for his 'visiting' status. Mustn't complain, thought Alec. Perhaps that's how I'd gotten into academia in Buenos Aires and Bogota. But what the good Doctor was doing to science was quite another matter. The compatriots of the Doctor had long been enamoured with matter/mind interaction. A sentiment that Alec did not dismiss, but did not profess any allegiance to, either.

At least, not under the auspices of physics.

Alec pushed the papers aside, switched on the computer and typed 'EPR paradox' in the Google window. A number of titles lit up on the screen. Apparently at the University of Arizona they had tried to find a link between quantum mechanics and Consciousness. Alec would have found them more interesting if they hadn't come up with sexy names like 'Quantum-mind' and 'Quantum approaches to Consciousness.' He thought that one might be able to quantify I.Q., but hardly consciousness. He also thought that they should have invited Dr. Goudonov, or Goudoff— whatever his name. He would have fit in with these metaphysical psycho-physicists.

Alec was definitely not into the metaphysical angle. He had trouble enough with the imaginary travels of his youth, with his purported space-shifting, and recently with his recurrent memories of Sandra. Troubles enough without bringing them to the office.

His passion, if one could call it that, was observing the universe and attempting to explain it. He desired neither to appropriate the Quantum Theory, nor to confer on it his own spiritual needs or emotional frustrations. He had tried to resolve the paradox between quantum universe and continuity. But this had nothing to do with any myths. Alec was, or tried very hard to be, first and foremost, a scientist. He wanted to observe, to measure, or prove beyond any doubt, or at least within a high degree of probability, that some things cannot be measured. Both ambitions were difficult enough to last him a lifetime.

Or so he thought.

A boisterous knock on the door interrupted his meandering thoughts. Dr. McBride literally pranced into the room.

"My, you've changed, lad. I can harrdly rrecognize you!"

The old man danced around the desk and took Alec into his arms. Since he could only just reach up to Alec's chest, he matter of some considerable difficulty; yet his bear-hug was as firm as a man's half his age.

"'Tis great to see you, Professor, ah... Desmond," Alec returned the hug. Then, as he looked closer at the professor, he added, "I wish I could say the same for you. You've been working too hard again?"

"Therre is only so much a man can do, at my age..." At this moment Des interrupted himself, "Sorry about your father, Alec. Must have been a shock. It always is. Aye, it always is..."

"Sit down, if you have a minute. I'm afraid I can't offer you 'a drrop of the harrd stuff' as yet. I arrived just an hour ago."

"I know. I came over as soon as I could." And suddenly Dr. McBride's face got serious.

"What is it, Sir?"

"They're trying to get you on the mumbo-jumbo circuit."

"Oh, Lord. That's all I need...."

"I've been trying to get you out of the UCLA gig. You might have to come down with a sudden cold, or something."

"I know. I've been reading up on Dr. Goudoff's previous dissertations. Not quite my cup of tea."

There was a moment's silence. Then Dr. McBride looked up from his knuckles pressed tightly together. He looked as if he was getting ready to punch someone.

"Therre is anotherr way, you know, lad. A verry dangerrous way..."

"Kill him?"

"Nae, that's illegal. But 'tis the rright idea." And the Professor leaned closer over the desk. "You might trry killing him with worrds, lad. Now that would not be illegal."

"And it could be a bit of fun...." Alec's eyes were already shining. For the last five years, four at McGill and a little more than one at Caltech, he had developed a bit of a reputation as a practical joker. And now, glory be, now he would be paid for it!

"The game's afoot." The Professor looked down at his watch. "Let us meet in my office at seven. I can't think with a drry thrroat. Be therre, lad!" he commanded.

Before Alec had a chance to agree, the door shut behind his old friend.

About half way through the second tumbler, Alec looked up from his golden liquor.

"I'll need three accomplices, three two-way ear plugs, and a lot of luck," he declared, as though talking to himself.

"Thrree? That's rather expensive. But, if you and I threw in a couple of bucks, we could swing it, eh lad?" The professor instantly guessed Alec's intent.

"We would prove beyond the shadow of probability—or would it the penumbra of possibility—that Cosmic Consciousness is alive and well in UCLA. And then run like hell," he chuckled.

"I'm affrraid not, lad. We would have to stick behind and admit to the Prress that it was all a hoax."

"But wouldn't that kill the objective?" Alec didn't quite follow.

"It would kill the theorists who bastarrrdize science. And that is the object of the exerrsise, isn't it lad?"

"'fraid so, Sir. You know, Des, you are a sneaky devil."

"You've only just discoverred?" The Professor looked genuinely pleased.

"You'll be sitting here, laughing your head off, while I'll be risking my life."

"No, lad. You misjudge me. I'll be procurring the best malt you've drrunk since the last best malt. In fact, this one's not bad at all, is it?" He held his glass up to the light.

"Aye, Desmond McBrrride. "'Tis not bad at all." Alec was getting good at imitating Des's accent.

The plans have been laid. If anyone ever took Cosmic Quantum Myth seriously again, they would remember

UCLA. Caltech would have done its, or their, bit. For the glory of science. And for the red, white and blue. And for...

"What haven't we drrunk to yet, lad?"

Alec's eyes focused on Des's face, then widened in disbelief. "Good night, Sirrr," he said, hardly slurring his words at all. Then he bowed deeply and took his leave with just a minute wobble.

He still had his old digs on campus. Eventually, he'd have to find a larger place, so that Suzy might visit and stay longer, if she could. The good thing about his present quarters was that all he had to do was to cross the lawn and he was home. Such as it was.

Miraculously, he ran down the two flights of stairs and pushed the door to the outside. As the fresh air hit him, the Scotch in his blood became more evident. He leaned back and waited for the trees to settle down. They didn't. It was the wind, after all. His initial anger had long dissipated in McDes's Scotch. Poe would have been proud of what Alec saw. And what he saw was just deserts for plotting scurrilous, conniving, underhanded attacks on the enemy.

It was, yet another, dark and stormy night.

***

Remembering

The human race is the basis on which heaven is founded.

Emanuel Swedenborg
1688–1772
Scientist, philosopher, mystic

7
Who is Sandra?

The lecture at MIT went splendidly. The day after the lecture, the professional reviews were cautious but friendly, and certainly without any 'metaphysical' connotations, although MIT's sister, Harvard University's Department of Physics, did exhibit some rather exotic overtones. Actually, Laboratory for Nuclear Science had sponsored the lecture. This fact alone might explain the down-to-earth, pure science type of reception.

Alec was grateful—no matter what the reason.

UCLA was quite another story.

Being younger, Alec had been scheduled to deliver his lecture first. They were keeping Dr. Goudoff for dessert, so to speak. And well they might. Alec had met him just before climbing the stage and found him clammy, rather like his smile. Even the doctor's hand had stuck to his. While Alec delivered his dissertation, Goudoff sat on the stage, a blissful smile on his overly full lips. As usual, Alec's lecture was followed by a question period. This was where and when the scheme he and Dr. McBride had concocted was to be put into operation. The questions had to come from the audience. With a feeling of now-or-never Alec looked up from his papers.

"And now, ladies and gentlemen, are there any questions?"

A number of hands shot up, wavered, and shrank back like tortoises into their shells. After all, this was Los Angeles, and LA is in California, and California had more unorthodox, ah... philosophers per square inch, than any other part of the civilized world per square mile. Only, hardly surprisingly, they weren't sure of their ground.

However, since the principal speaker was well known to all the amateurs of quantum-myth theories, the audience was peppered with gullible students, eager to prove the metaphysical connection. As such, they were ideal subjects for Alec's 'experiment'.

For the next little while there was deadly silence. Then, from the hesitant penumbra of the auditorium, an emasculated young man rose to his wobbly feet, bowed stiffly to Alec and asked point blank.

"What do you think about Quantum Mechanics and the Universal Consciousness connection."

They didn't waste any time.

"Could you be more precise?" Alec asked innocently.

"Well, I thought I was. Is there a connection between consciousness and quantum mechanics?"

"Of course!" There was a prolonged 'ahhh' in the audience. Alec waited until the intake of breath died down. "It is difficult to discuss quantum mechanics with someone who is unconscious."

Half the audience laughed uproariously, the other half wasn't amused at all.

"Are you making light of the theory?" a young lady asked.

"No, ma'am. Photons have nothing to do with it. I really meant what I said."

More laughter. Then Alec raised his hand.

"I just finished speaking on the subject of what could be described as omnipresent information. Just as other fields may be traced in interstellar space, so, I believe, can information. What form this information takes is another story. If you wish to call it consciousness, that's your prerogative. But if you do, it still does not prove any link with quantum theory."

"But what about the photons in the DPR paradox?"

"What about them?"

Silence. But a silence which some like to call: pregnant.

Alec thought time was ripe to conduct his experiment. The experiment was based on Einstein's statement about infinity. Old Albert had once said that 'Only two things are infinite: the universe and human stupidity, and I'm not sure about the universe'. The theory was often quoted but never proven.

He tapped the tiny listening device in his ear and immediately heard quiet confirmations. 'B34', seconds later 'P14' and 'K29', all confirmed their presence and locations. His coconspirators were in place.

"Do not confuse information with other forms of communication," Alec said in a slightly pontifical tone. "It is one thing to assert the presence of information, quite another to be able to access it. And not all information is accessible. For instance...." he raised his hand as if to quiet the audience, then raised his eyes to the ceiling. "The lady in the seat number B34 has a book in her handbag. The book is entitled 'Maternity'. She is completely preoccupied with this subject matter."

Heads turned.

Alec looked down at the audience, his voice down to a whisper. "The information is there. But I, for one, have no idea why the lady in B34 finds the book so important. Very few of us can access such information. Don't you agree?"

There was a momentary silence, then a giggle followed by a startled exclamation. A young lady from the 34th seat in row B jumped to her feet.

"How on earth did you know that?" She waved a book with '*Maternity*' splashed across the cover in red letters.

"I didn't and I don't. I only know that the information is there. Had you not confirmed it, it would still be there. Right?"

"I suppose so..." She sounded doubtful but slowly sat down.

"And what about me?" A young man waved his arms from the rear of the hall.

"What about you, Sir? I am not a mind reader..." A gentle, almost hesitant laughter followed Alec's assertion. "But I can tell that you are in row P, seat number 14. That much is self-evident." Alec was looking at the other end of the hall as he said that. Then a wave of heads turned in the direction of the young man.

"You couldn't possibly have known that!" the young man exclaimed.

"Of course not. I don't know that any more than I know that the gentlemen in seat K29 just stuck his chewing gum under the seat in front of him."

There was a stir in rows L, K, and M as people looked in the direction of the young man, who got up and fought his way over people's toes towards the exit.

"That's not funny!" he threw over his shoulder. And he was out. The sooner the better, Alec thought .

"So you can see that the omnipresence of information has little to do with Cosmic Consciousness or Quantum Mechanics. It's just there. For anyone to pick and use as they choose. Is it true? Isn't truth whatever you believe in?"

With this enigmatic question Alec gathered his papers, nodded to his audience, the visiting lecturer, and left by the back door. The hall was in total uproar. The crowd was milling around for a look at the girl with the book on maternity. Others pushed to examine the chair in front of seat 14 in row K. They appeared to have no interest in Alec's lecture, in the Information Theory, nor even in any cosmic or quantum connotations. The only thing that seemed to matter to them was magic.

The miracle?

It seemed to be of absolutely no importance to them how the 'miracle' was accomplished. In no time at all they'd released the girl, first making sure that the miraculous book was left behind with them. They passed it from hand to hand, flipped through it, looking for some explanation. They shook it, shuffled the pages and finding nothing they shook their heads in wonder.

By the time the public had settled down, Alec, Desmond and their three young accomplices, were sipping their 'lights' in Pasadena. Before the session, at the very last moment, Alec had advised the UCLA people that he could give the lecture as scheduled, but he would not be able to stay for a *tête-à-tête* afterwards, nor hear Dr. Goudoff speak. He regretted it very much but he had an urgent meeting that just couldn't be cancelled. "Something to do with National Security. No, he had no idea what. He'd just had a phone-call and was told to report to his office as soon as possible after the lecture. It could have been a crank call, Alec admitted, but whoever it was sounded very, very serious."

Thus the ground had been laid.

Frankly, Alec regretted not being there to hear the Russian deliver what everyone apparently wanted to hear. Or almost everyone in the hall, that is. Alec wondered just how much wind he'd taken out of the good doctor's cosmic sails. Now sipping a light beer, they were considering a plan of action.

"So, what's next?" Alec asked a little nervously. "Do we own up?"

"Oh, we'll own up, alrright," Dr. McBride assured. "In fact we've alrready done so."

"We what?" All four young people looked up.

"I wrote a detailed descrription of how the mirrracle was accomplished and sent it to all thrree prrincipal dailies. As I slipped it into the mail-box just beforre yourr blarrney; they should get it by the morrning post."

"I hope there is no extradition treaty between Pasadena and Beverly Hills..."

"Don't worry, lad. I made it all legal. I explained why it was done. All in the name of science."

Alec took a deep breath. "Thank God for that..." he whimpered without conviction.

"Oh, and I left a copy of my little *exposé* in a sealed envelope on dean's desk. Old grumpy Hezeldorff will enjoy it. I know the man. He's really on our side, only he lacks, excuse my Latin, lassie, he lacks balls." McDes was so excited he'd forgotten to roll his r's.

"I thought I had a malt, coming," Alec wailed also downing his glass.

"That you have, my lads. And lassie, of course. You'll all be rrichly rrewarrded in due courrse. That you will." Desmond reverted to his Scottish ancestry. "Only firrst let us get away frrom herre. I saw no reason to involve the young'uns. Officially only Alec and I put on this show. You thrree are clearr. It's one thing to wrrite letterrs, anotherr to meet y'rr enemy face to face. When you get to be my age, you'll want to keep y'rr teeth in y'rr mouth."

The three youngsters got up.

"Thanks for the fun, Sir. And you Dr. Baldwin. And thanks for the beer." With respectful nods the sophomores filed out in a single file.

"Come tomorrow, they'll be famous..." Alec mused.

"Though I would give up one of them just to hear Dr. Goudoff talk his way out of that one!" When Alec looked blank, he added, "One of my teeth, lad!"

"Me too," Alec agreed.

Alec gazed after the three youngsters. They reminded him of himself, barely three or four years ago. They did not consider their participation as a good deed for science; they were in it for the free ride, for the fun of it. He sighed almost imperceptibly.

As he and Dr. McBride also rose, the Professor turned to Alec with a satisfied grin.

"At least they won't botherr you, lad, anymorre with that nonsense. Not anymorre."

"Oh? I thought I might become a *cause célèbre* in some circles. Surely, you don't think the believers are going to accept your explanation of..."

"My? Why lad, it's you who signed the letters!"

And suddenly Alec didn't feel quite so well. He wanted to disappear into thin air.

"You know, Des, you are a bit of..."

"...son of a bitch? I know. Isn't it fun?"

"I was thinking more in the firearms' department." He grinned. "But if you insist..."

A day after Alec's venture into the occult, Suzy arrived for a weekend visit. It was a longish flight from Montreal and she was looking forward to a quiet rest. Alec had just rented a bigger place, two bedrooms and a decent L-shaped living room overlooking the San Gabriel Mountains. He hadn't had time to furnish it, hoping that Suzy would give him a hand. When Suzy saw the empty walls, she sat down on the floor in the middle of the large living room, and wiped her eyes.

"It's so empty..." she whimpered. "How can you live like this?"

"Darling, please, darling." He tried to embrace her but she held him off. "I've only spent one night here. I was hoping that you'd give me a hand with the furniture."

"B-b-but, I live in Montreal..." The tears wouldn't stop.

"But surely you'll join me after we're married?"

"Ma... ma... ma... what did you say?"

He repeated his last statement.

"You want to marry me?"

"I've only asked you a dozen times!"

"B-b-but not since last week...." Nevertheless, the flood was coming to an end. "You don't have to get down on your knees since we are already on the floor." A smile illuminated her face.

"You mean you will? Finally?"

"You first asked me after the tango. I was fourteen then. And ever since I've thought you were too young."

Alec spread his arms. "And now? Do I have to get the Nobel Prize before you say yes?"

"It would be nice," she sighed. "Mrs. Alexander Baldwin, Ph.D., N.P."

"There is no such thing as N.P."

"There should be."

"Could we delay this discussion until after I get my Nobel?"

"I don't know. Without it I would be just a pheee'd."

"A what?"

"How do you pronounce Ph.D., isn't it pheee'd?

They spent the night on a single mattress laid out in the middle of the master bedroom. About midnight Susan agreed to become Mrs. Phee'd, providing he'd continue to live with her. She said that living in Montreal while he had all the fun here was not fair.

She was right, of course. What's the point of getting married if you are to live a continent apart? In their case, something like 4000 kilometers as the crow flies. They agreed that Suzy would try to resign her post as soon as possible, but at the latest to leave Montreal before Christmas. Alec would go home for the holidays, to see her parents and his own mother, and then they would sublet their apartment in Montreal and move to California.

Dr. McBride's secretary offered to take care of the immigration formalities. The application stated that Dr. Alexander Baldwin was gainfully employed in the US of A, and, according to a statement by the Dean of the Department of Physics, he absolutely irreplaceable'.

On Tuesday, the furniture arrived. By the end of the day the apartment looked presentable. Unfortunately, next morning Suzy had to return to Montreal.

"My parents would never forgive me, you know," she said at the airport.

"Oh, yes...?"

"You've forgotten already!" She kicked him none too lightly.

"Ouch! What have I done now?" He hopped on one leg away from her.

"The wedding, silly? We can't do it here. My parents would kill me."

"Of course…" he agreed, still hopping. "We must do it in Montreal. It really hurts, you know."

"What, the thought of marrying me?" She came closer and massaged his shin. "I'm sorry. I really must learn more self-control. Forgive me?"

"Only if you marry me soon."

And then the loudspeaker announced that her plane was ready for boarding.

Alec drove back. His rented car was expensive, but their other car was in Montreal. Unfortunately, one could not live in LA without wheels. An automobile was taken for granted, just like the morning fog and smog and red-rimmed eyes. It came with the territory.

His, or really their, new apartment, also quite naturally, had air-conditioning. Another thing taken for granted. If you wanted to breathe, that is. And every time Alec thought of having Suzy with him on a permanent basis, he wanted to breathe for a long, long time.

Yet, even as he was thinking of his life with Mrs. Baldwin, the memories of Sandra began to insinuate themselves into his awareness; not competing for attention, but rather, in a strange way, participating. What a peculiar way to remember Sandra, he thought. Sandra who was already part of him, even as Suzy was about to become.

But it wasn't the same.

There was never a question of competition.

Who was Sandra? Or better still, who *is* she?

Had Alec been a religious man, the answer would have been simple. My soul, he would have said. But Alec didn't indulge in escapes into metaphysics. He had problems enough with the memories of his early exploits. Some of them he remembered as vividly, if not more so, than his experiences of last week.

What was it about Sandra that once made her so close? So immediate? He remembered her words: I'll always be with you. He even had both explicit and implicit recollections of the 'merging', of becoming one with Sandra. But it was one thing to relive the experiences of his teenage years, and another to accept it all with a mature, adult brain. He could not deny what happened on that 'Third Step,' the step he'd taken at her bidding, the final step of becoming 'one'. Or was it One with a capital O? His mind trained in scientific, inductive and deductive reasoning did not quite open wide enough to place that experience in its proper place.

Who is Sandra?

When he was a little boy, he was lonely. What boy isn't, on occasion? Especially if he is the only child. But to create a personality as complex as Sandra's would have been near impossible for a fourteen-year-old. In some respects, it might prove even more difficult for an adult. Yet Sandra was no less real today then she was then, only in a different way. Then— she was immediate, tangible, palpable. He could see her; on the 'Home Planet' he could touch her.

Alec did not suffer from inability to accept, what might be called, the invisible world. Indeed, his career was centered on 'things' he could neither see, nor smell, hear, taste, or touch. Things that did little more than, under conditions of almost absurd pressures, leave fleeting trails behind them. Things which came into being, 'physical' being, for fractions of a second and were instantly absorbed back into a world as yet inaccessible to men. He wondered what Sandra would say about his profession. Would she approve of physics? Particle physics? A science that seemingly competed with her to gain a foothold in the visible world?

Somehow Alec harboured an inner conviction that, in a certain way, he couldn't do anything Sandra didn't approve of. Rather as with Suzy, only... he had to face it, only infinitely more so. He might take liberties when Suzy was in Montreal, but with Sandra? Sandra was always with him. She'd said so.

On the other hand, it seemed that Sandra's powers, compared to his, were near infinite. Also her concept of morality, if there was such a thing in her term of reference, was vastly different from the human version.

And the Home Planet was another problem. Did he really invent its reality, as Sandra had implied? But if so, then she'd as good as admitted that he had also invented her. The tangible, palpable her. Only he knew he hadn't. Or if he had it must have been at such a deep, not merely subconscious but unconscious level, as cannot be reached by an act of will; certainly not by an act of will of a mere, fourteen-year-old stripling. Perhaps the great gurus, the swamis of the mysterious Orient, might be capable of such things, but not a young sailor, a budding tennis player, or a generally confirmed prankster. And, at the time, he'd been all three.

So, who is Sandra?

Carl Jung might call her his anima—perhaps his Superego. But if that was the case, then did he create Sandra or did Sandra create him? Had she been biding her time, revealing herself to him only when he was ready? She'd said something of the sort. But if that was the case...

If that was the case, then, in a manner of speaking, he wasn't Alec at all. He was the out-picturing of Sandra herself—the outer sheath of his inner Self.

Or was he just raving because Suzy had left and he was lonely.

Like a little boy...

The questions just wouldn't go away. But they had to. After all, he was getting married. He just couldn't keep two women in his heart. Could he?

And then, quite out of the blue, Alec remembered the words of his idol: *"I am going to tell you what nature behaves like. If you will simply admit that maybe she does behave like this, you will find her a delightful, entrancing thing...."*

Only Richard Feynman wasn't there to tell him who Sandra was. Perhaps she was just part of nature's behaviour pattern. Perhaps the doctor, the man who traded ideas with Einstein and Bohr, the man whose brilliance was only equaled by his chutzpah, could have told him. Alas, he wasn't there either.

Sandra was his, and his alone to discover. To rediscover? It was almost like trying to get to know yourself—only much, much more so. But of one thing he was sure. Whatever Sandra meant to his youthful fancies, it was time to grow up. It was time to be and act like the scientist that he was. Regardless of what his emotions might call for.

Goodbye, Sandra, he whispered. And then he added even more softly, Goodbye my love...

***

8
Wedding Bells

Seven more lectures across the United States, two in Europe, three stints at the Supercollider in Texas, a dozen articles in scientific publications—all in addition to his regular teaching post at Caltech—kept Alec in good form. He didn't have time for any sport, let alone for his beloved but oh... so time-consuming sailing, but he hoped all this would settle down once Suzy moved to California permanently.

The scientific establishment would never accuse Alec of playing the same tune, of marching to the same piper. After all, this was *their* specialty. There have been rare moments when Alec thought he was sinking into the comfortable embrace of scholastic stagnation. He suspected that he was on the verge of becoming brain-dead. To new ideas, that is. He would never admit it to himself, let alone anyone else, even Suzy, that Sandra was the one and only source of every original idea that ever crossed his mind.

And Sandra was dead. Dead and buried.

He should know. He was the judge, jury and the undertaker.

Surely, it was by sheer coincidence that, to the degree that he'd succeeded in dismissing Sandra from his mind, his joints began, once again, to ossify—to stiffen, to say the least. Particularly in the morning, getting out of bed was becoming a problem. He had to lie still for a while, and will blood into his extremities. And it wasn't just the joints of his limbs. His brain, too, was starting to feel fossilized, as though sluggish deposits were forming up there, somewhere.

He decided to do more exercise, and dismissed the matter from his mind. Life was too good to miss. "A few hard games of tennis and I'll be as good as new", he assured himself. Only there simply was no time for tennis. Or for any other exercise. Not at that moment. And frankly, he was a bit too stiff, already.

On the other hand, after only six or seven months of the lecture tours, Alec had already learned to repeat the same beaten track, to avoid phrases which might be too controversial, hypotheses which might offend the academia.

He was becoming one of *them*.

Only *that* he would not admit, even to himself. Not outside of rare moments of weakness. Or were they moments of remaining strength? On the last lecture tour Dr. McBride wasn't there to hold a rod and a staff, to give him comfort. To guide him. And the Press? The Press was euphoric. They were finally beginning to understand what, the now famous, Dr. Alexander Baldwin was talking about.

Or so they thought.

Once again, Alec was becoming angry.

Of course, in Alec's chosen profession everything was only as permanent as the next academic year. Not only because he might be replaced by a fresh, possibly cheaper, budding genius, but because he might have to move, in search of better opportunities for the development of his ideas, of his mind. Or both. Or just simply to advance his career. And by now his Information Theory was making headlines across three continents.

Dr. Alexander Baldwin was an up-and-coming scientist in great demand.

Academia had finally accepted that he was not yet another crank trying to marry the Occident with the Orient in some sort of Cosmic Quantum Consciousness concoction. The little game he and Des had played at UCLA died a natural death. After making headlines for a couple of weeks in the back pages of the local, and some not so local, press, it hadn't been mentioned since. On the other hand at Caltech he'd became an overnight sensation. On that account, Dr. McBride had been right.

"You've got to act like an aging Hollywood she-starr. It matterrs not if they talk 'bout you well or badly, the imporrrtant thing is that they talk!"

And they certainly talked.

For better or for worse, Alec became the new resident celebrity. He was invited everywhere, by everyone, all the time. Obviously, the vast majority of engagements he refused due to lack of time, previous commitments, and an array of the usual excuses. But one invitation he didn't refuse. It was addressed to Dr. Alexander Baldwin, Ph.D., NP. Before he even noticed a Canadian stamp, he'd guessed immediately what the envelope contained. He'd just been invited to his own wedding. The next day his joy was heightened even further when he met Desmond McBride in the corridor.

"So y'rre tying the knot, lad, arre'ye? 'Bout time, if I may say so. 'Tis a gorrrgeous lassie that Susan of y'rrs. Gorrgeous indeed!"

Dr. Desmond McBride had been invited also.

The following morning, for some reason, Alec's aches and pains subsided to an unexpected degree. As did his fluctuating anger.

Alec flew to Montreal a week before Christmas to give Suzy a hand. Some months after the event, Suzy told him that nothing had hindered her in the preparations as much as his presence. His constant insistence on helping laid an extra burden on her. But everything went off without a hitch. The wedding ceremony was conducted in the small, interdenominational chapel, with just her parents, Alicia, Desmond McBride, three of Suzy's brothers and some old school friends—one of whom brought her husband, and, of course, Pete. About fourteen people.

Pete was Alec's old school buddy.

They saw each other about twice a year, plus a few extra times during the holidays, to play tennis and down a few Molsons or Labbatts for old time's sake. At the time when Alec lived with his parents, Pete had lived next door. Alec moved on, Pete stayed behind. He married early, 'had to', as they say, and was a proud father of a two-year-old son. He worked at the Municipal Library, hoping to make Chief Librarian when his boss retired. Peter did not pretend to be a smart guy, 'like you, Alec', but he was by far the best-read fellow Alec had ever met. Pete ate books for breakfast, lunch, supper, and a couple for in-between snacks. He was definitely in the right profession. And... he could still beat Alec at tennis. But only just. That was, of course, before Alec's joints begun to stiffen up.

Pete's parents and his wife had also been invited, but they were all out of town. It was the first holiday they'd taken together since the baby was born. They deserved it.

All in all, in addition to the young couple and the vicar, there were fourteen guests. The vicar was Suzy's mother choice, a kindly old man who'd married her and John, some thirty-two years ago. Suzy insisted, and Alec heartily concurred, that a wedding is a private occasion, an event to be shared only with the very closest friends. It was a matter of declaring one's love for each other and asking the closest friends to bear witness to that love. As the Normans had moved to Kingston, some years ago, they agreed to have the small reception in Alicia's house. Alicia, needless to say, was overjoyed.

"So many new memories..." she cooed. "Just wonderful. Just wonderful!"

Suzy was anything but a hostess committed to staying in the kitchen. She could perform marvels when she chose, but not for sixteen people. She called the Ritz-Carlton and arranged to have a feast delivered to the Baldwin address, together with two waiters and all the plates, glasses and other paraphernalia needed for the reception. There would be no washing up on her wedding day. Not even one fork.

But first there was Xmas. The five of them, the parents and the hosts, sat down to Christmas dinner in Suzy and Alec's apartment. It was to be their last meal there. Tomorrow, the various pieces of furniture would be disposed of, in various directions. Whatever they were not taking with them, which was almost nothing, Suzy got rid of in good time. Their best furniture would go into long-term storage, most of what remained she hoped to get rid of at a garage sale, while the rest was scheduled to be picked up by the Salvation Army. Suzy'd made arrangements to hand over the keys to the apartment before the end of the month, and their wedding was scheduled for the 31st. They would start the New Year as Mr. & Mrs. Baldwin.

"As Dr. & Mrs.," she corrected her mother proudly.

For their last days in Montreal, Alec and Suzy would move in with Alicia. However, there was not enough room for all of them in one house. The Normans would have all their meals at the Baldwins, but, since Pete's wife and parents were conveniently away, they would sleep next door.

There was nothing particularly special about the Christmas dinner, except that it carried overtones of the Last Supper—a little out of season. It couldn't be helped. Alec came to Montreal not just to get married, but also to see his mother, and Suzy, of course, wanted to spend a few days with her parents before moving to Los Angeles. When all was said and done, this Christmas implied an atmosphere not so much of a reunion, as of a farewell party. And then, there was something else missing, and not just Alec's father. Suzy put her finger on it.

"After all is said and done," she said, "after the traditional, all too often stereotyped, wishes have been exchanged, there is still something missing. I think we all know what it is."

The smiling faced turned toward her expectantly.

"What's missing are little children," Suzy continued. "What is missing is seeing the candlelight dancing in their eyes, wide open eyes filled with the uncertain yet avid expectancy of what gifts the wrapping paper was hiding. It has always been their day. Their holiday. Christmas is really a celebration of the smallest amongst us. And without them, something is missing."

This was true for all except Alec. His eyes were shining, as though he'd just unwrapped the biggest, brightest, most wonderful present of his young life.

"You've done it again," Suzy smiled with sudden understanding.

"What have I done, sweetheart?"

"You've peek-a-boo'd again."

But there was no anger or annoyance in her eyes. Just understanding. Suzy smiled because quite suddenly she knew exactly what Sandra was doing.

***

"I do," Alec said in a firm, steady voice.

He'd had plenty of practice. He'd said it a dozen times on the airplane, and a dozen more times after he got to Montreal. "I do," he had repeated sipping his Scotch at his tiny bachelor's party. "You bet your life!" he'd tried for size. "Most certainleah," he'd affirmed, mimicking his father's British accent. "Arrr!" he'd pictured Desmond McBride by his side in a tartan kilt.

"I do," he repeated, as if making sure he'd been heard.

The vicar nodded with a slight smile.

"And you, Suzanna Joanna Norman, do you...."

I wish he'd get on with it, she thought. Of course, I do. Would I be here otherwise? What does he think I am doing all decked out in white, pulling my stomach in to fit into mother's dress that is half my size?

"I do!" she almost shouted.

She was afraid that if she held her breath any longer, the dress would give way. "Gotch ya!" she purred under her breath for only Alec to hear. "I gotch ya and I'm gonna keep ya. And I love ya."

"You may kiss the bride!" the vicar announced.

"You betcha!" Alec was already at it.

And for an instant there, it seemed as though he was kissing her for the very first time.

The reception was an unmitigated success.

It wasn't as though the young Baldwins wanted to get away quickly to hit the sack. After living together, on and off, for what Alicia once stated 'practically all their lives', they loved being surrounded by friends. This was as good as it got. His mother, the Normans, Sue's two brothers (one couldn't come due to a case of stomach flue), her three friends, all the way back from schooldays, Professor McBride, and last but certainly not least, his old buddy, Pete. The vicar excused himself after one glass of Champagne. He, the poor fellow, was no prude, but he had... a funeral to attend to. Only Suzy knew this and she didn't share her knowledge. Not even with her mother.

After *hors d'oeuvres,* the Ritz served *Chateaubriand,* and all sorts of side dishes Alec couldn't even pronounce. They ate and they drank, and they laughed and there were the usual speeches, and more speeches, all funny, all with a tinge of sadness, as good speeches at a wedding should be.

And then came the first bombshell.

Suzy, who contrived to open the zip at the side of her dress without anyone noticing it, took a deep breath and got up holding her flute.

"My friends," she announced, for which she got a well-deserved applause. "If there were one stranger here, or even the wonderful vicar, I would be of two minds about sharing this news with you. But," she looked to her left, her right and behind her, "we are all alone!" Another applause.

"What is it darling?" Alec was as curious as anyone.

"I should not be telling you this without first speaking to my lover, my husband, to the father..." John Norman looked up, "...to the father of my child. Our child."

And before the news penetrated Alec's scull, she raised her glass and said, "Ladies and gentlemen, I offer a toast to Alec Baldwin the Third."

Alec found himself as close to fainting as he'd ever been.

Peter was grinning allover; Alicia's and Joan's eyes and mouths had never been opened wider. But it was Desmond McBride whose voice rose above all others.

"Alexanderrrr Baldwin the Thirrrd!" he announced and downed his glass in a single gulp.

The others followed.

And then they all spoke at once. When? When is it... when is *he* due? Are you all right? Shouldn't you sit down? You mustn't drink, dear. Not any more. John managed to get close enough to his daughter to whisper, "I love you, my pet." Joan was by far the most excited. Did you see the doctor? Are you sure? How...?

"How?" Suzy repeated in disbelief, "don't you know how, mother?"

Luckily nobody asked 'who'?

And then Alec took Suzy in his arms. He didn't say anything. He just held her. And suddenly there was total silence. Only slight whimpers come from the two mothers, and a single though powerful thunder from John, clearing his inner tubes.

"Ah... what a lucky couple," Desmond mused half-aloud. "Theirr whole life beforre them. And just look what a marrrvelous starrt they got..." And the Professor wiped a wee tear from his own eyes.

Slowly things returned to normal, or as normal as any wedding can get. They all returned to their seats. The plates were cleared and eventually the dessert was served. It was then that Pete was unanimously delegated to open the presents.

And the party went on, hour after hour. People changed seats, exchanged conversational partners, even those who had never met before, by now, became friends. Not just acquaintances but real friends. They learned so much about each other that they began caring what was happening in each other's life. Even Suzy's brothers, who had virtually become strangers to their own family, seemed to recover the family fervour. They chatted with and embraced almost everyone, particularly Suzy's old school-friends, and promised to keep henceforth in close touch.

This was more than a wedding. This was a veritable love-fest. They were celebrating marriage, succession, the future, the dreams to come, the unfulfilled but yet to be realized desires, the possibilities.... And by some miracle of the occasion, they all seemed deeply convinced that virtually nothing was impossible, nothing was beyond any one of them, if they really wanted to succeed.

"And you should've seen their faces when I told them about the chewing gum!" Alec was recounting his UCLA prank to the flushed faces around him. "If I hadn't been the speaker, I would have burst out laughing myself!"

Quite true, Alec thought, while Desmond picked up the story. But why is it, he wondered, that people keep searching for the elusive fountain of life in some imaginary mystery, like 'Quantum Buddhism' or some 'Quantum Consciousness', rather than attempting to create it, or at least find it in their everyday life? And just for a moment he recalled the facility that once had been his, the facility to visit the Home Planet, a state of mind wherein he created virtually any reality at will. This strange ability of his had suddenly stopped. For a long time he couldn't figure out why. Now, suddenly, like a bolt out of the blue, it came to him.

Some five, six, or even ten years ago, he had needed to reassert his creative spirit. Then, when he started studying physics, for the first time in his life he began doing exactly what he wanted. He began studying the subject of his dreams, in a way, an inner reality. He no longer poured over curricula

set by others 'for his own good'. And even as he made his
dreams a reality, right here and now, the doors to the Home
Planet had closed. Forever? He doubted it. Ever is such a long
time... But for as long as his creative spirit was sated with his
creative will, there was no need for other realities. And then a
tentative cloud hovered at the edge of his mind as though
trying not to be seen. "Am I still as creative as I once was?"
he asked himself.

"...and then I signed them with Alec's own name! I
didn't even attempt to copy his signaturre. I just wrrote it in
big, fat letterrs, like a five-yearr-old. It was obviously a
forrgery. Alec could have always denied it, orr, if it suited
him, to say that it was his. A win/win situation. Ha, ha!"

A short applause and more ha-has followed. Des
McBride was having fun. He told stories, a number of them
connected with Alec. Most of the time he kept the party in
stitches. Alec's brief departure into his past went unnoticed.
Except for Suzy, of course. She spotted his far away look
immediately. She also noticed when 'he'd come back'.

"Still love me?" she asked.

"I am living my dreams, darling. Thanks to you."

Their hands met under the table.

Alec was grateful to the Professor for entertaining his
guests. The news that he was about to become a father was
only now beginning to catch up with him. He was overjoyed
and scared out of his wits. Simultaneously. He could just
imagine sailing with his son at the helm of their new boat.
We'll have to get one, he thought. Bigger than the old O'Day
27. Much bigger. Bigger than the 37, too! Or maybe he'll
enjoy a good game of tennis? He could teach him the AB, a
service he developed as a lad. It worked pretty well on Pete,
even now. He could teach him that. And swimming. He could
teach him to swim like a fish. And so could Sue. The three of
them could out-swim any other trio, anywhere. He felt sure of
that. If only my joints didn't hurt so...

The pain that receded some days ago, now began to oscillate here and there, as though looking for a place to settle permanently.

"Do you think he'll like physics?" he asked Suzy.

She looked at him for, what seemed like, a long, long time, and then burst out laughing. It may have been the tension of keeping her good news under her belt, literally and figuratively, for such a long time, but she just couldn't stop laughing. Tears filled her eyes, and she laughed as though she hadn't laughed for months on end.

"What have I said?" Alec sounded hurt. Or he thought he was hurt. Shouldn't I have been? This fatherhood is very confusing stuff.

Finally she quieted down. Only still, for a while, her body shook sporadically. Then she got herself under control.

"Of course, he will, darling. I can see it in his eyes."

"You what!!!"

"Well, I am sure he'll have your eyes. And you do love physics, don't you?"

Suzy was a mighty clever girl. Woman. Mother?

Suzy was mighty clever, he thought.

And then it was time to say goodbye. The past week she and Alec had stayed with Alicia. Tonight they would spend their nuptial night at the Ritz. Tomorrow, they would go back home, a small walking distance from the Ritz, for lunch, after which Alec's mother would drive them to Dorval Airport. For some reason, the French Canadians liked to change names. The airport was now renamed the P-E Trudeau International Airport, after a fairly recently demised, very popular though long despised in Quebec, Prime Minister of Canada, who had now risen to the ranks of local superheroes. The *Québécois*, like all people, needed idols to worship. P-E stood for Pierre-Elliott, exemplifying the marriage of the Two Solitudes, as the French and the English people were often referred to. Alec thought the *Québécois* were lucky that the powers at large decided to abbreviate the late PM's name. Had they not, the new name of Dorval would have been the Joseph Philippe Pierre Yves Elliott Trudeau International Airport. A mouthful for any taxi driver.

Alec, Suzy, and all their friends, still called it Dorval.

Baptismal rites for the airports notwithstanding, all the newlyweds had to do now was to say goodbye to everyone, and disappear. It was easier said than done. Joan Norman, who normally seemed most reserved, now held Suzy in conversation, giving her a litany of advice. On cooking, furnishings, travelling arrangements, feeding the baby, teaching him to walk, read, write, history, geography...

"But sweetheart, you're flying to California. That's the other side of the world. I might never see you again."

"You will, Mother. You will. More than you care to."

"And you must write."

"I will"

"Often!"

"Yes, Mom. Often."

"Every day..."

And so it went on. Each time Suzy tried to say goodbye to anyone else, Joan appeared at her elbow, hung on to it for dear life, and continued to impart the wisdom of her years. Dad, John Norman, watched from a distance, his eyes following Suzy's every move. Now and again he blew his nose. For a long time he said nothing. Then he approached.

"Come, Mother," he said, and took Joan gently by the arm. "Come, we must go. So must they." It wasn't easy for John Norman. It wasn't easy at all.

Gradually they all gravitated toward the small entrance hall. Dr. and Mrs. Alexander Baldwin were about to be driven by the proverbial limousine to their bridal suite. There was nothing more to be said. The final embrace, the final admonition, the final kiss...

And then a telephone chimed in somebody's clothing. Professor McBride reached into his pocket with some embarrassment. As he listened his face relaxed. He folded and put the cellular away.

"Ladies and gentlemen," he announced. "I am pleased to report that the nomination for the youngest recipient for the Nobel Prize in the history of physics has been accepted." Then he walked up to Alec.

"Congratulations, my lad. My heartiest congratulations."

The rest of them, including Alec, just stood there.

They were all stunned.

***

9
Alexander Baldwin III

On June 25th, at 1.30 a.m. PST, Alexander Desmond Baldwin III was born at the Good Samaritan Hospital. He displayed the requisite number of fingers, a good complexion, excellent vocal chords, boisterous energy and, what promised to become, a horrendous mop of hair.

"My son!" Alec exclaimed, the first time he held him in his arms. "My son," he repeated, as though not quite believing his own words. And then, terrified of his boldness, he laid him gently by his mother's side.

During the last few days, even hours, they'd tried to get back to Canada, to assure their son's Canadian birthright, but there simply wasn't time. Till that very last moment Suzy had felt and looked good, relaxed, hardly complaining about the extra load she'd been carrying. If it hadn't been for her flushed cheeks and the sparkle in her eyes, one would have thought that she'd simply put on just a little too much weight. Well, perhaps a trifle more than a little, but to Alec, and certainly to Desmond McBride, she'd remained the most beautiful woman around.

And thus, Sacha, which Desmond said was a Russian diminutive for Alexander, was born a US citizen. Alec thought that the Russian diminutive, which they all loved instantly, was a nice twist. A sort of balancing act. A Russian/US citizen. Nevertheless, when Sacha was naughty, Alec, remembering his own father's idiosyncrasies, called him 'a bloody foreigner'.

After flying in from Montreal they'd settled in their new apartment with just a twinge of nostalgia. They missed the view of the lake, the sunsets, and the comfort of the warm, cuddly indoors, when they came back from a brisk walk during the Canadian winter. On the other hand they did not miss at all the slush on the sidewalks, the ramparts of dirty snow when they had to cross the street, nor the need to don galoshes over their shoes each time they wanted to go out. That last chore, or inconvenience, Alec used to hate with a passion he'd normally reserved only for intellectual inadequacy.

Within four weeks or so, Suzy had turned the apartment into a cozy nest, as only a woman can do. Men tend to be neater. They tend towards *chaque chose à sa place* attitude. Not all men, of course, but most who needed an orderly mind in their work. Women are freer. They accept asymmetry as a state of being. They go for balance rather than for mathematical precision. Alec was growing capable of both.

"My, you've cerrtainly made a bonnie place, lassie," Desmond said, the moment he came in.

The Professor had become a frequent guest, virtually a member of the family. He was always welcome. Dr. McBride's wife had died almost twenty years ago. He never remarried, and his only surviving child, a man now, a broker of some financial clout, lived in Australia. They kept in touch by email. It seemed to suffice for both of them. Desmond welcomed being adopted by the Baldwins.

"Soon now you'll be looking afterr two childrren..." he quipped, referring to his own age.

"When the time comes, you'll be welcome, Des," Alec assured him.

"When that happens, make surre y'put the harrd stuff in my bottle. I don't take kindly to milk."

But before all that, a lot had happened.

Once the apartment had been fixed up, Suzy had begun looking for something constructive to do. She'd toyed with the idea of teaching, again, but, after due consideration, discarded the idea. At least for the present. In a few months, four to be precise, Sacha had been expected to join their family. She'd thought that starting work, and then taking maternity leave so soon would not be fair to the school, nor the pupils. Students, as they called them here. Actually, they also started calling the children students in Canada. She had no idea whether it was pure ignorance or just a gradual deterioration of the everyday language. Students, in her opinion, were people, young or old, who listened to lectures and made their own decisions about what to learn. Mostly they studied matters of their own choosing. Pupils were not given such a choice. Pupils were told what they must learn 'or else'. You stopped being a pupil the moment you left school. A student—you remained all your life. Or should.

Finally, Suzy decided to study art.

Perhaps it was Alicia's influence, but when they'd stayed that last week in Montreal, Suzy had grown closer to Alec's mother. What had drawn them together was, among other things, Alicia's love for art. Of course, Alicia has been painting for years. She'd had a number of successful solo exhibitions, and not just in Montreal. There were galleries in Toronto, and a small one in New York, that welcomed her work.

To her disappointment, Suzy soon found out that there were no undergraduate courses in art at Caltech. But within easy walking distance of their apartment, Suzy discovered a private school, which did not delve into the history of art, nor into the finer aspects of fine arts. Instead they believed that anyone could learn to paint. All it took was a little money for the tubes of paint, lots and lots of paper, a few brushes, and infinite hours of practice. This was exactly what Suzy had been looking for.

To her own surprise, she exhibited considerable aptitude for harnessing colour and form, and particularly in the use of her powers of observation. She saw the world in a very personal way. She saw, as did Alicia, beauty where other people failed to see it. Often in the most unexpected places. Perhaps this is what being an artist really means. An artist at heart, that is. Until the middle of June she'd painted at least four to six hours a day; that was in addition to the art course she was taking. All the while she remembered what her instructor had told them at that first lecture:

"You are not here to talk. You are not here to think. You are here to paint." The instructor concentrated on freeing the intuitive artist within.

And paint she did. Soon the spare room, 'Sacha's room', became a depository of her voluminous papers, canvases and even tablets of pressed wood. She painted on anything she could lay her hands on. Quite indiscriminately. By the middle of June she'd moved her considerable output to the storage space they had in the garage, and spent the next two weeks painting directly on the walls. By the time Sacha arrived from the hospital, his cradle stood in the middle of a jungle. The walls, ceiling, even the window frames had been completely covered with vines, leaves, and exotic flowers. Gnarled faces peeked from behind twisted branches, their equally twisted smiles rustling of unspeakable secrets. The doors became mysterious caves cut through giant red cedars and western firs, where fairies made their home; the blinds hiding the windows opened and shut as though branches swaying in the wind. If Sacha didn't grow up loving the mysteries and beauty of nature, no one could possibly blame Suzy.

"Welcome to Eden," Suzy said as she laid him down for the very first time at home. "Welcome to Paradise...." she whispered.

Yet, during those final months of waiting for Sacha, there had been moments when she and Alec still found time to go for a walk, or to sit back and just talk. About a month before the birth, they found themselves, as often after dinner, chatting; Suzy curled up, comfortably on the sofa. He'd asked his wife, by then radiant in her expectation, what she'd meant by the comment she'd made way back, after the Christmas dinner.

"The peek-a-boo business. You haven't mentioned it lately."

"That's because you are doing exactly what you want to be doing."

"And this means...?" He was baffled.

"And this means that Sandra and you are one."

Alec smiled, leaned back, then got up and started pacing the room. He had considerable reservations about Suzy's conclusions.

"Are you trying to tell me that I 'peek-a-boo,' as you call it, only when I am not engaged in something which calls on all my attention?"

"Partly. But more so, when you are not doing what you really enjoy."

"Why would you say a thing like that?" He was completely lost.

She pulled him down next to her, and cuddled under his arm. They sat like this for a while. They enjoyed moments of silence almost as much as when they exchanged ideas.

"You remember when I first told you that you've been shifting positions? It was in Montreal. At the time you already had your doctorate, but you'd been unemployed, restless, one might say not very content with your *modus operandi*. You, I would also venture to say, you'd been stifled, unfulfilled. You started shifting."

"Assuming that you're right, how come I don't have any recollection of it?"

"Well, this is the hard part. It is not really you who are shifting, although your body does appear to change position. Sandra is the one who is really shifting."

"What!? What does she have to do with this?"

"Actually, everything."

Alec wanted to get up but she held him down. He thought he'd buried Sandra. He'd done it for her. For Suzy. For his wife.

"Wait," she said. "Let's think this through."

Grudgingly, he complied.

"From everything you've ever told me about Sandra I gather that she is that part of you that cherishes, or you might say that which, or who, personifies absolute freedom. She appears to have her being outside time, outside space, in fact she does not recognize any limitations whatever."

Suzy turned to face him. He nodded. "Bull's eye, so far."

"But there is one other trait which you never mentioned to me, but which is obvious to an outside observer." Suzy seemed to be taking a deep breath, as though the trait was not as obvious as she'd claimed. "I am talking about Sandra also personifying your happiness."

Rather than jumping to his feet, or denying her words, Alec's eyes drifted to those far away places to which only he had access. Again they sat in silence, close, in a half-embrace. Time seemed to drift on, leaving them behind. Alec was thoughtful, yet happy. It seemed to him that Suzy, dear, dear Sue, had found another piece of the puzzle that had baffled him for many years. Could it be that Suzy was right? Was Sandra that state of consciousness that rejected suffering, rejected unhappiness, refused to recognize that anything, anything at all, was impossible?

And as he sat there feeling Suzy's warmth, he knew, with growing certainty, that his wife was right. As usual, he thought. What is it about women, he wondered? What gives them the right to offer through inherent intuition what men can only achieve through deduction?

He kissed her eyelids blessed with such great vision, then the lips, which gave him greater understanding of himself. And then he put one hand on Suzy's stomach and he said gently: "You are a very, very lucky man, Sacha."

The day after that particular discussion Alec woke up with virtually no stiffness in his joints. Happiness or not, Sandra definitely had something to do with his emotions. His emotional body? And it seemed that there were occasions when his emotional body, if such there was, had been, on occasion, stronger than the physical one. Whatever the truth, his back was giving him less pain.

But as he regarded himself in the bathroom mirror, he shrugged the idea away. "'Tis a fine scientist y'arre Doctorr Baldwin," he muttered, aping Des's quirk. "Next you'll await ferr the fairries to curre you, orr maybe a wee leprrrechaun... 'Tis a fine scientist you arre indeed?"

It was about a month after they discussed this matter that Sacha was born. A few days later he was installed in the jungle of Suzy's making. He either didn't notice his odd surroundings, or was too busy sleeping to notice. At least, he didn't seem to complain. Not much. Considering he was sleeping in a jungle.

His partents' life changed substantially.

There were no more walks, hand in hand, along the green slopes of Santa Monica Mountains, no more visits to the ocean shore to look at yachts they'd been hoping to buy, one day, soon, the moment Sacha was big enough to come sailing with them. The days became equally divided, as were the nights, by feeding times, a schedule in which Alec insisted to help. At least, once Sacha'd matured to a bottle.

A few months later things became easier. The frequency of the schedule was reduced. The feeding times grew further apart, in direct proportion to their size. Alec calculated that if Sacha were to continue eating in proportion to his size for the next ten years, his son would grow to be well over ten feet tall. Gradually, life returned to normal. Almost. Or perhaps they just got used to the new regime. A regime imposed by Sacha without the slightest effort on his part, yet with total and absolute confidence that it was completely his due. But even as Sacha changed, so did Alec's attitude towards his son. The proud father no longer regarded Sacha as a *Fabergé* Egg, which he was greatly afraid to touch, but as a living entity, with bright eyes, showing promise of intelligence.

Yet, the first time Suzy entrusted Alec with sole charge over Sacha, the proud father was completely terrified.

"There's nothing to it, darling. Really." She tried to reassure him.

"But... b-but..."

"Really. People have been doing this for years. Generations. Millennia," she smiled, vaguely amused.

"I ah... I s-s-suppose so," he nodded, but he didn't really believe her. People didn't do it, he thought. Women did. That was different. But he said nothing.

She'd left all the instructions, what to do if and when it became necessary, and left for her art class. For the first time Alec remained completely alone with his son. For a while he just sat there, looking down and listening to the regular breathing, the utter peace emanating from the countenance too young to have, as yet, any personality. The face still belonged to one unaware of being apart from the rest of the world; one still accepting universal membership as a due and natural state of being. It was strange gazing at his tiny face. It was the face of an angel, untouched by any awareness of duality.

Then Sacha opened his eyes.

For some nondescript time, the expression in his eyes hovered on that thin line between dream and reality. Alec looked deep. What he saw was not just the absence of any good or evil. He saw bliss. Perhaps... absolute bliss. Sacha was not claiming membership to the universe—he was the universe. Total, complete, with nothing missing, nothing encroaching on, or detracting from, its wholeness.

Sacha *was* the Universe.

The stars, nebulas, galaxies, were but his toys. His domain no less than infinite space. Neither past nor future invaded its wholeness. It was the eternal present, the singularity of existence, which transcended time and space and any other limitation. There was nothing—nothing to limit or hinder him in this singular realm.

Then Alec detected a pang of hunger—a rude awakening into the physical world.

Until recently, all Sacha's needs had been taken care of immediately. He'd been hardly aware he had any. His consciousness had been less than rudimentary, rather like a tree being aware of having sufficient water to feed its leaves. It could never have been described as human. Now... now Sacha had to fight to satisfy his needs. This effort came to him quite naturally. He took a lungful of air and let it out through a squeezed larynx. Something between a scream and a whimper. It worked. Food came soon after.

Alec offered the bottle: pre-prepared, waiting, the right temperature, the right mix of nutrients. For a minute or two Sacha became quite human, preoccupied with his physical body. Then...

Then, but a few seconds later, Sacha returned to Eden. Alec followed his son's retreat into a realm of indescribable bliss. They both did it quite easily, as though it was the most natural thing to do. For a short while Alec hung suspended in the universe of his son's making. Inexplicably, he shared his son's overwhelming joy.

So this is Paradise? No wonder the Hebrew word for pleasure is Eden....

But Sacha was not to remain there. Not yet. For the next few moments Sacha was draped, helpless, suspended over his father's shoulder. After a sigh of contentment, Alec laid him with infinite care in the cradle surrounded by the tropical jungle, or what Suzy so aptly named *her* Eden. Instantly Sacha fell asleep. Alec withdrew, as though respecting his son's privacy.

Alec sat for long time—thinking. There were memories storming the ramparts of resistance he'd built between his youthful daydreams and the reality he'd chosen to live in. The physical reality, the realm in which he could experience the fastest, the most efficient mode of becoming. The reality he'd chosen; the reality that punished mistakes, even as it rewarded commitment, guiding him ever forward, ever towards greater successes. He'd thought he'd found satisfaction in the realm of physics. The micro- and the macro- cosmos met there, in an amalgam of astral to sub-nuclear branches of his chosen disciplines. His research had been so intensive that he's completely forgotten that the other realms, his private domains, had once been just as real.

There was a great deal more that he'd forgotten.

If it hadn't been for his son, he might have forgotten forever. He might have lost all he'd learned on the Home Planet, or in the Far Country. Now, in that single communion with his son's consciousness he realized that one cannot give up one reality in order to serve another. He needed to be whole, even as his son was still whole. To be complete one had to recognize one's total make up. One's total being.

But the most fundamental revelation that his son had brought to him was that in his pursuit of a dream he'd forgotten about the dreamer. In order to just live, as Sandra had once put it, he forgot who it was that did the living. By intensive becoming he'd lost the power to just be. He'd lost the very essence that enabled him to pursue his dreams.

There comes a time when one must become, once again, a little child.

Only children hold the keys to paradise. Now that he'd recovered his key, he decided never to lose it again. And for some inexplicable reason he felt as though something within him wanted to sing a song of joy, of glory, of happiness, as though bliss was his to achieve.

"Thanks Sacha," he whispered. "Thank you, my son. I'll always be grateful to you for this moment. You've taught me more than I can understand at present. You reminded me who I am."

Yet soon Alec's eyes filled, once again, with apprehension. Am I too late? Would this precious key, this knowledge, still open the gates to my inner worlds?

***

10
Back to the Drawing Board

A **lec knew instinctively** that the revelation he'd had
when gazing into Sacha's eyes would affect every
aspect of his life. His, by now, famous equation, a
concept rivaling Einstein's $E=MC^2$ was just part of it. Alec
had proposed a theory that reduced matter and energy to
information. His equation simply stated that $I=MC^\infty$. 'I'
stood for Information, 'M' for mass and 'C' for the velocity
of light. The funny figure eight lying on its side was the
symbol for infinity. At first glance, to a mathematician, or a
theoretical physicist, the equation did not appear to make
sense. After all, anything multiplied by infinity became
infinite; on the other hand, in the practical sense, no more
could square the speed of light.

But that was the very purpose of the equation. No limits
could be set to Information, nor to its omnipresence in both,
mass and energy.

Essentially, the equation represented an expression of a
philosophy; an attempt to express a philosophical concept in
mathematical terms. It appeared too simple—even as
Einstein's equation made this impression on the previous
generation of scientists. People hate new concepts, new ways
of thinking and particularly when, in order to accept them,
they have to give up the lackadaisical, false comforts that
only mental stasis can offer. All established organizations
detest changes. So do the ruling members of political
systems, religions, and regrettably members of academic
hierarchy.

Alec was a harbinger of change.

A deeper examination of the theory provides that matter
and energy in their initial state are *beyond* both time and

space. Beyond spacetime. The theory stipulated that Information, which is extant in both, had to have existed before the universe came into being.

Before the original Big Bang.

In the SSC at Waxahachie, the world's biggest, most powerful Superconducting Super Collider, scientists were trying to recreate conditions that they thought existed immediately *after* the Big Bang. They assumed that matter became more complex with time, even in the first few millionths of a second. To discover the origin of the universe, they were endeavouring to find the original building block of the universe, a particle so tiny, so 'primitive' that Dr. Leon Lederman once called it the *God Particle*. Alec grinned as he recalled how Dr. Lederman subtitled his book: *"If the Universe is the Answer, What is the Question?"*

People had forgotten what the question was.

"Who cares what the original particle is," he smiled sardonically at his own thoughts, "if you don't know what to do with such knowledge?"

"We want to understand the nature of life," Dr. McBride had said. "We must never forget why we are physicists. All we learn must have a purpose. Otherwise... we are just dilettantes indulging in snobbish pursuits."

Einstein put it more bluntly. "I want to know the thoughts of God," he'd said, "the rest are details."

Alec wondered if intellectual snobbism wasn't the worst kind—the most harmful. For too many years, too many scientists have concerned themselves with details. They've been hoping to discover particles so small they would have only two dimensions. They called this pursuit 'the super-string theory'. They thought they would discover minute squiggly pieces of energy that held nothing but information. The information would be held in the specificity of different vibrations—or something to that effect.

"They cut the pieces into ever-smaller pieces until there simply was no knife sharp enough to cut any further," he told Suzy.

Until the SSC. Until they could smash matter into such small particles that they could neither see them, nor measure them, nor do anything with them. Why?

No one quite knew. Some people just like smashing things.

Alec had other ideas.

In the meantime, Sacha kept growing.

Suzy, forgetting her artistic aspirations, concerned herself with Sacha's welfare to the exclusion of almost everything else.

"The first three months are the most important," she would say, time and again. "They can leave an indelible mark on the rest of his life, you know."

Alec knew. He'd read the very same books she'd read. He took part in Sacha's early days as much as he could. He'd also bought a compact disk player to assure that Sacha would experience the harmony of Mozart's genius for many hours at a time. Right from the beginning.

Suzy went much further.

She'd learned that the owners of their building were thinking of converting the apartments into condominiums. Even before they officially announced their intentions, she made an offer to buy not only their own place (it wouldn't do to move Sacha so early), but also the one bedroom apartment next door. The offer she'd made was absurdly low, but the owners needed money right now, to cover the initial legal and permit expenses. It was a provisory down payment to be credited against the rent, if the deal didn't go through. Suzy was showing first signs of financial astuteness.

She sketched her own plans as to how they would interconnect the two apartments into a single, beautiful home. The 'new' living room would become Alec's study and a spare guestroom, if necessary. Since Sacha's birth, Alec worked a lot more at home, and needed more space. In addition, the extra bedroom in the adjoining apartment was large enough to accommodate a settee, which could open into a double bed, should her parents want to visit. The rest of the time it would serve as her studio. The extra bathroom would be very useful whenever they had guests, and the open counter of the extra kitchen would make for a wonderful bar 'for the Professor', while the rest of it Suzy proposed converting into a 'wine-cellar' with some extra storage space for her paints and brushes. Not the happiest of mixes, but Alec was too busy to point it out. To crown her proposal, Suzy negotiated extra storage space in the basement and garage space for two cars. If the condo conversion went through, they could be happy there for the foreseeable future.

"You are not going to run out on us to some other university or something, are you darling?" Suzy asked. Alec certainly had no intention of doing so.

In fact, Alec approved her plans all the way. He was grateful that she was not only taking care of Sacha's welfare but also his own. The additional income he was earning as a guest lecturer on a worldwide circuit made the proposal well within their means.

The only problem that remained was that both Suzy and Alec were growing more and more tired.

Sacha put considerable strain on Suzy—as babies usually do. Alec, while enjoying his extracurricular visits to far away places, was burning the candle at both ends. Even as he was growing in demand on the lecture circuit, more students attended his regular program. He needed more time for research, mostly to keep up with the work of other physicists, which meant reading voluminous publications. His theory had been picked up by a number of brilliant postgraduates, who began to expand on its implication in a number of diverse and imaginative fields. Alec could hardly keep up with the avalanche he'd created.

But what really unnerved him were the thoughts that crowded his mind as the direct result of his communion with Sacha. He knew that he must go back to the original experiences he'd had as a boy. Not the daydreams of buccaneers and polar explorers, but to the essence of, what he'd called at the time, the Home Planet and the Far Country. A dozen years ago he understood those visions, or concepts, as much as a fourteen-year-old could. This was no longer enough. He had to dissect the experiences in a more scientific way. He had to find a way to accept the past events not just emotionally but to integrate them into his psyche—intellectually. They had to make 'scientific' sense. He'd dismissed, as best he could, the concept of a personalized Sandra. He could not dismiss his own, personal memories.

First he tackled the Home Planet.

He recalled, in incredible detail, his first few visits to the imaginary world, wherein he had been apparently capable of experiencing, or even creating, whatever he put his mind to. There was a question, though, that could completely change the equation. Had it been he who had decided what to see and learn, or was it the dead-and-buried Sandra who had directed his development? And if it had been Sandra, then, for the thousandth time, he was back to square one. Is there, or had there ever been, a dichotomy within his psyche that would forever haunt him, invade his peace of mind, interfere with his scientific mindset?

Who was Sandra?

If the psychologists were right, then we all incorporate more than one aspect of our perception within the entity we call man. The id, the ego and the superego, correspond fairly closely to the emotional, mental and perhaps the spiritual aspect of our individuality. The 'spiritual' aspect, of course, had no equivalent in science, but the concept of superego has been accepted in psychiatry. If Sandra corresponded to his superego then he could at least study this concept. Freud had introduced the *superego* of which the key component was the *ego-ideal.* Whatever that meant was another story, but at least old Sigmund, for better or for worse, had been an avid atheist. This precluded any spiritual connections, should such prove 'undesirable' in some circles of the 'scientific' community.

Alec tried hard to maintain an open mind.

What he found fascinating, though, was that Freud placed the key components of the self, namely the id, ego and the superego, squarely in the unconscious. What of consciousness? Probably it was the *result* of the three. Not the essence itself, so to speak. The old Austrian had also assigned to the superego a set of moral values, or self-critical attitudes. Is this what Sandra is? And if so why, at least in his experience, had she been 'externalized' within his youthful experiences?

In a later structural model proposed by the father of psychoanalysis, a more complex psyche emerged. It introduced a struggle among the three internal agencies: the ego, id, and the superego. Alec found no real evidence of any struggle between his experience of Sandra and his own emotions or intellectual needs— other than occasional longing for the awareness of Sandra's presence. A search for understanding was definitely a struggle, but that had nothing to do with the Freudian context. Anyway, the result of such a struggle as Freud proposed was neurosis, and Alec, rightly or wrongly, did not recognize himself as a neurotic.

On the other hand, does anyone?

After a prolonged search, Alec found a greater affinity with the Jungian tradition. Marie-Louise von Franz defined Self as *'an inner guiding factor that is different from the conscious personality and that can be grasped only through the investigation of one's own dreams.'* If his images of Sandra could be relegated to dreams then he was on the right track. Before he'd experienced the 'unification' with Sandra, she could have been definitely described as his *'inner guiding factor'*, and equally as certainly she'd been *'different from the conscious personality'* he'd then espoused. If Sandra could be defined in terms of psychology established by Dr. Carl G. Jung, then Alec could finally accept that she, Sandra, was not a figment of his imagination but an expression of his inner Self.

Finally!

Finally Sandra became a concept acceptable in more precise scientific terms.

A valid, scientific, respectable concept.

So what?

So nothing. But Alec, having been trained as a scientist, needed such an affirmation so as not to become... neurotic. And a nominee for the Nobel Prize should not allow himself to become one. It might be frowned upon. Even in the fairly lax circles of Caltech. Finally, Alec felt that he was on safer ground—even if his ground did rise to the infinity of the Far Country. Infinity was something he could deal with. He'd used the concept in his own Theory of Information.

He took a deep breath.

Back to the Home Planet.

The concept of Home Planet, even by Sandra's definition, was a construct of his own, needed to externalize his 'inner guiding factor' which Freud called the superego, and as some of the modern movements referred to as the 'Higher Self'. In his childhood, he'd managed to externalize this part of his self in order to derive the greatest benefit from the Freudian 'set of moral values or self-critical attitudes', or the Jungian 'inner guiding factor'.

Things were beginning to fall into place.

Sandra fit into both categories. She had been definitely his guiding light, and the arbiter of his moral values. He'd trusted her implicitly. She couldn't lie, he remembered. And... and she was always with him. This last should have been a dead give away. Only an integral part of himself can *always* be with him. And Sandra always insisted that, in a manner he couldn't understand at the time, they'd always be together.

"Like two peas in a pod," he recalled her exact words. Words she'd repeated, then, many times.

So the purpose of the Home Planet was to impart on his young psyche certain values which could not have been understood, certainly not at that time, without such drastic, if for the most part pleasant, experiences. He'd learned responsibility for his actions. He'd learned to reject all limitations, to rely on his own self. He'd even learned to recognize that everyone travels his or her own, individual path. A path that was neither better nor worse than any other—just different. And all this he'd learned as a boy of fourteen in such a profound way that, if called upon, he could recite Sandra's words even now. What a marvelous, complex structure man is... he mused. Even a boy has the potential to understand the most profound tenets of ethics. The respect for others, the love of one's neighbour...

And suddenly he realized that these were not some ancient, perhaps outmoded, religious dogmas, but that this information had been stored in aspects of his inner self from before he was born. Before his private universe began. The information was always there. All he had to do was to find access to it.

$I=MC^{\infty}$

An infinite index, took the equation beyond time. Beyond physical reality.

No wonder it made so much sense. Only at the very beginning he had no idea why! The equation was easier to understand in terms of the Far Country, the image generated by his mind, than in terms of the Home Planet, which dealt with quite different concepts. The Far Country seemed to have an affinity with the equation itself. The Home Planet explored the flexibility of time; the Far County virtually denied it. Or, to turn tables on all three factors, the Far Country suggested the absence of time and space, and suggested that he, himself was the light...

"Time is a very funny thing," he remembered saying.

"It helps to arrange experiences into a sequence. It stops them from happening all at once," she'd replied.

Sandra sounded as though she knew every answer. Every answer to every question. To everything. Even the thoughts of God? Einstein would have been jealous indeed. She'd acted, and had spoken, as though information was always there for the taking.

Always.

And then...

Some indefinable period later... he saw the mini-universe taking the shape of his earthly contours. Galaxies joined by sparsely populated segments of space, individual stars hanging in the middle of nowhere, clouds and nebulas churning, gathering angular momentum, preparing for the stars yet to be.

"I am the universe," he heard his own emotive thoughts.

The trillions upon trillions of atoms of his mental body began to dissolve, once more, into impenetrable darkness. They'd only been sustained by his mental effort—yet only for a little while.

'I am the universe,' he echoed his own memories. And immediately he recalled his image of Sacha: 'Sacha was not claiming membership to the universe, *he was the universe. Total, complete, with nothing missing, nothing encroaching on its wholeness.*'

My son, a universe unto himself. All the Information that ever existed or ever will exist was there. It was embodied in his son.

Gradually, in slow, painstaking stages, Alec relaxed.

The meaning of his youthful exploits was finally coming home. Even Sandra made 'scientific' sense. It was inevitable that she and I become one... he mused. We always have been. Inseparable. Like two peas in a pod...

"We merely restored the balance," he smiled at his own thoughts.

And there was no contradiction between his inner and outer, or his imaginary and physical worlds. The realities were not many. What differed was our ability to recognize the

Truth. In one way, there were as many realities as there were intelligent, self-aware beings throughout the universes. In another, there was but One Reality.

Yet, if he could forget the deductive process, if he could return to his younger days, even for a moment, he'd do so at once. He had never admitted to himself, let alone anyone else, how he missed not being able to talk to Sandra. Sandra had been his best friend, his mother, the elder sister he'd never had, his confidante, his tutor, his absolute authority, the rock upon which he could lean in moments of weakness. Also, in a way he could not fully comprehend, she was the source of a strange, enigmatic power. He would give half his life to have Sandra by his side.

But... aren't I and Sandra one? Are not all my thoughts accessible to her?

Conversely, are not her thoughts available to me? Perhaps I must just re-learn to listen.

To myself?

Apparently.

Isn't that just a trifle neurotic? Sounds stupid listening to oneself. I've never found myself a very interesting fellow. Perhaps that was why, as a youth, I tried so hard to escape from myself.

And now?

Now I'm stuck in my body.

How dull.

And then Sacha spoke clearly in his head.

You are not stuck, daddy. You're as free as you decide to be!

He looked down at his son reposing, carefree, in his crib. No questions roiled, as yet, the bliss of his being. No problems to solve, no enigmas to churn in his mind during the late hours of the night; no tossing and turning. His tiny face showed nothing but utter bliss.

Is that the answer? Just... total bliss?

Yet Alec rebelled against a life with no challenges. Time enough for being after a life of becoming. Time enough for rest after I solve what I am destined to solve. After I find out who I really am.

But he didn't. Not yet.

At some level of perception he could not accept that there was an agency, Sandra, or any other concept, which, or who, would interfere with his own personal freedom. Even as his scientific mind was beginning to accept her, his ego rebelled. His ego needed to be supreme. To be the only God he answered to. A God he and he alone could control.

Next morning he couldn't get out of bed. By noon an ambulance took him to the hospital. After three days he left the neurological department in a wheelchair. He had no control over his lower body. And the stiffness was moving up. Daily. He dreaded the thought that it might reach his brain. The neurosurgeons appeared helpless. After a dozen ECG, EEGs, MRIs, CTs and other fangle-dangle scans, he was declared healthy.

Only he couldn't move.

***

11
Christmas in California

Neither of them would ever admit it to each other, but both Alec and Suzy had spent the first few months in California expecting an earthquake to happen at any moment. Alec had gone through this period well before Suzy, but her time followed. Apparently most new arrivals go through it. Alec admitted later that before he'd rented the new apartment, he'd had an engineer from Caltech check out the structural plans for safety. Apparently all the new buildings in the Los Angeles area have been over-designed with earthquakes in mind. Alec trusted his colleague and thought no more about it until Suzy brought it up.

"I should have asked you before... before we brought Sacha home..." she began haltingly.

"Well, darling, why don't you ask me now?" This wasn't like Suzy. She was usually a very direct person.

"Well, now that Alicia and my parents are coming..."

"You've already asked them?"

"You did say I could!"

"Darling, you don't need my permission to do anything, but this is not what you want to ask me, is it?"

"No!" When Suzy was angry it took her a few seconds to settle down. As with a smouldering volcano, Alec knew better than to get too close.

"It just crossed my mind that if both, Alicia and my parents, and you and Sacha and I and the Professor were to be here for Christmas, and there was a really big earthquake..."

It had to happen. A wonder it took so long.

"Darling. If we die, we die. But seriously. Before I handed over my first rent cheque, I had the structural drawings looked over by a friend of mine."

"I knew you did! I mean would have..." she sounded flustered. "You know something, I really love you." But she was still simmering.

"I was beginning to wonder..." And he only just avoided one of Sacha's tiny slippers aimed at his head. That was when Alec was still able to dodge missiles coming his way.

Since Alec moved into the wheelchair, the concept of dying had taken on a new meaning. There was talk of Lou Gehrig's disease, but the prognosis was not supported by all the symptoms. The physicians refused to commit themselves to any one diagnosis, though they were considering every imaginable neurological disorder in the medical books. So far they'd drawn a blank. Alec refused to subject himself to a psychiatric examination. His mind was doing pretty well, he claimed. "Come to one of my lectures," he'd said many a time. He also refused to reduce his schedule.

"Darling," he told Suzy, "it's all that keeps me going."

She didn't say anything. In fact, Alec refused to discuss his creeping paralysis with anyone. "It will go away," he told Suzy when she begged him to take it easy.

But the day he returned from the hospital, a male nurse accompanied him. A big man who would have made more money as a professional wrestler than a nurse. But Matthew needed to help people. That was his professional motivation. It had something to do with his parents having survived the holocaust by being helped by others. Without Matt, Alec wouldn't have been able to get out of bed. The big man also catered to all of Alec's sanitary needs.

Other than that, life went on as usual.

In some ways, Suzy's temper tantrums, as well as the sudden concern for her own safety, were amusing. It hadn't always been so. Not quite. Alec had sailed with her so many times he'd lost count. She had never been afraid of anything. He recalled when on one occasion a combination of her temper and *bravura* had cost them a mast. They'd been sailing on their beloved Lake Champlain in rather tempestuous weather. Normally, it's safer to be out on the open sea in such conditions than in restricted waters, such as a lake, where a good gust could put you on the rocks in just about any direction. But it's OK if you use sound judgment and have a modicum of experience.

This had not been a dark and stormy night. It had been a magnificent day, but a high was approaching from the south at a good twenty to twenty-five knots. While in the lee of any island, which by the way pepper the whole lake, they hadn't felt the need to reef the sails. Nevertheless, Alec always felt responsible not so much for himself but for anyone on board and even for the sailing vessel itself. When he'd heard on the radio what was coming, he told Suzy to steer into the wind so that he could reef the main a band if not two. Suzy obeyed. But just as he'd gotten to the mast to ease the main sheet, Suzy had pulled hard to port, and before Alec could get back to the cockpit, they cleared the lee of the small isle. The wind hit them with such force that the shrouds on the starboard gave way. Suzy immediately tried to get back behind the island, but it was too late. The mast above the spreaders snapped like a matchstick. Once they were safe again, Alec asked Suzy what on earth had made her take such a peculiar action. Still fuming, though by now most certainly at herself, she'd snapped:

"You should've said 'please'!"

And that was that.

All this happened years ago, when Suzy was no more than seventeen or eighteen. Since then, she'd brought her temper well under control. An odd plate or two, maybe a slipper aimed at him, often with quite amazing precision, would be as far as she would go. But truly, today Alec would trust Suzy with Sacha's and his own life in the middle of the Pacific. Temper was one thing, irresponsibility quite another. But some remnants of her disposition survived time. They'd clung to her like the memory of her youth. Just enough to make life more interesting. Just enough to feel that she belonged half-straddled across the San Andreas Fault. Well... almost.

At any rate, at the time, Alec's answer regarding the earthquakes seemed to have satisfied her concern for her family, though it did nothing to ease her state of mind in other respects. Perhaps not so much her mind as her poor, exhausted body. Sacha took it upon himself to fill the jungle in which he resided with resounding... singing? His performances sounded like a cross between crying and singing. Something boisterous and very loud, she said. And Sacha did it only—*only*—at night. During the day he woke up at regular intervals, gulped down the prescribed nourishment, and reverted to the blissful existence from whence he came. During the initial six weeks, his lungs developed sufficient power to wake the dead, which is what Suzy felt like after the first few of his nocturnal concerts.

Suzy was getting very, very tired.

In addition, after the initial few weeks, Alec could no longer contribute his share of parenting.

The night after Alec had come back from his last lecture tour, he and Suzy had had a peculiar exchange. They'd argued. Alec was becoming really concerned for her health. And Suzy wasn't fully over her previous qualms regarding earthquakes. But really, a sort of cumulative starvation of not having enough time to talk had precipitated their squabble. Really talk, like they used to back home, in Montreal.

Yes, Suzy still referred to Montreal as home. Alec suspected that when he was out of the country, she was lonely. She must have missed her friends. Even her new 'painting' friends had to wait until Sacha gave her more time. At the time Suzy was still half-dead from having missed a good night's sleep for at least a week. Alec had suggested that they take on a baby-sitter for a few nights. They might have asked Matt, he slept in the adjoining apartment, but taking care of a baby wasn't his job. He was a nurse, not a nanny. But Suzy would have none of it.

"You think you are immortal?"

"Aren't you? I thought you knew that we all are," she snapped back.

"Who told you that?" He was too surprised to say anything more biting.

"You did!"

"I never told you anything of the sort."

"You told me yesterday..." and even as she was saying it, she looked up at him in a peculiar way.

"But yesterday I was out of town," he replied, meeting her eyes.

"I know," she said slowly, and then remained silent.

After a while of tense silence, Suzy murmured under her breath. "Something boisterous and very loud."

"What dear?"

"Sacha's midnight concerts. Something boisterous and very loud. His performances usually last from midnight till about three in the morning. Sometimes till four. Then he goes to sleep as if nothing's happened."

"Yes, you told me that. So?"

"Alec, have you been peek-a-booing again?"

"How do I know? You're the only one who's ever noticed it. Or so you said."

"And I'm not around when you're travelling, am I?"

Alec froze. "You're trying to tell me that, in some form or another, I disturb Sacha's sleep when I'm not here?"

"Disturb? Hardly the right word. You're playing with him in the noisiest way imaginable! He made exactly the same sounds when you were playing with him this afternoon." She looked him straight in the eye. "*Something boisterous and very loud,* remember? That's what I told you Sacha was doing when he first raised the racket in the middle of the night.

"And he stopped when I got back... at night, that is," Alec mused, not altogether displeased.

"And restarted when you were busy all day," she accused.

"Suzy, it must be a coincidence..." Now he pleaded.

But neither of them believed in coincidences. Not any more.

There were minutes, sometimes hours, when Alec felt life in his lower limbs. He would feel a prickle and a tingle, like blood returning to legs that had fallen asleep. The next moment, as he was ready to get up, he would fall over the side of the wheelchair. On one occasion Matt had saved him from falling down the stairs. Stupidly, he'd decided he could make it.

At times, he was ready to give up. Not just physically but mentally as well. He wouldn't tell Suzy but his reputation at Caltech had probably suffered permanent damage. Somehow, the diagnosis that he was physically OK had leaked out. The sophomores began referring to him as Dr. Alexandra, the Histeron Prosteron. A sort of reversal of logic, and erroneously implying hysterical connotations.

He could cope with that. He, too, had been cruel to his lecturers in his sophomore days. What was harder to take was his relationship with Sacha. Whatever 'inner' abilities he'd once had were gone. What was the point of being able to play with Sacha 'at a distance', when he had absolutely no recollection of it? At least his paralysis seemed to affect only the lower part of his body. It didn't affect his lungs or his heart. It was as though he was not allowed to walk. To move forward. As if he was forced to keep still.

Behind the stillness anger stirred, churned, and grew even as a volcano churns and boils before an eruption. He drew on his reserves of will power to contain the storm brewing inside him. For his own sake as well as his family.

He and Matthew, now his constant shadow, had spent over two weeks touring Europe and then have been contracted for one more week; this time for a tour of South America. Alec had categorically refused to cancel any of his engagements.

"If Hawking can do it, so can I," he insisted. Stephen W. Hawking, a theoretical physicist and one of Alec's heroes, had been stricken with ALS, a motor neuron disease, many years ago, yet continued to function more successfully than most of his academic colleagues.

Alec had also dreamt of going on such trips with Suzy, but it was not to be. Not yet. He returned exhausted, to find Suzy even more so. Sacha demanded a lot more attention than Alec ever imagined. He began to appreciate all women who performed maternal duties in their stride.

And then they found an answer.

They'd invited Alicia to join them for the week before Christmas. At this time of the year Caltech was on slow revs, and Alec could spend much more time at home. Not that he could do much. Most of the time, Matt proved more useful than Alec. Matt was simply a very nice man. Willing to be of help to anyone, at any time. They'd agreed that with Alec's— or really Matt's—help, Alicia could look after Sacha, while Suzy would fly to Kingston, to spend a few days with her parents. She would then return with them to spend Christmas, all together, in California. Luckily, the apartment next door was still free.

Alicia agreed at once and actually offered to come much sooner, to give Suzy a longer rest.

"Don't even think about it, mother, not till you meet the heir to the throne. Believe me, one week will be quite enough!" Alec warned.

Neither Alec nor Suzy mentioned Alec's condition. His mother would find out soon enough, when she got to LA.

When Alicia did finally see Alec, he slapped his thigh and sighed, "The old war injury, m'dear. Playing up again, you know!" He said it with such a perfect imitation of his father's British accent that his mother burst out laughing before she had a chance to worry. The details came later.

Even with Alec and Matt and Alicia in the house, Suzy, just before leaving for the airport, began to waver.

"Are you sure this is a good idea?" She was looking down at Sacha nestling happily in Alicia's arms.

"Yes, dear," Alec assured her. "It's a very good idea."

"But Sacha is not used to being without me, do you really think it's wise..."

"Yes, dear, it is wise."

"But...?"

"Go!"

"Are you quite sure?"

"Go! Go, darling," he repeated more gently. "We'll all be here when you get back. Promise," he added, when she'd again opened her mouth.

And so she went. She took a taxi. Matt offered to take her, but Alec refused to abuse his generosity. After all, he was paid to be his nurse. Period. Not a general factotum. The man was incorrigibly helpful.

"You did that rather well," his mother commented. "Your father had exactly the same problem with me, when you were Sacha's age. Funny how history repeats itself."

There have been minutes, sometimes hours, when Alec felt life in his lower limbs. He would feel a prickle and a tingle, like blood returning to legs that had fallen asleep. The next moment, as he was ready to get up, he would fall over the side of the wheelchair. On one occasion Matt saved him from falling down the stairs. Stupidly, he'd decided he could make it.

At times, he was ready to give up. Not just physically but mentally as well. He wouldn't tell Suzy but his reputation at Caltech had probably suffered permanent damage. Somehow the diagnosis that he was physically OK had leaked out. The sophomores began referring to him as Dr. Alexandra, the Histeron Prosteron. A sort of reversal of logic, and erroneously implying hysterical connotations. Not kind.

But he could cope with that. He too had been cruel to his lecturers in his sophomore days. What was harder to take was his relationship with Sacha. Whatever 'inner' abilities he'd once had were gone. What was the point of being able to play with Sacha 'at a distance', when he had absolutely no recollection of it? At least his paralysis seemed to affect only the lower part of his body. It didn't affect his lungs or his heart. It was as though he was not allowed to walk. To move forward. As if he was forced to keep still.

Behind the stillness anger stirred, churned, and grew even as a volcano churns and boils before an eruption. He drew on his reserves of will power to contain the storm brewing inside him. For his own sake as well as his family.

Suzy returned from Canada a new woman. Had she been a soprano, she would've made Verdi proud with a joyful *"Ritorno vincita!"* Luckily, Suzy couldn't, or at the very least wouldn't, sing a note. A single week in Kingston had achieved a number of positive results. It cured her longing for Canada. How? On her arrival it took her three-and-a-half hours to get home from the airport in Ottawa. The snowplows just couldn't cope with the exuberant white stuff.

"It hasn't snowed at all this winter," her father had said, on taking her in his arms. "It all came down just for you!"

She could have done without it. The snow, not the hug.

The next day it snowed again. In spite of it all, she went for a walk, but after an hour decided that California wasn't such a bad place to spend winters in. Skiing was all right, as was skating, but not the slush. She'd spent the next few days being pampered by Joan and John, to within an inch of her life. She wasn't allowed to do anything. No cooking, no washing up, no clearing the table.

"That's not what you are here for," her mother assured her. Joan was radiant at having her daughter back, even for just a few days. "When I was having your brothers, I dreamt of such a week. Even a few days. Now that you have them, I can enjoy them almost as much, vicariously."

"Wasn't I any trouble at all?" she asked, almost hurt.

"You were never any trouble," Joan said. "At least, not while you were little..."

Suzy preferred not to ask what trouble she'd caused in her later years.

"But it all ended just right, didn't it darling?"

"Better than you can imagine," Suzy agreed. Suzy was certain that mother was referring to Alec who'd made an honest woman of her. And she smiled at her thoughts. And then, thinking of Sacha, she added: "did he ever..."

They'd arrived in LA on the 23rd of December, a little after four in the afternoon. The day was sunny, bright, and even the smog decided not to interfere with the family reunion. This time Matt drove the car, with Alicia holding on to Sacha. She didn't believe in the new intricate car seats required by law. This was the first time Sacha experienced the expressways of California. They say that if you survive the expressways in LA, you'll survive anything.

Upon Suzy's return, Desmond McBride joined them most days. He would come for a meal, a drink, or just for a chat. Alec suspected that he 'had the sweets', as his dad would have said, for his mother. It felt funny, thinking about dad in this context. At any rate, the Professor 'chatted up' his mother, offering to show her the hot-spots of LA, praising her only son, claiming that he had already practically adopted him, and that thus they already had a great deal in common. Yet all this apparent wooing was done with a great deal of humour tempered by his considerable innate reserve. Desmond was also painfully aware of the difference in their ages. Alicia was a good twenty years his junior.

"But one can dream, can't one?" his eyes seemed to be saying.

Alec decided to help his old friend.

"If it wasn't for Dr. McBride, Mother, I'd still be an unemployed Phee'd in Montreal," he said loud enough for all to hear.

"An unemployed what...?"

"That's what Suzy calls Ph.D.," he explained.

With his sparkling sense of humour in evidence, Desmond became even more a man of charm. Also, he was so different from Alicia's late husband that it could never be a question that the Professor might fill the void left by Alec's father. It was a completely different attraction. It was as though the Professor had performed a balancing act, completing an aspect in her that she was never aware of. He was his own man, knowing precisely what he wanted from life, living his life to the fullest; living it in the present. He didn't really make plans, at least not for himself. He helped others make theirs, especially 'the young 'uns', but his own self-appointed function was to live and let live, and to hell with tomorrow. In this respect, he was probably younger than any one of them.

As for Alec, the Professor had not mentioned his condition even once. He treated Alec as though nothing had changed. When he first saw Alec in a wheelchair, he'd looked up from the papers on his desk and remarked: "Been skiing again, lad?" And that was that. He knew the truth of course. But he chose to keep quiet. At least until asked.

And then, came Christmas.

With Sacha as the centerpiece, particularly when he was awake, the atmosphere couldn't have been more different than the last holidays they'd shared in Montreal. Although Sacha spent the majority of his time in the 'jungle', each one of them would, in turn, call for absolute hush, open the door to Sacha's verdant domain, and tiptoe in to steal a peek at the sleeping boy. Sacha didn't seem to mind all this adulation. He slept and ate, and smiled, and once or twice even burst into his famous *concerto grosso* without any instrumental accompaniment, or, for that matter, without sharing the limelight with any other soloists. The joy emanating from his throat had quite a different effect when limited to five or even ten minutes, than when conducted at length, in the middle of the night. But those nights, gratefully, were over.

Suzy, now fully recovered, slept like a log. She woke up each day looking bright, happy and relaxed. She even seemed to be getting used to seeing Alec in a wheelchair. And if not, she was doing a darn good job at pretending.

And it was mostly thanks to her, that in spite of Alec's conditions, it was by far the best Christmas they recalled ever having. And they didn't even miss the snow, though a few flakes wouldn't have done any harm. The Christmas tree dominated the livingroom, the candles on it were real, with real wicks smelling awfully when extinguished. But this was part of Christmas—even as were children. And a single child among them made children of them all. They laughed without any apparent reason, all their memories seemed to be pleasant ones; they had no cares that would interfere with the joyful holiday.

It was two days after Boxing Day. Suzy took Alec to one side. She looked baffled.

"What is it, Sue?" There was also a look of concern on her face.

"I don't quite know how to put it," she started, and then seemed to change her mind. "Oh, it's nothing, I'm sure."

Alec was ready to drop it, but she held him back.

"No, it wasn't. Only it doesn't make sense."

"Just tell me what it is?" Soon the Normans and Alicia would be around and their privacy would be lost.

She looked him straight in the eye. "I talked with Sacha," she said, her eyes daring him to contradict her.

"Darling, I talk to him all the time," he smiled his understanding. This wasn't like Suzy. She didn't normally make mountains out of molehills.

"I didn't say *to* him," she stressed. "I said *with* him."

Alec got it. He remembered the universe hidden in Sacha's eyes when he'd first been alone with him. This experience was never repeated. It had been a once in a lifetime event. Even then he had thought himself lucky.

"You talked *with* him," he repeated slowly. What was there to say? Then he added: "Do you remember what... what he said?"

"Yes. He told me to be away from LA next week."

During breakfast Desmond made a proposal none of them could refuse.

"I have this wee cottage by the sea," he said, almost as if he was musing to himself. "She's standing therre all by herrself, furrlon and lonely."

No one said anything, wondering where the Professor was heading.

"Last week I drrove there, and told Marria to fix up the place, in case anyone wanted to inhale some salty airr. Therre arre thrree bedrrooms, and if Alec and Suzy agrree to take Sacha into theirrs, we could all fit in ratherr nicely," he continued to muse aloud. He didn't mention Matt.

"Why, Professor," Alicia looked at Desmond, her eyebrows arching. "Are you suggesting what I think you're suggesting?"

"It neverr crrossed my mind, Mrs. Baldwin. I'd sleep in the salon, of courrse!"

The Professor looked really shocked. But the twinkle in his eye said something else altogether. There was a slight problem with this logic. Dr. McBride's plan would put Matt squarely in bed with Alicia. Assuming Matt was invited.

By Saturday they were all packed into two cars, and heading south. Alicia and the Normans rode with the Professor in his British-racing-green Jaguar, with Alec, Suzy and Sacha following in their bright-red Saturn, with Matt at the wheel. Alec was beginning to wonder how they'd managed at all without Matt even before his 'skiing accident'. Matt had quickly become an integral member of the family— or, at the very least, a sort of butler factotum, only more so. The 605 took them to expressway 5, which in turn led them all the way to Solana Beach, some 20 miles north of San Diego. In a little over two hours they were all reclining on a broad terrace overlooking the Pacific Ocean. Maria was serving Sangria, her specialty for as long as the Professor could remember.

"You've never mentioned you had such a delightful place, Des." Alec's voice was semi-accusatory.

"Neverr had any need to beforre, lad," and the old man who, during the last few days contrived to look about twenty years younger, stole a glance at Alicia. "Neverr had any need to, beforre," he repeated, as if weighing his words.

Alec smiled, and got busy trying to determine what options were available to him. The house was on a single level, with only storage spaces down below. On the way to Solana Beach, he'd noticed a bicycle path, and occasional snippets of a well beaten-down footpath along the upper edge of the shore; and, of course, the highway. That would offer ample opportunities for suicide seekers. He doubted anyone would slow down for a wheelchair; Californian drivers seemed always in a hurry. The one thing he could not negotiate, not even with Matt's assistance, was the horrendous flight of stairs leading down to the beach.

On the ocean side, there was an extensive covered terrace overlooking the beach. This'll be my domain, he thought. And even as he looked at the sand down below, he expected his paralysis to release him from its grip at any moment. He formed a fist, and then tried to curl his toes inside his shoes. The next moment he slammed his fist on the armrest. Luckily no one seemed to notice. Except Matt. He laid his hand on Alec's shoulder. That was all, but this simple act had an immediate calming effect. Alec's breathing returned to normal.

Even now, after all the non-conclusive medical examinations, after visiting a dozen specialists of all sorts, Alec refused to accept that his present condition was permanent. And anyway, soon there were bigger problems he had to face. The following Monday the TV screen was filled with reports of the worst riots in the history of Los Angeles.

***

12

The Game's afoot,
Mrs. Holmes

When **Alec first heard** about the riots, he didn't put two and two together. Not immediately. Suzy had. Instantly. She'd looked at Alec and not finding confirmation in his eyes, left the room. She half-expected Sacha to look up and say 'I told you so'. But Sacha didn't say anything. He was much too busy sleeping the sleep of one aware of a job well done. Or maybe all babies looked like that when they sleep?

"Thank you, my pet," she whispered. And just as quietly as she came in, she returned to join the others. By this time Alec was fidgeting, searching her with his eyes. "Did you see him?" he seemed to be saying, nodding in the direction of Sacha's bedroom. She nodded and then smiled. With a smirk she went outside. Alec left the rest of the gathering glued to the TV and joined her on the terrace.

"Well?" he asked, not quite knowing what he expected to hear.

"He said: 'I told you so', and then he went back to sleep."

"He what???"

And before he could recover, she began laughing. She doubled up and roared with tears flooding her eyes.

"Well... ha, ha... what did you expect him to say?"

"Very funny," Alec admitted, but it took awhile before he laughed himself. Usually he managed to get the better of Suzy.

When they'd both quieted down, they sat, side by side, looking out onto the ocean. Very little was said, but their thoughts seemed to meet on some distant cloud over the horizon. In direct contrast to Los Angeles, the ocean, true to its name, was at peace, the blue sky clear except for some local thermal cumuli forming probably over San Clemente Island. It felt like a quiet before the storm. For Alec, though, the storm pointed to his inner world, not to the endangered serenity around them. Nor to the human storm they'd escaped thanks to Desmond. Or, had Sacha dipped his fingers into the currents of time?

"You know, Sue, things have a habit of changing, steering you in directions you don't necessarily want to go."

He talked softly, as though thinking aloud. Suzy was perched on the swing-chair, swaying to and fro. After the horror pictures of the LA riots, the atmosphere of peace was palpable.

"What got me into physics, and kept me going, I suppose, was a powerful, if subliminal, desire to escape from my childhood..." he was looking for the right word.

"Your childhood reality. It was just too rich, for an adult. Too willing to accept the unacceptable...?" she offered.

"I was too influenced, or might have been, but for some atavistic archetypes, perhaps implanted genetically, which I thought of as old wives' tales; as unproven, imaginary, or just quasi-religious nonsense... Or, at best, psychiatric mumbo-jumbo. I have been attempting to explain reality in terms of theories, patterns, mathematical equations. And now, it seems, more and more, that an individual is the only reality. I think Jung said so. He also implied that the further we stray from the individual, the more likely we are to fall into error. Or something like that."

After a moment's reflection he added: "Do you think I'm wrong, Sue?" He was looking down at his flaccid legs.

Suzy smiled. She was half listening to him thinking aloud, half lost in the shimmering horizon, which seemed to be drawing her outwards with a persistent force. Alec hardly noticed the alluring beauty. He didn't find it easy to admit that the road he had travelled these last six or seven years may have taken him on a tangent from his real destination. He tried to relax and hear the whispers of his unconscious.

He shook his head.

Slowly, deliberately, as if searching for confirmation of his own thoughts, he continued, "And now, that from which I tried so hard to escape seems to be, or to be becoming, the motivating force. Is it because I am a scientist that I cannot opt for ignorance, that I cannot ignore the facts which, no matter how improbable, no matter how 'scientifically' inconvenient, are staring me in the face?"

A large ketch moved slowly across his field of vision. It looked suspended, half way towards the unknown. Alec felt that aboard that vessel time had stopped, or, at the very least, carried a completely different meaning. He saw himself at the wheel, his feet astride for balance, his eyes scanning the rigging. For an instant he thought he saw the mainsail billowing under the steady breeze.

"We could have been there," he muttered to himself.

And then, again, he shook the cobwebs out of his head. Not yet, something inside him was saying. Not quite yet. "Sandra..." he all but cried aloud.

"What, darling?" Suzy was looking into his eyes. "You are not going to peek-a-boo on me again, are you?"

"No, Sue. I don't seem to have time anymore."

Now, what made me say that? I must get hold of myself. I must. There is so much to do... And again, he wondered: do what precisely?

"Time for what...?" she asked.

"After all the soul searching, the repeated attempts to dismiss the evidence before me as imaginary or superstitious, or whatever... Once again, I must follow Mr. Sherlock Holmes's admonition: If all probable explanations fail, then we must accept that which seems impossible. Or something like that." He reached out for Suzy's hand. "The game's afoot, Mrs. Holmes. The game's afoot." And with that he drew her onto his insensate lap and kissed her long and passionately.

"Why, Mr. Holmes, I never..."

"Oh, yes, you did. And you did very well, I might add."

And before they ventured into truly dangerous territory, she pushed his wheelchair back to rejoin the rest of Desmond's guests. The Normans and Alicia were still gathered around the TV set, where the newscaster was busy telling everyone whose fault it was that the riots had occurred. The Professor was missing.

"Earlier this year, in my broadcast on March the 23rd..."

Much earlier, Alec thought. What had I been doing on March 23rd? Probably getting more and more nervous about becoming a father. It's a wonder that people have children. They are nothing but worry, they scream and demand as though only their needs and desires were of paramount consequence. They are tiny worlds of absolute egocentricity. And, to top it all, the world is vastly overpopulated. And yet...

And yet he wouldn't give up Sacha for all the tea in China...

"...and whatever else you do, do not leave the security of your home. Bar the windows, if you have bars, close the shutters. I'll keep you informed. Trust me."

The undying trust was interrupted by a cacophony of a dozen police cars racing from three different directions towards a single car stalled on some undefined ramp, leading to or from an expressway. The sirens were wailing, the tires emitting bluish smoke. On the nondescript ramp, a man was standing in front of his stalled car, his hands high above his head. The police cruisers came to a screeching halt some twenty yards from the unarmed man. The fugitive was black, of course. Assuming he was a fugitive. At least twenty officers of the LAPD, guns drawn, approached the man in semi-crouched positions. Had the man been white, probably only ten of the LAPD finest would have drawn their firearms. The whole picture made Alec vaguely sick. He shrugged and wheeled himself back to the terrace.

Sitting at the other end, lost in something he was reading, was Desmond. Alec approached him slowly, as not to disturb his old friend. Strange that, he'd known this Professor for such a short time, yet besides his immediate family, no man was closer to him than the 'r' rolling, Scot expatriate.

"Ahh, therre y'arre." Without looking up, the Professor waved Alec to wheel himself closer. "I've been reading your latest open dissertation."

An open dissertation was a lecture open to the general public. In such speeches, or lectures, Alec tried to avoid specialized scientific terms, equations, or other references, which only made sense to physicists deeply involved in that specialized field. The Professor was almost through. Alec peeked over his shoulder.

"...while photons can be regarded as either waves or quanta, in general the electromagnetic, gravitational, and now the information-field are not quantifiable in the same manner as matter is. Nevertheless, while the quanta of energy consist of particles of essentially identical characteristics, the underlying constituents of the Information Theory do not conform to this pattern. Although the wave characteristic remains, its components do not appear quantifiable."

"You sure about that?" The Professor ran his finger along the last sentence. Alec smiled and said nothing. He wasn't sure. He just found that the equation only worked when he made this assumption.

"...of matter which is subject to quantum theory. The Information Field is a field where all knowledge appears suspended, available to be drawn upon, explored, used, applied and when no longer required, ignored. When no longer required, it reverts to its original form, or lack of it, even as the gravitational field in essence does not exhibit any form though it does follow certain patterns. But there is no essential difference between the heretofore known fields and the field that I am proposing. The known fields are generated and/or are interchangeable with matter. Hence, $E=MC^2$. The same is true of the Information Field. The only difference is that it precedes both matter and energy. You might think of it as a matrix, which defines what characteristics matter and energy will assume, if and when it becomes manifest, or emerges, from the virtual reality. The Information flow seems to supply the impetus to organize matter from the available quanta.

And thus, to repeat, while other fields vary in intensity in relation to matter, the Information Field appears to be uniformly distributed throughout spacetime, as though a part of a virtual universe from which physical universes are born. It also appears, that the efficacy of the IF is somehow related to the recipient or the object drawing on the field, almost, as our covert organizations would say, on a need-to-know basis."

"Pretty good stuff that, lad. But what really got me, was what you wrote before about the Information Field preexisting the big bang. That should upset a goodly bunch of the old fusspots who think that their theories are the only theories."

Desmond had forgotten to roll his rr's. Alec was too old to blush, but the Professor's approval gave him a pleasant glow.

"But, after you get through all this theorizing, don't forget to get back to basics, lad. Don't ever forget that."

"Which are?" Alec asked. The old man was always full of surprises.

"Don't ever forget, lad, that the individual is the only reality."

Had Alec been standing, he would have needed to sit down. All things were coming to some kind of a climax. He was under assault by his Suzy, possibly Sandra, his son and now apparently the Professor. A little too much of a coincidence, he thought.

"Yes, Sir. I won't forget," was all he could utter.

Maria laid out the goodies for lunch. Out here, by the ocean, Desmond referred to many things as goodies. Including food. John Norman switched off the offending TV to get further away from the LA upheavals. The newscaster was right, at least to a point, that the riots had been predictable for some time.

"When the disparity between the rich and the poor becomes too great, you cannot continue forever as a two-class society. In LA, the balancing factor, the middle class, has all but disappeared."

The newscaster was uncharacteristically fuming, waving his arms. He might have been thinking of his own multi-million-dollar 'class'.

The middle class used to be made up of professionals, the group performing the necessary services for which they have been inadequately rewarded. Now, this group could no longer be defined as the middle class. They remained in the lower fifth of the income brackets.

These days, the truly offending members of society were the CEOs, presidents, chairmen and other VPs of multinational companies; the upper echelons of Banks and Investment Houses, who not only drew exorbitant salaries, but influenced boards of directors to award them multi-million dollar bonuses, even in fiscal years during which their companies sustained financial losses. In the past, such excesses remained *in camera*, hidden within the corridors of power, sequestered by their grossly overpaid lawyers and accountants. Now, their disgusting abuse of public funds, not public in terms of tax money—some loot they'd left to the politicians—but still public, because the companies they exploited were publicly owned.

And then there was that ever-growing class of professional 'sportsmen'. True, some of them did work hard to make their countless millions, but so does a neurosurgeon. Yet the salaries of professional baseballers, brawling hockey players, brutal football gladiators, golfers whose intelligence appeared sated by spending their whole lives, their total energies, in absolute commitment to rolling a little ball into a little hole, with a stick. Their get incomes, or even appearance fees, vastly exceeded those of cardiologists, oncologists, or even teachers responsible for the intellectual development of our children. Perhaps morons should get a greater share of the liquid wealth we call money. But during the last few decades the ratio has become vastly exaggerated.

Finally, one of the most offending groups were the seemingly innocuous youngsters, often no more than sixteen or seventeen years old, who were paid millions of dollars for a half-hour segment of third rate TV farce. They could neither act nor even enunciate their lines. Many never went to school to learn the rudiments of acting, not to mention basics of elocution. Like their equally retarded confreres, the rock 'musicians', they screamed and shouted or mumbled their lines without any regard for the wonderful heritage that the classical theatre offered. Most probably they'd never heard of Shakespeare or Mollière or even the modern playwrights of quality. The new scriptwriters of TV fares disqualified themselves by the mere fact that they passed the age of sixteen. Perhaps at that age they were in danger of thinking, and this fact alone, in the entertainment industry, was deemed a profound no-no. Nevertheless, those artless actors, once established, continued to gather millions, then buy themselves toy husbands, or toy wives, by the dozen, amass diamonds to flaunt them on Oscar nights, which had became no more than a vulgar display of a society of mutual adoration.

Hence, the riots.

"Can we go swimming after lunch?" Suzy asked, if for no other reason than to change the subject. She found discussing riots acutely depressing.

No one moved. "Why don't you all go for a walk? I'll look after Sacha," Alicia offered.

Joan, John and Desmond opted for a quiet nap, instead. This left Suzy and Alec to accept Alicia's offer. They did. After coffee, Suzy changed into shorts, while Matt took Alec outside, and led him to the footpath, winding its way along the shoreline. Then, as Suzy joined them, he withdrew. The sand at the side of the footpath was inviting. In segments, Suzy walked barefoot alongside Alec's wheelchair. It felt good to be walking barefoot again. It's been a while. You had to be a Canadian to really appreciate it. For his part, Alec enjoyed the exercise his arms got trying to keep up with her.

After a while, they stopped for a few minutes' rest. Suzy sat down, smiling at the waves below. Alec parked his wheelchair next to her, at the very edge of the sand. As he leaned back, his eyes followed a lone airplane, which, at great altitude, appeared to be moving incredibly slowly. The silver fuselage, picking up the shimmering rays of the sun, seemed to crawl across the cloudless sky like a far-distant comet. In a way, it seemed outside the confines of time.

What if it weren't there, Alec thought.

The silver dot lost its luster and melted into the blue background. "Like the Bermuda triangle," thought Alec. "Only it will reappear in a minute." But it didn't. "Probably just a refraction of light," Alec smiled, as he looked down at the water.

For him, the ocean possessed a magnetic property that had nothing to do with magnetism. It had the same hypnotic draw as an open fire.

"Will you accept a shell, instead?" Suzy asked.

"What for?"

"I don't have a penny. For your thoughts, silly."

What would I do without Sue, he wondered? Not once had she said anything contrary, let alone complained, about his legs. She must have evolved her own opinions. Perhaps she, too, like his sophomores, put his paralysis to hysteria. She'd never said a word. And even now, he mused, if it hadn't been for her, I would be constantly lost in thoughts that would take me on a wild goose chase—more often than not.

"I've been thinking of the echo effect. Of synchronicity. Of reconciliation. Of many things. Even of the Bermuda Triangle," he spoke slowly, haltingly.

She didn't interrupt. She leaned back against the slope, until she was looking directly at the sky. The same sky that hung suspended over their home in LA, over their old apartment in Montreal, over her parents' house in Kingston; the same sky over such different territories, different cultures. Different people. Different, yet in some ways almost identical.

"All things have already happened. Not to you, or me but they have happened. In their potential form. All matter and energy, in their endless varieties, combinations, complexities, permutations, in their infinite relationships... they already exists. All things already exist in the matrix of the universe. The physical or the virtual universe—but they already exist," he took a deep breath.

"This is the assumption of your Information Theory, isn't it?" She knew but sought confirmation. Alec's Theory was not the easiest theory to fathom.

"Yes. That is the crux of it. If all things already exist, then the information that enabled them to exist must also be available. If only we could find the way to access it. The universe is like a giant computer with unlimited memory storage. Everything is there..."

"It sounds a bit like magic," Suzy mused aloud.

"Ah, yes... the science of tomorrow."

Alec's eyes swept the distant horizon. Then he spoke again, weighing his words, as though finding his way through a complex labyrinth.

"And all those things must be arranged in order. If they happened all at once, we would have another big bang. Time puts them into a sequence. But the sequence is flexible. Different people learn different things at different times. The sequence can be changed, and it is, it must be, possible to oscillate between various points in the sequence. One of my post-doc friends has already shown that mathematically it makes perfect sense."

Suzy's thoughts took her on a different tangent. For now, she kept them to herself. She suspected that peek-a-boo was little more than Sandra using Alec's body for reasons of her own. Or perhaps, she was just using the information that his body represented even as he continued to use hers... without ever acknowledging her presence or asking her permission. Peek-a-boo could be nothing more than tit-for-tat.

"...and if you can really visualize it..." Alec's voice reached her from afar. A deep furrow divided his eyebrows.

People further down the beach began shouting and waving their arms. Alec and Suzy followed their hands pointing out to sea. A great surge was forming just this side of the horizon. The wave was some five kilometers away, but some people picked up their belongings and retreated to higher ground.

"What the hell is going on? Shouldn't we be moving away from here?" Suzy was up and pulling Alec's chair to join her.

"Relax," he said quietly. "Just relax..."

He continues looking at the incipient tsunami. For a while it continued to advance toward the beach, then it appeared to change its course. Almost. Rather than continuing on its path, it began fumbling in place, fulminating in apparent confusion. After a short while, it retreated into the vastness of the ocean. Soon only a vague memory of it remained.

"All things, all conditions already exist," Alec repeated. "In this or the virtual universe. The information is there." And he released the breaks on his wheelchair. "Let's go back," he said.

There was so much confidence in his command that Suzy, who hated to be told what to do, followed him without a word.

"There is also polarization of light, which can give you invisibility," he said, without breaking his pace. This time, his strong arms moved the chair faster than Suzy could walk. "And there is the weather, the climate, the movements of air..." He seemed to have changed the subject. Suddenly distant thunder reached them and an enormous bolt of lightening struck the place where the tsunami had been."

"Of course, it could be dangerous. Very dangerous."

And only then did he look as though he had just become aware of Suzy trotting at his side. He stopped and pulled her into his arms. Right there, in the middle of a public footpath. Not that such a display of ardour was unheard of in Lower California. Or on the beach. But it was certainly new to Suzy. She was a private lady.

"I'm sorry, darling. Forgive me?" And then looking even more guilty, he added quite unnecessarily, "I've been miles away. I'm really sorry."

Miles or years, she had no idea. But she promised herself that someday, some fine day, soon, she would go there with him. Wherever it was. No matter what it took.

For a moment she felt annoyed at Sandra.

Even as Alec moved his chair along, he continued connecting with the Information Field. Only he didn't quite realize it. Not as yet, but it would come.

With vengeance.

***

Time

If we could travel into the past, it's mind-boggling what would be possible... I have no idea whether it's possible, but it's certainly worth exploring.

Carl Edward Sagan
1934 – 1996
Astronomer

13
Atlantis

There are three stages of existence, not two as is normally accepted. Being, becoming and stasis. The last corresponds to death. Real death. Not the cessation of biological functions. When in stasis, one is outside time. No wonder so many religions compare this condition to eternal damnation."

They were all sitting on the terrace sipping the ever-present Sangria, looking out at the brooding ocean.

None of them had any desire to check on the events in Los Angeles. The broadcasts of the last two days had been so saturated with the riots, reasons for riots, proposed solutions, mayhem and murder, that any subject seemed better than more TV. Nevertheless, the subject under discussion was a direct result of the last session of the newscast, wherein the reporter and his guest—some local ecclesiastical authority, had discussed the morality of killing people who detract from the public good. They'd all had too much pseudo-philosophy.

"It's like being, then?" Suzy suggested.

"No. In being there is bliss, if the concept of bliss has anything to do with the chaos theory. I know it's far fetched, but I have my suspicions that there is also an infinite potential in this state, which is the driving force of our evolution. Perhaps it is the awareness of this potential that results in bliss. Anyway, in stasis, there is nothing. No awareness of self. It is a condition of absolute absence."

"We have that sort of thing in absolute zero," Des offered. "At the theoretical point of minus 273.18^0 Centigrade, there is no molecular motion. A form of stasis."

"That would make hell the coldest place in the universe," Alicia mused, fascinated at the prospect against her will. "I wouldn't like that. I wouldn't like it at all," she affirmed with a shudder.

"So the religious concept of hell, fire and all that, does have its echo in science?" John asked.

"I don't know enough about the old or new metaphysical trends to argue," Alec admitted. "But to me, stasis is not defined so much as an expression of something negative, as in Desmond's absolute zero, but rather by the absence of everything, positive or negative. It is a state of, well... of indifference. Like the ultimate state of the universe proposed by some static universe theorists. What do you think, Des?"

"First, I don't think that absolute zero is mine," he wagged his finger at Alec, "But I understand your point." Then the Professor turned to face John, as if Suzy's father had earned an explanation. "What Alec is referring to is entropy. It is a thermodynamic measure of the amount of energy unavailable in a system undergoing change. With no thermodynamic differential no change is possible."

"I don't quite follow..." haltingly Joan joined John. Her eyes registered an equal lack of understanding.

"Imagine a universe," Alec tried his luck, "wherein all the suns, over billions upon billions of years, gradually died. They'd all burned out their hydrogen, their fuel, and they'd become white dwarfs. All their thermal energy had radiated outwards, and eventually became equally distributed throughout space. The temperature everywhere would now be a fraction above absolute zero, but there would be no differential temperature that could stimulate any motion. You might call it a thermodynamic indifference. The whole universe would be suspended in total inertia. In stasis."

"Still sounds like hell," Alicia put in. She didn't like such extremes. They interfered with her cultivated sense of wellbeing.

"My point precisely," Alec agreed.

Joan threw up her arms in despair. "How on earth did we get on such a dismal, depressing subject?"

"Because..." the Professor said pontifically, rising to his feet, "because the ignorant have been mouthing off on TV again."

"What Desmond means is," Alec stepped in, again, "that when that oaf said we should kill people who detract from the public good he meant that, until there is absolute uniformity in all things throughout society, there will be no peace among the masses."

"Like stasis...?" Joan finally got the message.

"Like stasis. Only in the social, economical and every other non-thermal sense, I presume," John put in. Then, after scratching his head he added. "Wouldn't work, would it?"

"Not even if it were possible, which I sure hope isn't!" Alec agreed.

The Professor, who'd remained standing since his last pronouncement, looked down at them from his advantageous altitude.

"Y'rre looking like a bunch of lazy bones. Now who'll get up and join me on a constitutional along this prrristine beach?"

"I presume you want to go for a walk?" Alicia looked up. She liked looking up at Desmond. When they both stood, they were exactly the same height.

"Isn't this precisely what I just said, lassie?" Desmond confirmed.

"I'm game," Alicia rose to her feet.

"If only..." The Professor muttered under his breath.

John and Joan preferred a walk to the local store. They had some essentials to buy and they'd hardly seen the 'other side' of the house. This suited Desmond just fine as he'd been trying to get Alicia alone since they'd arrived. Although

Sasha hardly needed constant supervision, Alec and Suzy remained with their firstborn. By some quirk of fate, Matt was nowhere to be seen. He was always there when needed, but not otherwise. The man must have been a mind-reader.

Soon Suzy and Alec were alone.

Having the terrace all to themselves was just fine by them. For a while they sat in silence, enhanced by the gentle hum of the ocean and a whisper of the breeze, playing hide and seek among the roof rafters. Suzy had a little sleep to catch up on, and this was an ideal opportunity. Alec was, as so often of late, lost in thoughts. The distant horizon was once more getting hazy, gradually merging with the sky above. Finally the ocean and the sky joined into a single, continuous canvas on which an occasional erne drew a fragmentary line. Then, the line dissolved also.

Alec awoke in the body of a man about twenty years his senior. The man's head was supported on a short and stumpy frame, wrapped in a toga-like garment, flowing from his disproportionately broad shoulders and exposing his equally short and stumpy legs. Rather hairy, he thought.

What a funny dream, he mused. And what's more, I know that I'm dreaming. Only why am I so short and hairy?

He searched his memory. *Maybe I'm a Roman. They were quite short, and being Italian, so to speak, they could have been quite hairy, couldn't they?*

This realization relaxed him a bit. The next moment he, or the body he occupied, got up from the sofa. He was only vaguely aware of propelling it himself. Actually the sofa looked more like a *chaise longue* that could also have been of Roman origin. Even if vicariously, Alec experienced the familiar movement of legs. He held his emotive breath. 'I'm walking,' he thought. 'My, God! I'm walking...'

His host body approached a large opening in the outside wall. Wherever Alec dreamt he was, it was a beautiful place. The Home Planet? No. On the Home Planet he was always himself. Younger or older, but himself. And here...? For a moment he mused if this was one of the bodies he'd occupied in his previous lives; then he dismissed the idea of reincarnation as *non sequitur.* It's neither here nor there... he mused.

He looked out through the... window? A glassless opening.

Pity, he thought. The reflection might have shown me what the rest of me looks like.

As far as Alec could see, the rolling landscape was peppered with villas peeking from behind abundant Cypress trees. From a distance the villas seemed large—luxurious was a better word—with pools of water reflecting the bluest sky he'd ever seen. The grounds separating the villas were also richly landscaped. It all looked about halfway between what he remembered of the Home Planet and what he imagined ancient Rome might have been like. Or...

Suddenly it came to him: *I died and gone to heaven. Not a bad place heaven... I could be quite happy here.*

Only something was wrong.

If this is heaven, then why am I so hairy...?

Next he wondered if the owner of the body could detect his presence, or his thoughts. He tried to still his mind.

An airplane without wings, appeared out of nowhere and the next instant come to a very rapid stop. Anyone subjected to such deceleration would have been smashed against the wall of the... of whatever it was. A rocket? If the dream were to make any sense, the rocket itself would have fallen apart. But it hadn't. Even at a considerable distance, Alec could see people getting out of the airship and walking towards the villas. They seemed in perfectly good shape.

They'd overcome inertia! Alec smiled in delight. *What a place... what a dream!*

Even as he continued to look out at the serene landscape, another cigar shaped object rose from the ground, rose slowly upwards to about two or three hundred feet, then... virtually disappeared. This time, though, it left a slight trail of vapour in the direction it went. Flew. The direction it shot. And the direction was straight up. As though going into orbit. Or...

Or higher?

For a moment Alec completely forgot that he was dreaming. He even forgot that he was in a strange body. The problem of overcoming inertia commanded all his attention. Inertia was the tendency of any mass to remain at rest, or to keep moving in the same direction unless affected by another force. Theoretically, once an object left the gravitational attraction of the Earth, and then overcame the pull of the sun, it would fly forever, barring being trapped in the gravitational field of another planet, sun or galaxy. But there was an awful lot of space between galaxies. About ninety nine percent of space was, for the purposes of inertia, void. You could go virtually anywhere in the universe, if you avoided the gravitational fields.

If these people have overcome inertia, their interplanetary travel would be child's play. They would need hardly any energy to pop up to the moon, or Mars, or anywhere. Just for fun. For an after-dinner spin...

These people...?

This is a dream, he reminded himself. Slowly, with disbelief in his eyes, he looked at his short, hairy legs. A funny sort of dream, he mused, shaking his head. And then he gazed at his stumpy legs, again. My God, he thought. I am moving them. I am moving my legs. His legs?

I am walking!

He moved away from the window. Strange how walking comes naturally to me... It took me months to lose the ability, and just seconds to recover... He was already treating the host body as his own.

On the wall opposite the window there was a large map. The island it portrayed, though seemingly large, was quite unknown to him. He looked closer. In the right bottom corner of the wall—a map, really, that covered the whole wall— there was some sort of scale. At least it looked like a scale. It referred to units that were meaningless to him. They could have been miles or kilometers in another language, but he had no idea.

Nest to it, he found a series of buttons. He pressed one at random. The wall shimmered and then solidified into a dark background with little bright balls suspended here and there. He took a step back. Then he froze. The coloured points of light, little round spheres, were moving. They were following a regular trajectory...

"I'm looking at the solar system!" he said half aloud. "Only..." he stopped. He heard himself speaking with a very strange accent. He kept his eyes on the map.

At first he couldn't figure it out. It was almost like the solar system but it wasn't. The third planet from the sun was recognizably the Earth—bluish, with off-white patches.

I am back on Earth, he corrected himself. But something didn't add up.

Then he had it. Between the orbits of Mars and Jupiter the asteroids were missing. There was no Ceres, no hundreds of even smaller planetoids to be seen. Instead there was a single sphere, in graphic terms, about the size of Mars. And talking of Mars, our neighbour wasn't red, but bluish-green, with puffy, yellowish clouds, reminiscent to Earth.

It's amazing what one can see in a dream...

He reached over to press another button. He thought he would have to switch the present one off first, and in the process he turned it a little to the right. As he did, the map got brighter, and hundreds, many hundreds, of little dots began drifting through the space between the planets.

My God! He caught his breath. *These must be spaceships!*

They were all moving. Scooting through space as though it were the most natural thing in the world. There were literally thousands of them. They moved in a jerky motion. Very fast, then slowly, then fast again.

Inertia means nothing to them, he nodded, confirming his previous suspicions.

And then he stepped back, again.

"Who are these people?" he spoke aloud.

He chewed on the question for a moment or two. "If I am dreaming, and I must be, then what am I dreaming about?" Again he was taken aback by his own accent. It was completely strange to him—as if spoken by someone else.

He blinked, repeatedly, wondering if he might wake up. It didn't help. The living map was still there.

This was Earth, but not the Earth he knew. There were some different scientific laws, or rules, here. The problem of inertia had not been solved in Alec's time. There had been some experiments, but his colleagues were a long way from applying them to anything outside lab conditions. No. This was certainly not the Earth he knew. But it was Earth.

I must be stealing a glance at a very, very distant future... he mused, now less concerned with the nature of the dream, as with the things he'd witnessed.

And then he froze for the second time.

If I am looking at the future, then what on earth is the extra planet doing between Mars and Jupiter? And whatever happened to the hundreds of asteroids? Have they glued themselves together?

But even as he speculated on the dream's facility to glue together large chunks of terrain into a single continent, he knew that he was sailing on a completely wrong tack. He was looking into a distant past. He was looking at the Earth before the planet between Mars and Jupiter came to an untimely end.

Back to the original map.

Alec had to find the scale of the thing. The map was beautifully moulded, the contours rising and falling as if he was looking at this great island from far above. He turned the knob on the right. The map shrunk, the oceans surrounding it retreated till the whole Earth seemed to have formed a sphere, with just one large island remaining at the very center. It was like looking at the Earth through the wrong end of the telescope. Only it was a peculiar Earth. Not resembling the continents at all. It was a sister planet, beautiful, mysterious, where the laws of inertia had already been overcome; a planet for a physicist to study and admire.

Now, why did I think that? Half spoken thoughts seemed generated by someone who had access to his mind.

He turned the dial the other way.

The island grew, swelled before his disbelieving eyes, until it filled the whole wall. He continued turning the dial. The map kept growing until the oceans disappeared and land began sliding off the edges of the wall. Next, a pinpoint light began blinking at the geometric center of the screen. The map grew in direct proportion to his turning the knob. Quite suddenly, a city appeared.

Not exactly a city, but an undulating terrain with villas attached to the slopes of rolling hills. They all seemed to be located as though to optimize the view from each building.

What marvelous people...

In each direction there were long vistas, some with intermittent lakes as serene as Alec had once seen in the far North of Canada. Only this was a balmy climate, neither hot nor cold A gentle breeze was wafting through the large wall openings. Yes. By some freak of nature, he actually felt the breeze on his face. Or perhaps, all things were possible in a dream.

"Maybe this is the Garden of Eden..." he muttered. "Or maybe I'm a transcendental comedian?"

And then he turned the knob all the way. In the same instant he jumped back as though bitten by a deadly snake. He stood facing a short, stumpy man, who was looking at him, his mouth open, the mop of hair on the man's head reminding him of someone. In spite of the gaping mouth, the man Alec faced exhibited bright, intelligent eyes, and a powerful physique. What made Alec jump was not just the presence of a living being before him. It was the suddenness with which the other man appeared; that, and a deep conviction that the man he was staring at was... himself.

Himself—in his borrowed body.

The man wore an identical tunic, his eyes were at precisely the level of his own and, most of all, the man jumped back when 'he' saw Alec. A Doppelganger.

"I must wake up!" Alec whispered through his teeth. "I must wake up, now." And as he reached for the knob to turn off the unnerving image, his hand trembled. *Shall I still walk when I'm awake?*

But he didn't wake up. Not yet.

Closing his eyes he took two steps towards the offending dial and turned it to the left. Then, mustering all his courage, he looked again at the map. The man, his spitting image, was gone. He breathed easier.

There were three more knobs on the wall. By now, Alec was a little nervous. Actually, he was more nervous than when he'd first arrived there. The shock of seeing 'himself' was more than he cared to admit to himself.

What if Suzy jumps at me in some other body? What if she's hairy all over?

Dream or not, the thoughts were disconcerting. He returned to the *chaise longue*, leaned back and tried to work out what was happening. As this is a dream, he reasoned, none of this has to make sense. Not really. On the other hand, many great scientific discoveries had come about because of dreams. If dreams were a source of inspiration, then this one was loaded. And then another strange idea came to him, perfectly consistent with the dream concept. In a way, whatever he imagined happened. He'd always been fascinated by inertia. Here, he saw inertia resolved. He wanted to find out where he was, he needed maps—they appeared. He didn't exactly locate his whereabouts, but he knew that he was on a continent surrounded by water, with a balmy climate and a very advanced civilization. Very advanced.

Then he wanted to locate himself in time. A map of the solar system appeared out of a wall. He saw the planet between Mars and Jupiter still in orbit.

Why did I say still?

Next, he wanted to find out what he looked like. He got that, too. A living mirror. Scary as it might have been, a nightmare rather than a dream, but it was an experience that he hoped he'd remember when he woke up.

One way or another, whatever he needed, or wanted, or desired, even at a very subliminal level, came to him. There were different laws here.

Alec remembered the many Sci-Fi writers who warned that one should never change anything in the past, as it could affect the future. They warned about the dire consequences of breaking this particular law. Alec didn't think it applied to dreams, but there were dreams and there were dreams, and this dream was a lot more real than any dream he'd ever had.

"Have I changed anything?" he asked himself half-aloud.

And then he remembered the asteroid belt. *Damn, I shouldn't have made that planet!*

He jumped up, ran to the dial and switched on the solar system. He zoomed in on the inner planets just in time to witness a ghastly explosion, as the fifth planet from the sun burst into a minor nova. The planet was no more. And even as he watched, a string of giant rocks began to take on an orbit about halfway between Mars and Jupiter. Within seconds he watched, aghast, as the fourth planet began to lose its blue hue. The atmosphere on Mars was gone.

"My God! What have I done?" he shouted, his throaty voice reverberating in the large chamber.

He looked away from the cosmic disaster. For some inexplicable reason he felt sure that both Mars and the planet that had just exploded had been populated by his own kind; by hairy, intelligent, perhaps brilliant, very advanced people.

He turned towards the *chaise longue* and caught his breath. Lying on the sofa was the body he presently occupied. It looked limp, one hairy arm hanging over the edge; the eyes, lifeless, staring senselessly at the ceiling. Alec reached over and, instinctively closed the man's eyes. Then his own. He'd seen enough.

Suzy looked worried. She was bending over him, a glass of water in hand. Her eyes wide open, filled with disbelief mixed with admiration.

"You've done it again, darling," she whispered. "Only it was different this time. Wasn't it?"

"I have?" He rubbed his eyes, as though not used to the light.

"You've peek-a-boo'd..." she said. "Only... here, take a sip of water." Alec lifted his head and obeyed.

"I remember... some things..." he said. "Some things..."

And then he glanced at his legs. He tried moving them. Not even a quiver. They were as flaccid as a half-hour ago. Or had it been a million years? He felt beads of perspiration forming on his forehead. *The man was dead when I left his body; physically, mentally and emotionally, dead. And when he died he was an old man. Like me. An old man of twenty-five.*

"Like when you were fourteen?" He imagined he heard Suzy's thoughts.

"What? Oh, no. Nothing like that. Nothing like that at all."

For the next few moments Alec seemed to vacillate between two realities. Only this time he knew he was in Suzy's hands. Dear Sue. *Had you come with me, you would have seen me walk. Like in the old days. And now? Now I am dead. At least my body is. The beautiful hairy body I walked in.*

"God forbid," he muttered remembering the exploding planet.

"What darling?"

"Thank God I have you, Sue. You can't begin to realize how much I need you."

And the next moment Alec's eyes seemed to close of their own accord, and unwittingly, he took a short, dreamless nap.

Throughout all this time, Matt had remained immobile, standing within a few feet, yet deceptively invisible. When he saw the Suzy and Alec relax, a vague smile played at the corners of his mouth. Then, making no sound at all, he withdrew to the terrace.

***

14

Reconciliation

Dr. McBride left immediately after breakfast. He needed to go to his office. It had something to do with the reports on an experiment he was overseeing, which had just arrived from Waxahachie. The Professor had spent a short time on the cellular, and left almost at a trot. As Joan had once put it, Christmas didn't stop the Collider from smashing the poor atoms. There was a long line of scientists waiting for a chance to conduct their experiments.

In early afternoon Des was back. He looked deflated.

During his absence, Alec and Suzy took it upon themselves to replenish the fridge. Maria gave them a list as long as her arm. Alec asked Matt to drive him all the way to San Diego. While Suzy took care of the food, Alec searched for a malt Scotch good enough for the Professor. In spite of his good intentions, they failed to find the Professor's favourite Single. Thanks to Matt, however, Alec made a discovery that even Desmond might find acceptable. It was an impressive glazed ceramic bottle worthy to house a genie. The blend was called: *King of Scots*. Officially it was labeled a 17 year old, but on the back of the cask, the explanations assured that the figure 17 referred to the youngest ingredient, not the oldest. Alec wouldn't dream of indulging in such a luxury for himself, but his debt to Desmond was beyond his ability to pay him back. This was but a small token. When they got back from shopping, the Professor was already on the terrace, stretching on his deckchair.

"The place is dead," he said, reaching for the Sangria at his elbow. By then, Sangria consisted mostly of fruit and carbonated water, with just enough dry wine to give it zest. Alec decided the Scotch would wait till the evening.

"Caltech?"

"No, the whole city. There are no people in the streets. Even the expressways are empty. Like after a major earthquake. There aren't any riots, either. There is a general sort of malaise in the air that is quite palpable. It's as if people were overwhelmingly fed up." The Professor was as much reporting as thinking aloud.

"With what, exactly?" John wanted to know.

"Oh, I don't know. With just about everything. I only met with a few of them—the security guards, the janitor, two or three students. I got my paper from the fellow on the corner. Usually he gives me a 'Hi doc'. He didn't even look up. And he was the only man on the street. It was as though he didn't care..." Des continued.

"...about?" This was Joan.

"About anything. Whether he lived or died. My secretary came in only to make sure I got my documents. She's always spreading cheer. Today, she didn't say a word. Almost. She looked not so much worried as indifferent," the Professor shook his head from side to side, as though not quite believing his own words. "It's some kind of sickness, a virus, only it seems to affect people's hearts."

"Whatever brought the riots to a head was a long time coming. People expected the government to do something about it all, but... could it be, that those in power dipped their fingers in the extortion." Alec put in.

"Extortion? Isn't that illegal?" Alicia didn't accept her son's speculation.

"Look it up in the dictionary, mother. Extortion means the practice of extracting money from people by undue exercise of power or by the exaction of too high a price. Try not paying your taxes. Or refusing to pay full price on something where the profit margin is over a hundred percent, and you'll end up in jail in both cases. Isn't that akin to extortion?"

"But people must make a living..." His mother tried to defend the guilty.

"Yes, they have a right to do that. But not when the extorter's income is ten times that of the person who's being exploited. Look at the lawyers' fees, at the cost of medication, look at insurance premiums, even the cost of education... Each can jointly and severally ruin people who need those services. And God forbid you should break a leg without insurance coverage. You would keep paying with your blood for the rest of your days. Isn't that so, Desmond?"

"Pretty close. There are also the vested interests in Washington, as I am sure there are in your country, if not to the same extent, which abuse the public trust. They are there to line the deep pockets of our elite..." the Professor admitted quietly.

Alec looked out to sea. His mind drifted to the luxurious villas hugging the gentle slopes of the verdant city; a 'city' for people who appeared to have everything. Whom did they exploit? Where did the 'workers' live? Who invented this dream?

"I had a dream..." he murmured still looking out towards the hazy horizon. "I have a dream," he changed the tense, "of a place where all people have all they need, yet never at someone else's expense."

"We've all had such a dream, at one time or another," Desmond nodded, "but we—Homo sapiens—are not ready for it yet, lad. Not by a long shot."

"I wonder..." Alec held his ground. "I wonder..." he repeated but wouldn't say any more. He was thinking of creating such a great wealth within that it would spill over to the outside. That the wealth would not be drawn from other people, only from a source that never runs dry. That people would not accumulate wealth, because there would be no need to. The source would always be there, open. He saw such a world already existing, knocking on the doors to be allowed in. Into people's consciousness. Like his Information Theory.

"Alec!" Suzy shook his arm. Then she leaned over to his ear and whispered, "you're shifting."

He wasn't aware of doing anything of the sort. But he'd given up arguing with Sue. If she'd said he did it, he must have done it. It seemed that whenever he felt strongly dissatisfied, something happened to restore his mental and emotional, equilibrium.

"Sorry," he murmured.

But his mood swung the other way. Most people are walking in circles, he thought. Some are going completely the wrong way. Others have stopped, before they could get too far on the wrong track. I suppose they are the lucky ones. Then he looked down at his legs.

Perhaps they are the lucky ones, he repeated silently. But he doubted his own thoughts.

I am little more than an observer. I live in a wheelchair. This morning even my arms hurt. My bodily functions are discharged without leaving the chair. That drove Suzy crazy until we got Matt to live-in with us. To dress me, wash me, and clean me in moments of incontinence. And now Matt's salary is paid by my mother's inheritance.

I am dead. Or might as well be dead.

Sandra...

Alec argued long and hard against such a financial arrangement. But Alicia dug in her heals. "I can't take the money with me, Ali, and you have Sacha to look after."

She'd won.

Actually, the whole affair was vastly exaggerated in Alec's head. The lion's share of Matt's salary was paid by Alec's medical insurance. The extra amount did not place undue hardship on Alicia or anyone else. And Matt himself expressed little interest in money.

Later that afternoon Alicia stayed with Sacha, and the 'young couple', as everyone except Maria called them, went for a walk. This time the beach was less inviting, but Alec insisted on a little exercise. He thought that using his arms would stop, or at least delay, the progress of, what was beginning to look like some sort of muscular atrophy. He hasn't exercised nearly enough lately, and propelling the wheels with his arms for a few miles was the least he thought he could do. Keeping to the higher ground they only just managed to evade young cyclists pelting along, who were presumably imagining that they were on the *Tour de Californie*. On their left, the tide was at its highest. After a mile or so, Alec slowed down. His arms hurt badly. He pulled to one side, his eyes searching for answers in the rolling breakers. The waves seemed to waver, roil in a confused manner, then retreated about forty feet down the sand; retreating under his gaze. Like the tsunami? Perhaps on a small scale—only this time it was much easier. Alec grinned, turned his wheelchair, and continued along the bicycle path.

"It's nicer now," Suzy murmured. She'd hardly said a word since they left the villa. She seemed to sense Alec's discomfort. "I think the wind is dying down."

"Could be," he smiled, grinding his teeth in an effort to keep rolling. All his attention was again directed toward moving his arms. He was only vaguely aware of having had anything to do with the retreating waves. Ever assuming that he had. He simply thought that the inner and outer realities should be brought more in line. That, in a way, all realities are a question of faith. Of belief. Or it could have been just his imagination.

To his surprise, his arms seemed to hurt less with each stroke.

He knew that, sooner or later, he must become reconciled with the power that was welling up inside him. He must stop setting himself apart from it. Perhaps he didn't have to apply scientific principles to absolutely everything in his life. Nobody else seemed to. They relied on their emotions, instinct, and intuition as much as on their intellect. Perhaps he could, and should, be a little more flexible. Suzy accepted the evidence of her eyes, no matter how improbable. On the other hand, since nobody else seemed aware of his peek-a-boo antics, perhaps she was not espying him with physical eyes. Did that make any sense?

Sacha was quite another story. He seemed to enjoy it—his reputed shifting.

Does the lad know something I don't? Does he see a reality that neither Suzy nor I can perceive? What is reality anyway? Isn't matter mostly empty space?

As a physicist he knew that it was. Some 99.9999% of it.

The same old questions returned to him with renewed force. Like the breakers, which now seemed to come back, echoing his inner strife. What once had been happening only in his dreams he now seemed to retain in his waking hours.

Am I retaining some peripheral ability to affect reality? Or am I loosing my senses.

At the same time, if it were true, if these weren't just ravings of a disconsolate mind, he felt it wasn't his power. He had no idea how it worked, nor did he even know whence it came. It had its origin in his subconscious, perhaps deeper. He only knew it was there. It was in the same category as Atlantis.

Now why did I think of Atlantis?

"You know, Sue, when we were on the terrace together yesterday…" Alec stopped his chair, reaching out for Suzy's arm.

"Of course, darling. You were really away..."

"I was in Atlantis!" he said, keeping his voice from shaking when he said it. "Do you think I'm going crazy?"

"Why would you ask such a thing, darling? Do you feel as though you are?" It was meant to be a joke.

"Sometimes..." He wasn't smiling.

They resumed their way. Since yesterday, Suzy felt that something very traumatic had happened when Alec fell asleep on the terrace. After a while, without breaking her step, she asked him why he thought he'd been to Atlantis.

"After all, how would you know?" she asked. "After all, no one's ever been to Atlantis."

Alec chewed on that before answering. There was a problem. If our planet Earth were to collapse into a black hole, it would be about one centimeter in diameter. The whole of the 'empty space' would have been squeezed out of it, and... well, it would become solid. Really solid. Conversely, if the process were to be reversed, Earth, the planet Earth, would be mostly empty space. Like we all are. Even now more than 50 trillion solar neutrinos pass through an average human body every second without even slowing down.

What is reality?

After another half a mile, the wind died down considerably. Alec stopped again and pulled Suzy down to sit beside him on the sand. They were close to the spot where they had rested the last time. Only on higher ground.

"Frankly, I have no idea. It just came to me. You know," he hesitated, then nodded to his thoughts, "it was the same with the Information Theory. First it came to me, and then it took me eighteen months to work it out to be able to put it on paper. Inside, I knew it all along. But it just wouldn't come out. Now that it's in the open, the theory I mean, most people, at least in my circles, accept that it might be valid."

And just as suddenly and unexpectedly, Alec's memories retreated to his childhood.

The Home Planet, the Far Country, the many jaunts he did as a boy, it was all part of the same thing. Reality was defined by man, the individual. Not man by reality. You created your own universe. It wasn't fixed, immovable; it was as flexible as the waves that agreed to stay farther down the beach. It was as flexible as the feeling of joy or sorrow, or even love and hatred. We all create realities. We explode into riots, rebellions, against the abnormalities of our own constructs. None of us should ever blame others for our fate. We are the sole creators of our destiny.

"But isn't Atlantis a little farfetched?" Suzy prodded gently.

Her question brought him back. He weighed it before answering. His mind was still elsewhere. He was beginning to long for the state of consciousness that once allowed him those journeys into the unknown; journeys that provided so many answers. But, of course, then there was Sandra...

"Back in Montreal, I read some books about Atlantis, Lemuria, the Kingdom of Mu—that sort of thing. I forget the author, the title also for that matter, probably because I didn't take any of it seriously. But I was a student and you wouldn't move in with me, and I'd lost the ability to 'project' as the book called it... well, I'd been reading the book because it reminded me of my own escapades. And, as I said, you wouldn't move in with me..."

"I heard you the first time. Now, you know why."

"That's not fair. I got the book *after* you refused..."

"I was just kidding." She looked at his furrowed brow. Alec was not smiling. Something was eating at him. From within.

"Oh, of course. Well, anyway, the book made some interesting assumptions. It said that periodically the whole world changes. That a certain critical mass is achieved by humanity, and then there is a sort of cosmic leap in consciousness. The previous states just cease to exist—new ones are formed."

"That doesn't sound so far fetched." Suzy's tone was conciliatory but still a little doubtful.

"No. Not really. Evolution is said to advance in leaps, not in a continuous curve, or even a jagged line like a chart in the Wall Street Journal. Between those leaps, there is virtual stasis, until the next leap takes place. Something must happen to Homo sapiens, or a good percentage of us, before the next leap can occur. At least the book suggested that..."

"It seems to echo the old Hindu theories that there has been a golden age, followed by silver, bronze and iron ages. In Esoteric Buddhism humanity seems to be on a descending spiral, rather than ascending..." There was a time when Suzy read avidly on Eastern Philosophies. As a feminist by nature, she started with Helena Blavatsky.

"Not so much spiral as periods of relative stagnation separated by jumps. My book did not specify in which direction the human race was jumping. Up or down."

"Like a yo-yo?" Suzy put in.

"Not really. I don't think that it is really a question of up or down. It could well be a lateral movement, only, as I've already said, into a different set of coordinates."

Suzy was looking up at Alec, her eyes misty.

"What?" he asked. "What is it?"

She smiled. "You sound very wise, and clever, and learned, when you talk like that."

"I thought we were having a serious discussion," he shrugged.

"We are, darling. You can't blame me for admiring my own husband," she looked hurt. Actually, she was only pretending. With the hurt, not the admiration. She brushed her lips against his. When he didn't respond she kissed him.

"Alright! All right, I forgive you..."

"For admiring you?"

And they sat silently for a little while. As always, they enjoyed the periods of silence as much as when they talked. It was as though they continued to communicate on some different level.

"I suppose we should get back...?" she said.

"Don't you like it here?"

"Sacha..."

He turned his wheels at once.

"I am sure he's all right, I just... well, I miss him," she admitted. "In a certain way I seem to miss him virtually all the time. And then, sometimes, I seem to feel he's right here, with us, or with me, when I'm doing something. I wonder if all mothers feel that way about their babies."

"You are not all mothers," Alec affirmed with conviction. "But Sacha does seem to have a peculiar ability to communicate his presence. I've felt it a number of times."

"You too?" She was surprised. She assumed it was a mother's prerogative to have such feelings.

"I don't think it's anything to do with *our* perception," he addressed her unspoken question. "I think it's something to do with Sacha himself. Some kind of ability that may be latent in all of us. There are so many abilities we don't seem to use."

"Or lose…?"

They were at the front door of the cottage when Alec stopped once more.

"You know, this Atlantis business? I just remembered," he sounded excited. "Actually, it's more to do with cycles. As you've said, there's been the golden age, then the silver and the bronze. And now we are in, what you once called, Kali Yuga," Alec had a near-photographic memory for names— names that mattered to him. "Well, if that is true, then the next cycle would take us back to the golden age, right?"

"Yes, darling," she agreed, but her eyes were saying 'so what'? She didn't want to tell him that in Hindu philosophy each age was spread over hundreds of thousands, up to almost two million years. The Grand Age which incorporated cycles within cycles was said to last some 4,320,000,000 years. Bit long to hold your breath.

"Then..." He was interrupted by Sacha's joyful troll. "We'll talk about it later," he said, and pushed harder on the wheels.

The Professor, the Normans and Alicia were all sitting in a semi-circle watching Sacha give his performance. Maria was peeking through a crack in the door. Matt, as usual, contrived to remain inconspicuous. There seemed to be moments in which Sacha was so happy that he felt the need to sing. It was as if something occurred, or perhaps was happening, that gave him great joy. Obviously, no one had any way of knowing what that something might be. Alec had actually attempted to relate his son's more boisterous moments with whatever preceded them. No cake. There were various possible explanations but, he conceded, one had to be six months old to know what makes a six-month-old happy. Apart from the bottle, that is.

It was time to present Desmond with the prize Scotch. Suzy took Sacha, who was evidently going through his last coda, to the bedroom, while Alec wheeled himself to the kitchen, got some ice and fetched the King of the Scots.

Desmond was almost as elated as he'd been when he had announced that Alec's nomination for the Nobel Prize had been accepted. However, when Alec offered him ice, he very nearly exploded in disgust. Rising to his full five-foot-six-and-a-half, he wagged his finger an inch from Alec's nose, and thundered:

"Arre ye crrazy, lad, putting frrozen waterr into the nectarr of the Gods?" The Professor looked aghast.

"But you always..." Alec decided to stop. There was no reason to tempt his fate.

"I always nothing, lad. I neverr always anything. I judge everrything on its merrits. And this King of Them All deserrves morre rrespect than being diluted with a common solvent!"

The Professor took the bottle defensively in both palms as if to protect it from unworthy hands. Then he looked sideways at Alec and added in half tone.

"But if you pass y'rr glass a little closerr, I'll let you have a drrop orr two."

Alec did and got his generous drop or two. He thought himself lucky that John and Joan had gone to freshen up before dinner. It saved both, his face and reputation. He would never again offer a common solvent to anyone sniffing anything more ancient than a twelve-year-old.

As usual, the dinner was simple. None of them liked to eat a lot before retiring. Suzy laid Sacha in the tiny cot, which Maria had brought for him from her own home. Maria, in spite of the Professor's five guests, not to mention Matt, was a tower of strength. She took looking after them all in her stride. She acted more like a mother hen, than a maid. Suzy developed a genuine affection for her. Maria had never complained, never been too tired to do anything. If only there were more Marias in the world, she'd once told Desmond.

"Ah, they don't make them like Maria anymore. She's one in a million. She's been looking after this shack for over twenty years. She was about sixteen when she started. And she was as good then as she is now."

"Is she single, then?" Suzy was taken aback.

"Don't you believe it. Last time I visited her home, she had three little ones and she confessed that the forth one was on the way!"

"How does she manage all this then? My hands are full just with Sacha."

"As I've just told you, lass, they don't make them like Maria any more. There is, of course, her mother who looks after the children when Maria's here. And her auntie, and grandmother, and probably half the village."

And here, she now has Matt to help, he almost added, but pulled short. He couldn't quite figure out Matt.

No one could.

With Sacha asleep, Suzy picked up a book and stretched out next to Alec's chair. After a page or two, she put her book down.

"What did happen exactly, yesterday? In, you know, the place you visited?"

Suzy found the Atlantis story a little corny. Like a *cliché* dating back to Alec's youth, at which time his imagination took him to all sorts of unlikely places. She tried hard not to sound flippant about the whole thing.

For a long time Alec didn't answer. She was used to that. Many years ago she used to think that Alec hadn't heard her. By now she'd learned that Alec never answered unless he thought about his answer first. His thoughts may have been spontaneous but his words were invariably measured.

"It's not just what happened, it is rather how it happened," he said at last.

She waited. She knew that, given time, she would get an account worth waiting for. He'd never disappointed her yet.

"Well, first of all, the reality there seemed to have responded to my curiosity. When I wanted to learn something, conditions appeared that enabled me to satisfy my wants. In fact, in hindsight, it seems they responded to my subliminal thoughts."

Here Alec described the strange relationship between his desire for information and its apparent availability. As best he could he described the wall-map of the land, ocean, and later of the solar system.

"It was quite incredible. The moment I wanted to learn about my whereabouts, the map appeared on the wall. When I became interested in the historical context, the solar system appeared. And this was the punch line: our solar system with an additional planet. Such a planet, between the orbits of Mars and Jupiter could only have existed in the very distant past where the present asteroid belt is."

He didn't tell her how he apparently reverted the solar system to its present configuration. Frankly, he was scared to even think about it. This was the case when the reality responded to his subliminal thoughts. The extra planet collided with his perception of reality. What he did tell her, though, was about the apparent resolution of inertia. Finally, he told her about his desire to find out what he really looked like.

"I don't mind telling you that it scared the living daylights out of me," he admitted at last. "I hardly looked human at all. Can you imagine? A living mirror? Those guys who inhabited my dream were more advanced than we shall be hundreds of years from now. And yet, they seemed to be living in the distant past..."

In all this time Suzy hasn't said a word. She listened looking at Alec, as though afraid that he might peek-a-boo again. She's heard about lucid dreams, but this was well beyond anything she'd read.

"You know," Alec started again after a long pause, "in Atlantis I'd lost my physical body but retained my own power of imagination. Or, except for my physical characteristics, I remained myself. I wonder what might happen in other realities in which I might also lose my imaginary powers. Like the difference I'd once experienced between the Far Country and the Home Planet. If you recall, one was based on the powers of imagination, the other on our mental conceptualization. Not the same, by a long shot."

"I remember very well, darling. We discussed it many times. I almost feel as though I'd been there with you," Suzy said.

It was apparent that she resented not being able to have 'traveled' with him. It was a part of him, which, it seemed, they could never share. Not fully.

"You must have thought about it…" he turned to a different subject, "the only difference between animals and humans is that animals are in a state of being, while humans––becoming. I am not talking about biological evolution only of consciousness, which takes advantage of it. Becoming is a conscious process. Sacha is still mostly in the first, or primal or perhaps the transitional stage. For becoming we need self-awareness, and in him this condition is just awakening…"

Suzy loved Alec expounding his theories.

"By those standards not many people would qualify to be called human," she put in with a grin. "But, you may be right. I've read somewhere that in the biological sense, evolution advances at a rate somewhere between dead slow and dead slow. I think it was James Burke, the science historian, who'd said it. Barring accidents, evolution would not advance at all. But now, for the first time in history, we, humans, seem to be standing at the edge of taking charge of our evolution. I'd think that once we've defined the genome, fully, the rest would be just hard work."

"You're right, of course, but it's not quite what I had in mind. I was thinking not of the development of our genes, our physical envelope, but of that, which resides in it. That is, if the two can be treated as separate concepts. Like id, ego and superego we discussed before."

She nodded and closed her eyes. Her knit brow indicated that she was concentrating on Alec's every word.

"I'm beginning to suspect that the realities of the past, such as Atlantis, or Lemuria, or any other civilization which appears only in esoteric literature, or seems buried in the hoary past, do not disappear as though never having existed. Somewhere, in our genes, there seems to linger a distant echo. An archaic memory of something not easily accessible."

Alec pushed his chair against the wall and leaned his head on the partition for support, as though against a headboard. His eyes, as was usual on such occasions, were searching the horizon that he could just see through the corner window.

"Past civilizations," he went on, "continue in some kind of limbo or virtual reality, which may or may not be accessed and/or even populated by intelligent species. Now that I think about it, the body I occupied in Atlantis may not have been human at all—unless we redefine what we mean by human altogether..."

Suddenly Alec stopped.

He recalled that the body he'd occupied in Atlantis was dead on his departure. Perhaps the man, if it had been a man, just died on my arrival and I'd only used his body for convenience. This concept was too involved for an instant analysis... perhaps later, he mused. This subject was the one thing he didn't share with Suzy. Confessing to the possibility that in that reality he may have been a zombie was not a pleasant realization. There was one other detail: that man's eyes had been almost red, as if blood shot. Could the sun have affected the population of the Earth differently then? Assuming it was Earth...

"You mean as referring to self-awareness rather than a particular species?"

"Precisely. If they look similar, and exhibit self-awareness we would or should probably accord them human status."

"How generous of us..." Suzy did not approve of human superiority. In Montreal she was a part-time member of a society that was involved in forming cells of political pressure to restore ecological balance. She thought that the biblical statement in the first book of Genesis that, in the interpretation of fundamentalists, give man the right to exploit and subject all other species on earth, was a pathological misnomer.

"I didn't mean this in a condescending way," he looked up at her. "Surely, Sue, you know me better than that?"

"Sorry. It's just that with the riots and all, we're hearing so much about exploitation of man by man, it begins to sound as if some of us belong to a different species right here and now." There was a trace of sadness in her voice. Suzy wanted all people to be nice and generous. She'd never asked herself if she was.

And then they both stopped talking. They both looked, simultaneously, at Sacha. He was lying quietly, breathing deeply as though enjoying the sea air. But it was his eyes that startled them both. Sacha wasn't sleeping. His blue eyes were wide open, and they could both swear that he smiled his approval at their musings. As they both leaned over his cot, Sacha let out a long, joyful, high-pitched note. A single, melodious tone that swelled, rose, and then diminished to almost a whisper. Then he closed his eyes and slept without uttering another sound.

Suzy and Alec decided to follow his example. As if by magic, there was a gentle knock on the door, and Matt's massive frame filled the doorframe. He lifted Alec from the chair, and placed him on the bed with the ease with which Suzy handled Sacha. His task done, the giant withdrew without a word.

Only then Alec realized that he hadn't told Suzy about being able to walk in the other body. The hairy, dead man's body. Somehow, right now, it seemed a lot less important. Also, he detected in her eyes a certain reticence to accepting his attitude towards his experiences. If felt as though she was humouring him—not actually denying that none of it ever happened, but giving it as much credence as one would to a vivid dream.

"Either that, or I need an extensive session on a psychiatrist's couch..." he murmured. He didn't like the sound of his own voice.

Yet, for reasons that were hard to define, they both wondered if they would ever learn to share their dreams. They both wanted to.

Perhaps...

***

15

Return to the Far Country

They **drove back together,** as previously, only this time they all ended up in the young Baldwins' residence. Suzy insisted that before her parents return to Canada, they should at least enjoy a late lunch together, and then she and Matt would drive them to the airport, while Alicia and Desmond could reminisce about the holidays while babysitting Sacha. Professor needed very little convincing. Alec remained silent.

As for Matt, well, he was becoming an enigma. Since coming to live with them, he hasn't taken a single day off.

"You never know when I might be needed," he affirmed.

He was right, of course. Alec not only couldn't get in or out of the chair on his own, but he couldn't even reach for a book on a higher shelf, reach for a glass to get some water, nor take care of his own sanitary needs. His arms, better for a short while in Solana Beach, were again loosing their strength. They thought of taking him to New York where a specialist claimed to have achieved some sort of breakthrough with back injuries, but Alec categorically refused.

"They've done all the tests on me that they're going to do," he stated with utter conviction." Then his voice wavered. "I can't explain to you how I know," he said, turning to Suzy, "but I am convinced that this is something I have to do myself."

"Perhaps, but how can we help you, darling?" She did her best to blink away tears welling in her eyes.

Alec looked up at her like a boy who was caught doing something naughty.

"There was a time, Sue, when I thought I was simply going the wrong way. Now? Now I seem to be walking in circles. Like people…" he added after a momentary pause, "Like people I've always looked down on."

Matt looked on at this interchange, his face, even as his large frame, frozen in Sphinxian immobility. There was pain in his eyes, only no one noticed.

After six days at Desmond's house on the shores of the mighty Pacific, Los Angeles looked and smelled overpopulated. Alec, in a moment of renewed hope, decided that the moment he could afford it, they would buy something further out, even if it meant commuting for an hour each day. Initially, the avoidance of driving for hours was exactly why he bought the apartment close to Caltech. He thought commuting was a waste of time. Now, he was having seconds thoughts. He apparently hadn't noticed that well in excess of five million other angelic citizens shared his newly acquired sentiment. This preference accounted, in large measure, for the homicidal tendencies one developed commuting on the Californian Expressways.

Later, assuming his eventual recovery, it would turn out that his new aspirations had been little more than a theoretical exercise. A place such as the Professor's, which Desmond, if a little unfairly, called a shack, did not come on the market under two or three million dollars.

"When I got my shack, m'lad, rreal estate prrices werre a frraction of what they arre today," Desmond McBride announced proudly.

The day after their return, they settled into their usual routine. The only difference was that they managed to convince Alicia to stay with them for the foreseeable future. This gave Suzy much more freedom. Matt did a marvelous job tending to Alec, but Sacha needed a woman's touch. Within a couple of days, Suzy returned to her painting classes. Within a week, however, she discovered that she could learn much more from Alicia than from the less-than-successful teachers at the school. Both ladies began painting with vengeance. Suzy said she'd never had so much fun before. Outside sailing, that is.

Alec, thanks to Matt, was again busy with his lectures.

Some days later, completely out of the blue and without any preamble, Suzy asked Alec point blank: "When we were sitting on the beach, and later when we took the same stroll, did you notice something peculiar happening with the ocean? The waves, I mean?"

"Yes," he conceded, turning away. He wasn't quite ready to discuss the subject.

"It was you, wasn't it?" She wouldn't give in so easily.

Alec hated discussing phenomena that were as incomprehensible to him as the velocity of thought-waves. Assuming there were such a thing as thought-waves.

"I didn't command the waves to retreat, if that's what you mean. I can't. Oh, believe me, I tried! I tried it and nothing happened. I know that I can't. Yet, well, the elements, if you will, seem to respond to something inside of me."

"And you have no explanation at all?"

"Not as yet," he was hedging. She sensed it but didn't press. He, on the other hand, knew that she wasn't buying it. Not altogether.

"You know, when you're writing a thesis, you write the beginning last." He sounded as though he'd changed the subject. "It's a sort of resume of all your conclusions, which, when presented at the beginning the reader knows what the paper is all about. The body of the work then serves as an explanation of how you've reached your conclusions. Do you follow me?"

She nodded.

"Well, it's not as simple as all that. When I had to write my conclusions, I remember sitting in front of my computer for four days, not being able to even start. I had no problems with the body of work, you understand, but the conclusions, the quintessence, the crux of the matter, just wouldn't come in a comprehensive form. I knew, of course, what it was, but... well, as I've said, it wouldn't come."

He looked up at Suzy, as if gauging her attention. Satisfied, he continued.

"On the fifth day, I decided to put the Theory of Information to the test. I opened my iMac and closed my eyes. I then told myself that all the information I need is available in me, and is ready to be put into word. I sat there till I convinced myself beyond a shadow of doubt that the Information was there to be had. I then sat still, not even trying to write anything at all. This was after a four-day mental block, you understand. Well, the next thing I knew, all my conclusions had been neatly typed. So neatly that they did not need a single correction. Oh, I wrote them all right. I remember watching my fingers do a machine-gun staccato on the keyboard. Only I've never been quite so neat before. The clock said that it took me less than three hours. Under normal condition, a couple of weeks of painstaking work checking all data, comparing different sources and so forth would be considered fast."

There was a prolonged silence. At long last Suzy sighed as if making up her mind.

"Did you know," she asked, "that is precisely how Mozart is said to have composed? He didn't start till he knew the entire composition, and then just wrote it all down. No errors, no corrections. As if it was all there, ready and waiting for him."

"So I am not crazy?" Alec was only half-serious, but there were signs of his tension dissipating even as Suzy spoke.

"Darling," Suzy smiled her reassurance, "painters do that sort of thing all the time. Sculptors talk of just removing the unwanted pieces of stone to reveal the sculpture that was always there, within the block of rock, ready and waiting to see the light of day. It is the most natural creative process I know."

Alec, for all his studies of physics, didn't know that. After a while the usual far away look returned to his eyes. "My thesis, Mozart's music, waves, even what we used to call 'inner travels', they're all to do with our perception of reality. And the relationship of reality to consciousness. Or whatever we are aware of at our deepest level, in, well... in our heart of hearts as poets would say..."

He looked at Suzy. She nodded, but again didn't push.

"When consciousness leaves our bodies—we die. I don't mean leave the body partially, as in sleep, daydream, or even profoundly, as in a coma. But completely. You cannot stay alive without consciousness. We say a stone is not alive because it is not conscious. In those terms, you can define consciousness as life itself. People who define life as God, would have to assign the same appellative to consciousness."

"God is consciousness?"

"Something like that. Full consciousness that is, to which few, if any of us, can lay claim. But total awareness is awareness of totality. That, I always thought, is what people mean by God."

'I am Life' Suzy remembered her books. "Who is I, in that case?"

"I am. *I am* is the awareness of life and *I am* is the expression of consciousness. The two are inseparable. You might say they are one. Not as Cartesians say 'I think therefore I am', only 'I am conscious, therefore I am'."

"Or I am consciousness..." Suzy added wonderingly. "It's a simple as that?"

"I don't think it was ever supposed to be complicated. The religions made it complicated. They would not recognize that we are more than meets the eye."

"I thought that's exactly what they said."

"No way. According to all the religions I've laid my eyes on, the various theologians claimed that we are nothing, sinners they call us, but the big Ju-ju is somewhere out there, granting or not granting us higher traits. In fact what defines man is the degree of his awareness of his totality or wholeness. Without this awareness a man is hardly human."

"You've said something like this before, haven't you?"

"Probably. I'm fed up with the blind continuously leading the blind. It ceased to be funny."

Alec's ideas, if one could call them his, were beginning to find a semblance of order. He was a long way from full understanding, but he'd taken the first step. He accepted that just because he could not dissect something with a scalpel or smash it to smithereens in a Super Collider, it didn't mean that that something did not exist. The acceptance of this premise was, for him, a continuous process of reconciliation of his mind with that over which he had much less control.

"And all this has something to do with moving oceans about?" Suzy smiled in spite of herself.

"It all has to do with reality as we know it. Back then, I imagined the ocean different than it was. I didn't question if I or anyone else could do it. I didn't doubt that it could happen. I just assumed that it could. I think I held a 'why not' type of cavalier attitude. But, simultaneously, I was deadly serious about it. I thought that if it could happen, then it would. I left it at that."

"I see," Suzy said quietly. She decided not to ask him any more questions. Some of his answers had been worse than her questions. If he was right, then why couldn't he cure himself?

Alec must have read her thoughts. He glanced again at his legs. And at some level of perception he began hating Sandra and all she stood for. He rebelled at his total inability to oppose her power with his own will. He was rebelling against her interference. This frame of mind was the beginning of the darkest depression he'd ever suffered.

He was on the verge of giving up.

"Giving up what?" he asked himself. But he heard no answer. He'd lost the ability to listen.

It seems that dreams were the only thing in Alec's life that kept him sane. The night following their last discussion on the nature of consciousness, Alec made his first 'trip', for the want of a better word, to the Far Country. It was a return trip, the first after many years. He actually smiled at the thought that nothing had changed. Well, almost nothing.

Somehow, his universe has grown. It was hosting more stars, a greater variety of nebulae, of galaxies of different shapes and sizes. Whirlpool galaxies spun on their axes creating currents that extended for many light-years. Their spheroidal sisters, some dressed in cosmic sombreros, others arranged in vast clusters, so vast that light took a million years to shine upon itself. All these, and so many, many others, enriched this universe, which Alec thought he'd once known so well. Yet it was all so familiar. Perhaps the universe hasn't changed, after all.

Perhaps I have. Am I really the only reality?

His thoughts seemed to come from so deep within, almost as if they weren't his own.

Alec also found that he wasn't attached to any particular segment of space, but rather wandered about until his attention became anchored to a particular point of interest. Then, the object, or group of objects, grew, expanded, the colours previously diluted by distance increased in intensity and diversity. Only all this took place faster that he could think.

He turned his attention towards the familiar Crab Nebula. For more than a thousand years it spread its influence across the vastness of space. The fragments of its body were still expanding at more than a thousand kilometers per second. At its source an ashy orb attested to its former glory. Alec had no idea how he knew of its precarious history.

I was born of the white-bluish dwarf still at your heart...

Only then Alec realized that he was not aware of his body. Not just his of his legs, but his whole body. The memories of his previous visits to this realm flooded his... his what?

My soul? What is soul? The questions came and disappeared with the velocity of light. *My consciousness? That's right. My consciousness.*

The realization of his own beingness flooded his awareness.

My awareness is the mirror of whatever I come in contact with by placing my attention on it. But am I not just conscious of the reality I myself created?

The Nebula continued to expand.

So what is attention?

He directed his mind at a distant star which shimmered as though with new light. It was as far as his attention could reach. The next instant, he was witnessing the explosion of a gigantic sun. A cosmic wind shot by him and through him, without touching his senses. He didn't even feel the heat. Almost simultaneously the eternal silence of Outer Space was filled with a sustained roar as a billion, billion thunders that raced after the photons spreading the news of a new beginning.

Attention is....

He almost had it but it... the attention, had been distracted by the Super Nova. The brightness was awesome.

How come it doesn't burn my eyes? And as the question formed that answer was there, apparent: *I have no eyes...*

He could see without eyes, he could feel without a body, he could hear without his ears.

Who am I. Who am I... who am I...?

I am...

I AM

That was all that formed in his awareness. Just that. I am.

"I am that I am," his mind mirrored its own definition. And for some inexplicable reason this still incomprehensible knowledge filled him with unbelievable joy. He laughed at the stars; he embraced the individual atoms with contentment. He impregnated each photon with his pleasure. The countless particles flying in all directions became saturated with serenity. There was another word for it back on Earth. They call it love, down there.

Here, it felt more like Oneness.

What would he give to have Sandra by his side...

But there was no Sandra. He'd killed her. He destroyed his memories of her. Or tried to. He alone would rule these inner worlds. No one would dictate to him the nature of true reality. No one! He and he alone would find the source of his power. Within himself. Within or without his body.

What would I give to have Sandra by my side...

Within the impenetrable darkness of the night, an even darker shape detached itself from the wall and bent over Alec's body. For a moment the shape stood there, stooped, as though checking if all was well. If one could see in the dark, one would detect concern on the man's angular features. A deep concern born of something akin to fear. Only it wasn't normal fear. It was dismay born of compassion.

In the morning Alec's depression got worse. Suzy had already left the bedroom some time ago to look after Sacha. She always tried to leave the bedroom before Matt came in. It was, she thought, less embarrassing for her husband.

When Matt came to get him out of bed, Alec dallied.

"I feel tired," he lied. "Just let me be."

Matt withdrew and sat at the far side of the room.

"I don't need you here," Alec barked. "I don't need anyone. No one at all!" He all but shouted.

Matt didn't move. He sat as immobile as though cast in granite. After some fifteen minutes, he got up and set about preparing for Alec's morning ablutions. The special clothing he wore, a sort of outsized swaddling band that went under the name of adult diapers, took care of his nocturnal emissions. But, on occasion, the outer clothing also had to be changed. As often the sheets. Each morning they went through this embarrassing procedure. Hardly a word had been uttered. Matt worked quickly, efficiently, and with minimum effort imposed on Alec' part. He was in no position to help.

Then Matt administered a massage to restore at least partial circulation into the parts of Alec's body that remained immobile. This took a good twenty minutes. When Alec still attended to his duties at Caltech, all his lectures had been scheduled for the afternoon hours. This gave him and Matt plenty of time to do what was necessary.

Usually Alec wheeled himself to take breakfast in the nook of the living room. Today his arms, even hands were numb. Matt took him to the table and waited.

"Well?" Alec asked without looking up. He was leaning over the table.

"Is there anything you would like for breakfast, Sir?"

"Surprise me," Alec sneered with an air of abject indifference.

Matt went to the kitchen, prepared a poached egg and toast, and brought it to Alec who was still slouching over the table. Matt sat next to him, and with infinite care began feeding him. Now and then, Matt put down the fork and held a cup of coffee to Alec's mouth, aiming the plastic straw between his lips. The whole procedure was eerie for its absolute quiet. After breakfast Matt broke the silence.

"What is your agenda for the day, Sir?" Everyone called Matt by his first name. Matt didn't reciprocate. He maintained his distance.

"I don't care," came the answer. "I just don't give a shit."

Matt bowed in silence and withdrew to clean up the bedroom. He was back within a relatively short time. Alec hadn't moved. His eyes seemed to wander over some non-existent horizon. Slowly he looked up at Matt's impassive face. This is a man I've learned to love, he thought. This is a man... but he refused to think any more. Resignedly, he withdrew even deeper into his shell. A shell that was rapidly becoming empty.

***

16
Magic

Thursday nights were long reserved for dinners with Desmond. Not that Old Des never dropped in on other days, especially now that Alicia was gracing the young'uns' nest with her presence. But not only Desmond—everyone looked forward to the Thursday get-togethers. Usually, they met early for a few long, relaxing drinks. Ladies sipped wine, while Alec and the Professor did a little justice to Scotch. Luckily for Alec, who recovered partial use of his arms and hands, Scotch was of the common garden variety, and Alec had not incurred the excessive wrath of the Professor's gustatorial ethic by adding a 'fair amount of solvent to protect their gastro-intestinal systems', but rather to make the salubrious nectar last longer.

On March 18th, they celebrated Alicia's tri-months-versary.

The dinner had been preceded by a tour of Alec's office, Alicia's bedroom, and all the other rooms wherein the vertical surfaces that lent themselves for hanging a variety of canvases. The object of the exercise was to tell which paintings had been 'perpetrated' (as Alec referred to them) by Alicia, and which 'committed' (as Alicia called them) by Suzy. The Professor thought them all to be brilliant. In fact he offered to buy them all, providing someone would explain to him what they represented. This brought protests from both ladies, and a weak applause from Alec.

But not all of the remarks were that serious. There was a very discernible difference between Alicia's and Suzy's style. Not just in the application of the brush but the manner in which the two ladies approached their art. Alicia preferred oils and watercolours; her brush-stroke was warm, romantic

as though she'd been painting the love she felt for whatever
caught her attention. Suzy couldn't have been more different.
After only a few months she'd given up the brush for a
spatula, which progressively got broader as her confidence
increased. Her strokes seemed to suck out the essence of the
colours from her subjects, concentrate them and place them in
such relation to each other as to create the most explosive
effect. Her painting seemed to compensate for her temper,
which at least of late, she had managed to keep on a short
rein. Also she much preferred acrylics to oils, as the former
dried faster and were soluble in water. And the idea of rinsing
her spatula in water was much preferable to soaking it in a jar
of smelly turpentine.

Finally, the ladies decided to have a two-man, women in
this case, exhibition in the corridors of the Architectural
department of Caltech. Assuming the department would
agree, of course.

"Oh, they'll agrree, all rright," the Professor assured.
"I'll see to that m'self."

So that was that. The following Saturday Alicia was
booked on the midday flight to Montreal. The overtones of
sadness were hovering in the air even today. One could detect
a slightly forced gaiety. The Professor tried to recount as
many jokes as he could recall. In the meantime, Alec, who'd
recovered partially from his physical and emotional nadir of a
week ago, was busy offering Matt help in toping-up the
drinks. For her part, Alicia appeared none too keen to return
to the solitude of her Montreal home.

"You're all here, now," she said. "You're all I've got."

And with that she withdrew to her room to attend to
some forgotten chore. She couldn't face her son in the mood
she was in. He needed cheering, not sad faces.

Only Suzy held her own.

As of last week, Alec and Matt slept together in the
adjoining apartment. It was easier on Suzy when Alec called
for help in the middle of the night. She needed her sleep to be
able to give Sacha her best. And Suzy too would miss Alicia,

perhaps most of all. With the hours spent together, painting, they grew closer than most daughters and in-laws can grow. They also shared other interests, from their taste in books, to the love of sailing, and even to the dryness of their red wine. They behaved more like sisters than what their relative ages would indicate. Alicia, single-handedly, managed to fill in the gap left by Suzy's Montreal friends. And Suzy loved her for it.

After a week's break, Alec resumed his lectures at Caltech. More and more publications mentioned his Theory. More articles appeared in the scientific press, each requiring his scrutiny, correction if need be, to protect the purity of his concept. In some ways, Alec has become very much his own man. In others, he was no more than a spectator. There were no creative juices stirring his imagination. On the other hand, he no longer needed to hang on to Desmond's coat tails. He gave his lectures at Caltech and wrote such articles as have been expected of him to foster the advancing research done by other scientists in the field.

Nevertheless, for now, he delayed accepting a string of invitations for another Pan-American lecture tour. The thought that his physical condition was temporary kept him going. At work he kept busy. At home he spent hours just watching Sacha. For now, he'd achieved an innocuous condition of mental and physical stasis.

And then, for no apparent reason, he was swamped with a treacherous flood of doubts.

The Thursday after Alicia left for Montreal, Alec decided to talk to Desmond about his purported alter ego, Sandra. He resolved to divulge just enough to get the benefit of the older man's experience.

"You're not telling me much, lad," Desmond looked up at his favourite adopted son. Even when both were sitting, Des had to look up at Alec. "Don't you think you could trust me with the truth?" There was not even a suggestion of the

Scottish r's in Desmond's answer. There was concern and a little sadness.

"It's not very scientific..." Alec started again.

"I was a man before I became a scientist, lad. And I still am, no matter what they write about me."

There was a hint of smile in Desmond's tone. It helped. Alec needed to relax particularly when dealing with this subject.

"So you won't laugh?"

"That I can promise. But laughter never really hurt anybody, and many it helped."

Alec had spent the next hour and a half giving the old Professor a *précis* of his 'inner' life. It had to be brief, but Alec had learned to be concise and precise at the same time. His scientific training came in handy. After he finished, Dr. McBride continued to look pensive. He remained silent for so long that Alec suspected that he'd lost interest. But, knowing the Professor, he didn't interrupt. He waited even though the palms of his hands got a bit moist. It wasn't every day that Alec bared his soul to anyone. No matter how close. And, frankly, this could cost him his job. He was supposed to be a scientist. To think like a scientist.

"You've got to be scientific about this, if at all possible," Desmond said at long last. "Since Pythagoras, to this very day mathematicians have been trying to equate reality with a mathematical equation. The transforms, the fractals, they're all tending, to my mind, towards the same direction. Maybe they'll find that God, or Ultimate Reality, is a number, although Lederman prefers to think of Her as a beautiful melody. It would be unscientific to deny your experiences, as you call them, just because they do not fit neatly into your existing mathematical coordinates."

And again the Professor lapsed into silence.

Then, after some more pensive minutes, the Professor asked Alec a number of questions. They were as broad and far-reaching as Alec's story. Dr. McBride asked Alec about his youth, his imagination, his interpretation of his inner travels, his aspirations, even about Atlantis. Finally he asked the vital question.

"Does any of this fit in with the Information Theory?"

Alec explained his own understanding of how there was a link, though not as yet very tenable. But it didn't contradict it either.

"They're like two parallel lines. They appear to meet in infinity."

Although the Professor was strictly a theoretician dealing with quantum mechanics, he, like all theoretical physicists, was well acquainted with the theory of relativity. In an Einsteinian universe, two parallel lines did meet. Rather like longitudinal lines on the Earth represented on a globe. According to Einstein, space, due to gravity, curved upon itself.

"That's what you've got to be, lad. Scientific. If what happens contradicts your mind, then you'll venture into religion. If it doesn't—you're on sound ground. But... it's not going to be easy, is it?"

"No, Sir. Although, thinking of Einstein... he did say that science without religion is lame..." Alec looked for support for his cause which although it had nothing to do with any religion, it did sound like a construct of some New Age movement.

"...while religion without science is blind. Aye, he did say that. Make sure you are not groping in the dark and up a blind alley. At the same time, since we're banding quotations from our favourite relativist, he also said that the only real valuable thing is intuition," the Professor wielded both, the rod and the staff.

Then Desmond sat up and looked Alec in the eye.

"If you cannot deny what you experienced, then it must be true. Unless you are crazy. Are you?" There was little if any humour in the Professor's tone.

Alec smiled. "Why don't you tell me."

"I'm not a psychiatrist, and if I were, I doubt I would trust myself. But you don't have that luxury, lad. You must trust yourself. If you don't—who will?"

So it was all down to trusting one's intuition. No matter how improbable, how seemingly unscientific, how shrouded in mystery, he had to plod on. Einstein *and* McBride could not both be wrong. Not in Alec's mind. And then he remembered his original hero, Richard Feynman. The man, who'd made quantum theory almost palatable to mere mortals, once said: 'It does not do harm to the mystery to know a little about it. Far more marvelous is the truth than any artist of the past imagined!'

Three weeks later came that fateful night from which Alec took a good week to recover. Matt put him to bed at the usual time. Alec looked tired but relatively relaxed, content after a busy day. The dream started, like an ordinary dream. Alec found himself sitting on the sofa in the living room. He found that he was perspiring heavily, his pajama damp on his back, his forehead covered with beads of sweat. At the very edge of his awareness, he knew he was still dreaming. After all, he couldn't have walked to the sofa.

At the same time, he couldn't be sure. "Did Matt put me here…?"

Usually, on waking, Alec enjoyed vivid memories of his dreams. This time it took a while before he recalled what happened. It was almost as though he wanted to block the dream from his memory. But to no avail. First in snippets, little fragments woven into a jagged cloth, then with an overwhelming power the recall forced itself on his mind.

It hadn't been a dream, it was a nightmare.

He'd dreamt that he was going back in time. Not in a single instant, as in the case of Atlantis, but rather like a spectator watching disjointed events, as history unfolded itself before his chimerical eyes. It was like watching a movie. A flash of the Second, then First World War;

chimneys belching smoke of the early industrial revolution; a procession of magnificent buildings he'd associated with intellectual Renaissance. All this was over in seconds, as though viewed from a fast moving train. Finally his temporal regression reached the dark ages.

That was when the nightmare had started.

None of it made sense. Not waken sense. He felt drawn by tremendous forces—struggling for supremacy? It was as though he were pulled in all directions, at once, by powerful tides of human psyche. He saw images of devils with fiery eyes, demons with tails split into multiple prongs as depicted by various medieval artists, who must have made the same chimerical journey. Dante's inferno was little more than a foretaste of what had been really taking place in peoples' minds, perhaps their souls. Hatred was palpable; the desire to kill and exploit permeated the air the breathed. People were being burned at the stake, not for any transgressions or purported blasphemy, but for fun. The perpetrators, clad in lay and priestly robes alike, danced around the funeral pyres, rejoicing and screaming praise to their dark masters.

Next he witnessed a senseless, convoluting mass of human bodies, contorting in wild, ritualistic gyrations at some satanic rock concert. The cacophony of noise and blinding lights complemented the image of utter desolation.

The image shifted to a large group of people, their faces frozen into immobility of expectation. They were looking up to a wooden platform where men in long red coats and skullcaps were readying themselves to flay a woman. Not just to scalp her, but to strip off her skin as one might skin a hare or a rabbit. She'd been tied, hand and foot to a pole, naked. She was still alive. Alec covered his ears with his palms in a futile attempt to block her agonizing screams.

It must have been at that moment that he'd crawled out of his bed and staggered to the living room, where he'd collapsed on the sofa. He must have managed it on his own. By the time he'd awoken, his mind refused to support the memories. Now, they were creeping back. Slowly, vividly. In minute detail.

Had such things really happened? Ever?

He shook his head, then closed his eyes against the flood of new memories. He refused to allow them into his conscious mind. By shear effort of will he blocked them out. He hoped, permanently.

"Let them remain in the darkness were they belong," he whispered, wiping his moist forehead for the tenth time.

At first light, Matt found him asleep on the sofa. Gently, he returned Alec's limp body to his bed. The expression on the big man's face gave nothing away. Not even surprise at Alec making his way across the room on his own.

The following day, Alec still had no idea why this nightmare had been thrust upon him. Discounting the Atlantis experience, he hadn't experienced any dreams that vivid since the time he'd found himself suspended in the center of the universe, in the Far Country. He was thirteen then. There and then he'd learned that wherever and whenever he was, his presence defined the center of the universe. Not other people's but his very own, particular, subjective universe. "I am the only reality," he remembered hearing his own thoughts reverberating in the vastness of cosmos. What of others? What of the people who led saintly lives; of monks and nuns, of hermits or martyrs of all religions? What of the monsters of today's nightmares? What were their universes like? Were their universes as real? Was there any similarity? Should there be? Why? Why was it that every man, woman, and child, had to build, create, their very own, their unique, individual universe? Why was it necessary?

Then Alec remembered the dark ages, during which autocrats, demagogues tried, often by force, to impose their realities, their universes, on others. Some time later he suspected that, at long last, he understood the reason for his nightmare. He was to think twice before attempting to convince anyone of the validity of his own reality. No matter how good or bad. The consequences of authoritarian, theocratic dogmatism had been too dismal, too lurid, too ghastly to contemplate. He could share his findings, offer them as a free gift, but never, never impose them on others.

But the most frightening thing he'd discovered was that the vast majority of those self-styled fanatics suffered from a deep-seated conviction that they were doing the right thing.

The following two weeks passed without any unusual incidents. Sacha was growing at an alarming rate. Suzy resumed her painting. Alec recovered reasonable use of his arms—at least up to the elbows. He could move his shoulders, but only with considerable pain. Matt continued to remain practically invisible.

They were all reasonably content with their fate.

Following his discussion with Desmond, Alec had taken a week off to digest the menu of philosophical *hors d'oeuvres,* before returning to serious work. He needed a clear mind, unimpeded by extracurricular factors. Finally he'd settled down. He didn't question, didn't meander from his chosen field, but stuck to the straight course. He was happy just living. Alas, it didn't last. The memories of his nightmare continued to haunt him.

Then it happened again.

It came upon him suddenly, without any apparent cause. As always, it happened at night. He felt it coming. He sensed it without being able to explain his premonitions. He rebelled. Another hallucination? He braced himself for the worst.

"Why me?" he asked the dark walls that seemed to close in on him cutting off any hope of escape.

"Why me?"

The walls remained silent. They stared back at him in stoic indifference. With a superhuman effort he managed to transfer his weight from his bed to the adjoining wheelchair. He rested for a minute, then pushed the wheels towards the window. From the vantage of the fourth floor street laps extended east and west like a string of golden nuggets marking the way to the unknown. Perhaps the past and the future? Here and there, a dark shadow of a man, his shoulders hunched, as though trying to shrink into non-existence, shuffled along the sidewalk.

"Is he a universe unto himself?" Alec couldn't help wondering. "Is he searching for the meaning of it all, whatever *it* might be?"

But the distant shadow wouldn't answer either. He could just hear the click-clack of stiletto heals of a working girl, her legs casting grotesque long shadows along the sidewalk; returning, dejected, from her night vigil?

"What of her universe?" he mused, a bitter smile, a snigger, momentarily distracting him from his own woes.

The night, the trees, the street maintained a covenant of silence. Only his heart wanted to scream, or at least to shout again and again in a recurrent protest to whoever might listen... "Why me? Why me?"

Silence.

"There are six billion people on Earth. And there are a trillion, trillion Earths scattered throughout the universe. And each entity here, and everywhere, must discover his and her own answer to the eternal question: *Why me...?*"

And as his hands moved his wheelchair back towards his bed, he perceived a nagging pulse in his heart, in his veins, in every cell of his body whispering, insisting, demanding to be heard, acknowledged.

Because I am, because I am, because...

Throughout this time Matt hasn't moved a muscle. Now he got up, lifted Alec from the wheelchair and carefully placed him back in bed. He covered him with a blanket—as carefully, as gently, as a mother would cover her baby. Without a word, in eerie silence, Matt returned to his own divan. Soon his breathing was once more slow and regular, that of a man at peace with himself.

Alec did not share Matt's serenity. He was not meant to rest much that night...

He was gazing at a large plaza. He stood, immobile, seemingly relaxed, looking down from the third story balcony of a sprawling palace. He was also much taller than he was in the reality he'd left behind. In his bed. Sleeping. But most of all, he *stood*. Yet something else was wrong.

"I don't belong here," he muttered. He was hardly aware of a disdainful sneer half-hidden by his thick moustache. A pointed beard hung loosely halfway down his chest.

"I don't belong, here," he repeated, this time out-loud. His voice was deep, raspy, seemingly used to giving orders.

The body he occupied didn't appear to mind. Alec knew he was elsewhen the moment he looked down. Even before he realized that he was standing on his own feet. Yet the next moment his identity began to waver. Not just his own body was missing but his emotional make up. He was already enjoying his new, seven-foot physique, his surroundings, his evidently exalted position. He enjoyed towering over others. Over the vassals. Masses of them.

His sneer widened his cruel mouth.

"Peasants," he spat out. "Bah!"

It was a judgment of mental satisfaction, even acceptance, without any emotional contentment. The next instant he sensed strange currents churning in the darkness behind him.

He shrugged. No one could harm him. *They can plot, but they have no power to carry out their puny schemes. Not any more.*

Outside the darkness became less acute. The moon, having cleared the clouds, offered enough light to permit the workers to continue with their labour. There was no time to stop. It could be too risky.

The towering gods had been hoisted, one by one, to face the ocean—to protect them all from the evil spirits. The gods, their expressions grim, immobile, frozen in stone forever, towered over the landscape, threatening anyone who would dare to approach their coast. The last colossus would be raised tomorrow; then, he could rest. From the day they'd started erecting the barrier, he had to use all his powers—great powers—even for the Third Son of the Third Son of the First King. Only his magic maintained the horrendous waves from smiting his people.

"People? Little more than slaves to their fears," his mouth twisted still farther, now reminiscent of a satanic grin. He alone offered and maintained protection from the enemy who rode the unprecedented surges.

The masses laboured below—sweat on their backs glistening in the moonlight. But the Goddess was waxing. They had to finish soon. They could only work at night, to keep their secret.

"Only my magic is strong enough," he affirmed, taking his powers for granted. Powers that by now he found intoxicating.

He held out his arms before him. Immediately, even in the relative darkness, he could see the workers turning their heads in uncanny unison, and slowly lowering themselves to their knees. Not to honour him, nor to give him praise. They did so out of abject fear. Out of inbred cowardice. They all knew that a single thought from his dark mind could kill any one of them easier than an arrow carrying fragments of Little Jewels on its tip. Some recovered from the poison of the worms, none from his wrath. Ever. So great were his powers. The powers of darkness.

That is what they all believed.

"Fools," he interrupted his own dark thoughts.

He'd never killed anyone. At least, not for many years. Yet, legends have a life of their own.

When he'd risen to the throne, his predecessor had attempted to kill him with his own evil spells. But he'd been well versed by his mother on how to fight them off. In that alone lay his real strength. He'd learned early, not to direct his own power at others, but to reflect their own evil at them. He'd never killed anyone, but he'd helped many to kill themselves. That was the real secret of his ascendancy; only no one suspected this truth. Not even his closest guards. No one was ever tempted to find out.

Occasionally people died. People who had dared to oppose him. They'd died in a variety of ways. He alone knew that the choice of death his enemies succumbed to had been their own. They'd chosen the horror that they'd wished upon him. This was the real essence of Black Magic. It wasn't really black; it was just highly polished. Like the Ancient Amulet on his royal chest.

For once, he smiled a benevolent smile.

It was the amulet his people have noticed. Their eyes were used to the darkness resulting from the constant, onerous, cloud cover. In recent times, fragments of moonlight were rare blessings. His enemies had darkened the sky. For them, the pale moonlight was like the dim sunshine they enjoyed on hazy days. Raising their arms and stretching them upwards in humble supplication, they slowly lowered themselves to the ground into a posture of absolute obeisance. He was not their master. He was their god.

"Arise!" He heard his own voice. He stepped back. His voice sounded like a horn blown by a bull elephant.

The Divine King had spoken. His minions could return to work. By his grace.

Alec slept late that morning. Images of a dark island... forest of tall monoliths towering over the waves... kept flooding his mind. He'd waken up a number of times, but the dream kept coming back like a mosquito trapped in a tent. As though he was meant to learn something. As if he would not be set free until he knew what lesson he was to memorize. Could this have been Sandra's doing?

Finally he awoke, feeling a stranger in his own bed. He found his six-foot-two frame meager, not sufficiently commanding to impress, to intimidate his people. He sensed a wave of disappointment.

And then he sat up with an ease he hadn't experienced for months. He looked around. Matt was still asleep. It was at this instant that Alec realized that he was still held in a vise of power. Only he wasn't wielding it. It was someone he'd once been. Portrayed? One wielding absolute power over life and death. And suddenly he was afraid. Afraid of the capacity that still lingered within him. Nothing, nothing was as despicable to him as the sensation of absolute power. Of power over others. Of controlling other people's minds. Of being someone else's god.

He shook his head.

Am I to be wary of my work? Is there such power in knowledge alone? More questions. What exactly am I to learn from my peculiar visions? And even as he formulated the last question in his mind he fell back on his pillows. Listless, prosaic like a rubber doll deprived of its dilating air. Once again he was hardly aware of his body.

"I am still just an observer," he whispered in amazement. "When shall I start living?"

And once again he rebelled against his fate. He felt anger. Anger at God, at Sandra, at fate, or just at his mental and physical ineptitude. He turned his eyes towards Matt. His massive body stirred, then relaxed again. But Matt couldn't offer to solve Alec's mounting enigma. It wasn't his job.

***

17
Hades

"**It must have been Lemuria,**" Alec told Suzy over breakfast. He'd already given her a rough sketch of the dream. "The South Sea Island was unmistakable. So were the statues."

"And I suppose you enjoyed playing god?" She'd decided to humour him. She had little to lose.

"I wasn't playing god, I was..." somehow even the joke of being a god over others was repugnant to him. He wondered how some people managed to sit in judgment over others, to control others' lives, when they had no idea what intricacies wove their avowed subjects' particular realities.

It was time to 'go' to the office. His arms retained enough dexterity to do his work. He couldn't quite propel himself in his wheelchair with his arms, but the electric motor took care of that. At least after last night's experience, once his anger subsided, he felt neither physically tired nor mentally exhausted as he had been after his glimpse of the Dark Ages. He hoped he would never have to witness the depth of human depravity again. Never.

"But the images of me cut in hard stone weren't bad at all," he confided after he finished the last sip of coffee. At least he imagined so. He felt it. He'd never actually saw himself there and then.

They chatted for another few minutes. Suzy remembered the time when Alec would run out, sprinting, like a student who might be late for his lecture. Actually, even in those days, he'd seldom scheduled his lectures for the mornings, but he enjoyed running. If he didn't have to carry a stuffed briefcase, he jogged all the way.

Suzy felt a tear forming in her eye. It was all such a very short time ago. Seemed like yesterday.

Alec was convinced that both dreams, or nightmares, had been etched in his subconscious for a purpose. It might have been to stop him from ever attempting to impose his views on others. He was to stay away from looking for converts to his own particular view of reality. History was replete with examples of insidious harm perpetrated by men who tried to impose their views on lesser minds. Even with the best of intentions.

But surely, it had nothing to do with the Information Theory. Was there power dormant in its equations? Or was it a question of casting pearls before swine?

He also had been shown that the emotional nature was cruel in the extreme. He strongly suspected that the religious imposition of beliefs had more to do with emotions than with intellectual appreciation. It was levying a strangle hold on people's feeling, which in turn would not allow their minds to function. In Lemuria, as he now called it, the power of the intellect was made evident to him. It was pure and simple black magic. There, in that strange body of his, he did not control people's emotions, he held a psychic garrote on their minds. Mind control was not emotional at all. It was cold, rational and calculated for maximum effect. If you controlled their minds, you were their God. If you controlled their emotions, you were more like Satan. He was not quite sure there was that much difference between them, although Satan did appear to be more cruel. Gods demanded obeisance. Satan hungered for blood. Both repelled him—virtually with equal force.

Suddenly he remembered that for the first time he'd forgotten to kiss Sacha when leaving home. He felt guilty. And then his thoughts of Sacha overlapped with the memory of his dream. He thought of Sacha's eyes. It came to him that even as good reflects only good, so evil can only reflect evil. We all live in houses of mirrors, he thought.

He was nearing Caltech.

Whatever else happens to me, he told himself, I'll do my darndest to avoid travelling in time through the Dark Ages, or any ages where a few wielded absolute control over the many. He hoped, dearly, that the horrid past was not making its way back to the present. There was considerable evidence that some men wielding power in the world today were practitioners of both emotional and mental control.

Right now.

Not in some God forsaken demagogic middle-eastern potentate, or some far-eastern oligarchy, but right here. At home. In the dear old US of A.

Alec got to the Institute feeling more alive. He could neither walk nor run, but he could think. He was ready for a good day's work. The Information Theory was not the only subject of Dr. Alexander Baldwin's lectures. He had developed informed opinions on a variety of subjects. They were all related to physics or often, more precisely, to mathematics. The subject was as broad as it was fascinating. He tried to present physics to aspiring scientists as a subject that would be to man today what religions once were. It was a search for truth. He recalled some of his early lectures in which he pointed out that early Greeks, or Athenians really, as Greece had not been at all homogenized in those days, accepted Apollo as their chief god.

"This Apollonian allegiance" he'd said in that early lecture, *"distinguished the rationalistic theology of the West from the mysticism of the East. And this was not only true of the early Pythagoreans, but of later philosophers to whom mathematics was the very foundation of philosophy. And mathematics will lead us to the truth, even as logic delivers us from evil."*

He'd taught this, believing firmly, at the time, that he'd been preaching the gospel of Truth. Now, he was not so sure. He still espoused mathematics as the only way to define objective reality, but... and this was the problem, his view of reality was becoming, quite unwittingly, more and more subjective.

And that he couldn't teach. It would not be 'scientific'. It would not be guided by logic alone. It seemed to him, that scientific or objective reality was a compromise. A sort of average derived from the countless individual realities, countless individual points of view.

Could it be that there was a link, a common ground, where the objective and the subjective realities met in a union of understanding? Could it be that God is both, a Number *and* a beautiful Melody? Why should we put limitations on the Infinite? Would that be a virtual oxymoron.

"And if He or She or It is, more power to Them, the Three-in-One," he muttered, grinning to himself.

Could it be that both the East and the West must seek a common ground to finally step on the right road to an objective reality that all man could espouse? Enjoy?

Or was man destined to remain, forever, the only reality. Forever trapped in the reality of his own making?

He feared the latter.

It was at moments like this that Alec needed support. He feared stagnant, though to others he was still the bright kid on the block. He was the one who was supposed to provide answers. That was his job. This was not a kindergarten where the boys and girls were led by the hand. This was the place, the agora, where you threw ideas in the hope that some of them would strike fertile ground. You didn't tell people what was right or wrong. You told them what axioms have not as yet been disproved.

"It is up to you, each one of you, to find your way," he told them, repeatedly. "I cannot tell you what is your subjective reality. There, within your realm, you are gods. The only gods. *And ye shall have no other gods before ye...*" he quoted from memory.

Suzy would have liked that last one. She liked to read up on mysteries of the East, even as he liked the logic of the West. And yet they loved each other. Perhaps this was the secret. Perhaps it was all as simple as that. Two peas in a single pod. Different peas, one pod. Now—was that mysticism or just plain logic?

"I must ask her," he promised himself.

And then there was Sacha. Sacha still sang, trolled, on special occasions. When he did, his eyes shone, sparkled, as though heaven had opened and allowed the stars to twinkle within them in celestial harmony. He had an incredible affinity for happiness. Not that he never cried. But his displeasures were few, far between, and normally well substantiated. Usually it had something to do with a food. The intake or the exhaust. Both were of vital importance. Perhaps, Alec thought, they should be more important to us all. We seldom think when, what, and how much we eat. We seem even less concerned with the reverse gear. We do not assign special times to the evacuation as we do to the intake. Perhaps we should. Perhaps if we did, we would be as exuberantly happy as Sacha was.

But food was not the sole preoccupation that stimulated Sacha's psyche. On occasion, both, Suzy and Alec noticed that Sacha attempted to manipulate their wills.

"It was as though he was checking how far he can push us. I had a cat once, in Montreal. When still a kitten, he did that to me a number of times. Or tried to." Then she laughed. "It's a little hard to admit, but he often succeeded!"

"I suppose we all try to find our ground. As a sort of base of operations," Alec agreed.

"Oh, but Sacha goes much further. A few times I had the distinct feeling that he was honing me, at night, during sleep, to do something to his liking," Suzy persisted.

"Just how would my son succeed where I have failed repeatedly?" Alec demanded.

"Very funny," Suzy ignored Alec's feeble attempt to steal the limelight. "Explain to me, why, on some days, I wake up with an overwhelming desire to take him to the park?"

"Perhaps you like taking him to..."

"On a day pouring with rain?"

They reached no conclusions, but agreed that their son is a very special son. Alec refused to suggest that perhaps, just perhaps, all parents feel that way about their first-born. But joking apart, he also tasted some echoes of Sacha's will. He also thought that Sacha was *much* too young to understand that trying to impose one's will on another was a nono. He wondered if he should tell him that in his sleep. They say that the subconscious never sleeps, he recalled, and when the body reposes, the ego is not there to object to outside interference.

But when push came to shove, the very opposite happened.

And the funny thing was that Alec was grateful.

As so often lately, the Sacha incident took place when Alec was a sleep. At least it felt like sleep. As usual on Saturdays, Sacha had been left in Alec's care, while Suzy went shopping. With Matt's help, Alec had stretched himself on the sofa, and began flipping pages of some scientific dissertation, until be began to feel drowsy. Sacha seemed happy on the floor, surrounded by his favourite toys. After a while, Sacha leaned back, uttered a few unintelligible syllables of the goo-goo-goo variety, and closed his eyes.

The next thing, Alec found himself floating in the Far Country.

Alec's first reaction was to reach out for the Home Planet. Nothing happened. Only then he'd noticed that there was something very wrong. This was the Far Country, surely... only where were the stars? Where were the galaxies, the wonders of the infinite universe?

"Where am I?" he marveled.

He was reacting to the potential within himself. A potential trapped, static, unfulfilled. He was replete with thoughts, which weren't yet thoughts. It was as though he'd held all the unwritten symphonies in the palm of his hand ready to be put on paper, to be conducted, played... Only there was no one to write them, let alone play them. And his hands were empty? He had no hand. He, in an absurd way, wasn't there at all.

Where is there? Here?

He suspected he was some sort of mental construct, a mental state of being. Not yet becoming—the incredible potential welling within... within what?

If this is heaven why is there no bliss? A stasis? Perhaps patience is a divine virtue. It's easy if you're immortal... Immortal? There is no life here. You can't be immortal if you are not alive.

But if I'm not alive, who am I?

I am dead. I am in Hades. Sheol. Gehenna. In hell. Why? What have I done to not-be? Lethe has washed over me. Oblivion? Is this what hell is? Not-being? Who am I? If I am not, who is it that is aware of my not being?

Why don't I like it? Is this where you abandon all hope?

It was at this instant of non-time that he heard laughter. He saw, he felt, he sensed Sacha's carefree laughter. In that same instant, that same fraction of whatever measured duration before time was born, he wanted, wanted with the whole power of his non-being, to see Sacha. He felt that Sacha and he would be somehow similar. That Sacha would be his mirror. That he would learn the nature of his own beingness, even in non-being.

He desperately wanted to create a mirror. To see the potential in a mirror he needed light. And there was no light. There was no darkness either. There was nothing.

Just stasis. Hades. Not the land of the dead. Was this the land of not yet being? Of them that never were? Not yet?

He wondered if he'd ever live again?

Sacha?

And the first real emotion was born in his state of non-being: a first motivating impulse of the worlds yet to be. It would take the vastness of time to create his own mirror—a mirror that would show him his innermost potential. A mirror of what he could be—of what he could become.

He sighed with great pleasure. He was aware of being aware.

I am, he repeated nonverbally; this single thought permeating the awareness of his being.

I am, I am, I am...

Joy and love, and the sense of oneness, the forerunners of bliss, came into being simultaneously... then, the bliss of self-awareness.

Now he was ready.

He looked and there was light. He'd taken the first step that would lead, in the fullness of infant time, to seeing himself in the perfect mirror of his own creation. The living mirror of becoming.

Even as he hovered in the original void, the Nothingness resolved itself into a glorious darkness. And against this darkness the substance of his mental body shimmered against the rich, velvety background. Soon, first tenuous, then, discernible against the ocean of Nothingness, gaseous clouds came into being; followed by great nebulae, luminous mysteries—giants that call the vastness of space their home. And then stars shimmered, salting the expanse with the joy of light. They twinkled shyly, as though not sure if it was time, yet, for them to appear. The ancient denizens of timeless infinity...

All moving.

There was no more stasis. No more Hades of the lugubrious ancients. In Hades there is no hope. Here ideas fulminated in effulgent glory. What made such a diametric difference, he wondered? What really underscored the difference between heaven and hell? Were they not both but states of consciousness? One of absolute absence, the other of absolute potential.

The latter was also the source of ultimate bliss.

For a long time Alec remained motionless on the sofa. Sacha continued sleeping, content on the carpet. Alec wondered what would have happened had he not heard his son's joyful laughter. Can one hear without any ears?

Apparently.

Bliss, he'd learned, contrary to many religions, must be earned. It may have its being in the infinite potential, but it can only be experienced for services rendered. Without the due process of becoming, bliss is a sister of stasis. A state to be avoided. Nor is it accorded out of mercy of some agency so many people worship. Nor is it something that exists in its own right. It needs a mirror.

There is no bliss without awareness of bliss.

Like everything else, it is a state of mind. Of consciousness? The Far Country is as far as the mind can reach. Beyond that, there is just pure being. All is potential. Lemuria, he now understood, was but an illustration of a mental realm. Of magic gone wild. He sensed its pathological echoes in the Middle Ages, finally becoming subverted by uncontrolled emotions. Exploitation of weaker minds by the stronger. This motif repeated itself throughout history. Alec smiled sadly.

It continues to flourish today.

Could it be that the lessons have already inscribed a full circle?

"What happened?"

Suzy's hands were full of plastic bags she carried from the garage. It took two more trips, hopefully just to the elevator, before she deposited the last load on the kitchen counter.

"I'm sorry darling…" He didn't know what else to say. Watching her carry the groceries while he remained utterly useless.

"I called your cellular three times and you didn't answer. I was worried." She looked at her husband, concern in her eyes. "You've been away, haven't you?"

"I thought it was just for a moment," he still had no control over his sudden 'departures'. 'Away' in their vernacular, meant asleep, day-dreaming, completely lost in work, and, in Alec's case, in Atlantis, or Lemuria or suspended in the very center of the universe. She was learning to detect, from his eyes and facial expression, which it might have been.

"It was really far, this time, wasn't it? Then she smiled and faced the mess in the kitchen. "Let me unpack and then I'll also tell you something."

Matt had already put the heavier articles away. Suzy never understood how Matt did those things. Surely she'd only turned her back for a few seconds?

She turned to Alec. She never asked her husband, well, almost never, what precisely happened. She'd learned to trust that he would share his insights with her, if he possibly could. Some things came out only a month after the 'event'. Some… perhaps some she would never know.

"They have to be experienced," he told her. "They just don't make sense when broken down into words. There's only so much you can reduce to a 'horizontally structured communication'."

He meant writing or talking. Sometimes the omission of a seemingly innocuous detail changed the whole impression. You could never describe a whole event simultaneously, as it had been experienced. You had to break it down into a sequential order.

Meanwhile, Sacha decided that whatever was happening around him was not sufficiently interesting to wake up. He turned his head a little to one side, commented a perfunctory 'goo-goo-goo', and returned to wherever he'd been before.

They both smiled.

"I still say he knows something he's not telling. I think he spends an awful lot of time in heaven, or some other paradise we know nothing about," Suzy knelt down, kissed him gently and returned to the kitchen. Matt withdrew with his usual bow.

Finally, the lunch dishes were cleared and the kitchen restored to its acceptable, if not pristine, order. With Matt's help, Alec sat down on the sofa facing Suzy. Their legs were entwined, as they leaned back against the two opposing armrests. Suzy slowly massaged Alec's feet. Matt had told her that she couldn't do that too often. With her other hand, Suzy caressed a glass of Chilean Merlot, while Alec sniffed at a brandy that Desmond brought him last Thursday.

"It doesn't even smell like Scotch," the Professor confessed accusingly, thus disqualifying it from being fit for human consumption.

Alec liked Armagnac. It couldn't match Remi Martin for the *bouquet*, but it was softer on the palate. Frankly, Alec liked anything that was remotely alcoholic. He drew the line only at some French concoctions that seemed produced for the sole purpose of giving man a lockjaw. Like Pernod, or that bitter red poison, which he was sure only the French could drink after some ten generations of futile attempts at acquiring the taste.

Later, when finally alone, Alec gave Suzy an outline of his 'dream'. It was harder and harder to call these visions dreams, but also he could not call them visions because he did not 'see' them— he was right in them. 'Experiences' would have served except that everything was an experience. Meeting an idiot was an experience, as was meeting a sage. They still didn't find a word to define Alec's peek-a-boo's. And even peek-a-boo, whatever meaning the expression acquired was not exact any more. Alec no longer shifted positions before and after such events. Suzy did her best to take Alec's escapades seriously. It wasn't easy, but when she managed to do so, she insisted it was all Sandra's scrambling for attention.

Alec described, as best he could, the unfolding events, up to the point when he thought he was dead, in Hades, wherein 'abandon all hope ye who enter here' flashed though his awareness. At this point he stopped and tapped himself on the forehead. "You won't believe this," he muttered, "but something very similar happened to me when I was a kid." He thought for a little while and then he quoted as though reading his own thoughts:

"....I remained in the non-space for aeons. I filled the endless void with innumerable possibilities. Countless, wondrous possibilities. With ideas that heretofore had their being only within myself. Within my mind? Wherever I looked there was my presence. Virtual presence. My presence did not exist as yet, but it had the potential to become anything, perhaps everything. Only the ideas remained just that. Just ideas.

And I dreamed for a few more aeons...."

"In a way, this was just a continuation of the exposition of the same creative process. Or perhaps, what preceded it. Only how you can precede anything when there is no time is beyond me... That's the trouble, you see, with trying to describe a gestalt image in a sequential order. When you are 'in it', time is of no consequence. None at all."

"It seems to me that when you were little, you were spared the unpleasantness of stasis, don't you think?" Suzy's intuitive perceptions were working overtime.

"How clever of you. Had I witnessed the utter emptiness of the... you know, of where I'd been, I probably would have gone crazy. I must be much stronger now." And then he remembered. "But didn't you say you had something to tell me also?"

She smiled. "I'm afraid my esoteric experiences don't match yours, darling. Not by a long shot, but, well, I might as well tell you. About half-an-hour after I left, I was about halfway through my shopping list, when I heard distinct laughter. It was somehow familiar, though quite impossible to accept. Only the laughter didn't sound like ha-ha, ha-ha, only more like it was saying round and round pa-pa, pa-pa, pa-pa. It doesn't make any sense, does it?"

Alec didn't say anything. So he hadn't imagined Sacha calling him from the void. Suzy had heard him even as he had. Does everything have to make rational sense?

"Yes it does, Sue. It makes enormous sense to me." And he recounted to her the rest of the dream. Suzy sat quietly, listening and gradually—believing. When Alec was through they both looked at Sacha.

But Sacha said nothing. There was no need to.

***

18
Mu

There were good days, and there were bad days. The real problem Alec had to face had little to do with his legs, although, it was all interconnected. After the Hades experience, he had recurring moments of facing imaginary monsters, perhaps evils is a better word. But even that wasn't the dilemma. The real problem was that in those moments he became acutely aware of his infirmity. Usually paralysis means that one has no sensation of feeling. But in those moments, his limbs, his back, his upper arms were filled with pounding dull pain. Perhaps imaginary, but that didn't make it any easier to bear.

The attendant agony was that he was unable to move. He couldn't run, couldn't escape. He had to face his enemy. He was paralyzed, waiting to be devoured by his own fears.

In such, fortuitously brief, moments, he embraced death as his only deliverer. He regarded his body not just as an inconvenience but as a prison sentence with no possibility of parole. The actual pain subsided quickly, but the resulting depression lingered on for hours, sometimes for days at a time. If it hadn't been for Matt's stoic tolerance and staunch imperturbability, Alec would have found a way to end it all. With Matt around, he couldn't. Matt seemed to have access to his subconscious and always appeared at his side when things seemed darkest. And recently, the dark moments increased in frequency to an intolerable level.

During his late teens, Alec had read about the Kingdom of Mu. It was described in the same paperback that introduced him to Atlantis and Lemuria. The same book had chapters on other ancient civilizations, the Bermuda Triangle, and even Flying Saucers. He was grateful that, so far, he'd managed to elude little green men and other nonsense of immature, if not demented minds.

But he did not escape the Kingdom of Mu.

He tried.

On the last few occasions, the moment he'd felt the sensation of falling, which often preceded his ventures into the unknown, he'd forced himself to remain fully alert. A number of times he'd succeeded. But whatever had been forcing him to advance his knowledge of some other realities, be it in the realm of imagination or, perhaps, in the deep atavistic recesses of his own mind, had not been easily discouraged.

While fighting a loosing battle, Alec began reading some books Suzy had given him on ancient religions. He had no desire to switch professions to a country preacher, nor to start his own, tax-free-all-expenses-paid church of the New and Unexplainable, although the latter would certainly benefit his pocket. After the first three books he came to a conclusion that no church in existence today had anything to do with the ancient teaching to which they auspiciously and overtly claimed allegiance. Nothing whatsoever. Even the official pronouncements of their leaders were at odds with the reputedly holy words, the words of God, as they said. Alec tried to open his mind, to suspend all judgment—all to no avail. Whatever the great avatars of the past brought to earth has been long dead and forgotten. Loving one's neighbor—rather then killing him, not stuffing one's pockets and/or stomachs like starving pigs, which most North-Americans resembled, choosing the middle ground, not seeking revenge... wherever he looked, at home or abroad, the original teaching was gone. And often the closer one got to the administrative headquarters of the cult, sect, or church, the greater both mental and physical debauchery. Not always, but all too often.

What happened?

On Thursday he asked Desmond.

"Religions were what all the Great Masters came to destroy, lad. They came to free humanity from the oppression of priesthood. That's why they were slaughtered in the first place."

"You're serious?" Alec didn't quite dare to go that far.

"Look at the scriptures. I don't know much about the Hindus and Buddhists, but in Judaism and Christianity, or Islam for that matter, the records speaks for themselves."

"Just what do you know about scriptures, Des? I thought they weren't quite your cup of tea?" Alec's eyes were growing larger.

"They're not. But they were once, or I thought they might be," Des smiled, seeing the disbelief in Alec's eyes. "You think I've always been such a cold fish, do you, lad?"

"I never thought you were a fish, Des. But I also never thought you were a sheep."

"Ah, you're thinking of our colleague again: 'In order to be an immaculate member of a flock of sheep, one must above all be a sheep oneself.' Ha, ha. Albert did have his moments," Des admitted.

Few people realized that a number of world-class physicists would make an even better living as professional comedians. Einstein was no exception.

"Sorry, I didn't mean to..."

"None taken. I don't take offense easily. If I did, I couldn't deal with the politicians, which I have to do to run my department. But, let's get back to your question. Before I took up physics, I gobbled up libraries of esoteric stuff that would make your ears curl. There are tons of the stuff, and the vast majority not worth looking at. But there are some exceptions, ah... the angel cometh..."

"Good evening, Professor, how are you today?"

Desmond got up with the agility of a young man. He must have been exercising in secret. He kissed Suzy on both cheeks and sat down again. "That must keep me going till next Thursday," he said miserably. And then, almost as an after thought, he reached in his pocket and pulled out a little box. He handed it to Suzy.

"See if you like these, lass" he muttered.

Suzy opened the box that had the appearance of long years of use. The blue velvet on the outside was wearing thin at all corners. Inside was a beautiful necklace of brown and yellow amber. The translucent fossils shone with a variety of deep if muted lights as though coming from different sources. Gingerly, Suzy took it out. The necklace was long enough to go twice around her neck.

"Professor! May I try it on?"

"Why not, lassie, it's yourrs if you like it?" Desmond's rolled r's always reappeared when his emotions were involved.

Suzy apparently hadn't heard him. She run out into the hall and faced the mirror. There she dressed the necklace around her neck, then rolled the beads twice over, and finally reverted to a single long strand. With the necklace sill around her neck, but also holding on to it with both hands as though refusing to let go, she came back and faced the Professor.

"Do you like them, Des?" she asked. Alec could swear that her eyes were shining.

"Me? Why should I like them? They'rre yourrs."

"What? Mine? Why? Why today? Mine?"

She couldn't have heard his first offering.

"Aye, that appearrs to be what I've just said," the Professor remained cool, almost distant, but Alec knew him well enough to note that Des enjoyed the effect the necklace had on Suzy. But when his dear wife, instead of thanking the Professor politely, threw herself at her benefactor, he'd 'lost his cool' completely. He held her as she kissed him, again and again on both cheeks, then embraced him, and then kissed him again. All this time Dr. McBride gave the appearance of trying to extricate himself from her bodily assault, though... not very hard.

"Why, lassie, you'll squeeze the life out of me. Now that'll be quite enough. It'll last me a month. Two months! Maybe longerr..." But his eyes suddenly misted.

"You're so very, very kind, Desmond. You are by far my favourite uncle."

"Aye, you'rre even like a niece, ney, like a daughterr to me, lassie. Now you see that you enjoy them," he admonished when at last he regained his breath.

Only later did they learn that the necklace was in Desmond's family longer than he cared to remember. He found it some time ago, but only this morning he'd decided that it was wasting, just lying there, in the drawer. He brought it over at once.

"To whom could I possibly give it to?" he asked wistfully. Alec mused that had Des thought of the necklace sooner, his mother might have been the lucky recipient. At the very least, it remained in the family. It turned out, much later, that the ambers were Desmond's last link to his own past. He was now a free man.

"We were talking about religions?" Alec tried to return to the previous subject without seeming ungrateful. The Professor needed to get his teeth into something less emotional.

"Aye, that we were," Desmond affirmed, his voice a little steadier.

"You were talking about the volumes that had been written on esoteric subjects," Alec prompted.

"Ah, yes. Well, after a couple of years of midnight oil, I discovered that all the ancient wise men taught just about the same thing. It became equally as apparent that humanity was nowhere near ready to adopt their teaching. But that's only a byproduct of my research. What I really wanted to find was the philosopher's stone. Only I didn't want to change base metal into gold, but ignorance into knowledge. Or, as our departed friend put it, I wanted to know the thoughts of God."

Alec knew all of Einstein's famous expressions. It seemed that, in their heart of hearts, all scientists were searching for the same thing. Only a great many of them, human that they were, got sidetracked. They started building bombs instead.

"And...?"

"And I didn't find it—as if you needed telling. The old religions teach us how to live. Or how to go to heaven, not how heaven works—as the clerk defending Galileo had put it. There is some overlapping, but that's only marginal. They tried to teach us how to survive. Since then, of course, the sacerdotal fraternity perverted the teaching into a 'how to die' nonsense. Everything has been changed into the after-death type of philosophy, as if any single one of them had any idea about whatever happens after death. Anyway, they never explained if they were talking about the physical, emotional or mental death, but judging by the way they amassed gold in this life, they certainly learned how to live happily in the here-and-now."

There was neither passion nor rancour in Desmond's voice. He simply stated the truth as he knew it. He even sounded as though he felt sorry for the 'sacerdotal fraternity' for having lost all meaning of life. Certainly, it seemed, neither he nor the said fraternity appeared to have found the 'thoughts of God'. Not in the ancient scriptures.

"So," he continued after a little while, "I started looking elsewhere." He looked into Alec's eyes. "And, lad, as you can well see, I'm still looking."

They never touched on the subject again. While they talked, Suzy was preparing dinner. She prepared it—the men cleaned up afterwards. Des and Matt. They also laid out the table and served the drinks and wine. As Suzy ventured from the kitchen to the living room, to the corner where the dining table was laid out, she lingered longer then usual. Alec suspected she didn't quite like what she'd heard, but she didn't have sufficient arguments to oppose the Professor.

"Especially after the necklace..." he thought. "It simply wouldn't be nice..."

But, Suzy reconciled herself that Desmond's words rang true. He didn't condemn, he simply confessed that what he was looking for lay elsewhere. The divine thoughts he wanted to hear were not recorded in the same books. There, God talked on other subjects, the essence of which the Professor was practicing all his life. There was no need to dwell on them any more. It was simply the right way to live. Right belief, right resolve, right speech, conduct, occupation, effort, right contemplation and right ecstasy. The eight-fold path of Buddha. Why were these guidelines so difficult for the western man to adopt? Then she smiled at her own thoughts. The East, frankly, was not doing so much better, she'd conceded.

"More cheese, Des?"

The dinner was running to its satisfying close. The Camembert was just right, the Roquefort also, and the red Burgundy complemented both perfectly. Next came coffee, and then, as was their custom, a brisk walk around the block. In the days when Alec still walked, this was the only time they left Sacha asleep in his jungle unattended. The walk took just under fifteen minutes. Sometimes either Alec or Suzy would get back to Sacha, while the remaining two would make another round. By ten the streets were fairly empty, the stroll cleared their lungs before retiring. Ever assuming there wasn't a smog warning posted.

Neither Alec nor Suzy knew, nor would they have guessed, that this would be the last time they'd be enjoying a pleasant dinner-for-three with the Professor. No, it wasn't because Sacha was ready to join them at the table. Not yet. Yet the custom they'd grown to enjoy so much had run its course.

Last night, Alec had, once again, some unpleasant chimerical flashes. Each time he dozed off, he had wakened almost immediately with a feeling of profound distaste. Only short snippets of the dreams came to him, as though the past had been presented to him in tiny fragments torn out of the fabric of time. Each segment lasted no more than a few seconds, two or three minutes at most—of real time, that is. Thankfully the ordeal, if one could call it that, did not last too long. After about a half-hour he finally succumbed to a relaxing, uninterrupted sleep.

The following morning he felt a lingering nausea similar to that which he carried with him for a week after the original horror he'd 'witnessed', during his nightmare of the Dark Ages. These new snippets had not been as intense, nor as cruel nor horrifying as that first nightmare, but they did seem to make a statement that human kind had a tremendous propensity for inflicting pain. Alec wondered, as he had after each such dream, what was the purpose of his subconscious torturing him on such a regular schedule. There were no obvious answers. When he'd talked to Suzy, she was as stumped as he was. In spite of her almost inerrant intuition, she'd drawn a blank.

"But there is always a reason, for everything," he insisted.

"But the reason may well be buried deep in your own subconscious," she'd replied. "It may be accessible only to you and no one else, don't you agree?"

He had to agree. From the time he was a little boy, he'd experienced dreams that did not seem to trouble anyone else he'd ever met. Neither then nor now. Was it his early evolution, his willingness to escape into the chimerical world of daydreams for which he was now paying? Or was there a more sinister reason?

He still hoped that somewhere, somehow, the secret of a cure for his paralysis lay in those enigmatic visions. He dissected them with the precision of a seasoned surgeon. All to no avail. More and more often he felt that his time was running out.

As was usual in such circumstances, he threw himself into his work. He lectured, conducted experiments, wrote articles—kept as busy as is humanly possible. At the very least he was determined to hold on to his mind. The rest of the time he played with Sacha. He asked Matt to take his son for walks, while he, when no longer propelling himself with his arms, buzzed along on his motorized chair. This gave Suzy a chance to do some painting. By the evening Alec was so tired that he slept peacefully, unhampered by any sadistic demons. It was then that he'd promised himself that should he ever venture into the world of dreams again, he would do everything in his power to bypass any and all Dark Ages. However dark the past, he'd turn his face and his mind only towards the future. In the evening, he remained in his wheelchair for as long as possible, to stay awake as long as he could.

It worked for a while.

Yet, apparently, there was one more lesson he had to endure. Luckily the prologue to the main event, as he'd recounted it later to Suzy, was almost free from satanic connotations. It had taken him into the land as ancient as to be completely unrecognizable. It might have been on another planet.

The sand stretched in all directions as far as the horizon. From his vantage point, he could see the undulating pattern of dunes, and its mirror image only much darker, no more than a dozen feet above his head. He arrived there after yet another, though mercifully short, series of flashes through the cycles of human depravity, which apparently formed deep scars on the sequential order of human evolution. These scars had occurred, it seemed, throughout history—probably prehistory. There had been the countless tribe leaders wielding both absolute and uncompromising power over their more ignorant subjects, the underground societies, which had terrorized men and women for many decades at a time, only to be reborn elsewhere and elsewhen to continue their demonic cults. He was then shown the horrors of primitive religions so similar to the original cults yet whose crimes had been committed in the name of One who was not there to deny them or to defend Himself. The One invariably battled for supremacy with other 'Ones'—the births pangs of monotheism.

And after these and many other depravities, he'd been thrown into a virtual stasis. Not the stasis he'd experienced in the no-space-no-time zone, but a reality that was suspended halfway between physical and nonphysical mode of existence.

He has been placed in bodies of men, if men they were, in different parts of the Kingdom of Mu, the name that was firmly etched on his mind, though it had nothing to do with what Augustus Le Plongeon described the sunken continent. This had nothing to do with anything that made any sense…

This time, Alec was more an observer than an active participant in... in whatever the inhabitants of the Kingdom did. It seemed to have been very little, until he saw that the activity was not really connected to or dependent on the body he'd occupied. The body was no more than a suit of clothing, having little or no will of its own. If he had not enlivened it with his presence, it would have remained in a state of rest. A stasis.

It would have remained in abeyance.

When he found himself placed, progressively, in the third 'body', he attempted to look through its eyes.

He was standing on top of a low dune; its surface slightly undulated, as the top of an ocean swell would be in a gentle breeze. Indeed, he was in an ocean of sorts. It was an ocean of sand. As far as the eyes could see. Above him was an equally endless and equally undulating ceiling, perhaps of thick cloud, almost water, so heavy as to barely rise above the sand.

The body that served him was equipped with very good eyes. He could zoom in on the grains at his feet, for the flat portions at the end of his stumps must have been feet. They seemed more suited to standing than moving. Apparently there was no need to develop more functional feet. Legs for that matter. He moved by willing to be in another body and immediately he was elsewhere. He realized, immediately, that his host body remained in the same place. What moved was his awareness. His point of view. Only there seemed little point to this exercise. For wherever he transported himself, seemingly by magic, the environment was identical to the one he'd just left.

What could have been the point of it all?

And then he saw another pod on similar stumpy supports looking at him. At least its eyes were directed in his direction. He zoomed in on those eyes and he saw nothing. An emptiness that can be seen in the eyes of a man in a coma. Perhaps these pods, these people, were not awakened yet.

He had no idea into what life they would come into. There seemed to be no life here, as yet. As yet? Was life here yet to evolve? Was this the beginning?

He looked at his foot-pads and imagined a plant.

Nothing happened. The sand remained dry, useless, undisturbed. He looked around, his eyes swiveling a full circle, and faced once more that other pod standing some two hundred feet from him atop another dune. The other pod had remained completely static. Dead? Yet... Even from this distance he saw that the pod was staring at his own feet. He looked down himself. And there, a single stem was moving upwards, winding itself around one of his stumps. Instinctively he jerked his 'leg' to free it. The little stem hovered and fell back on the sand. It was dead.

Alec, for he still thought of himself as Alec, felt a strange sadness.

"I could have let it live," he thought. "I didn't need this body."

He tried to imagine the plant again, but this time, even after waiting a long time, nothing happened. He'd lost his chance. The plants wouldn't trust him again. Not to be born, not to live. Pain constricted his heart. He felt great remorse.

After a long while he looked up from his luckless stumps. The pod on the other dune was still there. It looked different. Very different. He zoomed in on it. From head to toe it was covered in a mesh of winding, interlocking vines. And in some places, tiny, extremely tiny leaves were just breaking out from their buds.

And then there was only darkness.

It was night when he awakened. Still in his chair. Matt never interfered with his wishes; unless they threatened his physical wellbeing. He would not put him to bed against his will.

For a long while Alec couldn't figure out the purpose of this dream. An exercise in fear and stupidity? Or just a lesson in the force of destiny…

There could be so many answers to so many questions.

Next day Alec was back at work. He was busy putting together preliminary proposal for the elusive, the improbable, virtually impossible, Unified Field Theory. A theory that would, with a single equation or a series of equations, unify all the physical laws and forces and show their interrelationship to each other. The Information Theory was the key. The rest was just hard work. Finally the force of gravity would 'join hands' with the other universal forces.

But each day, the moment he got home, the Kingdom of Mu kept returning to the forefront of his awareness. The same questions, the same enigma. Why all this sand? Why no water? How can anyone survive without water? Why would they want to?

And, worst of all, who made, or built, or created those pods? There was no other life there. None at all. Just pods. Skins waiting to be filled with life? They seemed inanimate until Alec showed the other man, the occupier of the other pod, how to make a plant grow. And later, how to destroy it...

The following day, while thinking of something quite different, Alec caught his breath. His thoughts continued to come back to that single concept of fear. Was that the beginning of all evil? That single unthinking, irrational reaction of fear? The only thing you must fear is fear itself, he remembered. Was that what it was all about? Could it be that the previous snippets of history, each and every one of them, had their origin in fear? Was this why man killed, tortured, debased himself?

He recalled the anguish he'd felt when the plant he'd just created wilted and died at his feet. It was his heart that had failed him. The heart that had been short on courage. On rational action. On being more human?

What does it mean, really, to be human?

He wondered what the Kingdom of Mu looked like today. There must have been thousands upon thousands of pods covered with plants. Perhaps forests. And maybe they would learn to grow new pods, and make them mobile, like men. Perhaps the pods and the plants could coexist in harmony—or would it have been seeded with the germ of fear.

Alec pressed a button and the wheelchair rolled silently towards the window. And as he looked out onto the cityscape below, he knew. He knew exactly what the Kingdom of Mu looked like today.

And yet, he still missed the most important lesson of the Kingdom of Mu.

***

The Return

Heaven is under our feet as well as over our heads.

Henry David Thoreau
1817 – 1862
Author, Naturalist, and Philosopher

19
Sacha and other Youngsters

When it happened, it happened quite suddenly. One moment Sacha was playing on a rug in the middle of the living room, the next instant he was a foot to the left. Suzy swallowed hard, picked him up, inspected him from all sides, held him protectively for a while and, finally, though with a vague reluctance, put him back on the floor.

Sacha was no longer willing to remain in his playpen. He could be induced to stay there for a short time, as when lured there by a new toy, but that was about it. The rest of the time he roamed wherever a physical barrier would not impede his progress. Desmond called him a tourist. Who knows where else he went when he shifted, Suzy thought, her heart beating a little faster.

"He did it," she told Alec the moment he got back from the Institute. And before he could ask 'What?' she told him. "Sacha peek-a-boo'ed."

Alec smiled. "Darling, Sue..."

"He peek-a-boo'ed, today, right on the carpet," she insisted.

"Well, did you clean up after..."

"And it's all your fault!" she added.

He had to dodge her slipper aimed with great precision at his head. His wheelchair no longer afforded protection. He'd have to watch his step, so to speak.

"All right, so he peek-a-boo'ed," he acceded. According to you I've done it dozens of times and I am whole and hale. Perhaps it's the most natural thing to do, only no one's ever noticed such things before. For all I know, you do it all the time. Perhaps we all do it..."

"What!!!" She was removing her left slipper.

"Just kidding," he assured, but made a precautionary dodge behind the table.

Only Alec wasn't whole and hale. When Sue quieted down, his mind returned to his last excursion. He'd moved from pod to pod without legs, he was virtually independent of the pod he inhabited, through which he'd acted. And it still had been in his power to do 'good and evil'. We are not our bodies, he affirmed firmly. After millions of years of evolution we've learned to identify ourselves with our physical envelopes. But... but we are not... We are what we seem to be.

"You don't believe me!" Suzy sounded as angry as she was sad. This was about Sacha, again.

And the next moment, without the slightest warning she stooped over the wheelchair, threw her arms around Alec's neck. Her head jerked with uncontrollable sobs. He wondered, incongruously, how would he feel if she really would peek-a-boo now and then. Would he be as worried? He stroked her golden hair.

"It's all right, Sue. Everything's always exactly as it should be." He had no idea why he'd chosen these particular words of reassurance. Perhaps they'd worked the last time. Apparently he was right. Suzy was a great believer in Divine Providence.

"Nothing bad could happen to him, could it?"

"Of course not. You know that?"

"Yes. I know that. But...."

Five minutes later she was calm. It was being alone and having to witness her son following his father into the unknown, where she had absolutely no access, that bothered her most of all. Long before Sacha had shifted positions she'd resented that she couldn't join Alec on his wild escapades. She didn't care if they were real or not; she wanted to be with him. Always. At all times. Forever.

"Everything's always exactly as it should be," Alec murmured under his breath. Had Suzy looked, she would have seen a light come into his eyes that had been missing for quite a while.

For now, Sacha remained perfectly 'normal'. Other than trying to break down the structural stability of most pieces of furniture with whatever he could get hold of, he was a perfectly normal child. Perhaps they'd both imagined that he 'appeared' to them in certain circumstances. Why not? There were great many things they'd imagined. Suzy imagined her innumerable paintings, Alec—the invisible particles integrating themselves into a predictable mathematical patterns. Both creative endeavours were neither more nor less demanding on their imaginative faculties than visualizing father's attributes in his son, or feeling his presence when in need of such.

"The human mind is a strange and complex machine," Des said the last time they'd met. "Aye, when we fathom the mind, we'll fathom the universe."

What neither of them could figure out was if the mind was the originator of reality or just a means through which this reality manifested itself. In the first case, the mind was the prime cause. In the latter it was a means. Either way its scope appeared limitless.

During the last few months, Alec was attempting to tackle the reconciliation between gravity and the other three forces. After the quantum theorists got through with the weak force, things didn't get any easier. The strong and the electromagnetic forces suffered a little less. But the force of gravity was quite a different problem. While we all recognize it's presence, since it stops us from flying off into space with the rotation of the Earth, at the atomic level it's effects are so insignificant that most nuclear physicists leave them for the astrophysicists to deal with. This divisive gap remained to Alec's day.

And even Alec's present theory was not new. The ancient Greeks had been toying with the idea that had been resurrected towards the end of the eighteenth century by a fellow called Boscovich. He'd thought of atoms as of particles that had no size, rather like Greek geometric points. Alec picked this notion up, only he defined the points as units of information. The points had specific characteristics. What remained was to show the relationship of how different points affect those characteristics. It was like writing an equation wherein all particles had a common denominator—so that you could express each one in terms of the others.

Easy, right?

Easy or not, Dr. McBride rejected the first three drafts Alec produced to explain his theory. They seemed quite clear to Alec but, alas, not to anyone else.

"You sound like Beethoven explaining his symphonic structures to a man who is deaf. It wouldn't be too bad, if it weren't for the fact that Beethoven was deaf himself."

Alec was not exactly pleased with Dr. McBride's comments.

"I'd better put my nose back to the grind stone and keep honing my ideas," he said, explaining to Suzy Desmond's remarks.

"I like your nose just the way it is," she threw over her shoulder without taking her eyes off the canvas. She was working on an acrylic for a friend. It was a commission. Her first. "Aren't you mixing some metaphors there somewhere?"

According to the Professor he'd been mixing a lot more then metaphors.

"But that was the whole idea. To put them all together..."

But Suzy wasn't listening. As long as his nose remained roughly the same shape and size she was happy with whatever else he did.

Desmond approved the fourth draft for publication. Not as a theory but a direction in which a solution might be found. It was really a means of protecting Alec's ideas, his name, in a way. In physics it mattered if you published first. It mattered a lot. Officially, Alec no longer required Dr. McBride's blessing to publish any of his work. He was now a fully accredited lecturer, with total autonomy over his research. There were two reasons why Alec chose to seek the Professor's approval. One, it was polite. And two—certainly equally, if not more, important—Alec was still very young. He jumped into the fire before checking if there was any water around to put out the flames. He was impulsive. He needed someone looking over his shoulder. Not to guide him, or push him, or do his thinking for him, but to hold him back. The young stallion needed strong reins. Luckily Alec was mature enough to know that. He didn't expect his work to send shock waves across the scientific world, but he hoped it would be a step in the right direction.

When Desmond finally granted his blessing, Alec relaxed. Regrettably, he was not very good at doing nothing. He was fine for a day or two, but his nature was such that even two days of leisure brought him a feeling of restlessness. Probably he was, what is erroneously called, a workaholic. Alec always hated work. He thought that life should be so automated that all his time could be dedicated to pleasure. That's all he ever sought. And sought actively. It just so happened that what he did at the Institute gave him more pleasure than almost anything else. And now that the period of depression he'd suffered released its grip over his emotions, he needed to slake his thirst for work more than ever.

"If I want to work, I'll go sailing," he once said. "Now, that's work! If you don't, you drown."

In spite of his self confessed aversion to any form of exertion, sailing, as he mentioned periodically, was still drawing him. He never imagined that his legs, or lack of them, would ever stand in his way—he grinned, or rather groaned, at his pun when he'd first thought of it. He felt that once his eyes had been opened by his venture into the Mu territory, his confidence in his ultimate full recovery was a given, not a vague hope.

The next time 'it' happened, it did so in a simple, most natural way.

Once again, after publishing his latest paper, Alec spent a few days at home. He used the free time to allow Suzy some time off from looking after Sacha. Most of the time sat in his wheelchair, gazing at his son. He felt comfortable and relaxed knowing that Matt was somewhere around. Later, he recalled feeling guilty about repeatedly taking Matt for granted.

This time there were no time warps into Atlantis, or some desolate deserts of Mu. Instead, he felt on his face a gentle breeze from the sea.

"Watch your feet!" he shouted when a wave broke a little too close to Sacha.

"Don't worry, Dad, I've been here before," Sacha assured him.

This was the first indication Alec had that he'd again slipped into an altered reality. In dreams, one usually witnessed some embroidered fragments of one's past. This was new. By now, Sacha was perfectly capable of enunciating a dozen words or so, but not a complete sentence that not only made sense, but also referred to past events.

Alec looked around.

Could this be the Home Planet? He was sitting on a sandbank that fell quite steeply toward a vast ocean. The sun was hot, but the wafting breeze from the water kept him comfortable. He was wearing his shorts and a tee shirt. Sacha was playing in the waves, running in and out of the water in quick succession. He was trying to dodge the bigger breakers—escaping their fury only at the very last moment.

Alec looked at his son with a mixture of pride and pleasure. Sacha was only eleven months, but he moved like a three-year-old. In fact, here, wherever 'here' was, he *was* a three-year-old. Alec wondered if it had been he or Sacha who'd chosen this particular age.

"You can't choose for other people here, dad, remember?"

In an instant Alec understood it all. Sacha and his Princess were still one. When you're a little child you don't break down your personality into disjointed fragments. That comes later. Why? He had no idea. But Sacha and his Princess, or his Superego, or whatever you chose to call it, were still one. That's why he could read my thoughts, Alec realized. That's why he could make it here under his own steam, so to speak. That's why he'd as good as said that he's been here before. And then, out of the blue, Alec remembered a phrase from a book he'd read as a schoolboy. The phrase said: 'Be ye like little children.' The words took on a new meaning. It seemed that, at a certain time in our lives, we all were whole. Complete. Only later we separated, fragmented our essence, and spent the rest of our lives trying to put ourselves together again. To revert to our original ground.

To return home.

Alec remembered his attempt at the Unified Field Theory. There was a driving force that fired his imagination, ignited his mind, sated his innermost desires. Making things whole was all that life was about.

"Papa, look..." Sacha was smiling. He was looking at the shimmering air beside the spot where Alec was sitting. The air seemed undecided what to do, then, gradually solidified into a human form.

"Gosh, you scared me you two," Suzy looked more disappointed than angry. "I looked for you everywhere," she added. She seemed completely at ease.

However beautiful she was on Earth, in physical reality, here she looked like a wizard's amalgam of herself and Sandra. She was more than a Princess. She was a Queen. This must be Paradise, Alec thought.

And at this very same moment he heard Sacha's ditty. If angels could sing...

...only Sacha was sitting on the floor at his feet. Suzy had just walked in from the apartment next door.

"I've been calling you," she looked worried. "Where were you?"

She didn't know, Alec thought. Not yet. But she is close. Very close.

And somehow this idea made him more happy than all the scientific papers he'd ever published.

Alec found it difficult not to talk about their meeting on the Home Planet. He felt, however, that the very fact that Sacha was more advanced in the reality transfer than Suzy, might set her back. He decided to hold his joy within, knowing that sooner of later the real world would be theirs to share.

This was the first time that he fully recognized the inner worlds of his childhood as the Real Worlds. Within those realms there were few questions he couldn't answer. The inner universes seemed created to please anyone who found his or her way into their gentle embrace.

Yet, the two, the Far Country and the Home Planet couldn't be more different. Perhaps they, too, would be reconciled one day. He remembered from his younger days that there had been other people who knew of them, other intelligent entities visiting the Home Planet, but no one he'd ever met on Earth. At least he didn't think so. Like attracts like, he remembered Suzy saying. And if the saying were true, then by now he would have met someone who shared his dreams.

In the meantime, Alec had to get on with his work.

Publications were the icing on the cake. The lectures, the scientific journals, the keeping up with the scientific Joneses, remained. It wasn't always fun, but courtesy demanded that if Alec expected others to read him, he must keep abreast of other people's efforts himself. A *noblesse oblige*?

Yet, truly pathetic some of these efforts were.

It became more than apparent that every university Professor, or lecturer, felt compelled to publish a certain number of papers per term, or at least per academic year. It was expected of them. Some of the stuff Alec read sounded as though they'd been written to satisfy the prescribed requirements of publication, whether the author had anything to say or not. *Noblesse* indeed!

The other day he'd read another attempt, by a well-established physicist, to induce a forced marriage of Quantum Mechanics with Universal Consciousness. It wasn't just that the author's conclusions were scientifically unsound and unsubstantiated, but even assuming that some of the wrong assumptions were correct, they still didn't hold water. Yet, it seemed that there was some underlying need, even a hunger within the younger generation of theoretical physicists, to reach out beyond 'just numbers'.

Finally, alone in his office, Alec began wondering, "Could it be that I am wrong?" he mused aloud.

"Not for as long as you want to call yourself a physicist, lad," came from a head peeking through the half-open door. Desmond knew instantly what Alec was doing. "I too have my drreams and desirres, but publishing all of them in scientific jourrnals is not one of them."

Then the rest of the Professor followed his head into Alec's office. He leaned over his desk. "Come to the cottage, lad. Bring yourr lassie and the wee lad," he said. "'Tis the best time of the yearr. We'll talk some morrre."

It was early June. According to the Professor, every time was the best for going to the cottage. Out there, Dr. McBride felt as though he were the head of a family.

Two weeks later, they were ready to go. Suzy had packed the essentials last night; Matt took them down to the car. They wanted to leave as the moment the rush hour was over. Sacha walked down to the garage 'on his own', testing the elevator walls for structural strength with a rubber mallet. He must have inherited this engineering propensity from his grandfather on Alec's side. Apparently the walls had passed the test, and just to make sure that the passengers were equally as sound, Sacha gave a good whack to a lady in front of him. She smiled, but got off at the next floor. Probably a wise decision. Once in the car, Sacha let out a single prolonged note, commenting in his own inimitable way on the idea of going da-da. Actually Sacha had already acquired a considerable vocabulary but he reverted to the original expressions when he deemed it appropriate.

As on that first occasion, they got to Solana Beach in well under two hours. Desmond had said that he would be there ahead of time, to get the place fixed up. It turned out that he had another reason for the 'fixing up' chore.

As the door opened, they'd been greeted by... Alicia!

Alec froze, shook his head, and then propelled his wheels forward almost knocking his mother down. She jumped aside just in time, but returned to embrace him. What happened was that Alec hadn't used the accelerator button. He'd used his own muscle power. He'd used his arms.

No one seemed to have noticed. Except for Matt, of course. There was a surreptitious smile hovering at the corners of his mouth. As usual, he made no comment.

Then it was Suzy's turn. She placed Sacha on Alec's lap and gave Alicia a long hug. Both women emerged from the embrace with tears in their eyes. Finally Alicia reached over and took Sacha. He didn't seem to mind the attention, kissed Baba on her cheek but then demanded to be put down. Baba was Russian for Grandma, as Desmond had once explained to them on hearing that they'd chosen a Russian diminutive for their son.

"When? How?" Alec and Suzy asked simultaneously.

"To answer your questions—a week ago, I flew. How else?" Alicia laughed.

How Alec missed that pearly, cascading laugher. He tried to remember if he'd ever seen his mother angry. Or even unhappy. He couldn't think of a single time. And only then he remembered his host. All three of them were so overjoyed at seeing each other that they had completely forgotten about

Desmond. He was standing back, watching the reunion, a broad grin on his face.

Alec shook his hand. Suzy followed with a hug. Matt bowed from a distance. The Professor didn't speak. He continually kept clearing his throat as though getting ready for a welcoming speech. But he didn't make one. The delight at seeing three of his favourite people so happy was all he needed right now.

"I thought you might like a li'le surrprrise?" he uttered at last. It was a rhetorical question. "Come in, all of you." And he led the way.

Sacha was promptly installed on the terrace, which had been fitted with string netting along its whole length. Alec recalled seeing such nets on boats when people sailed with infants. It reduced the need to fish them out of the water too often. The net was one of the reasons why the Professor got here a week early. The other, the principle reason was equally obvious.

On the south side of the terrace Maria had already laid out the table for lunch. It was a little early, but no one minded the view and a cool glass of, what else... of Maria's own Sangria. They talked all at once, interrupting each other, trying to catch up with the intervening months.

It soon transpired that Desmond had visited Montreal about two months ago and again a fortnight today. He had some business to attend to in Toronto, he said, and had dropped in to Montreal to make sure that Alicia hadn't come to any harm.

"You can neverr tell what a lassie will do, when left on herr own," he affirmed knowingly.

Alicia just loved being called a lassie. First she thought she was being compared to that graceful dog from the old Hollywood Westerns, but soon accepted the Scottish version.

"And he calls me that in public, would you believe it? In LA? I have to twirl my skirt and curtsy to live up to my new title."

Alicia looked at Desmond with such affection that Suzy began to suspect that there was much more to it all than met the eye.

Just then Maria brought in the first course. Suzy got up to greet her. Maria was practically a member of the family. This morning Alicia had insisted on serving her breakfast while Maria had to sit still, eat, and tell her all about the immediate neighbourhood.

After lunch, when Maria offered to look after Sacha, the ladies took the stairs down to the beach. Not to swim, but to walk barefoot along the shore. Desmond accompanied Alec along the footpath, keeping a keen eye on both ladies below. Matt? Matt, when not needed, was playing his usual role of an invisible man. He must have been somewhere around.

After some five hundred yards, for no apparent reason, Suzy took Alicia in her arms and hugged her to within an inch of her life.

"So you'll be here?" she asked, her arms flapping as though she was about to take off.

The men looked down at the two women.

"What's going on down there?" Alec wanted to know. They were only about ten yards away.

"Des! Didn't you tell Ali yet...?" Alicia wagged a finger at the Professor.

"Didn't quite get 'rround to it, lassie. But I'm beginning to suspect the lad alrready knows..." Desmond looked very uncomfortable.

"Why is it that we, women, must always do all the work?" Alicia flung her arms up in exasperation. "Sue, you tell him."

"Why me?" Suzy was laughing with tears in her eyes. "Just look at the Professor. Imagine that this man had given more public lectures than all of us put together!"

Seeing that Desmond was embarrassed beyond his due, Alicia walked up the sloping sand to the footpath and put her arms around the Professor's neck. "Ali," she said without taking her eyes off Desmond's, "What would you say if I moved in with the Professor?"

"What and live in sin?" Alec was shocked.

"Neverrr," the Professor finally came to life. "We alrready have a piece of paperr that makes it all legal!"

"A piece of paperrrrrr?" Alec looked down his nose at the Professor who once again seemed at a loss for words.

"We thought you young'uns might want to witness ourr vows in a chapel," he added miserably.

"A CHAPEL?" Alec roared, loving every minute of it. This was the first time since he'd met Dr. Desmond McBride that he held the upper hand. Not for long though.

"That's quite enough, Ali," Alicia brought her son down to earth. "In the chapel, next Saturday. We thought that you might be Desmond's best man and Suzy my bridesmaid. We don't want anyone else, except Sacha and Maria, of course."

Strange that no one mentioned Matt.

Ten minutes later the congratulations were over.

"I suppose I'll have to call you daddy?" Alec smiled. He was on the verge of chuckling.

"You'll call me as you always called me. Or at least the last yearr orr so, laddie." Authority returned to Desmond's voice.

"And me?" Suzy asked.

"You can call me anything you want, lass. Anything at all, but call me!"

And they all laughed.

They decided to get back and raise a toast to the lovers. Alec's worries about being so far from his mother were over. Suzy didn't have that problem. She had three brothers in Canada, and her parents were still very much together. Alicia, on the other hand, has been all-alone, and Alec simply couldn't look after her from across the continent. Thanks to dear ol' Des, she'd no longer be stranded. What's more, Suzy would recover her painting companion.

As for what was happening in the hearts of the 'young couple', no one would ever know. But on the way back,

Alicia and Desmond walked together, hand-in-hand, like a pair of youngsters. Every dozen steps or so, Alec and Suzy heard Alicia's unmistakable cascade of laughter reaching them from the water's edge. Whatever else fate would deal them, they would have many laughs together. The Professor was as young at heart as the circumstances permitted. And the new circumstances were all in his favour.

And then Suzy looked down at Alec at her side and stopped dead. Her eyes were as wide open as her mouth.

"What is it darling?" he asked.

"You're a-arms... y-you are using your arms," she half-stammered.

"Oh? I hadn't noticed," he lied. But his heart was as full of joy as his wife's. He could now hold his son in those very arms of his. For the first time in months. Thanks Sandra, he whispered.

He closed his eyes and held his breath. Just for a moment. The ground was just below him. He decided to put his feet down, on earth, before he got dizzy. This was like the difference between dreaming and a waken state. His senses responded to the environment in quite 'normal' fashion. Here, he was standing on his own feet.

"Why here? Why now?" he wondered. "I thought..."

"I thought you asked for me."

The voice came from just behind him. Alec was standing in front of the same old archway in the wall he'd visited so many times in the past. So similar to the one on Atlantis, only this was definitely Home Planet. He felt it, he was sure. And Sandra was just behind him. He would recognize her sweet voice anywhere, on earth or in outer space. He spun on his heels and nearly collapsed. Facing him was Suzy. Only more beautiful, more radiant, more exquisite.

"I cannot be quite as you've seen me before. After all, I am really within you. I'm the servant of your image of me." And the smile she flashed was as coquettish as Suzy's ever was. The Sandra he looked at was a beautiful woman, a little girl, a wise matron, all in one. She was also Suzy.

"H-how... d-do I call you?" he stammered.

"You already did. I am Sandra. I always have been. That is why you are Alec-Sander, remember?

"Alexander..." he corrected automatically. Then he laughed. "But you are also her!"

"I am anyone you choose to make me. Don't forget that here, on the Home Planet, you are the absolute creator. The boss, so to speak," a disarming smile never left her lips.

The lips he'd kissed so many times. Only here, they were even more desirable.

"I think you'd better leave that part of it for the earth..."

She was definitely teasing him. This was Sandra all right. No matter what she looked like. He remembered the old days, when he'd been hardly fourteen—the awareness of the difference between boys and girls only just invading his youthful consciousness. This was different. Very different.

"I get the message," he murmured. He didn't have to. He also remembered that Sandra could always read his thoughts. After all, in a way, she was also him.

"Now you get it!" she encouraged.

"So finding you desirable is like... like making love to myself?"

"Not quite. But man has been told to love others as himself. So..."

"Isn't that religion?"

"What is religion?" Sandra did not give in. Perhaps she was as stubborn as he.

"It's a method of controlling people," he answered at once. "Of controlling their minds."

"You are talking about the people administering religions. The priesthood. Of them it has been said that they have the keys to the kingdom of heaven, they do not enter themselves, yet they don't allow anyone else to enter. Suzy told you that some time ago."

"Well?" He was standing his ground.

"Well what? I am talking about a number of great men who found a way to reach within themselves, as you did when writing your thesis, as Mozart did when writing his Requiem, as sculptors do when exposing the sculpture hidden within the stone. Other great men reached within and found wisdom which could benefit all man."

Sandra was quite up to date. She knew of his recent discussions with Suzy.

"Of course I know. I am you. When will you accept that? You are no longer a little boy. You should not pretend as little Alec did. You have to face the truth."

Alec knew all that, but he still found it confusing.

"It is not really confusing if you accept that you are more then meets the eye," Sandra was not as complaisant as she'd once been.

It was definitely time to grow up, he sighed.

"Precisely!" she concurred.

Alec laughed. "It's like talking to myself..."

She didn't say anything. But he knew he was right. He also knew that he had a choice of pretending that all this was a dream, or that he was on the verge of growing up. Only this growing up required a complete metamorphosis. He would have to give up his independence, his personality, and submit to Sandra within him. Submit to her will.

"Would that be so difficult?"

"It would be a form of dying. Man does not find dying easy..."

He actually said this aloud. And in that instant images of millions and millions of men slaughtering men, during thousands upon thousands of years of wars, pogroms, concentration camps, induced plagues, earthquakes, tidal waves and a thousand other cataclysmic events throughout history of man... all these seemed to fill his mind simultaneously. And then he saw the crowning glory—an atomic bomb fulminating its horrific yet spellbinding beauty as the mushroom rose towards the sky.

"Are you quite sure of that?" Sandra's voice was deep inside him.

"To die, perhaps to dream no more..." there had been others who dreamt of dying. "To dream no more. Does this mean living one's dream instead?"

"There is only one way to find out."

In all this time Alec was standing motionless, facing Sandra. For some reason she didn't offer any more answers. Was he to find them out himself? Or were the answers already etched within him. Hidden inside his mind even as a sculpture is hidden within a block of granite. That last was the obvious explanation. Was he sculptor enough to bring the unseen reality out into the daylight? To his waken awareness? Why is it that we must all find our own, individual way to the truth? Wouldn't it be easier just to read a book and follow the instructions?

Perhaps there was such a book...

But the concept of death never came easy to Alec. Life, or what he recognized as life, that energy within him, was such a powerful force. His unspoken promise to Sandra was by far the most important commitment he'd ever made. Yes, a conscious commitment. All his inner travels, even as a little boy, had been really a celebration of life. The problem with death was that it was so final. It seemed so permanent. That's what was wrong with death, he thought. It was so permanent.

And then it struck him with a clarity he'd never experienced before.

"You want my ego to die, don't you Sandra?"

But Sandra was nowhere to be seen. Once again, he was alone.

He woke up in the middle of the night. His first thought was that of being angry with himself. He was angry with himself for having wanted to ask Sandra so many questions. Even in his dreams. He refused to admit to himself that he'd been dreaming about seeing her for a long time. For years. He

wanted to ask her so many things, more things every day...
How did the ocean waves act the way they did? Why was
there thunder and lightening after the first tsunami on the
beach? How do sculptors know what is inside a stone? How
could Mozart know the whole composition before he took
pen to paper? And, for that matter, how was it that he seemed
to have visited Atlantis? And Lemuria? And...?

So many questions.

But the next thought in his troubled mind had to do with
Suzy's, or had it been Sandra's, smile. There was something
whimsical in that final look. It was as though he'd made a
mistake. As if he got things quite wrong...

At this precise moment Sacha sang a single, joyful note.
It climbed and climbed towards heaven, lingered there for a
timeless moment and resolved itself into cascading laughter.

And then Sacha returned to sleep. And so did Alec.

He dreamt a normal dream in which he was able to walk.
And run. People do not appreciate the simple pleasure of
walking. The almost sublime pleasure... Next morning he
awakened with a broad smile. He was finally ready to accept
his fate.

***

20
Wisdom of the Past

The first time it happened, Alec was scared out of his wits. He fought to get back into his own body, his own time, his own consciousness. It took him a long time to relax, whatever 'long time' represented in the inner realm. But whatever impulse brought him to experience the great minds of the past, wouldn't let go. He felt like a schoolboy who must do his set homework or he wouldn't be allowed to advance to the next class. He occupied other bodies, at least he thought he did, but not like this.

"Something is playing with my atavistic memories buried deep in my subconscious. Probably stored at the genetic level."

Suzy looked worried. "Well? What else can it be?" he asked defensively. "Or I am just stark raving mad," he muttered, too low for her to hear.

On that first occasion, Alec found himself in early sixth century BC. He had no idea how he knew that, since the people here, or there—depending from which time frame you were regarding them—obviously had never heard of Christ. Perhaps he'd only dated the experience after he got back. Of late, his inner and outer worlds became inextricably overlapped. Anyway, to the people he'd visited, it was just another day.

But what a day it was!

The air was so pure, so refined, that for a moment Alec derived pleasure just from breathing; although, he soon realized, they were not his lungs that languished on this sea air. Evidently, neither was it his body. Contrary to previous experiences, he had no control over its functions.

So it happened. I am finally and irrevocably paralyzed.

The body was lying on a straight, rather hard cot, its eyes closed, its muscles in total repose. An instant later he sighed in emotional relief, realizing that the body he'd entered was asleep. Alec explored his host's subconscious. He soon ascertained that he was in Miletus, a harbour on the balmy Aegean Sea, in Caria, near Sa   mos. The host, whose personality and name remained to be determined, was proud of his city, which apparently had been designed on a modern, rectangular layout, by the best planers in Caria.

Alec also learned that his host was both, a philosopher and a scientist, as well as a practical man, a skilled manipulator of market trends, and thus a man of substantial wealth. Miletus itself had already been recognized as the hub of progressive thought. It also flourished in business and was later credited with having been the cradle and inspiration of science and philosophy, which evolved into Western Civilization.

He'd also discovered, there and then, that the early Greeks never claimed to be forefathers of major philosophical or scientific trends. They were well aware that not only Cretans but Mesopotamians and Sumerians, not to mention the Egyptians before them, had been their precursors by several millennia. Only later, much later, we, of the Western Civilization, thought of the Greeks as the true fathers of modern science. But the error of this assumption came to Alec only after his return.

What am I doing here? What has all this to do with me?

Alec 'saw', if one can use such an inadequate expression, the thoughts of the day through the eyes of Thales, or what the eyes of Thales had accumulated over the years. For Thales turned out to be the name of the host who, so conveniently, decided to take a nap at the right time.

"All things are made of water," Thales declared.

I am also reading his past thoughts. What an incredible storehouse of information is a man's subconscious. Is this what I am supposed to reach into?

For no reason that made any sense, after only a cursory scan of the ancient Greek's mind, Alec returned in his own time. The whole visit seemed fragmentary, without any particular point, rather as though it formed part of his general education and served only as a background for some later purposes.

On his 'return' Alec thumbed through books he'd not seen since his schooldays. Thales counted as one of the wise men of the Greek Tradition. He had not only advanced the knowledge of his day, but was well versed with science dating back to Babylonian records. He appears to have been a learned, cultured, and astute man.

Even as with Thales, on a number of future occasions Alec had been placed in other ancient bodies, perhaps minds is a better word, minds of men of unprepossessing knowledge, but even more so, of impressive strength of character. None of them had given an impression of being woozy headed philosophers, detached from the stream of everyday life. They'd all been active participators in the development of their civilization. Not at all like some specialized wool gatherers Alec had met in his own time. Not one of the ancients seemed afraid to state the truth as he saw it, regardless of the consequences to himself or his reputation. Those condensed snippets of knowledge from the past, which Alec gathered, emanated from a number of minds, but only, while the consciousness of the host body was sedated by a relaxing sleep.

There had been a number of men whose character could serve as a paradigm for us today. Perhaps that was the lesson Alec was meant to learn. Perhaps today we also need men we can look up to. Not idols of the stage, film, or the arena of professional sports, nor the inflated egos of political puppets.

Perhaps, what we needed today, he mused, are our own giants.

Giants of the mind?

Alec recalled but a few of the minds he'd touched on. Anaximander, not just a scientist and philosopher, but an inventor, and a man versed in practical aspects of everyday life. Later Pythagoras who'd established a more mathematical tradition and introduced the notion of universal harmony. Heraclitus who'd developed this concept of balance, a view of the world that relies on a balanced adjustment of opposing tendencies.

Behind the strife and struggle between the opposites, there lies a hidden harmony or attunement, which is the true nature of the world... Alec read in his mind.

"Good God!" Alec exclaimed, while recounting some days later his experiences to Suzy. "This was five hundred years before Christ!"

"Could Jalaludin Rumi have said it any better?" she mused, equally as stunned. Rumi live in the 13th century of the present era.

Alec grew more and more pensive.

Have we really advanced from those days? Are we really more developed as human beings? Or do we tread the mill in the ever-recurring present. All things are made of water... he recalled Thales' words. *Does water symbolize a constant stream of thoughts? Churning and churning, round and round, without ever going anywhere? Is this where we have our being?*

In time, Alec had been shown the minds of other great men. Always strictly as an observer. He couldn't probe, search for items of interest, outside what was readily available. Even at the very beginning he'd felt instinctively that taking over an advanced mind would be a horrendous crime, akin to black magic.

In sleep, however, even if the men, on waking, were to be aware that someone had visited his dormant consciousness, he would have assigned it to dreams; and dreams then as now, had not been fully understood. Even today Alec was aware of an enormous variety of dreams, from symbolic communications from one's own unconscious, through purely relaxing and therapeutic images, to settling some antagonistic subliminal conditions, all the way to vivid, extremely real and palpable experiences, with which he was very well versed. Anyone attempting to create a Unified Theory of Dreams would be condemned to dismal failure.

"No disrespect intended, Sigmund," he smirked, with just a tinge of condescension. Freud was one of Suzy's heroes. "Our conscious mind is to our subconscious as the tip of an iceberg is to the remainder of its submerged body."

"He never denied it..." she attempted a feeble defense.

"Perhaps that is why the Home Planet is so rich in texture," Alec continued, lost in his own thoughts. "So prolific in everything. We can always imagine whatever we've ever experienced..."

"...or haven't as yet," she added. This time Alec nodded in agreement.

What he did not tell Suzy was that the unconscious lay far beyond the reach of even our subconscious. The Far Country was the realm of the unconscious. Of virtually pure thought.

There was another advantage to visiting men while they slept. Their own consciousness may have been taking its own trip to other realms. Alec could not only explore their subconscious, but what had been equally fascinating, he could hear and thus witness at least some of the waken activities of others within reach of the host's body. He'd discovered that the subconscious never sleeps. It was like using a time machine which, though it could not move from place to place, it could provide information on its immediate surroundings.

Does this have something to do with my legs? My partial paralysis that defies diagnosis?

But here he came across a new problem. While the subconscious stored its data in images, when attempting to espy activities 'live', language became a barrier. But even so, at least the emotions had been well discernible.

That was the good part.

The bad part was that when exploring the subconscious of another, one sacrificed one's own. And this was why, particularly on the first few occasions, Alec had felt so completely lost or, as his father would have put it, discombobulated. He not only hadn't known where or when he'd been, but *who* he may have invaded at the time. Literally. He was no longer aware of his own beingness, yet did not feel integrated into the new mental environment. In time, he developed a sense of allegiance to the alien nature, to the mind in which he'd found himself a temporary visitor. And frankly, whatever subconscious he visited in those few days it, or he, felt as alien as anything he could imagine.

We think we know one another, but this simply isn't true.

Within the depth of our being, we share almost nothing. We are as different from each other as a cockroach would feel finding itself within the body of butterfly. It would have to become cognizant of wings with which to fly, of the eyes with which to see in a completely different spectrum. It would have to learn to recognize different colours, different smells, even different impulses driving sexual attraction.

It was *almost* as bad among humans.

Alec found that the range of human emotions was spread over a very wide field. Also, it was conditioned by such an incredibly divergent environment that it was subjected to moral and ethical codes, which had been interpreted differently by each human subconscious he'd entered. It seemed that what made us human was not our capacity to unite, but to differentiate from one another.

Could this have been the underlying reason for human strife through the ages?

And yet, at some level of our being we long to be one.

When Alec observed the minds of giants of the past, he'd detected a trait in their humanity that defied our weaknesses, or apparent predisposition towards all that sets us apart. The trait wound its way through the ages, never to be broken in man's gradual progress toward greater self-awareness. Perhaps toward the awareness of Self? Only Alec suspected that the Ultimate Goal, identical for all, if hidden as yet from our eyes, had been and continued to be approached from countless diverse directions.

Hence the apparent alienation.

It took Alec hours, sometimes days, to decipher what he'd experienced, not to mention to interpret the acquired knowledge into a sequential, logical order. What had been right and logical some twenty-six centuries ago did not always mesh with the present reality. Not immediately. While a great deal of the past may be regarded as 'out of date' in terms of our latest discoveries, our forefathers entertained highly advanced attitudes, which now appeared lost for reasons which were hard to fathom. The greatest among them, it seemed, was the incredible diversity of resourcefulness the past giants had exhibited. They each encapsulated a gamut of interests akin to Leonardo da Vinci's. Alec became determined to widen his view of the world—to become more aware, at least, of his immediate environment; to live in a more intense state of awareness.

He also learned that among the early Greeks, science and philosophy had been integrated into a single discipline. What happened to set them apart? He'd learned the importance the Greeks placed on mathematics. Not just the axioms, which we used to this day, but the manner in which thinking was disciplined by mathematical logic. Much of this wisdom was still practiced by his colleagues today, but certainly not by all. While the world overtly conformed to patterns, to beautiful rhythms that could be expressed in mathematical terms, such knowledge seemed inaccessible to most people. Even the mathematical beauty manifest in the endless unfoldment of fractals remained a mystery to members of his own family.

"Is this my fault?" he wondered. "Do I share in the blame?"

Some of his theoretically minded friends, however, went as far to 'the other side' as the best among theological mystics. Were they the quislings, the *vendus*, or did they cut a new trail through the jungle of science by opting for theoretical concepts without any regard to the due process— the process of logical analysis. Of course, quantum mechanics didn't help. The classicists believed in cause and effect. Alec's 'quantum' friends opted for ultimate uncertainty. There was still a cause, perhaps a prime cause, but the effect was only in the realm of probability. It was as though there was still God, but She was no longer responsible for Her actions. He liked referring to God as 'She'. He thought he ought to balance the equation of thousands of years of machismo.

And thinking of gods…

Alec had soon discovered that search for the essence of reality, no matter how scientific, inevitably led to the realm of the infinite, even as his own Theory of Information had taken him to the very gates of the divine. Throughout history, it seemed, the search for truth had lead men to gods—no matter how absurd their arcane concepts might have been.

Recently, Alec had also learned that no self-respecting Greek philosopher-scientist could be accused of regarding his or her various gods the way the later generations looked upon theirs. Not the way the Hebrews, the Christians, or the Moslem looked upon their gods. The Greeks placed no reliance upon their divinities. They did not live in fear of their punishment, or worship them in the hope of rewards. To those early Greeks the gods had been no more than personifications of certain human traits, raised to their probable ideal. That was all. The ancient philosopher had relied on gifts he had been blessed with, perhaps the Prime Cause, perhaps

Evolution, to determine his own future, his own fate, his own Olympus or Hades. Not at all like later religions that made man no more than a servant of the invisible, invincible, omnipotent, adamant, reputedly all-merciful but as often utterly cruel deity, condemning the ignorant peons to eternal damnation. Ancient Greeks may have tolerated such beliefs among their uneducated masses, but such perversions had been neither taught, nor encouraged, nor accepted among men of philosophers' stature. The Greeks accepted the possibility of an inherent predisposition to the Universal Good, but that was all. The rest was up to them.

Alec leaned back and closed his eyes.

"All things are made of water," Thales declared.

And on that day modern science was born. Not because Thales was right, but because he motivated his successors to ponder of what we are made, and ultimately of who we are. He had shown that in philosophy, as in science, what really mattered were the questions you asked, more so than the answers that were given. From his day on it was up to us to steer our ships across the oceans of time and knowledge. At least they, the ancients, had steered their ships with courage of conviction.

What happened?

When did people draw a line between the gifts they had been given and the giver of all gifts? Is not Mozart's music still Mozart's even though played by his successors? Is not the composer and the composition irrevocably of a single nature? Are they not one, indivisible, forever united by the creative act?

Greeks had known the truth. We seem to have lost their ancient understanding.

"Wasn't Moses a historical figure?" Alec asked no one in particular. He tried to pit the early Hebrew philosophy against the knowledge of ancient Greeks.

The foursome was sitting on the terrace after an early dinner. The gentlest of breezes wafted over the waves, carrying a salty smell of faraway places. The sun was playing peek-a-boo with the low clouds over the horizon. The atmosphere was as serene as the Pacific itself.

Alec never owned up to his latest escapades, but he did raise some subjects ensuing from them. And there were many subjects. More than he could fathom on his own. The influence of the Torah on succeeding generations was just one of them.

"He might have been, for all the good it did them," Desmond replied.

"You mean he might have been more successful, so to speak, had he been but a myth?"

"They say that pen is mightier than the sword. And they assign a lot of books to Moses," Desmond affirmed. "And, by the way, never say *but* a myth. All religions are based on ten-percent fact and the other ninety on myth. Myth is the most powerful weapon man has invented to date."

For a moment Alec tried to figure out how many men died in the name of religions and how many as a result of atomic bombs. The myths won hands down. Desmond was in a habit of stating the obvious which no one seemed to have noticed before. Maybe he was a Greek philosopher in disguise?

"So why are you so negative about Moses?" Alec pressed on.

"Because Moses was virtually the first offender," Desmond explained. For some reason he's foregone his usual r's. "He'd been inspired with a superb set of rules which could have set men higher on their dismal perch, and what did he do? He told them that he'd been given those rules by a burning bush. Hardly surprising the people didn't take him seriously."

"Could he have told them the truth?" Alec sounded doubtful.

"Maybe he had, in a symbolic way, but how many among the masses were likely to understand esoteric symbolism? Have you met anyone lately who was actively studying the Kabala? As it turned out, the Mosaic method could hardly have served him any worse," Desmond smiled sadly. "And the second time round, he'd been told, reputedly, that the giver of the Ten Commandments was I AM." He drew great big letters with his index finger in the air. "Not you are, not He or She way-up-there-yonder is, but I am. And did he listen to his inner self, his I am?"

"Possibly not. But this time he did speak the truth."

"Only in a manner of speaking. He didn't tell them that he'd been inspired to give them the Mosaic Law. His Law. He implied that it came from an external source. Not from within. He wanted them to accept his god in lieu of their divine golden calf. Well, when you first tell people lies, thereafter they don't believe you. There is a built-in reflex in all of us to smell the rat. Our brain is wired to reject the improbable."

"And a body set in motion continues in motion until..." Alec didn't finish.

"What are you talking about?" Suzy cut in.

"I was quoting from Newton's *Principia*. It parallels Desmond's proposition, that once a religious leader, or any leader for that matter, starts lying to his people, he doesn't know when or how to stop," Alec said.

"One fellow did stop lying... didn't do him much good, though." Des murmured, seemingly to himself.

Alec did not know enough about the Bible to agree or disagree. He tried to imagine a world in which people had listened to Moses. Not his story about the tablets or the burning bush, but to his set of laws. The Greeks could not have improved on them much. And Moses was way back before the Greeks. There was one other Greek that fascinated Alec. A Greek who spoke the truth.

Alec's next peek into the past was even more unnerving. Had it happened in a dream, it would have been another story. His arms were getting stronger by the day, and the evening felt just right for some exercise. He could actually lift himself up from the bed onto the wheelchair by himself. Alec decided to take a hike along the coast, all by himself.

At some point along the bicycle-path, his mind wondered. He imagined he was running. Perhaps his synapses were making new connections. Next, incongruously, he thought he'd tripped, and fell flat on the ground. As he turned over, he was reclining on a long bench. He was propped up on a few pillows.

I must have hit the ground hard, he thought. By then he was elsewhere. And elsewhen.

He felt consciousness ebbing from him fast. He could hardly keep his eyes open. Around him he could just discern a small group of people.

"My friends," he thought. "My dear, dear friends..." he repeated.

More were not allowed. Even his closest friends were here only by special dispensation. Their faces showed concern, sadness, a few displayed anger. The guards stood further off, as if afraid of what his friends might do if they got any closer. His eyes were loosing their clarity of vision. He could only just recognize his friends' faces. The space around him was growing darker, less distinct.

"So much to do... No matter, Plato will carry on," he sighed deeply. "Unless they get him too..."

He felt very weak.

Minutes earlier, still walking, to let the poison circulate faster through his veins, he could just see the back of the South Stoa with the Law Court on the left, and Tholos beyond. The farther buildings were already veiled a darkening mist. Not of the air, but of the hemlock which was taking its hold. When he lay down his vision was even more affected. With an effort he raised his eyelids. Crito looked worried. Good old Crito, he thought, always faithful...

"Crito… listen," his voice was hardly above a whisper. "My truest and best part will survive my body..." Why do they worry about such things? I taught them for so many years... Why can't they understand that my body is but an insignificant part of me?

"What shall we do with…"

"….with my body? You can do with it whatever is usual. It is of no concern to me."

Why is it so dark? It must be time. He smiled with relief.

"Crito, I owe a cock to Asclepius—pay my debt for me…"

Alec hadn't tripped. He hadn't been jogging, either. His body responded to the rhythmic movement of his arms, the beat of his heart. It's been set on automatic. Not so the body his mind had just left.

One fellow did stop lying. Didn't do him much good...

Alec recalled Desmond's words. His friend had not been talking about the Bible. Alec's wheelchair came to a gradual stop. For a while, he just sat there. He sat there and wept.

He felt like Crito. Quite helpless.

"I really don't feel like it today, Sue. I'll stay with Sacha," he said.

It was early next morning. Bright, sunny, blissful. Not at all like his vision last evening. She tried to persuade him to take a stroll, but failed. Alec could be quite stubborn.

Matt helped Alec strip and left him seated on a stool in the bathroom shower. Alec could reach the faucets himself. He took a long shower, then, with Matt's help, dressed and spent the next few hours with the Bible on his lap. He'd never read the whole Bible. Like the vast majority of the Christians, he'd always relied on hearsay. Sue and Des were the only people he'd ever met who read the Bible cover to cover. They also read the Koran, the Bhagavad-Gita, Tao Te Ching, Rumi's poetry and who knows what other pearls of ancient wisdom. He'd read some extracts of the Bible in school, but later he'd given it up.

Science seemed more fascinating.

Not that he objected to the quintessential teaching, but he couldn't stand the constant talk of sinners, of the uselessness of man, of man's inadequacy, of man's constant reliance on external sources. But he still felt that any book to which one billion people pledged their allegiance must have something to offer. He was determined to find out what it was. What it might be. Frankly, his physical condition did not inspire him to delve into the reputed source of benevolence. Then he started getting desperate. At present, he had little to lose.

Alec had many reservations about the authenticity of the scriptures. For his mathematically trained mind, there were just too many contradictions, too many teachings which, judging by the evidence of his own eyes, had been completely ignored by people who claimed to base their faith on the scriptural writings. He was fully aware that the Bible had been written by hand, copied and recopied by equally fallible hands many times, then translated again and again from two dead languages into modern usage. This even applied to the King James Version, though the English of early seventeenth century did support, in his view, the poetry of language, perhaps of the original. This was lost in latter attempts at bringing the translations more up to date. He saw those in hotels, on his travels.

Alec was also acutely aware the text had been written for people who have been dead for more than 2000 years. Long-gone idioms, referring to long-gone images, probably made sense only to the contemporaries of the scribes.

No matter.

Alec was on the quest to find out who he was. Later he tried to do equal justice to the Koran. He hadn't fared as well. After some fifty pages he'd given up. Having found each Sura adorned with assurances of Allah the Merciful, the Compassionate... and then, on the very same pages, being told that this Magnanimous Deity is ready to dispatch him, under the slightest pretext, to eternal, fiery and altogether unpleasant damnation, he decided to get depressed easier and faster by reading the Financial Times.

Even in his unaccustomed studies, Alec suffered from one weakness.

When something began preying on his mind, he couldn't let go until he bit off at least a good chunk. And the Bible was no exception. Last night, and almost every night since getting to the villa, instead of a good night's sleep, he'd read in bed till after three in the morning. Finally he'd close his eyes only to be taken on a wild spin through the biblical stories, some pleasant, some full of gore. Last night he'd ended up in a stone courtyard. He found himself crouching on rough paving, his back against the wall, just to the side of an arched porch. It was still on the dark side of gray. The day was just breaking. His head was propped up on his hands, which in turn rested on his bent knees. He was not a happy man.

How could I have done it?

He knows I love him, and it was not really I that denied him. Someone did. Just as he said. But if he knew, why didn't he stop me? Does he enjoy seeing me suffer? If only he hadn't mixed me all up. He said that he was within me. If he is within me then maybe he denied himself? I wouldn't, I couldn't have done it on my own.

Never! No...

Not on my own.

And he also said that heaven is within me. Within him and me. Within all of us. And he said that the Father is in heaven. Well, if the Father is in heaven and heaven is within me, then how could I have denied him? It just doesn't make any sense. Not three times... Had I known that he didn't mean me to do it, I would have stayed at home. I've got friends! Not many, but I have some who would've put me up, right? And instead he lets me deny him thrice.

What could I have done? Should I have opposed his will? Contradicted him?

But isn't he always right? So what of my free will?
At least I didn't betray him. If I'd been chosen for that
job I would have hanged myself. I very nearly did, anyway.
Why can't I understand his words...?

Every time Alec had such dreams he would wake up
sweating. And lately, such dreams haunted him almost every
night. The dreams had been vivid. He not only saw and heard
whatever happened, but shared the full emotional impact, the
full anguish as he sat there, in the silent courtyard at the dawn
of a dismal day. Simon's thoughts may have been rebellious,
but his heart was broken. He'd suffered agonies like he'd
never suffered before. He'd been scared, not just for himself.
He couldn't even face reality. And there was nothing Alec
could have done for him. Not a word of consolation. Not even
a pat on the shoulder.

This just wasn't fun. Not any more. When he was a boy,
all Alec's dreams had been magnificent escapes. They'd been
filled with joy and daring, and danger and courage—and
invariably crowned with final victories.

What happened?

When I was a child... I thought as a child; but when I
became a man... Is this what happened? Were the early
escapades designed for children only? No wonder adults
don't dream as I do. They didn't put away childish things;
they just grew out of them. Perhaps all such dreams, dreams
of alternate realities, are hard on the dreamer. Perhaps...

"At least Peter also had his problems. So... I'm not
alone," he thought.

Somehow this realization made him feel better. He was
not alone. And, he felt he was getting there. Wherever 'there'
took him.

***

21
Who am I?

"**I am a biochemical machine,** which exhibits a cerrtain level of intelligence?" Desmond replied automatically. It sounded as much a question as a statement.

It has been a while since he'd given the riddle any thought. He wondered what had prompted Alec to bring up the question. Alec was at his best when at work at the Institute, but outside, he looked perturbed lately. Desmond could help him with math and logic, and with a lot of questions on physics, but this? What does he mean: 'Who am I'? Doesn't he know?

"Or am I intelligence which at some level of perception guides biochemical processes by the encoding of intelligence or instructions in the gene to produce a biochemical machine which enables this intelligence to enjoy the process of not necessarily just physiological becoming..."

"...but rather the pleasure of partaking in the advancement of arts, of creativity, of intellectual pursuits, music or even just free thought?" Alicia made her contribution.

"Did you know that Krishna in Hindu means 'All Pleasure'?" asked Suzy.

"I like that. I like that a lot," Alicia approved.

"I thought you might." Suzy was pleased. The two ladies shared a lot together, not the least among them being their view of the world.

"What do you think, Des?" Alicia was leaning on Desmond's arm.

"I definitely think Krrishna was rright. Especially since I've met you." Desmond sounded dead serious.

"I love you too, darling," Alicia whispered in his ear.

"You have to. We'rre getting married tomorrow." He gave her the naughtiest of winks.

Tomorrow came very quickly.

The church was small; perhaps two hundred could fit in, if most remained standing. Maria had made all the preliminary inquiries. She found three small churches that met Alicia's description, and later she and Alicia drove around to pick one to Alicia's liking. Actually the church was little more than a chapel. Originally it was Roman Catholic, but now, with the decline in church attendance, it had opened its doors to all denominations. It stood on a hill, as all good churches should. It was covered with stucco that looked freshly whitewashed. Leading up to it was a narrow winding road, little wider than a path, with edges overflowing with Bougainvillea dressed over a low stone wall. Red over white.

"Canadian colours," Suzy remarked. "How nice!"

It was nice.

At three in the afternoon the church was empty, holding its breath for the wedding. Maria, dear Maria, made sure that the main altar would be awash with flowers; all local, all fresh, all festive. Even Desmond was impressed. He wasn't as artistically sensitive as his wife to be, nor did he accept that religious rites should impede on his private union with Alicia. In fact he wasn't quite sure what all the fuss was about. They'd already recited their lines at the civil ceremony as required by law, and that was more than good enough for him. Didn't the Good Book say 'thou shalt not swear'? Or 'swear not at all'? Something like that. No matter. Nobody listened to the Good Book anyway. Least of all the padres. I suppose they had to make a living, Des thought, and people wanted to swear. They thought they were making a commitment. They needed that formality. It gave them, they thought, some kind of handle on their future. Only it didn't work. Around fifty percent of first marriages in the States ended in divorce. A lot more in California, he suspected. Marriages were good for the priests and good for the lawyers. Not so good for the people.

Yet, when he saw Alicia in her wedding dress, the same one, incidentally, that she'd worn twenty-six years ago at her first wedding, he would gladly have driven her to hell and back, if that was what she'd want. Des had studied her family photo albums, and he defied anyone not to admit that Alicia was at least twice as beautiful now as she'd ever been.

"Sorry, lassie," he turned his head when he first saw her all decked out. He'd turned to wipe a tear. "But I've neverrr seen such an angel beforre..." And he blew his nose with considerable conviction.

As it turned out, the padre, or the priest, was the nicest man you could hope to meet. He was big, a little on the plump side, jovial and disarming. He came out, outside, to meet them, embraced them all as though he were an old family friend. He seemed to possess that rare trait of actually loving people. It was not a show of the so-called 'people skills' but a genuine love that could not go unnoticed. The joy in his eyes that two older people found love, and found it for the second time, seemed to fill him with great personal pleasure. He made all six of them feel that they were entering his personal home, that they were his personal guests, members of his family, and simultaneously the most important people in his life.

Just looking at the 'young couple' was enough to bring tears to Suzy's eyes. Maria was not doing any better. She seemed to have kept a corner of her heart reserved for the Professor for many years, and now, rather than losing him, she felt she'd gained another friend in Alicia. The Professor had been almost like a father to her. To her whole family. When her husband had lost his job some years ago, the Professor kept her whole family going until her husband found new employment. That took almost six months. No wonder they had to take time to dry their eyes before the ceremony could even begin.

"I most cerrrtainly do!" Desmond said in a strong, amazingly youthful voice. He thought himself by far the luckiest man in the world.

"I do!" Alicia echoed and not waiting for padre's permission kissed Desmond on both cheeks and his mouth. She proceeded to kiss the padre, Suzy, Maria in that order. Then, after a momentary hesitation she reached up on her toes and planted a firm kiss on Matt's cheek. The big man turned bright red. No one knew if the flush was due to pleasure or innate shyness. Matt had volunteered to be the official chauffeur for the young couple. Matt enjoyed volunteering. Apparently, it was in his nature.

When it was Alec's turn, she whispered in his ear: "Thank you, Ali."

For the wedding fiesta, they'd reserved a private room in a restaurant not far from the church. The padre, of course, had been coaxed into joining them. He spent the next two hours recounting the most hilarious stories about other marriages he'd presided over. Alec tried to make notes so as to pass them on to his colleagues at Caltech. But most of the time he was too busy just laughing.

Finally, they drove back to the villa. Neither Alicia nor Desmond wanted a traditional honeymoon. "We're in the loveliest place on earth, surrounded by people who love us," Alicia insisted. "Why would we want to go anywhere?" She had a point.

Desmond had a different reason. "I'm too old for that sort of thing," he admitted some time later when he was alone with Alec, "and it would have been too tiring. My idea of doing something all night is basically sleeping. And you can't do that on a honeymoon."

But on that day, he wouldn't dare say that.

By seven o'clock the newlyweds took a walk along the beach. The sun already sunk to a low angle, its rays skimming along the crests, spraying them with glittering fire. Alec and

Suzy sat on the terrace watching Sacha, who was still busy examining each square of the security string net. Maria's daughter, who'd been looking after Sacha during the afternoon, was sent home with one complete tier of the wedding cake. Matt? Matt was nowhere to be seen.

Alec felt great contentment. Whatever was upsetting his peace of mind lately evaporated into thin air. His eyes followed his mother and Des along the beach. They all felt happy.

"He's a good man," Suzy said.

Alec knew about Desmond's goodness. He counted on his judgment in more than just the scientific field. He respected the Professor's view of the world. Des was a little like Socrates. He didn't lie. Perhaps he didn't know how to lie. Alec recalled the Professor's answer to his question 'Who am I?' 'A biochemical machine…?' Is this all I am?

"You know, Sue, few people realize that scientists, the good ones, are people of very deep faith. They talk and sound like atheists, but that's because they dismiss the simplistic images of God which the sacerdotal fraternity promulgates to the gullible masses. Yet the scientist is a man who is continuously exposed to incredible mystery, beauty, harmony, order and wonder of the universe. We are more aware of this unimaginable affinity than any group of people who do not study the universe for a living."

"I must admit, I never thought of you guys that way. They all seemed at the very least agnostic," Suzy admitted.

"You say *they*, but how many have you really met?"

"True. I don't know enough of them to pass judgment," Suzy nodded again, "but you must also admit that this is a common misconception, such as it is."

Alec let that drop. She was probably right and anyway, he'd suggested as much. The physicists did sound detached from the commonly recognized and accepted religious superstitions. But this had little to do with faith. Only the motivation, the object commanding their, of our, faith carried very different connotations. Whether the question 'who am I' was an aspect of faith or science, remained a moot point. In recent weeks Alec read volumes on who, purportedly, he was supposed to be. Who anyone was. Or at least, on what role model we were to channel our research.

Alec was well aware that Suzy knew much more about this subject than he did. He asked her if she could make some notes for him.

"When we get back, of course," he added.

To his surprise she got up and came back with a copy of the Bhagavad-Gita. It was a well-worn copy, a book that she'd looked at many times over the years. The funny thing was that neither she nor Alec had ever had any religious attachments. Nor had they ever discussed the question of religious preferences. Perhaps they both just knew too much.

"You carry that with you?" He looked as surprised as he sounded.

"You took the Bible, so I took my Gita. Do you mind?"

"Not at all, but… why this particular scripture?"

"Well, that's partially your fault. It is your hero who said that, and I quote: 'When I read the Bhagavad-Gita and reflect about how God created this universe everything else seems so superfluous'."

"My hero? You must be kidding! My heroes don't often quote God."

"Albert Einstein did. These are his words…"

For the next half-hour each became lost in their thoughts. Alec continued to thumb through the notes he'd made on the Bible; Suzy was marking up some passages in her own text. The idea was that if the scriptures claim that we are created to reflect some sort of infinite potential they refer to as God, then lets find out as much as we can what they say about God. That should help us to get a handle on what we might be. Not very scientific, but he had to start somewhere. Dreams alone were not enough.

Soon Alec's list was ready. The notes he jotted down from the New Testament were short and unsatisfying. They were also predicated by the fact that Christians regarded the author of the statements as their God. He limited himself to statements beginning with the words 'I am'. This didn't get him very far, but the part about 'entering in and going in and out to find pasture' had an interesting ring to it. He made a mental note to look at this phrase later. As for being 'the truth and the life', well, that also needed a closer examination. If our belief system created our universe, then we all are the truth and the life within the confines of our reality.

The Old Testament fared little better, but at least it was more definitive. It said simply: I AM THAT I AM. This didn't give away much, but it was also not sending him on a wild goose chase within a symbolic labyrinth.

He did much better with some extracts from Nag Hammadi Library. He'd jotted them down in LA. The statements in the Gnostic gospels were considerably more explicit. He glanced at his notes: *I am he who was within me. Never have I suffered in any way, nor have I been distressed.*

This sentence established a dichotomy between the body and the mind, or the spirit. He found this separation expedient to explain some of his own experiences. Also Alec was not sure there was a difference between mind and spirit, as long as you didn't confuse mind with intellect. He continued reading.

I am the first-born son who was begotten.
I am the beloved.
I am the righteous one.
I am in the process of becoming.
I am the honoured one and the scorned one.
I am the silence that is incomprehensible.
I am the one before whom you have been ashamed.
I am strength and I am fear.
I am war and peace.

This last placed the 'I am' firmly in the realm of duality. Not in any imaginary heaven where, some seemed to imply, there was no differentiation between I am and the Whole. Alec recalled his early encounters with Sandra, many years ago, when she'd said that he and she, the Princess, were like two peas in a pod, but that all the Princes and Princesses were also an expression of a single larger pod. This had been fairly meaningless to him at the time, but now it suggested that our mind could be an individualized expression of a Single larger Mind. Rather like the Egyptians seem to have implied.

There were some other quotations, but he already had a mouthful of 'I ams'. Scientifically he couldn't use many of them.

But there was one 'I am' which particularly caught Alec's attention. It was the 'I am the process of becoming'. It caught his attention because he'd seen something very similar before. It was Plato who had said that our being is a perpetual becoming. How odd, he thought, so many centuries apart.

"Here you are darling. I hope that's enough for a start?"

Suzy handed him her notebook. It was more than Alec had expected. And she got it all just from the Bhagavad-Gita. Alec tended to scribble, Suzy's notes were written out in her neat, precise handwriting. One would never suspect it after seeing her paintings!

I am the taste of water, the light of the sun and the moon...

I am the sound in ether and the ability in man.

I am the original fragrance of the earth, and I am the light in fire.

I am the life of all that lives, and I am the penances of all ascetics.

I am the original seed of all existence, the intelligence of the intelligent, and the prowess of all powerful men.

I am the strength of the strong, devoid of passion and desire.

I am the Self, seated in the hearts of all creatures. I am the beginning, the middle, and the end of all beings.

I am ever detached, seated as though neutral.
I am the source of everything; from Me the entire creation flows.
I am seated in everyone's heart, and from Me come remembrance, knowledge and forgetfulness.

"There must be many others, of course, but these might keep you going," she added when he said nothing.

"Sue, you're a marvel. I may be sinful and vicious, but to you I'll always be beneficent."

"Ouch!"

"What?"

"You are butchering Mizra Khan. If I can quote from memory, he said 'To the sinful and vicious, I may appear to be evil. But to the good—beneficent am I'."

"Did he?" and Alec gazed at his wife with renewed admiration. "How on earth can you remember such things?"

"It's almost as easy as the hieroglyphics which you scribble on the blackboard when you give one of your lectures."

She had a point. He recalled the first physics lecture he'd attended as a student. He remembered it for one reason only. He'd understood almost nothing. It was that inability to comprehend that propelled him to study physics. He could never bypass a challenge.

Alec looked as Suzy's list for some time.

"You know? This whole list tells me only one thing. It says in many different ways that I am consciousness."

Alicia's laughter reached them from below. The bride had changed immediately after they'd returned home from the restaurant. The loose chiffon she now wore performed exciting acrobatics in the wind. It was evident that Des loved every second of it. He strutted like a young stallion showing off his first conquest.

"I knew it would be tough," Desmond announced at the top of the winding stairs. "I can harrdly keep up with this lassie."

"It is I who could hardly keep up with you, darling. You must have been cheating when you told me your age."

"I did it only to prrotect my poorr life," he fired back.

And so it went on.

Alec thought it was time for a drink. Since arriving, almost a week ago, they'd hardly drunk any alcohol at all. Not counting the Sangria and the wine with meals, of course. But no Scotch. It was high time to make up for the grave sin of omission.

In spite of their long walk and Desmond's protests, he didn't look the least bit tired. They seemed blessed with a new lease on life, or better still, with a new lease of youth. They both had decades of living to catch up on. Memories to share. Alicia did most of the listening. Until recently, she had had someone with whom she'd shared her dreams. Desmond had been forced to keep his innermost thoughts to himself for a much longer time. Never, never in his sober mind, would he have dared to imagine that now, in his early sixties, he would inherit a beautiful woman many years his junior, and, to all intent and purposes, a daughter and a son. He kept staring at Alicia, as though not quite believing his eyes. Now and then he got up, walked up to her as though to make sure she was real.

A little after nine, Suzy tapped Alec's ankle under the table, and pointed to the bedroom. He understood immediately. Only later that night did he realize that he had registered a semblance of feeling in his leg.

"All this fresh sea air makes me sleepy," he said immediately. "If you'll excuse me, I think I'll turn in."

Suzy stifled an imaginary yawn.

"May I join you my husband?"

"You'd better. I wouldn't trust you with this Casanova on the same terrace."

But no one heard them. The newlyweds sat looking into each other's eyes. They had to make up for many, many years.

Alec didn't shower but lifted himself onto the bed still in his swimming trunks. Suzy joined him smelling of perfumed soap.

"Love you," she said in half tone.

"What darling?"

"Say goodnight to Sacha," she said, this time her voice really sounding sleepy. There had been many emotions today.

"Goodnight, Sacha."

But Sacha was already out in the pasture, going in and out, at will.

Suzy switched off the light. She had no courage to say what she had to say facing him.

"I've made an appointment with Dr. Shulling for next Monday," she said under the protection of darkness.

Alec had seen Dr. Shulling three times. He was the best neurologist around. It was he who'd declared that there was nothing organically wrong with Alec's legs or spine.

"That's OK. We'll just cancel it," he said quietly.

"Alec, please..." There was pain in her voice.

"Switch on the light," he asked softly.

"Why?"

"Do it."

Alec pulled the sheets up over his chest.

"Look," he said in a loud whisper.

Suzy looked on as he moved first his left then his right big toe. Then he wagged them both in opposite directions. Up and down.

"I felt your tap on my ankle at the table," he said.

Suzy switched off the light to hide her tears.

"I l-love you," she repeated in half-whimper.

"I know," he whispered, "I know Sue..." He, too, couldn't say any more.

It's been a long time. There were times when he had virtually lost hope. When the paralysis had been moving up his spine, he'd read articles on muscular dystrophy. He was scared. Then came incontinence. Without Matt, he would have drowned in his own excrement. Later, he'd lost control over most of his body. Even his neck had stiffened.

Yet the physical degeneration was not the worst of it. There had been moments when he was losing faith in his mental capacity. The simplest scientific articles he'd had to read two or three times, before grasping their import. He'd had to stick to lectures on well-tried subjects, avoiding anything new. It had been then that he'd thought that he'd joined the establishment. That he'd become one of *them*.

"Is my pride at the bottom of all this? Is it my exalted ego?" he'd asked himself a thousand times. But most often he just cried a silent cry: "Why me?"

Last week he'd stumbled upon a possible cause for his insensateness and even a degree of mental stolidity. He became convinced that he's been denying his true nature. He wasn't sure yet, but it seemed that it wasn't his body denying him its efficacy. It had been he who, in some way, had been denying his body. He was shortchanging himself.

During the last two days he'd managed to use the bathroom. On his own. It wasn't a question of lifting himself from the wheelchair onto the toilet seat. It was a question of knowing when to go, and then getting there on time.

And now he moved his toes. Both of them.

"Sometimes you choke on fear," he thought. "Sometimes on pure joy. Dear Sue..."

***

22
Come Fly with Me

"**The earth is nothing more**, nor less, than a recycling factory," Alec declared next morning at breakfast.

"You've been dreaming again, Ali?" Alicia was watching her son masticating his second egg. Suzy just finished feeding Sacha.

Alicia should have been used to her son's sudden declarations. Apparently, over the last few years, she'd forgotten about some of his mental gymnastics. She'd always enjoyed, indeed encouraged his ventures into the realm of imagination, but hardly shared any of them. Certainly none since Alec has moved out to live on his own.

"Good morning, mother," he answered. "Come and eat with us." Alec leaned over to pull the chair out for his mother, and continued as though he hadn't been interrupted.

"Animals must eat animals, other members of fauna digest most of the flora, the bacteria break down the remainder into ever smaller particles, and finally the atoms decay—complements of the omnipresent weaker force. With a bit of luck, in no time at all, we end up as pure energy. And yet the Creator's genius is such that even the discarded materials fill us with awe, though here, on earth, we, as the rest of nature, are but a weak echo of our original beauty."

"Wow!" was all Alicia could contribute to this tirade.

Alec had been thinking of Suzy's breathtaking beauty on the Home Planet. And, he suspected, the Home Planet was only once removed from physical reality. How would she seem in higher realms?

"Some of us are as beautiful as we could ever be," Desmond affirmed, as if reading Alec's thoughts. He stood behind Alicia, his eyes on her golden hair.

"Good morning, Oh Delphian Oracle. But I beg to differ."

Alicia and Desmond brought their soft-boiled eggs. Maria had been given a day off, and Matt had his breakfast earlier.

"Delphic," Alicia corrected belatedly. "Delphic Oracle. Delphian sound too much like a fish."

"Dolphins are not fish, mother," Suzy butted in.

Alec threw his hands up in the air. "Whatever," he sighed. "The question is not how beautiful we are on earth, but how beautiful we could be if, for instance, the earth was transformed into a Garden of Eden."

"You mean no pollution of air, water, food, ears, eyes, lungs..."

"That sort of thing. And you forgot 'minds' or their physical equivalents, our brains."

"So what has this to do with recycling?" Suzy brought the meeting to order. She wondered if Alec was not just celebrating another successful evacuation of his bowls. After the last month or two, this would have been reason enough for exultation that he was overtly displaying.

"Everything. We, the sapient Homos, are not cooperating with nature. We are not recycling the earth as fast as she is ready to absorb our... our excrement."

Suzy sighed. 'I must have been right,' she thought.

"*Bon appétit*," Alicia murmured.

"All right, our refuse, offal, scum, dregs, sediment, trash, debris, dross..." he corrected.

"I think we get the picturre. Not much morre palatable, lad, but what arre you leading up to?" Desmond finished his egg and sat back to enjoy his coffee and toast.

"Frankly, after you two love-birds came in, I lost my train of thought. But I think I was trying to make a point that we completely misunderstand not only the purpose of physical life, but the environment in which we find ourselves."

Desmond looked at Alec questioningly.

"Therre is morre to all this than you'rre saying, lad, isn't therre?"

"Well, if the earth is a giant recycling factory, then who operates it?"

"The so-called naturre, I prresume," Desmond offered.

"Then you are crediting nature with inherent intelligence?"

"With inforrrmation. And I got that, dearr Doctorr Baldwin, frrom yourr own Theorry." Desmond's tone wagged a finger at his pupil.

The Theory of Information held, *inter alia*, that, at their most basic level, the so-called laws of nature are derived from the omnipresent information, rather as space is omnipresent, or as gravity is omnipresent in reasonable proximity to a given mass. The Theory further treats the whole universe as an interconnected mass. The interconnector is Information.

"*Touché*. But there should be, like you've just said, more to it than that."

For a while they just sipped coffee. Alicia entered into a whispering discussion with Sacha; Matt appeared, miraculously, to clear the table. With the exception of Alec, they evidently thought that it was far too early for a philosophical discussion. Or a scientific one for that matter. Alec was left alone with his thoughts. Finally Desmond took pity on him.

"Oh, all right, lad. Out with it."

Alec needed to share his ideas, though he wasn't sure that he was ready. Still, it wasn't often that he had Desmond's ear all to himself.

"We are in the process of continuous becoming..." he started, his tone not yet quite confident. He sounded as though he'd interrupted himself. The Professor did not say a word. "'I die daily', said Paul the Apostle," Alec continued apparently on a different tack. "I'm telling you that we die millions of times a second. The subatomic particles of which we are made up wink in and out of existence faster then we can become consciously aware of them, not that we ever could. Even our large, infinitely complex cellular structures subsist in a constant state of division and dissolution. And this, as you well know, is not some theoretical mumbo-jumbo, but pure science backed up by controlled laboratory observations. Physically, we are walking corpses, the living dead—zombies, if you like. Knowing this I find it important to find out if I am any more than meets the eye."

With this Alec leaned forwards in his chair. For a moment he looked as though he was ready to get up and pace the terrace. He felt better for having unburdened himself. Down below, the ocean continued its Sisyphean struggle against the sandy shores. What a waste of energy, Alec thought. Yet... I'm sure there is a reason for that, too. How does it fit into the recycling concept? Obviously it must. Only we are all so damnably stupid. We know so little. We are...

"And this really bothers you?" Desmond's voice reached him from afar.

"What? Sorry, I've been gathering wool again." Alec kept his eyes on the far, far horizon. "Yes, it does bother me. It bothers me because I'm not sure anymore if I am going in the right direction."

Desmond didn't say anything, but his face showed signs of concern. Long, long ago, he struggled with similar problems. Perhaps everyone did. He'd resolved them by keeping busy.

"Have you tried just living?" he asked quietly.

Alec gasped. The words had such a familiar ring... He remembered. So many years ago. 'Just living' was exactly what Sandra had advocated.

Last week the universe collapsed upon itself, and enclosed Alicia and Des in a warm womb of mutual self-discovery. Last night was quite different. It had more to do with the previous day, with the sharing of their joy not just with each other, but also with Suzy and Alec. It was almost like a renewal of vows. So soon after their first, but still, it was special. The altar, the flowers, the priest, the light coming in through the stained glass windows way up above them—the sun casting its multi-hued blessings on their union, it all made yesterday unforgettable.

Today they felt as though they've known each other all their lives. Not that the process of mutual discovery and exploration was over. That would continue for the rest of their days. It was because the last barriers that they'd originally erected to protect the most secret chambers of their hearts had collapsed. They became one as much as any two people can. Perhaps such unity can only be achieved by people of a certain age, a certain maturity. Or, perhaps nature, in her glorious abundance, steered them on such a course just to help Alicia deal with her son's problems.

They sat on the terrace, hands touching, the vastness of the Pacific stretched before them, a world unto themselves.

Later that day, Sacha remained with the McBrides. Alec bestowed this title, quite correctly, upon Desmond and his mother on the way back from the church, and it became his favourite appellative. He called them that at every opportunity. Actually, even before the return trip he'd started singing outside the church: "Here come McBrides, here come McBrides..." he chanted, to the tune of Mendelssohn's wedding march.

"Will the McBrides be joining us on the beach at this time?"

"No, the McBrides will stay and read a book. The Baldwins can go for a walk, if they wish," his mother replied. "I told Maria she can go home early. She's done so much for us in recent days."

The Baldwins went alone.

No one knew where Matt was.

Alec had asked Suzy previously, but he now posed his question differently. "Come, fly with me," he said. And, having said it, he had no idea why he'd chosen those particular words. He was in a good mood. As light as air? Perhaps he felt like flying. His heart felt a light as a feather.

They remained within speaking distance of each other. Alec was half-expecting to start flying, at any moment, or for both of them to soar into some strange reality. He continued to feel a strange expectation as though something momentous was about to take place. Only he had no idea what.

Nothing happened.

A light supper, sandwiches and nuts, was washed down with Scotch'n water, for the gentlemen, and Sangria for 'The Girls'. Desmond would not refer to the ladies in any other way. Suzy had lost her title of lassie to Alicia and resigned herself to being called just plain 'lass', and Sacha remained a wee lad. Only Maria managed to retain her baptismal name, although only just. On some occasions Desmond referred to her as La Zorrita, because, he'd said, no one dared to get near his property in his absence, because it was common knowledge that it was Maria who looked after it.

"La Zorrita would not let the ungodly get within a stone's thrrow..." he'd once told them. And he meant it.

For a while they all remained on the terrace, until the sea-air made them sleepy. They retired early. Suzy took care of Sacha, while Alec fell immediately into an uneasy asleep. He kept tossing and turning, agitated by—he knew not what. Perhaps his body was attempting to exercise. About midnight he woke up. Turning on the side meant dragging his legs, one over the other, with his hands. It didn't hurt but was frustrating.

In order not to wake Suzy, he lifted himself onto the wheelchair, and went to sit on the terrace. He found Matt sitting on the twin swing-chair suspended from the beams overhead. After a minute or two, without a single word, Matt lifted Alec and placed him on the swing beside himself. It wasn't the first time that Alec suspected Matt of being able to read his thoughts. But for the life of him, he would never ask him such a question. There was something about Matt that was both inviting and forbidding. He was an excellent hired help. Even a friend. Yet...

They sat, side by side, in silence.

The gentle sway, to and fro, seemed to echo the ripple of the waves washing the pebbles on the ebbing ocean. Alec found it soothing. The moon, low over the western horizon, bounced its rays along the water, picking up the very tops of the gentle swell. The night was filled with idyllic, carefree serenity.

Not so Alec. He felt he had something to do. Only... He opened his eyes.

Matt was gone. Suzy sat next to him. She'd raised his arm and cuddled underneath it. Without a single word they watched the moon spin its gossamer beams all the way to the dark horizon.

And then, finally, it happened.

"Come, fly with me..." he heard himself saying, only it was redundant.

They were flying, soaring really, or hovering easily from place to place, looking down on a spherical gaseous orb, still irregular, but gradually taking shape as the spinning motion smoothed its contours.

"Look," he said. "Up there."

He didn't point because he didn't have any arms. But Suzy looked. Above them, a little to their left, there was an enormous ball of fire. It appeared about twenty times bigger than the sun they were used to on earth. It was quite unbelievingly huge. Its raw power was such that they became aware of the roar of countless atomic bombs exploding, simultaneously, in an ongoing, horrendous holocaust. Only there wasn't any roar. The roar was born in their minds in response to that which there ought to be.

"Why am I not afraid?" she asked.

It was an emotive question. A question that Alec heard, and to which he responded in kind. She heard him. She was quite relaxed now. She was not aware of having a 'body', but felt being held by him firmly, protectively, as though he'd never let her go.

If we had bodies we would have been fried to a cinder, he thought. Suzy giggled. Obviously she heard his thoughts.

"This is your world," he smiled. "Do with it what you want."

It was at this moment that he became aware that he was sharing Suzy's subjective reality. Subjective, yet identical to that he remembered from his youth. I'm sharing her dream, he mused. Also, at this moment, he became acutely aware of Sandra's presence. Not apart, as in the past, but as integral part of his being. He felt whole, complete, as he did once, so many years ago.

I love you forever more, my Princess. You are my life...

He remembered the words he'd spoken to her outside the confined of time and space when he was but fourteen years old. Yet, it felt like yesterday. He became aware that by denying her presence, he was denying life itself.

He turned his emotive thoughts to Suzy.

"This is your world in which to create life. To turn it into Eden—into Paradise. It is your universe to rule and command and to learn how to be benevolent. To be kind to your creatures. You are all they have. You are their life. You dream them. You give them their reality."

"Who am I?" Suzy's mind asked.

"You are who you are. But to them, your children to whom you'll give life, you will be what each of them thinks of you. Each one of them will carry an image of you. And whatever that image, that you shall be to them."

Alec listened and tried to comprehend his own thoughts. It was Sandra speaking though him. The Sandra within him. Ideas, knowledge, raw unorganized, timeless, swirling information overwhelmed him with the might of their infinite potential. It was frightening, yet here, he knew, he was indestructible. Immortal?

It had been a long time since he'd heard Sandra's voice as his own. He'd forgotten how to listen. The answers really did lie within him.

"Always listen to yourself. There lie all the answers."

This was for Suzy. She was new to this realm.

Suzy was cuddled-up under Alec's arm. The swing-chair was swinging gently, to and fro... to and fro... Her eyes rested on the ocean, breathing the depth of its peace into her mind. She'd never experienced such serenity. Could Alec control the elements, she wondered? Something happened. Something she neither caused nor understood. The images were still floating before her eyes.

"Why wasn't I afraid?" she asked, again, only this time in past tense.

She knew the answer to her question, but still found it hard to accept. She was as sure as she was of anything that she and Alec had witnessed, together, the instant preceding creation. It didn't make sense. Preceding the creation of her reality? She had no idea how she knew this. The knowledge was part of her. It was intrinsic to her nature.

She nestled deeper under Alec's arm. All the doubts she had, for so long, about Alec's dreams, visions, even what she considered 'ravings', begun to recede into the mists of disbelief. She realized, instead, how hard it must have been for him not to be able to share what he'd seen and heard, what he'd touched with his emotive thoughts. No words could ever do them justice. Poets tried, composers turned those precious, enigmatic moments into symphonies, jubilant oratorios. But even they could offer but a dim reflection of the inner reality. There, she witnessed her own self—not with her senses, but with the essence of her being. I am that I am, she mused, her mind still caught in the wonder of that moment.

Ye are gods... she remembered reading.

Only now she was beginning to realize how much Alec had given up by remaining in the physical reality. Did he have a choice? Had he been waiting for her all this time?

"Have you been waiting for me?" she repeated her thoughts aloud.

"I knew you'd come. It was just a question of time."

"Up there, there is no time. Is there?" The stars shimmered in her eyes.

"I think there is. Only it unfolds very slowly. Perhaps it is we who give it its momentum. I rather think that time decreases its progress as we rise in consciousness. Somewhere up there, it stops altogether. But when it does, I'm not so sure we are still aware of it. That it stopped, I mean."

"I'm not sure I understand..."

And then the second magical thing happened that very same night. The moonlight swirled in his irises till they became iridescent. She looked into them and nodded. "I see," she said. "I understand," she confirmed again.

He hasn't said anything.

But for the hum of the waves washing the shore, they sat in silence. The night was too beautiful to go back inside; too silent to disturb it with voices. What they shared that night couldn't be put into words, anyway. Time slowed down, seemed to hover in serene abeyance.

"*I am the servant of My servant's image of Me,*" Alec whispered. "We must be careful, you and I," he added after yet another pose. "We must be very careful what images we create in our minds."

"Do I also have my Prince?" Suzy sounded as curious as she was fascinated.

"You and your Prince were there together. You can't get there on your own."

"But why can't I see him, the way you saw Sandra?"

Alec didn't answer. He asked himself that same question dozens of times. Why can't I see Sandra when I want to? Like I used to? He thought he knew now.

"I suspect it is the privilege of the young."

"How beautiful…" Her eyes were shimmering with playful moonbeams.

"You know, that last time I saw her on the Home Planet she looked just like you," he whispered.

She cuddled even closer.

The following day, after breakfast, Des took Alicia to visit San Diego. Alicia had never been there and she'd been long curious about the Salk Institute. She knew Louis Kahn designed it. There was a time when she'd hoped that Alec would choose architecture for his career. With his father having been an engineer, there would be certain continuity. It was at that time that she'd read quite a lot about architecture. She'd thought she would have had more to share with him.

It didn't turn out that way, but her interest remained.

Suzy took Sacha to the beach. Alec sat close to the rail of the terrace, following them with his eyes. Now and then he moved his toes. Then with an enormous effort he moved his right ankle. No more than a fraction of an inch, but he succeeded in contracting and relaxing his foot muscles by the effort of his will. It took all his concentration to breathe life into his feet. It wasn't easy to bring life to earth. People took it for granted.

Thank you, he said through clenched teeth. And then he tried moving his left foot. Beads of sweat formed on his forehead. Finally, he relaxed. He felt as though he'd climbed Mount Everest. He looked at his hands, now working perfectly. People never seem to realize what magnificent creations their bodies are, he mused.

Matt, looking through the window, nodded approval.

Sacha never seemed to get tired of wading in and out of the water—of splashing, kicking the approaching wavelets, and generally making a successful impersonation of an otter. He splashed in every imaginable position: standing: lying on his stomach, on his back, and any configuration of imbalance in-between. Alec thought that given half a chance he would swim. All by himself. Alas, Suzy would not allow him to wade deeper than his tiny ankles. Knees, at most.

Later, they sat on the terrace again, books on their laps.

"Where was it that we were, exactly?" Suzy asked. She wanted to ask him that since last night.

"It was obviously well into the pre-Mu realm. In fact pre-Eden, although I'm not sure which came first. It's the old chicken and the egg problem. Did we create Eden, or did Eden create us. I suppose it depends with which consciousness we choose to identify. Anyway, we were both bodiless."

Alec was aware that it sounded stupid, inadequate at best, when put into words. It sounded more like the stuff of fantasy. It couldn't be helped. After all, didn't it all happen in our minds?

"Did you miss my body?" she asked innocently.

He couldn't help laughing. "You have a one track mind." He'd missed her body for months now.

"Well, did you...?"

"I miss every single atom of your body that is not all mine to do with as I dispose."

Her brow tightened in concentration. Then she smiled. "I think I can live with that," she nodded pensively.

But Alec would never believe it. Suzy was anything but a submissive woman. She knew her own mind, and she knew it pretty well. He didn't say anything. He wouldn't push his luck.

"So each one of us is given a world to develop?" she returned to previous subject.

"I still haven't figured out if the stuff we see, out there I mean, is literal or symbolic. It could be that it is up to our interpretation," he said slowly.

"It was my very first time, but I gather from my impressions that *everything* up there is subject to our interpretation. You are what you believe yourself to be."

"I tend to agree, but the proposition is frightening. I just cannot imagine riding herd over a world. Being an absolute ruler. No matter who created it."

"But you're not, darling. 'You are what your servant thinks of you,' remember?"

"I am *where* my servant thinks of me," he corrected. "As for what I am, Rumi said 'I am the servant of my servant's image of Me.' In a way, that's even worse."

"Not if you grant free will to your creation..."

"As I've said, that's even worse. Can you imagine how great must be your love for your creation to grant them their own, individual reality? Even when you know that they are completely wrong?" Alec sighed.

"Isn't this what unconditional love is all about?" she said, lowering her voice. She felt they'd been talking about things that seemed 'holy'.

"Unconditional love is the prerogative of God!" he almost barked. He was rebelling against the knowledge thrust upon him.

Suzy waited a moment and then she said very softly. "And of creators..."

"Gagooooooo..." Sacha confirmed their conclusions.

The next moment they looked at each other and tried their best not to burst laughing. "Mustn't wake our young philosopher, must we," Suzy whispered.

Alicia was enchanted. "You should have come with us. Really. It was absolutely marvelous."

She carried on for quite a while—all in superlatives.

She reminded Alec of the mother he'd known some ten years ago. She seemed to have shed about as many years since she'd met Des. It was now evident that his father's death left a bigger scar on her than he'd originally realized. And the initial shock may have been exacerbated by the loneliness that followed. She'd never shown it. She was a good actress, when she wanted to be. Alec also suspected that his mother believed, and practiced her beliefs, that it was all right to share her joys—her sorrows she kept to oneself. Most people did the reverse.

Desmond sucked it all in. His eyes shone, a vaguely pompous grin seldom left his face. The McBrides obviously complemented each other in an incredibly fortunate way. For another while, Alicia continued praising San Diego, the University, the drive, the air, the whatever-she-could-think-of. When she finally finished, Desmond rose to his feet.

"The King of the Scots!" he proclaimed, holding a white, ceramic bottle above his head.

Suzy and Alicia genuflected, to pay homage to Royalty. Alec bowed deeply; Matt smiled and withdrew, while Maria run, giggling, to the kitchen.

"You may arrise," Des acquiesced unperturbed. "My dearr laddie," he turned to Alec. "The glasses, if you will?"

Alec spun his wheels, and still bowing retreated backwards to the kitchen in abject obeisance. He knew better than to trifle with the King of the Scots—may his name be whispered on blended knee. Alec was already in the kitchen when Desmond's voice reached him from the terrace.

"Make it fourr crrystals, m'lad. The lasses shall parrtake in the nectarr of nobility—just on this special occasion," he added, evidently surprised at his own beneficence.

Desmond, The Keeper of the Bottle, never explained what the special occasion was. Finally, if foolishly, Suzy asked him.

"Why, my wee lass, it is the firrst time that yourr motherr-in-law and I drrove to San Diego togetherr!" the Professor said collapsing onto a deck chair.

"How silly of me," Suzy apologized planting a big kiss on his forehead.

"Aye," Dr. McBride accepted the gift gracefully, "I cerrtainly deserrved that."

They all agreed that he most cerrrtainly did.

***

23

The Undiscovered Country

"**A**ctually, you've already been** to the Home Planet, remember?" Alec's tone sounded studiously matter of fact.

Suzy's eyes grew perceptibly larger. She wasn't sure if Alec was serious. He seemed too happy lately. She assumed it had been due to the gradual recovery of sensation in his legs. Actually his ebullience reached a sustained peak, a sort of arête, since they soared together in full consciousness. For some reason, Suzy found it perfectly natural, even as Sacha had that one time on the Home Planet. Have I been the only one to find all this so... so esoteric, Alec wondered, so mysterious? Suzy, with all her doubts, has been waiting for just such a thing to happen for so long that, when it did finally happen, she took it as long overdue. It was Alec, not she, who was beginning to lose hope.

"And just when did I accomplish that marvelous feat?" she demanded.

"We were there together," he assured her, and then added softly: "All three of us."

This made her sit up. She didn't mind not being aware of a dream-type trip, which could be construed, at a pinch, as a 'real' dream, but to dream together, not just with Alec but with Sacha, and then to forget it, well... this just wasn't fair.

Alec explained how and when it happened, and why he'd decided not to tell her about it straight away. After some five minutes of huffing and puffing, and unwittingly showing him one of her most luscious pouts, she calmed down.

"It is your consciousness that must expand, not your itinerary," he finally said.

She nodded. She got the message. Or, so he thought.

"When can we do it again?" she asked.

Alec sighed.

"It's not like snapping your fingers," he assured her for the hundredth time. "And it certainly couldn't happen when you're agitated."

"First, I am not agitated," she stated categorically, her voice rising with each syllable. "And second, why not?"

"Again, I can't be sure, but it seems that when we are tense, or angry, or involved deeply at the emotional level, then the doors to the reality which relies almost exclusively on your emotional content remains tightly shut. Your emotional condition ties you to the reality you are in at the time."

He remembered his many 'trips' into the past, yet always as a spectator. Not once had he succeeded in venturing into the creative realms.

She weighed his words for some time. After all, he'd been at it for more than ten years. For her, all this was new.

"It is like throwing an anchor and trying to sail at the same time. It just doesn't work." This was on her familiar ground, ah... water. This would sink, ah... float. Alec always had problems with metaphors. Even in his own mind.

"What you must do is to take me to Home Planet and the Far Country," she said slowly. She knew all about them from his many descriptions. "Or, if you prefer, in reverse order."

"Well, I thank you, my lady, for your gracious permission, but I fear I do not hold the keys to the kingdom of either. You and you alone can make the trip."

"But I don't know how, you know that!" Once again she was loosing her cool.

There was no point answering her, until she changed her attitude. After a while he tried again, softly: "Look within yourself and listen. The answers are all there. And remember you already found them. Twice."

Once again, her mouth started to form pout, but she didn't argue. She was disciplined and honest enough to know that Alec was right. And, in the meantime, it was high time for breakfast. Just before they left their bedroom, Alec began feeling sorry for Suzy. He recalled how he'd tried, often desperately, to contact Sandra, all to no avail. And then, somehow, she was there. He'd learned to expect Sandra, regardless when she chose to make her presence known. It sounded like a contradiction, but it wasn't. Or hadn't been. At least, not for him. Even as a boy, he'd learned to live in a state of grateful acceptance, rather than that of a demanding desire.

"I'll tell you what helped me, darling. Learn to expect the best. Learn to expect what you really desire. But concentrate on the expectation, not on the desire. Don't push it; just believe firmly that it will happen—when you're ready. Be grateful, as though it was already happening. Accept the gift, even if it is a future gift. Believe without even a slightest trace of doubt. No matter how seemingly impossible."

Suzy smiled, but her smile wasn't all that happy.

Alicia and Des had already taken a walk on the beach, laid out breakfast, and waited for the 'young'uns' to start eating. The eggs were still to be made, since it was Alec's turn to fry them. Being in a wheelchair was no excuse for slacking on his share of chores. He apologized for being late and donned the cook's apron.

In the meantime Suzy finished feeding Sacha, who already resumed his inspection of the netting at the balustrade. His new hobby was to steal forks and spoons from the table, and throw them as far as he could onto the beach below. By the time they'd noticed his new preoccupation, three spoons and two forks were missing.

"It is self-evident," Desmond declared with a straight face, "that the wee lad will grrow up to be a champion disc orr javelin thrrowerr. Prrobably both," he added, after due consideration.

They all agreed except for Suzy. She had to recover the tableware. But even before she finished trying to dissuade Sacha from exercising his tensors, Matt replaced the missing items on the table. They had been rinsed and dried. Then— Matt disappeared again. If it were up to Suzy, she would have sworn that he was peek-a-boo'ing. Only for extended periods of time.

After a leisurely breakfast, Suzy took Alec for a drive. The day was too cloudy for the beach, and Sacha seemed quite content to catch up on his dream-time.

"Do you know that this is the first time, since Montreal, that you have invited me for a drive?" Alec asked.

"Frankly, I hadn't thought about it, darling. Why, do you like the idea?"

"I suppose all you want to do is get away from Sacha, and The McBrides, and then park and neck?" He sounded hopeful.

"I haven't thought of anything else since Montreal," Suzy admitted. Then her tone changed. "What ever did happen to your Nobel Prize nomination?"

"No news is good news. If they haven't called, then I'm probably still on the long-short list. Des would know."

"You don't seem concerned. Why?"

"Well, I don't find fame that attractive. They start inviting you not because you've got something to say, only because you're a laureate. Often the winner is said to be just a political gesture. You can do a fair amount of good with the money, of course, but…"

"But you're still too busy living, to just sit back and be admired?" Her comment was as much an answer as a question. It would not have been true two weeks ago, but his mind seemed to have been opening up even as a new surge of blood began oxygenating his legs.

"Something like that…" he admitted.

My mind and body are irrevocably connected, he thought. The Romans had been right. *Mens sana in corpore sano*. Except for a few geniuses. Like Hawking or Beethoven. But how many Hawkings and Beethovens are there around?

Suzy drove slowly, admiring the scenery. They'd reached quite a high elevation. They were on a narrow country road, in the general direction of Escondido. Twenty minutes later they'd passed the town on their left and continued to climb the hills. Finally, Suzy pulled up at a rest area, big enough for no more then three cars. Luckily, there were alone. She wanted to take a panoramic look at the surrounding countryside. The car was facing west. The view was strange to say the least. They'd climbed above the coastal fog and could see the ocean emerging beyond its western limit. It looked as though the shimmering vastness was emerging from the clouds; the water and the sky embraced in some strange ritual.

For a while they sat, just looking. There was little to be said. Any description of the phenomenon would have diminished it. Neither of them wanted to lessen the magic. Then a single ray of sun punctured a hole in the coastal fog and revealed a sailboat making its way southward. A forlorn sail in an ocean of mystery.

"The light of our consciousness only plays upon the surface of the water..." Alec spoke in a whisper. "Just think of the depth to be explored..."

She kissed his sunburned arm and slid underneath it. With her head nestling against his neck and chin, his arm around her shoulders, she was content to let the world come to an end.

The sun grew bigger, much bigger, until it reached two or three times the diameter of the star they'd left behind. In it's orange light the skin on Suzy's arms gave a healthy glow.

"I made it didn't I?" she whispered. She was afraid to destroy the image before her eyes. As Alec before her, she imagined she was visiting Machu Picchu. Only the pointed crags atop the soaring mountains were much, much higher, and infinitely more beautiful. It was as Machu Picchu would be if it were perfect, and in its original glory. The buildings were all meticulously put together of pristine white marble.

They were sitting on a rock that was soft to the touch. The valley before them extended... forever and a day. Farther along, the boundaries framing it alternated between green slopes and forbidding pinnacles, some wearing halos of white, puffy clouds as tonsures, just below the pinnacles.

"I made it..." she repeated, hardly believing her own eyes. "You never told me it was so beautiful..."

What could he say? He'd told her a dozen times, but words had been so inadequate. They only gave you fragments of reality. They could never describe the whole, the gestalt vision in a single word. And here one witnessed it all at once.

"Did you create it all? All this?"

"Didn't you just say that you did it?" he smiled at her disbelief.

She was still too lost in awe to even think straight. It must have been the artist in her. Yet Alec realized that the view before him was richer, much richer, than anything he'd seen before. It must be her presence, he thought. She'd enhanced what he'd seen before. She'd added her own vision, her own dream, her innermost aspirations, which dwelled in her subconscious.

"You did it, darling. I merely... started, planted the seed. You made it grow and blossom," and I had help. He was thinking of Sandra.

"You and Sandra are one," she corrected him.

Once again Alec realized that even as he and Sandra merged into a single entity, Suzy and her Prince had never been apart. They'd always been one, yet her Prince was much closer to her awareness. What was missing was the realization. Acceptance? It explained so much. It explained her previous trip to the Home Planet. It explained the vision, or the experience, of the earth in its infancy. It explained her ability to join him in this realm.

"You are reading my thoughts," he marveled aloud. His voice sounded melodious even to his own ears.

Suddenly she giggled exactly as Sandra once did. "Do they make love on the Home Planet?" she asked.

For a timeless instant they merged in absolute unity. It was not an intercourse of their bodies. It was the joining of minds

"Oh, my God!" Suzy caught her breath.

"My Goddess!" he echoed.

It didn't last. The experience was too overwhelming to be sustained. When Suzy opened her eyes, the beauty of the valley remained.

They were floating in the center of the universe. The black womb embraced them, caressed them with its velvety softness. With sudden fierceness, the intense darkness was punctured with billions of stars. It was as though angels poured diamonds all around them. The sparks shimmered, and dazzled, and oscillated in diversity of forms, as if to awe them with iridescent light.

"The Far Country?" he sensed her emotive thought. "The Far Country..." the emotive resonance enclosed them in an enchanting symphony of light.

This was no longer just his domain. Not even his and Sandra's. The image has expanded again; it grew richer with each moment as Suzy added her own creative stream to the universe. The reality grew exponentially and their awareness grew with it. They too became bigger, perhaps greater, more able to grasp the inexplicable splendour.

"All this is thanks to you..." Suzy pointed her emotive finger at a solitaire diamond. Even as she did so, it approached them, its effulgent fury fulminating before them, seemingly at their disposal.

"The gods wield quite incredible power."

Alec felt Sandra's presence as never before. She sharpened his emotive senses beyond his wildest expectations. For the next fragment of eternity they absorbed the wonder of creation. Alec's consciousness continued to expand.

"Will you join me, my husband?"

The galaxies, which a moment ago had been scattered all around, now coalesced and blazed in all their glory within their consciousness. They became bodies made up of countless stars, of countless galaxies...

The two universes, hers and his, overlapped and then merged in a phantasmagoric fanfare of light. The two became one. There was no more darkness. They rose above and beyond the Far Country. They became beings of pure light.

They both heard laughter.

Sacha?

A globule of light spun around them, performed a dance of joy, and came up close, touching their auras. Here he was their equal, perhaps more mature. His consciousness felt at home, more aware of this reality. Look, Sue, after all, he'd only recently left it...

I never left it Ali, I am always here. My body might be elsewhere, but I always remain in my true home.

These weren't words, not even thoughts. It was a strange kind of direct perception. Sacha became Alec each time he addressed him, yet maintained equal contact with Suzy. This was the strangest realm...

Dad!

Alexander merged with another globule.

This time it was he who was caught in a dance of shear delight. His father was the essence of another being of light, pure light—yet definitely his dad. His own, dear, loving father...

Alec's heaven erupted in an outburst of rapture. All light merged as though a single photon expanded to infinity in all directions.

...they stood apart, light facing light, reflected in each other's glory, staring, not seeing, but being fully aware of the singularity of being...

"Sue.... Come back..." Alec shook her shoulder, "Suzy... Susanna!"

"Must I?"

The reluctance reached him from a distance far greater than that measured by men. Slowly, not wanting to let go of her true nature, she opened her eyes. She didn't let go of Alec's hand. His arm was still dressed over her shoulder, the fingers of his right hand and her left entwined. She still clung to him, as though seeking protection from the reality to which she was returning.

"I knew you could do it, " she whispered. "I knew you would take me there..."

And before he could assure her that it hadn't been he, at all, that was at the root of it all, she sat up straight, shook her head and exclaimed: "Sacha was there! And your father!" And then she started laughing, until tears filled her eyes.

"Sacha was there," she repeated her voice still filled with euphoria.

"My dad...?"

"And he didn't throw any spoons down from... where were we Alec?"

Alec smiled as he pictured his son, a globule of light, throwing spoons and forks at other globules. The image was too ridiculous for words. It was his turn to laugh at the image.

It took quite a while before they really came down to earth. A long while. After what seemed an eternity Alec looked at his watch. About twenty minutes had passed since Suzy had parked their car in the rest area. About ten minutes before they lost awareness of their surroundings, and another ten since they 'came back'. The Home Planet, the Far Country, and the Reality Beyond, must have lasted mere seconds. The Reality Beyond, he whispered. The Unexplored Country. Inner realities play by their own rules, it seemed. No wonder up there we are eternal, endless, infinite.

"Do you think we visited heaven?" Suzy was beginning to calm down. She felt dreamy, happy, sated to overfilling, yet, in a strange way, aware of a new hunger. A hunger she'd never experienced before. The hunger Alec had felt from the time he was a fourteen-year-old boy.

"Heaven is a state of consciousness. Even the Bible teaches that. In other words, heaven can be whatever you imagine it to be. Like a place filled to overflowing with virgins..."

Had she been standing, and not overflowing with happiness, she would have kicked him.

"That is not a place you are ever likely to go, my dear husband. Not if I develop any connections with Saint Peter," she warned but couldn't make her voice sound even remotely threatening.

Actually it wasn't the Christian heaven that offered such *deliciae deliciorum..* No matter. Alec thought it unlikely that one could enter any such state, or reality, on one's own. It seemed that the very act of union, of becoming one with someone, was the prerequisite for such an experience. Once there, the unity seemed universal. Maybe that is what heaven was all about. Of being whole, complete.

"I think so too..." she nodded. "And further more..."

"Have you been hearing my thoughts?"

"Why, I believe I might have been. Can you hear mine?"

I love you, I love you, I love you, I love... "You seem to be doing all right!" she said out loud seeing his expression.

"Is that all you think about? Love and..."

"...joining? Only this act in the upper spheres is immensely more satisfying."

"You know, Sue, I rather think that it was your, ah... obvious predisposition that got you to all the three realms," he said out loud again. Just transferring one's thoughts felt unsatisfying.

"You mean sex?"

"Well…" he raised one eyebrow.

"I've never heard you object to it before?" She was her old tease again.

"Welcome back," he murmured.

"You know," she said, her voice more serious, "that time when I'd first read your thoughts? Well, I think that people got it all wrong. We don't see with our eyes, we see through them."

"Sacha is doing it all the time."

"It must be nice to be so recently out of that bright place, before you lose all contact with reality..." Suzy's voice sounded dreamy once again.

"This is your first time, Sue, well, practically your first time, and already you call *that* state 'reality', not where we are now. Don't you find this strange?"

"No, Ali. For the life of me, I don't. That place, in fact all those places, seemed much more natural than, well, than the wonderful life we are having here..." Then she looked up and grinned, "you are right, darling. It is extremely peculiar!"

"But all those realities felt like home. The Real Home, didn't they?"

She didn't answer, but Alec followed her thoughts without speaking. Something happened on their last trip together, or perhaps it was the experience of the singularity they both felt in the Far County, that gave them both the ability to hear each other's thoughts. The unity they'd both experienced had been so intense, so profound that whatever kept them apart at the mental or emotional levels was gone. No secrets, not even secrets they didn't know were secrets. He suspected they could be a million miles apart and read each other's thoughts. Or emotions.

"It pales, a little, doesn't it," she said following his eyes and thoughts. He was looking at the ocean.

"And it was so beautiful before," he agreed.

"Oh, it's still beautiful," she insisted, "only... only..."

"Only our consciousness, here, is too used to the modality of physical limitations," he said.

On their way back they didn't talk much. They preferred to listen to each other's thoughts. The mind doesn't think in letters and words, in grammatical sentences. It seems to paint gestalt pictures, three dimensional, with colours merging and adapting as the emotions enter the visual arena. Alec was digesting the reality he'd visited for the first time. Had he been thinking in words, he would have spelled that reality with a capital R. Reality. Rather like Paradise, or Eden. And yet it was none of these. It was a realm where consciousness existed in perfect bliss. Not bliss achieved as a reward for services rendered, but bliss that was there, waiting, for anyone who would enter. It was the Reality from which all happiness emerged. It was the Hub, the Source.

If there were a still higher Realm, then Alec felt no need for it. What if there were? Surely when all Princes and Princesses merged into a single pod, their awareness of themselves, of their Isness would be gone. Alec had no such ambitions. He was unspeakably happy that he had found Sacha there. He was so preoccupied with his son that he didn't recognize his own father. He only saw him later, through Suzy's eyes.

He did discover, nevertheless, that Princes and Princesses did commune with each other. He also suspected that in that Reality he was really Sandra. Perhaps Alexander, but certainly not Alec. His personality, the one he wore daily on his sleeve, was gone. What remained was Individuality. Or indivisibility. He couldn't think of himself apart from all the other Princes and Princesses. That was heaven enough for him.

"You know, Sue, it wasn't a dream we shared. It is here, now, that we're dreaming. But it is my job to make this dream as exiting, as loving, as fascinating for Sandra as only I can. She's given me a glimpse of heaven. I'll give her the most wonderful dream she'll ever dream. She may be the dreamer, but I shall make her dreams come true!"

Suzy nodded a little sadly.

"Trying to translate what we just experienced into, what you once called, horizontally structured communication, is a mistake. When in Rome do as the Romans. On earth, act like a human. If we aren't the best that we can be, we probably would have evolved differently."

Why is she always right, Alec wondered, forgetting she could read his thoughts. "Essentially you're reiterating the 'just living' idea."

They felt like little children. They laughed most all the way home. Suzy even tried 'gagoooo'ing." She wondered if Sacha could hear her.

Lunch was great.

Maria prepared a feast of seafood, which they washed down with *Pouilly-Fuissé*. "It is a special occasion," Alicia declared gravely.

All heads looked up.

"It is the semi-versary of Desmond's first proposal," she added in an even more serious tone of voice.

"But you've been engaged hardly at all!" Suzy's math didn't add up.

"Not at all, we've been engaged for two weeks."

"What? I thought you said..." now Alec was also lost.

"I said *first* proposal. I turned him down. I told him that if he didn't take care of himself, start exercising, walking and that sort of thing, he would be too old for me."

"You said that to the Professor?" Alec's eyes were filled with disbelief. One doesn't talk like that to heads of departments at Caltech, let alone deputy Chancellors.

"Not in as many words, but he got the idea," she smiled gently at her husband.

"She wants to destrroy me and inherrit my forrtune," Desmond commented sadly.

"Darling, I had no idea you had a fortune!" Alicia looked at Desmond with disbelief.

"You mean you didn't fall for my money? Well, just as well. I don't have any. But I could have had. And wherre would you have been then?" he concluded triumphantly.

"I strongly suspect, right here," Alicia observed calmly.

"Thank God forr that. Forr a moment I though you would've left me forr a richerr man."

"Aren't you two ever going to grow up?" Suzy wanted to know.

"Not if I can help it!" they replied in perfect unison.

Right then Alec suspected that those two had on earth what Sue and he'd only just discovered in the Undiscovered Country.

Suzy nodded. She'd read his thoughts.

***

24
Delight

"**D**o you think **Adam and Eve** really walked around naked?" Suzy asked, sucking on a leg of a delicious Alaska crab. The lunch had been over a half-hour ago, but Suzy managed to find an odd juicy leg buried under a pile of empty shells.

"As naked as the leg you'rre chewing on, lass. They werre also rred, all overr, frrom the shame of it all," Desmond enlightened her authoritatively.

"Now, Des…" Alicia tried hard to make at least one of them grow up.

"She'd starrted it," Desmond replied defensively. "But now that you mention it, it could have been rrather fun in the old Parradise," he smacked his lips.

"You, my dear husband, are a dirty old man," Alicia declared.

"Thank you, lassie, but easy on the old?"

This paradise wasn't so bad either, even for hikers from other realms. One could easily get used to eating crabs' legs and washing down them cool wine.

"Anyone for a swim?" Des asked eyeing both ladies. "I can't prromise to be naked, but I'll pull m'shorrts a high as they'll go, if that'll please you?"

"You might try pulling them over your head, dear," Alicia suggested.

"Love to oblige, but wouldn't be able to see you, m'love," Des answered unabashed.

The sun finally dissolved the coastal fog but not the gathering cloud. The ladies decided on a quick dip. With the rolling breakers gathering force, Sacha remained with Alec and Desmond. Matt, as usual, lurked in the shadows.

As Alicia and Suzy ran down the steps, Des turned to Alec.

"I've been on the phone..." he declared, and when his announcement failed to elicit any response from Alec, he added rather bashfully: "...need a word with you, lad."

This wasn't at all like the Professor. When he was serious, Desmond invariably got to the point by the shortest route. His next words confirmed Alec's suspicions.

"I'm afraid, my lad, we didn't make the final short list," he sounded more annoyed then crestfallen.

"Des, making it even to the officially non-existent short list was quite a, ah... honour." Alec offered his reassurance.

Desmond stopped and looked up at his favourite, if adopted, son.

"So you're not all broken up about it?"

"I'm a bit young to start living in the past. I rather think that winning the prize would have cramped my style."

"That's the spirit!" Desmond approved heartily. His good spirits returned instantly. "I wouldn't mind it eitherr, if it werren't forr the fact that the leaderr on the shorrt-shorrt is a buckarroo who's got the quantum theorry all mixed up again with some sorrt of comic... I mean, cosmic converrgence. For the life of me I can't underrstand those Scandinavian morrons, I mean solons."

Alec loved Professor's multiple Freudian slips.

"The guy who's actually up therre could be that fellow Goudoff's cousin. Orr even himself!" The Professor threw up his hands. "What is the worrld coming to?"

"Perhaps there are other roads to the truth?"

"Perhaps. But I wish those journeymen wouldn't call themselves physicists." The rolling r's have subsided together with the Professor's pulse.

Alec didn't say anything. The Professor looked out to the sea and muttered, "It's all politics, these days. That's what it is. Politics."

So that was that.

Actually, Alec's reaction went a lot deeper than he'd let on. As he sat back, he felt a strange movement in his veins. Not just in legs and spine. In his whole body. The news seemed to have released him from the Democlesian sword hanging over his head, threatening to cut him down to mediocrity. To make him part of the dreaded "them". Des, Dr. Desmond McBride, was one of a handful of men who'd escaped being absorbed into the academic establishment. He remained young. In every sense of the word. He would probably die young.

Had Alec looked up, he would have noticed Matt studying him through the open door of the living room. For a moment or two, his eyes seemed to smoulder like two crimson embers, then the light was gone, and a satisfied smile replaced his impassive face.

The big man went inside the living room and sat down. His work was almost done.

Later, that evening, Suzy and Alec, tried to read on the terrace. It wasn't easy. The wind whined and whistled, palms swayed precariously, the house creaked. The Pacific was no longer peaceful. The swell was mounting higher by the minute; white crests raced each other, furiously, towards the shore.

Then came the first drops.

Just a few, large drops plopped on the terrace rail; practically in slow motion, as if with premeditation, some distance apart. Within the subsequent sixty seconds the sky released all its pent up energies. There was neither lightening nor thunder, but the roar of the downpour on the terrace roof sufficed to drown their voices. For a moment, they sat mesmerized.

Not for long.

At first drops, Desmond moved his chair as far back from the edge of the terrace as it would go. Alicia was about to call him a chicken when a furious gust of wind drove the torrent almost horizontally. Alicia, Suzy and Alec were instantly drenched.

Both women screamed, giggled, flapped their arms, and run for cover. Alec laughed. He was enjoying the downpour to the full. It was the next best thing to a swim he hadn't had for months. He loved the deluge pelting his body from head to toe. It made him feel alive.

"Would it be rraining a wee bit, lassie?" Desmond asked innocently.

Later that day, alone in his room, Alec raised himself to his feet. His legs gave way a second later, but he actually stood up on his own. Matt, always at hand when needed, caught him in time, and gave him a thorough massage.

For the next few days, mostly at night so as not to attract attention, Alec practiced standing up, and sustaining a vertical position, each time for a few seconds longer.

"It's amazing," he told Suzy later, "how we all take such elementary motions for granted. A child takes a year or so to learn how to stand. Perhaps longer. No one ever seems concerned with how many muscular movements must be coordinated, how much energy must be pumped and directed at an increased rate…" he sighed deeply. "No one ever wonders how many trillions of electrochemical reactions must take place in your brain, let alone the rest of you body, in the right order, for a man to stand up."

"I suppose we relegate all that to our subconscious?" she offered.

"The hypothalamus," he corrected. "It links the nervous system to the endocrine system via the pituitary gland… never mind that. The question is just how many people have you met who ever, *even once,* expressed any interest…"

"…in their subconscious?" she repeated.

"We inhabit magnificent, awe inspiring machines that man is apt to destroy by puling a trigger with a single finger.

We are so much better at destroying than at creating..." I was darn close to destroying myself, he thought, guilt showing on his face.

"We are the image and likeness..."

"Are we? I sometime wonder." His smile was bitter. "We are reputedly created unto the image of some superior being, but what we really are remains a mystery..."

Suzy put her arms around Alec's shoulders.

"We take so many things for granted," she conceded. "But I'll never take you for granted, my husband. I know who *you* really are, remember?"

In that moment, as though by a wave of a magic wand, the image of Sacha, globe of delight, of euphoria, of utter happiness, shimmered before his eyes. And just as suddenly, years of struggles, of search and frustrations, of transient successes and lasting disappointments—all in search of the nature of his being became worthwhile. Even the time he spent in the wheelchair.

"There is a reason for everything," he nodded to himself as much as to Suzy. "And you are reason enough for me to live."

For almost a week, Alec exercised daily. Not just daily, but most of the time. Some days ago, he'd asked Sandra for a sign. He got it when he'd felt Suzy kicking his ankle under the table. He would never forget that moment. It was all he needed. He no longer sat and read, and, on occasion felt sorry for himself, but made his physical body his priority. His mind was mending in parallel. Failure, if one could call it that, to be awarded the Nobel Prize, released him from exorbitant expectations. In many ways, it was a blessing in disguise.

For hours on end he lifted small weights strapped to his ankles. He held on to the furniture, and attempted little knee bends. He stood against a wall and tried raising himself on his toes. He did not believe in miracles. Throughout his life hard work brought him results. He applied the same philosophy to his legs. He was getting results.

Dr. Alexander Baldwin was a fighter.

As Suzy had once suspected, she and Alec were completely naked. It didn't really matter that much, because they both sported enough body hair to make Lady Godiva green with envy. Dark brown, actually, but envious, nevertheless. They were both so hairy that when Suzy first saw Alec, she couldn't believe her eyes.

"Take that stuff off at once," she commanded, "you look like a gorilla."

It should be mentioned that the sounds that emerged from her throat were precisely those of a large ape. A she-gorilla, to be precise. Or she could have been a chimpanzee. An orangutan? Alec was not an expert on simians. What Alec 'heard' were her thoughts.

But whatever the subspecies, she was the cutest anthropoid ape he'd ever seen.

"Agh, agh, aghrr," he replied politely, assuring Suzy that the hair was not only quality of his indubitable charm, but the aspect of himself he admired most.

Alec suddenly realized that he could see himself from her point of view. He looked at himself through her eyes. How very strange! How very different. To say that he was surprised would be a vast understatement. This is when the shifting takes place, he mused. He could animate his physical form to be able to see through it, to make use of its senses, but he could not enter it until he left Suzy's host. We are all one, but our attention decides where we are at any particular moment in the unfolding sequence. Just for fun, he tried to see himself through Suzy's eyes dancing the tango with himself many, many years ago. On second thought, he decided to wait until she was less hirsute. Less shaggy. Or at least until she stopped scratching herself allover.

"Thank you very much, you monkey!" She obviously retained the ability to read his thoughts.

"Ape," he corrected. "I am quite advanced on the scale of evolution. Whoever started this zoo must have done it quite a while ago."

They both had the facility to go in and out of their bodies, almost as easily as Alec once had with the pods in Hades. Almost, because contrary to his previous experience, the bodies they now occupied had achieved a rudimentary intelligence, enabling them to move from place to place, to feed themselves, albeit at a purely instinctive level, and, probably, to reproduce themselves. This last remained a moot point because, peer as they both did, they could not see any other living creatures in their vicinity.

"This must be just after I gave you my rib."

No matter what he thought, his mental activities were available to Suzy with only a minimum of attention. And vice versa.

"You mean we're in Eden? The Garden of Eden?" She couldn't quite believe it.

"It feels very much like it," he mused. "There is a certain virginity, a pristine innocence in the air. Don't you feel it?" The next thought that crossed his mind surprised even himself. "If this is time travel, then it's unlikely to upset any sequential order in the universe."

"Why would you think of such a thing now? Shouldn't you think of a way to get back?"

"You mean you don't like being in Paradise?"

Alec had to remind himself that he'd been travelling in strange realms since he was a boy. For Suzy this was still very much an untested experience. Both, in fact and figuratively.

"It appears that Eden is not all it was later made out to be," he offered, "or at least, what Moses transformed it into. Assuming he was a fundamentalist, which, frankly, I doubt very much. Nevertheless, I suspect there really is no 'good and evil' here. We can't expect the host bodies we occupy, to oppose the laws of nature. They must obey or perish."

"They haven't eaten the apple," Suzy was getting into the spirit of things.

"Precisely," he nodded his hairy head. "Their self-awareness has not yet realized that they can oppose, regardless of consequences. They really have no free will."

"Are you telling me that you are Adam and little *moi* is Eve?"

"Don't be silly darling. We both are Adam and both are Eve. The two are an integral part of a more advanced humanoid. I mean Homo sapiens. Adam symbolizes the conscious mind and Eve the subconscious, you know that?"

She knew that, but it was fun thinking otherwise.

"If a billion Christians and another billion Moslems can think otherwise, then why shouldn't I?"

Alec ignored that. He never wasted time on fundamentalist interpretations, which accepted in the scriptures only whatever suited them, and ignored everything else. This was neither time nor place for theological discussions. Not that he knew much about theology. He's always been too busy to waste time finding out more about his reputed biblical origins.

"You mean that the so called 'man's fall' was the irrevocable consequence of evolution?"

"Define 'man'. If you mean that our beingness, which we both experienced in the Undiscovered Country, became more and more entangled in material consciousness, then yes. It was definitely our fall. But if you think of this beauty which is housing my consciousness at this present moment, than it was a meteoric rise for them."

"But if we, beings of light—sort of... pure consciousness— want to experience life as a mode of becoming then, surely, we want to advance the entities we occupy as much as we possibly can..."

Suzy's fur was almost shining. Her apish eyes were filled with intelligence. She was right. In the physical realm we don't look with the eyes, we look through them.

"Precisely," he nodded once more. And once again he directed his brooding, blood-shot eyes at Suzy. She was magnificently put together. Her body functioned with ease, exhibited a great lightness of foot, enjoyed a superb sense of balance. He could sense all that. There was also an undeniable kindness about the bodies they occupied. Perhaps they hadn't learned to kill and maim, and take advantage of their fellow creatures. Alec suspected that, in those days, the earth had been so sparsely populated that the animals seldom if ever came in contact with each other. Just as well that these two had one another for company, he thought.

"There is a price to pay, of course. They became aware of duality, of good and evil."

"May I touch you?" He felt gentle probing of her fingers on his skin. It gave him pleasure. He didn't want her to stop. He experienced utter delight.

"Did you know," she probed his mind, "that in Hebrew, the word Eden means Delight?"

If he didn't before, he knew it now. And then he felt her smile. "You haven't changed much in this skin," she purred. He didn't know apes could purr.

And, as soon, the delight was gone. Only its memory remained. He sighed, almost like a human.

"It's strange," he resumed. "To experience delight, we must touch. Even a foot apart, we are completely separate. Lonely. Or they are. As I've said before, the Garden of Eden is not all it's struck out to be. The only way they can travel, to where we are now, is to make a full circle. They must sacrifice their innocence in order to regain it."

"They must die in order to come alive?" Suzy mused.

"In a manner of speaking, I am hoping that you and I are approaching our innocence once more, only this time we must do so in full consciousness. Maybe this is what it's all about. To go back whence we came."

"Only, as you said, in full consciousness..."

And for an instant of eternity two globules of light merged into a singularity of being... somewhere, somewhen, in the Undiscovered Country. Time stopped, the Wholeness was theirs. They were one again.

The next moment they became acutely aware, once more, of their hairy bodies.

"It's a long journey..." Alec marveled.

"...but well worth the years of evolution, don't you think?" She knew what he meant.

"To go back and dream, till the creatures of our dreams join us, up there, beyond the Far Country."

"Endowed with attributes that enriched their individuality during countless eons of growth..."

Eve moved her lithe body toward a nearby tree, and reached up over her had. "*...your eyes shall be opened, and ye shall be as gods, knowing good and evil,*" Suzy mused, completely lost in her thoughts.

"You know, it isn't true. Gods do not know good and evil. In God's eyes all things are good. God's cannot behold evil."

Eve's jutting jaw parted in a hideous grin.

Perhaps, she thought, perhaps though it was all merely symbolic, it had to be done. As of now, they were her creatures. She reached out for a round fruit, tore it from the branch and bit into its lustrous redness. Her brown teeth left an irregular scar on its pristine surface. Then she offered the rest of the fruit to her mate. He took it and started eating.

And it was good.

To this ancient day, the apes have eaten only berries, fallen nuts, whatever they could find on the ground. If it lay there, it was good. Yet in this singular moment of their journey they had taken a giant step. They had been given a choice. They could reach up or stoop down. They could say 'no'. "I will not eat that which is at my feet. I shall reach up and eat of a fruit from above. I shall exercise my choice, my will."

There was another aspect to the momentous event that happened simultaneously. Eve, reaching up for the apple, stood on her hind legs. Till this moment they've lived only on the ground. Today the trees became their new domain.

After Alec and Suzy left the apes' bodies, the two hairy simians remained motionless. They felt something very important had just taken place. They did not understand what. But their eyes retained some of the gleam which, till a moment ago, spoke of advanced intelligence. One day they would know exactly what had happened.

They would know that they'd just taken their first step towards the stars.

"You can't experience real bliss until you are fully conscious of it. No matter what the price, the apple was necessary." These were the first words Suzy uttered finding herself in her own body. She felt surprisingly naked without her hair. It was as though someone had shaved her all over.

"Yes. Apparently that's what it's all about." Alec spoke softly. Then he laughed. She'd forgotten he could read her thoughts.

"Well, you don't have X-ray eyes, so there," she snapped.

"Are you sure? I've been at this game a lot longer than you, darling…"

But she was right. Had he X-ray eyes he would have seen the slipper behind her back which, in the next instant, was propelled expertly at his solar plexus.

"Ouch! What's that for?"

"Just making sure you're in your own body," was her wry comment.

"Soon you will find out for sure," he said hoarsely. "You know," he continued, after clearing his throat, "our minds have grown too complex to conceive of the simplicity of Eden. That is why, some say, we all merge, periodically, into a single pod, to start again and experience the joys of real childhood. Like the breathing in and the breathing out of Brahma."

"You know about that?"

"I didn't want to accept it. The universe fascinates me so much that the concept of the Big Crunch, the awakening of Brahma, is abhorrent to me. I want Brahma to keep dreaming forever."

"And yet?"

"It's all different now. Now I feel much more part of Brahma than of the universe. No matter how beautiful, enchanting, mysterious, and all the other superlatives applied to it. I think I can finally accept that our glorious earth, and the abundance of wonders on it, is all an illusion. That my true self is always up there, where Sacha said he'd never left."

"And shall go in and out and find pasture..." Suzy quoted one of his notes. She unexpectedly realized that her power of recall became very different. The last day or so, she found she could recall anything she wanted to. There were no blanks in her memory.

"And we can actually create our own heavens, or Edens, right here, on earth, now, independently of other people. Within our individuality, each one of us *is* the total reality."

Alec's voice was filled with wonder. He knew what he knew, but he continued to absorb the wonder of it all at different levels of his awareness. Infinity takes a long time to absorb. Perhaps forever.

Suzy's smile assumed a dreamy quality. "Now that I can stand back," she picked up the scheme, "I see the real difference between Edenic and true Bliss. The real thing is the state of awareness of infinite possibilities. It gives birth to the cosmic splendour of the Far Country. To universes that are yet to come. The Far Country is only as marvelous as our thoughts make it. Bliss is pregnant with the possibility of countless, absolutely countless, Far Countries." Suzy shared her thoughts without uttering a word.

Alec agreed.

"Yet men whose minds are empty would find the Far Country an absolute hell. Imagine finding yourself alone in a universe of absolute darkness, not a single spark of light to keep you company. It would be almost as bad as I found it in the emptiness of the gray, indifferent reality of stasis—the hell beyond hell! Indifference is by far the greatest of depravities. And make no mistake, there are men who do not care at all about their mental development. They never examine their lives, nor the potential of their minds. I hope they never wonder into the Far Country by accident."

"An unexamined life is a life not worth living," she read his thoughts. He was thinking of Socrates.

Suzy's eyes remained filled with wonder. The incredible experiences were gradually impregnating her mind, her heart, her soul. She was metabolizing them, making them her own. Alec thought she was ready to start building their own Paradise, their own Eden, their Delight, right here on earth.

"On one condition," she sounded quite serious, this time speaking out loud.

"What is it, darling?"

"I don't care if we're naked. But I absolutely insist on skins."

Alec squared his jaw and replied in grave voice: "I'll see what we can do about it,"

And he's been doing something about it ever since.

***

Epilogue

What is the meaning of life? To be happy and useful.

HH the Dalai Lama

Just Living

After reaching out from the emptiness of nowhere, to the euphoria of the here and now, Susanna and Alexander came a full circle. They realized that all their trips began and ended in the 'present'. Great diversity of states of consciousness became available for them, almost overnight. They'd learned that life consisted of continuous becoming, and becoming meant change.

"I'll make all her dreams come true," Alec repeated often, his voice filled with gratitude. He was addressing both, Suzy and Sandra.

"We only just scratched the surface of infinity," Suzy said on their return to LA. "The sad part is, that we cannot share our worlds with others. I have just you and Sacha. Anyone else would regard us as crazy."

"There had been those who spoke of various heavens," Alec murmured, "Remember Saint Paul?"

Suzy remembered. "'I knew a man… such an one caught up to the third heaven', he wrote in his letter to Corinthians. Still others spoke of seven heavens…" she said dreamily.

"Do you think anyone ever took them seriously?"

It was a moot question.

Their holidays were over. The responsibilities Alec took on at the Institute demanded his physical presence. He raced across the park in his wheelchair, souped-up with muscle power. He was glad to be back. He was also glad to add his share to the fabric of the universe, to the matrix of the world he knew and loved. He was glad to be back.

"It's like having your cake and eating it," he defined his view of the world. "I dream my dream, I make it real, I improve on it, I solve the problems inherent in it, and, most of all, I enjoy it. To paraphrase Krishna: life's all pleasure."

Just living, they called it, though they could have said, just dreaming. "Life is an assortment of wondrous dreams, fragments of dreams, reveries and, on occasion, nightmares. Our innermost desires create them. This physical reality, no less so. Although, only in the Undiscovered Country I feel truly awake."

Suzy nodded. She was beginning to understand what he meant.

Sometimes, all three of them would wake up, together, in different reality. They took it for granted that they belonged there. That the universe was theirs to explore.

For almost a year, nothing much happened. Alec gradually improved; he worked hard, exercised as best he could, played with Sacha in his spare time. He found his slow progress annoying.

"It took you ten years, Sir, to reach this condition. It might take you a little while to come out of it," Matt volunteered a rare opinion.

Then, all sorts of things broke at once. Dr. Alexander Baldwin, Ph.D., did win the Nobel Prize, though, surprisingly, not for the Theory of Information. Without his knowledge, he had been a co-nominee, proposed by people in CERN. The prize went to the scientists who made the greatest contribution towards arriving at the Unified Field Theory. Alec didn't see much of the money. His mother took care of most of it. As for fame, it seemed that Dr. Desmond McBride took the honours virtually upon himself.

"I always told you he was a brright lad, lassie, didn't I?" Des asserted gravely, his cheeks pink with pride.

Using Alec's winnings, Alicia and Suzy opened a school of painting in Solana Beach. In their school everything was free: paints, paper, cloth, board, pencils and brushes were all provided by the school. Otherwise, it was doubtful if any children would come. Classes, weather permitting, were held in the open air. If not, they gathered mostly on the covered terrace. Suzy drove down, with Sacha, for alternate sessions. The best paintings of each of their *protégés* and *protégées* had been, in due course, exhibited in Caltech's corridors. Any proceeds went principally towards the purchase of artists' materials, and the money left over, if any, had been equally divided among the participants.

In some ways, Alicia was learning from her pupils. She found that children couldn't lie. When adults painted, they tended to improve on nature's version of the truth. Their vision was tempered by their expectations, or by desire to please a prospective admirer.

Children, she'd discovered, didn't do that. They seemed nonjudgmental. They neither changed nor augmented nature's portrayals, yet contributed their own, unique view. They painted the truth as they saw it with their pristine eyes. They had a way of extending their vision by incorporating love or admiration or fear or even dislike into their creative process.

All the while, Desmond was strutting at Alicia's side like a slightly over-aged peacock.

"The lassie is a verritable dynamo!" he crooned regularly. "She's neverr too tirred to help the urrchins. I wish I could teach them some physics," he added in a more somber tone.

"Try to find a practical side of physics," Alicia suggested.

In time he did. It was a joy to behold a gray-haired Professor sitting cross-legged on the beach, giving a lecture on elementary particles to a group of boys. Occasionally a girl or two would join them, but most of the 'wee lasses' preferred Alicia's classes. Des thought this was most unfair.

.

"After all the inner realities, the infinite wondrous, intricate patterns of the Far Country, the unadulterated beauty of the Home Planet, the inexplicable Bliss of the Undiscovered Realm, or the more humble pleasures of Eden with its frolicking, irresponsible childhood, it is good be here, right here, with you and... and... just live."

Alicia took Des and Sacha for walk, Suzy lingered on the terrace, cuddled under Alec's arm.

"It's overcoming the little everyday problems, mustering all my resources to face the big ones... or watching Sacha take his first steps..." she sighed.

"...hearing him say the first recognizable 'mama'," Alec continued dreamily, "...to watch the joy in his mother's eyes when she discovers yet a new gift in a gifted child... to hear Des roll his r's each time he's happy, all this and so much, so very much more, in our common, everyday-life, makes this the reality I want to abide in. I don't care if it is my own or even my wondrous Princess's dream. As long as she dreams also of you, I'll stay here for as long as I can."

He brushed her forehead with his lips.

"Up there, there is no passage of time," he continued. "Wherever I place my attention, I am there. Whatever I desire, I have it. It is not really a becoming—it is almost a state of being. Yet, strangely, I am only aware of this on my return."

A little later Alec grew pensive once again.

"I wonder why it took me so long to understand what Sandra was saying." There was self-deprecating disbelief in his voice.

"You're thinking of her 'just live' admonition?"

"Yes." The frown remained on his brow, but his voice recovered its confidence. "She didn't mean us to 'just live' at all. Not in the sense that most people would understand it. 'Just living' could easily be understood as living passively, in an attitude of indifference. It could be that in this sense many people 'just live'. Like little vegetables. That's not at all what she meant!"

"She meant for us to live in the present. 'Live now' is what she'd really said?" Suzy read his thoughts before he could enunciate them.

"Precisely. She'd meant that we all continuously create our realities. In the present. She meant that if we shut off the past and the future, only then we we'll able to experience 'just living'. When we live each moment fully..."

She smiled. She never felt as close to Alec as she did since they began roaming the universe together.

"But if we are all individuals, whose worlds are we aware of?" He heard Suzy's thought inside his own mind.

"Our worlds overlap. You and I like the same books, same paintings, music, flowers, trees, nature... if we share a great deal, and particularly if we share our beliefs, our universes will overlap. It's like sharing the genetic code. We merge. To the extent we share what we like—I prefer the term love, because love unites—to that extend we share our creations."

After a long pause she asked: "Are you my creator?"

"I am the creator of my image of you, even as you are of mine," he was speaking aloud. "The closer our images of each other get to the truth, the more our realities will overlap."

"When two or three are gathered in my name..." Suzy quoted an old memory. "the more your and my I am, our individual globules of light merge..."

"You are my light," he whispered.

The weekend was over. Back in LA apartment Matt stood at the door, his coat dressed over his arm.

"You won't be needing me, Dr. Baldwin," he said. "I'll be on my way, if you don't mind."

"What?" Alec got to his feet and took two steps towards Matt. He swayed, then staggered. Matt remained perfectly still. He didn't move one muscle to help him. Alec took another step towards his towering male nurse, the man to whom he virtually owed his survival. "B-b-but... but y-you can't, Matt. You just..."

"You don't need me any more, Sir."

The most Alec had walked at the time were three steps between the table and the settee.

"But were will you go?" Alec couldn't imagine having dinner without Matt sitting at the other end. "What will you do?"

"I have a ticket to Tunisia, Sir."

"Tunisia? Why on earth Tunisia?"

"There is a blind man there who needs my help."

"But how can you help a blind man?"

"I'll tell him, Sir, that Allah is All-powerful."

"Didn't J-jesus say s-something similar..."

Alec was bubbling. He was playing for time, searching his mind for something to say, to keep Matt for a little longer. He learned to rely on Matt far more than he cared to admit, even to himself. It would feel like loosing my right hand, he thought. Why do we take so much for granted? Was Matt really going? My God, how ungrateful I've been to him.

"So did a number of Hebrew prophets, Sir."

Matt glanced at Sacha who left his toys and was staring directly into Matt's eyes. Silence stretched. And then Alec felt that there was more light in the room. As if someone were playing with the dimmer switch over the dining table. Only no one was.

"You really are going, aren't you?" Alec was calmer now.

It was beginning to sink in. Suzy was standing, her arms hanging loosely at her sides. She had grown very fond of Matt, only she'd never told him that. In fact, they hardly spoke at all. How strange, she thought. Yet, I always felt that I knew him. I mean, really knew him...

"We all have our purpose, Ma'am," Matt addressed Suzy with his usual courtesy. He allowed his coat to slide onto the back of a chair. "We grow by fulfilling it." And he looked at

Sacha again. Their eyes met for the last time. Then he bowed and moved towards the door.

They haven't even heard his footsteps. Strange, Alec thought, incongruously, a man that size moving so quietly. Then he grabbed Matt's coat, staggered, then run after him into the hall. Matt was gone.

"Perhaps he won't need his coat in Africa," Alec mumbled. He felt lost, as if part of him evaporated into thin air.

Suzy, her eyes wide, was staring at her husband.

"What?" he asked. "What is it?"

"Y-y-you r-ran to the hall..." she stammered.

Alec smiled. "He did say I wouldn't need him. Didn't he?" And then he sat heavily on the nearest chair. There were beads of perspiration on his forehead. "He did say that, didn't he," he repeated, as though listening to his own voice.

One day, Alec and Suzy sat on the pliant stone slabs of their villa on the Home Planet, staring at the sublime view, unfolding even as they looked. It seemed to waver and solidify, as if fulfilling their innermost desires. They came here when tired, or when the trials of everyday life seemed a little heavy. Here they languished, filled themselves with beauty, which Suzy enhanced further on each visit. It seemed to them that there was nothing to stop them from staying here forever. For ever and a day...?

Time was such an elusive concept.

Tell me, Sue—don't you think I should go back and write all this down?

You mean your early exploits?

Well yes, to start with. But if people accept it, if people buy the idea, then I could write the second part, also. I could call the first part 'Princess', and the second, a sort of combination of Alec and Sandra. Together. We could call it 'Alexander'. After all, I've never really been Alec, have I? It would be a love story that started before time began and which will go on forever..."

"Let's go back, darling, Sacha is alone," she broke silence with a coy whisper.

"Really, darling, it's not necessary," Alec laughed, seeing the expression in her eyes. "Sacha is never alone."

And Alec peek-a-boo'd down to Earth, before she could deny his words.

A minute later Suzy followed him; and a little later, so did Sacha. They didn't even know he was there, listening to their thoughts. He wanted to remember what it was like to be a baby. A human baby. But that's another story. Who can tell? Perhaps Sacha will share it with us. One day.

One day soon?

So long...

If you enjoyed this novel, please don't forget to write a (brief) review on the Amazon.
I'm interested in your thoughts.

Acknowledgments

I would be remiss were I not to thank Bryn Symonds and Madeleine Witthoeft for their diligent editing, each in his and her inimitable way. I am indebted to my many friends for their meticulous proofreading, with particular thanks going to Kate Jones, who took great pains to perfect my manuscript. As always my gratitude to my wife, Bozena Happach, who put up with being a grass widow for weeks on end and then offered me her inspired insights.

Second Edition was studiously examined by Ronald Piecuch, assuring the continuity of the previous work. My thanks to all of them.

Sincerely,
Stan I.S. Law

A Word about the Author

An architect, sculptor and prolific writer was educated in Poland and England. Since 1965 he has resided in Canada. His special interests cover a broad spectrum of arts, sciences and philosophy. His fiction and non-fiction attest to his particular passion for the scope and the development of Human Potential. He authored more than thirty books, twenty of them novels.

Under his real name he published seven non-fiction books sharing his vision of reality. He also composed two collections of poems in his original native tongue in which he satirizes his view of the world while paying homage to Bozena Happach's sculptures. His poetry in English, as well as a number of articles and short stories, can be seen at Authors Den: http://www.authorsden.com/stanislaw

The story continues in
Sacha
The Way Back
Part Three of the Trilogy

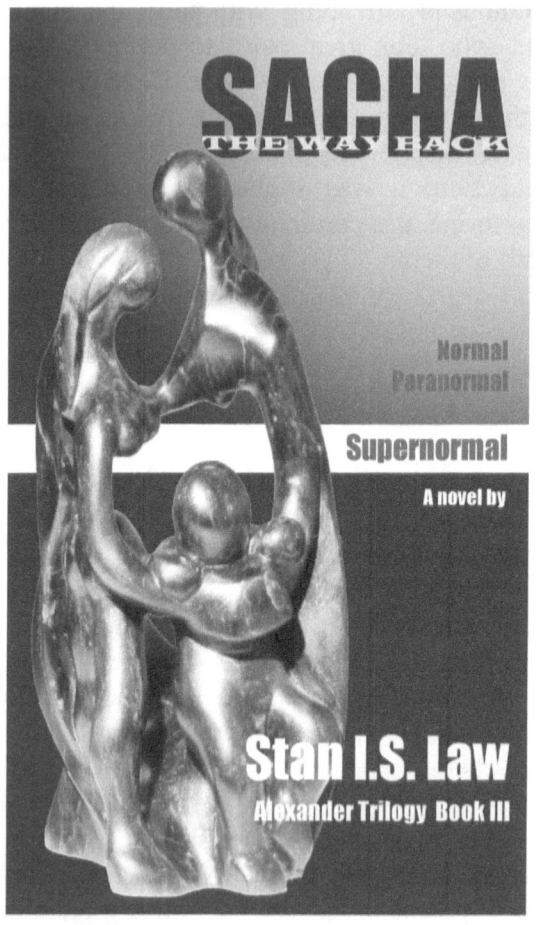

INHOUSEPRESS, MMONTREAL, CANADA
http://inhousepress.ca

www.ingramcontent.com/pod-product-compliance
Lightning Source LLC
Chambersburg PA
CBHW021437240626
47153CB00001B/188